W9-BUB-914

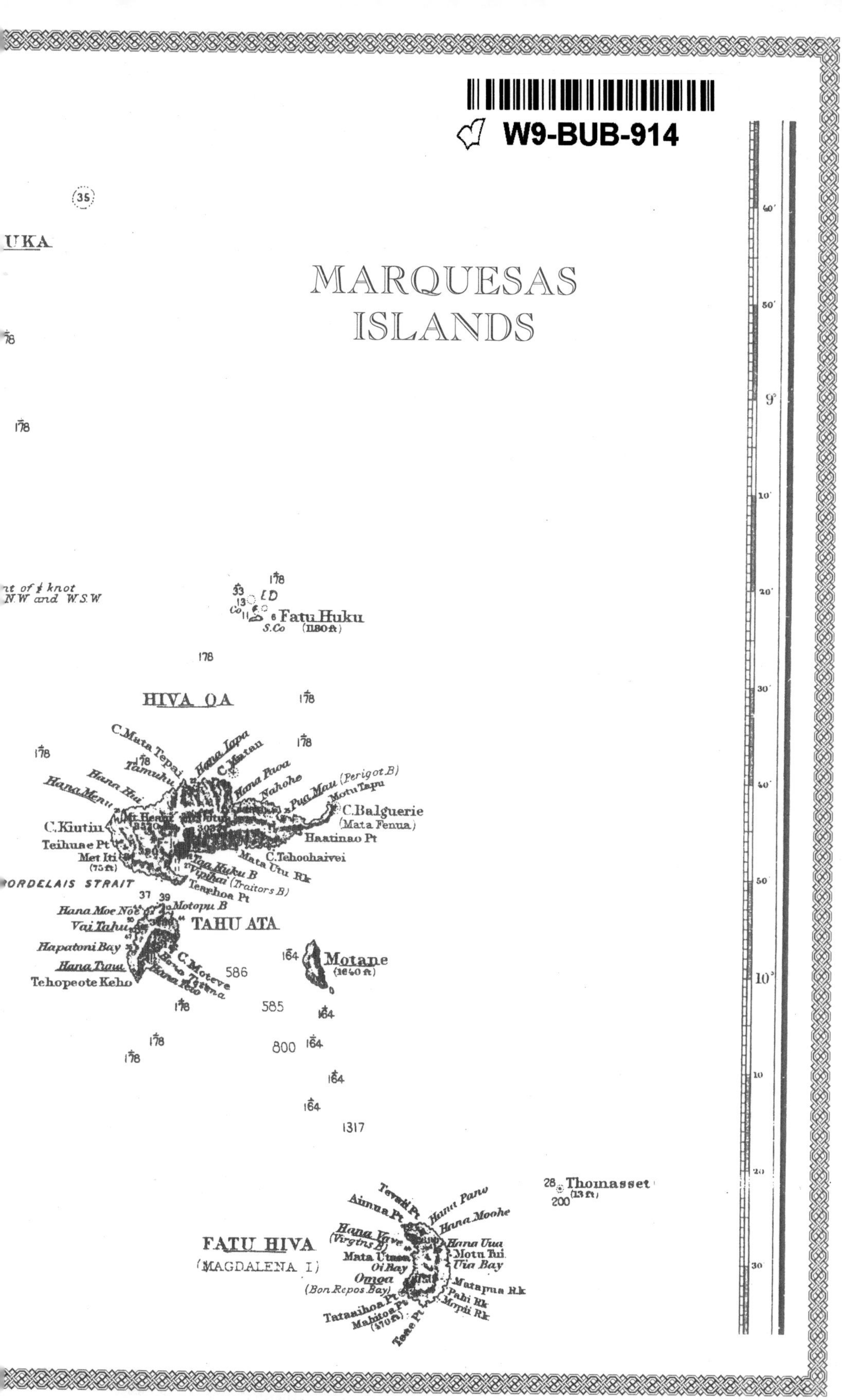

UKA

MARQUESAS ISLANDS

Fatu Huku (1180 ft)

HIVA OA

C. Mata Tepai
Hana Iapa
C. Matau
Hana Paoa
Nahoho
Pua Mau (Perigot B)
Motu Tapu
C. Balguerie (Mata Fenua)
Haatinao Pt
C. Tehoohaivei
Mata Utu Rk
Taa Huku B
Vaihai (Traitors B)
Teaehoa Pt
Tamuhu
Hana Hui
Hana Menu
C. Kiutin
Teihuae Pt
Met Iti (75 ft)

BORDELAIS STRAIT

TAHU ATA

Motopu B
Hana Moe Noe
Vai Tahu
Hapatoni Bay
Hana Tuau
Tehopeote Keho
C. Moteve

Motane (1640 ft)

Thomasset (13 ft)

FATU HIVA
(MAGDALENA I)

Tevaii Pt
Aimua Pt
Hana Pauo
Hana Moohe
Hana Vave (Virgins B)
Hana Uua
Mata Utusa
Motu Tui
Oi Bay
Uia Bay
Omoa (Bon Repos Bay)
Matapua Rk
Pahi Rk
Mopdi Rk
Tataaihoa Pt
Mahitoa Pt (370 ft)
Tease Pt

SEA *of* LOST DREAMS

ALSO BY FERENC MÁTÉ

A New England Autumn
The Hills of Tuscany
A Vineyard in Tuscany
The Wisdom of Tuscany
Ghost Sea - a novel
A Real Life

SEA *of* LOST DREAMS

a novel

FERENC MÁTÉ

W.W. NORTON NEW YORK LONDON

For the people of the
Marquesas and Society Islands

Contents

Printed in the United States of America
First Edition

ISBN 978-0-920256-66-4

Book design and composition by Candace Mátè

Albatross Books at
W.W. Norton & Company Inc., 500 Fifth Ave, New York, N.Y. 10110
http://www.wwnorton.com

W.W. Norton & Company Ltd., 10 Coptic Street, London WCA 1PU
1 2 3 4 5 6 7 8 9 10

SEA
of
LOST
DREAMS

a novel

Book One

El Dia de los Muertos

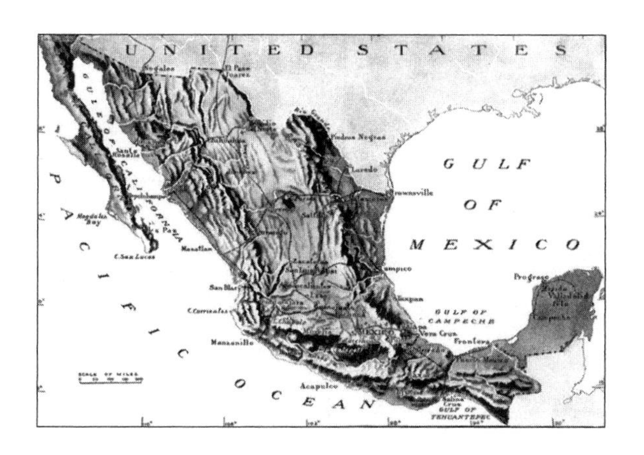

Chapter 1

Cabo San Lucas, Mexico, November 2, 1921

The Day of the Dead seemed to never end.

The sun burned white between the masts and the heat weighed anvil-heavy on the ketch anchored all alone in the crescent bay. Between the water and the craggy, parched hills crouched the town, its church steeple leaning, houses shuttered against the heat, *la plaza* deserted, and the ruined pier crumpled, like a felled beast, in the sea.

Dugger heaved the canvas bucket out of the water and splashed it on deck to keep the planks from shrinking, the seams from opening. The air filled with the smell of wet teak and hot tar. He poured the remnants of the bucket over his head, soaking his coarse white shirt and rolled-up canvas pants, then he stood barefoot in the puddle to cool his feet. Pulling his felt hat down to shield his eyes, he studied the blinding shore. Nello was nowhere in sight.

They had rowed through the predawn darkness speaking in whispers, with greased hemp around the oarlocks and the rifles rolled in blankets to keep them from knocking. The land breeze had grown hotter through the night and brought the smell of incense and decay. Below the pilings of the pier, they'd unloaded the rifles, then lugged them, five at a time, to the mouth of the arroyo where the old man squatted, waiting with the mule.

"You sure you're all right alone?" Dugger had asked.

"They want me alone," Nello said.

"And if they don't pay?"

Nello smiled. "Rebels are dreamers, Cappy. Dreamers always pay."

"Good," Dugger said. "I'm sick of beans and rice."

The old man cinched the rifles to the wooden saddle of the mule and covered them with bundles of dry sticks.

"Here," Dugger said, shoving the binoculars into Nello's hand. "Look out for the soldiers . . ."

"I'll be back before them," he cut in, but put the binoculars into his shoulder bag beside the pistol. "Anyway, they're hunting priests and nuns. Do I look like either?"

He stood, one gray eye smiling, the other squinting. His gaunt face, lined with gullies, had been eroded by twenty-two years at sea, and his graying stubble and long hair sticking out of his weather-beaten hat gave him an air of having just stepped from a wilderness. He wore a white shirt patched at both elbows with sleeves cut at mid-forearm to stay out of blocks and winches, sailcloth pants patched likewise at the knees, and boots that were old and worn, yet supple with seal grease. A sun-bleached black vest strained across his back. He touched the rim of his hat in salutation.

Dugger watched them climb the dead hill below the indigo sky flecked with stars.

She awoke with a start and thought, Where am I? She recognized the salon where she slept to catch what air moved through the ketch, but was baffled at the man's shirt and pants she wore and her bare feet, their tops burned by the sun. For a moment she had no sense of outside place or time, or who in her dreams was still alive or dead.

A man's face from her dreams hovered before her—long and stern—and she bit her lip trying to remember who he was. Come on, Kate, she chided herself, you have to remember. But she couldn't. Beyond three weeks ago, she could recall only senseless snippets from her life. The last lucid thing was a snowy winter night in an Indian village among islands and steep mountains. She remembered a snow-laden tree over the sea in the moonlight, and the smell of smoked fish along a stony beach where the tide melted the snow, and facing the beach an enormous shed with a bonfire in its middle, full of people, obscured by smoke and shadows. She remembered lots of mirrors stacked around the fire. One was broken. A long shard of it, streaked with blood, lay on the dirt floor. Shots were fired from all around above them, and then they were on the ketch.

All that was three weeks ago. But what had happened before? She had no life "before." It was as if she had been born on that snowy night. A mighty big baby, she thought. Then she looked in the small, bulkhead-fastened mirror at her young freckled face, and wondered, How old am I?

She remembered with crystal clarity every moment aboard the ketch in a gray and empty ocean, sailing from the mist of icy winter to the heavy heat of this bay. She recalled the boat's constant motion, a gentle rhythmic heaving, until one night a bludgeoning wind churned up the sea in just hours. Between the hard smoked clams of dinner and the first light of dawn, the wind had heaped the sea into towering cliffs around them, pointing toward a dismal patch of sky. And that incessant, maddening noise: the seas smashing against the hull, the rigging vibrating like violin strings until she could feel the tremor in her bones, the clattering and crashing of everything below—cans, tools, cutlery, pots—as the ketch rolled to one side, stopped, then rolled back again.

When the sea was calm, she'd read every book on the ketch,

hoping to ignite her memory: Slocum, Chekhov, one by another Russian in which a young man kills an old woman for her money but feels so bad he seeks punishment, and one by Conrad in which a man abandons his ship in panicked fear and feels guilty ever after. Fine, she thought, I'll seek punishment, I'll feel guilt—just let me remember for what.

She'd hurt her arm the day before when the boat plunged fiercely and she fell against a cleat. Now she hurriedly pushed back her sleeve and looked past the fresh bruise, thinking if she could find something—a scar, a mole, something from before—maybe it would all come back. My life might just flood back. But there was nothing on her arms; white, blank, unlived, empty pages.

She heard footfalls above. She went on deck. In her loose men's clothing she felt like an actor in the wrong costume, the wrong play. Nothing here is mine, she thought. Not even the shirt on my back. A sad smile crossed her face: The bruise is mine.

Climbing the companionway ladder, she shielded her eyes against the blazing sun. The day was still but for the pelicans, with beaks pointing down and wings tucked, plunging like lead weights, shattering the smooth sea. She stood opposite the big wood wheel and brass binnacle, looking into the empty cockpit where Dugger had lain with his bandaged bullet wound, his face drawn. How she loved his often-smiling green eyes, whose expression changed as quickly as the shadows of windblown clouds.

She watched him sloshing water onto the deck, moving with such a comforting sense of purpose that for a moment her unease vanished. In his drenched shirt he seemed too slight to work the ropes of a big ketch, but as he filled the bucket, his arms and back tensed with stringy muscles. He looped the rope and hung it on the horn of a cleat.

"Good morning," she said. "Are you feeling stronger?"

"Much," he said. "Did you sleep well?"

"Fine," she said, clearing her throat. "You?"

"Too hot." And he lifted up his hat and poured what was left in the bucket into it.

"Nello's not back yet, is he . . ." she said more than asked.

He forced a smile. "Mexico," he replied. And thought, What if they didn't pay? What then? The rifles were gone, their money was gone; the only thing they had left to sell now was the ketch. He couldn't quite think of what to say, so he raised his hand to touch her face, but something in her eyes made him hold back. It struck him that this was how she'd been at sea each morning: uncertain, guarded, as if they were meeting for the first time. Each night they were close. They shared soft whispers when the wind was low, and she'd press against him and moan softly in his arms. During the violence of stormy nights, they'd exchange fiery glances full of joy and fear; then, forgetting his wounded arm, she'd clutch him so hard he could barely breathe.

One starry night they drank rum and danced to the sound of Nello's harmonica, holding each other on the slowly rolling deck, with the sails of the ketch moving among the stars. She had swayed effortlessly to the roll of the ketch, all the while heeding his least movements—the lean of his legs, the turn of his hips—until he could no longer tell where he ended and she began.

Now she stood in the bright light, tying her auburn hair back with a string. Her face looked beautifully innocent, yet weary. Her long legs and thin arms made her look frail, and he felt an enormous fatigue from worrying about her and her recurring sadness. He caught himself thinking, Is love worth the trouble?

"I'll bring you a dress from town," he said apologetically.

Her face turned sadder. "We spent everything yesterday on provisions."

"When Nello brings the money, I'll buy you a dress,"

"Oh, good," she said brightening. "Like all the senoritas wear," and she drew a dipping line down to her breasts.

At her smile, Dugger felt relieved. "Lower," he said.

She undid a button on the shirt. "Like this?" she smiled.

A pelican crashed nearby into the smooth sea. "Like a mirror breaking," she said quietly, and sat down on the cabin. "Why do I remember a shard of a mirror, Dugger?"

He turned away. What could he reply? Because you stabbed your husband with it to save my life? He watched the empty shore in silence. Only a handful of fishing skiffs with sails furled lay askew on the blinding sand.

"I'd better go find Nello," he said.

He picked up his hat, pulled on his boots, climbed into the skiff, pushed off, and set the oars.

You have to tell me one day, she thought.

Chapter 2

Nello lay flat on the flank of the arroyo, with his hat over the binoculars to keep the sun from reflecting off the glass. He watched the horse soldiers come over the crest, kicking up dust, the sea breeze blowing it into long, playful plumes. The soldiers reined their mounts for the descent, pulling the horses' muzzles against their chests. They spread out on the path that wound down to the shore, close enough that he could smell the acrid-sweet sweat of the horses.

He focused the binoculars on the lieutenant in the lead: the deep-set tired eyes, the bony hand working the reins to and fro, guiding his horse's every step down the broken slope. Behind the lieutenant he caught sight of a boy. The boy rode carrying a strange black flag: a priest's cassock tied by the sleeves to his rifle. He had small, steely eyes and his jaw was set tight as he urged his horse ahead.

"Madonna puttana," Nello muttered to himself. "What a nasty-looking runt." He felt something bad in his gut about the boy. Then he saw the dead man. With skin whiter than his underwear, he was slung across a palomino halfway down the pack, his legs dangling and swinging to the rhythm of the horse.

He turned the binoculars toward the ketch and caught sight of Dugger rowing with long pulls toward town. If only the soldiers hadn't come back early. There was nothing to do but wait until the soldiers finished eating and getting drunk, and lay in torpid sleep with kelp flies on their faces. Without rising, he crawled backward among the rocks into the speckled shade of a dying mesquite. He leaned against its trunk, covered the pouch of gold coins with sand, pulled his hat over his eyes, and hoped he would dream of a place cool and dark.

With the skiff growing small in the distance, Kate stepped out of her ill-fitting pants and slammed them on the deck. Now, this is more like it, she thought. This is me. She stood half naked with legs slightly parted, her eyes as determined as if she were about to stand her ground come what may. She crouched to jump in when she saw the birthmark. It was halfway up the inside of her thigh, and like lightning came a clear image of a man kissing it, and she wondered if Dugger had ever kissed her there—before—in the time she could not remember. With a leap, she dove into the sea.

She let herself sink. I remember diving like that when I was little. But where?

Below the keel of the ketch she stopped; through the deep, clear water, she could see her shadow on the sandy bottom. She stayed under longer than she thought she could, and was surprised at how much she wanted to remain. So calm here, she thought. There's no place on earth so calm.

She swam with wide kicks like a frog, rounded the dark slab of the rudder, along the curve of the bilge, and then surfaced amidships on the ocean side of the ketch, out of Dugger's sight. She floated on her back and felt alone; completely alone. Almost happy. Then she swam deeper still, down at a sharp angle, toward the anchor that lay, flukes buried, in the rippled sand.

Dugger rowed the skiff slightly crabbing shoreward, alternately eyeing the town behind him and Kate standing on the rail, her white skin aglow against the dark blue sky. When he saw her dive, he held the oars. He counted: one second, two seconds. At forty seconds he spun the skiff and rowed back with such vehemence the oarlocks groaned. When near the ketch, he leapt with a twisting motion into the sea. The skiff rocked and the oars slid free.

He swam down and clutched the keel to stay under. He searched but couldn't find her. He twisted and turned until his eyes burned. Then his lungs began to burn and he had to surface. He dove again, spiraling down into the shimmering light, and far, far ahead, where the anchor chain hung in catenary, he saw her. Much deeper than he thought she could be, she was floating beside the anchor in the blue light, her long ghostly body paler than the sand.

He tried desperately to will away what lay before him, to roll back time so he could do something, anything, that would prevent her from being down in that blue light.

He shot up, gasped for air, then dove again. With tremendous pulls on the anchor chain, he rushed toward the bottom. He'd have to pull her to the surface, hold her against the hull, and squeeze her hard to jolt her diaphragm to pump the water from her lungs. His mouth on hers, sucking the last bit from her lungs until she coughed and breathed. Dear God, please make her breathe.

As the chain shook, Kate looked up, then waved. Kicking hard, she swam straight to the surface.

They hung on to the gunwale of the skiff gasping for breath. "I didn't realize I'd gone so deep," she said, going pale.

He didn't reply. Loving her and hating her, he lifted her and shoved her into the skiff over the gunwale.

No love is worth this, he thought.

SHE SAT IN THE SKIFF, shivering despite the heat. Dugger held her as one would a frightened child.

"I'm all right," she said. "I'm all right."

He pushed the hair out of her eyes. "You could have drowned," he said, keeping the anger from his voice.

"I saw the chain had wrapped around the anchor," she said. "You told me to watch for that in wind shifts. I went to clear it. Why are you looking at me like that?"

"Like what?"

"Like I'm crazy."

"I worry, that's all," he said.

"That I'll drown myself?"

Dugger didn't know how to reply.

"I'm not crazy, Dugger. I may be missing a few pieces . . . confused—that doesn't mean I'm nuts."

He kissed her forehead and her face and clutched her in his arms.

"Don't worry." She smiled. "I'm not going anywhere until I find out how this ends."

She gathered the hair that hung behind his neck and squeezed the water from it. Then she spread her legs slightly and pointed at the birthmark. "Dugger," she said softly. "Did you ever kiss me there?"

He wiped beads of water from her goose-bumped arms. "How could I have missed it?" he said.

She smiled. Then took his salt-cracked hand and held it to her lips.

"I better go find Nello," he said.

Chapter 3

The lieutenant held back his horse and let the steel-faced boy ride by. He watched the rest of his soldiers with mild disgust as they lurched awkwardly on their bony horses. Sad peasants riding in rope sandals, he thought, but he felt pity for their sadness and unease on the horses, when all they longed for was a bit of land and a hoe. Who knows? he mused. If the revolution comes . . . The only one he disliked was the boy, who held his rifle stiffly and rode with arrogant skill and unfettered pride. The boy loved his horse, his rifle, and his boots. He dusted and soaped the hard saddle with great care every night. The rest of the world seemed to mean nothing to him.

The lieutenant envied him this indifference, perhaps even hated, envied the intensity and relentlessness that propelled him out of bed each morning. He would have given anything to be as possessed as the boy.

The boy sat proudly on his horse on the hard sand of the shore and wished the horse would stop jittering so the breeze could billow his flag. Sometimes he wished the horse dead and stuffed or, better yet, made of bronze like the statue he'd seen in Guadalajara, with a proud general in the saddle. He could see himself finally receiving recognition, sitting amidst envious eyes forever.

He turned his horse and spotted hard-edged boot prints in the sand. They came out of the sea. At the mouth of the arroyo he saw the hoof-prints of a mule. The beast must have spent some time there: the sand was full of prints, as if the mule had danced. Looking far up the arroyo, he thought he saw something glitter under a tree. He rode up to the lieutenant and excitedly began to tell him his observations, but the other rode by without a word or glance. The boy felt his face redden with rage and shame. I'll show you, he thought in a sudden fury. I'll show you.

The tramp steamer that plied the coast was a whole day overdue. Its handful of would-be passengers sat silent and weary in the thatch shade of the cantina, some reading, some sleeping or staring unseeing ahead. No one moved. Only a mongrel under a table rose, looked out into the sun, then slowly collapsed again. A barefoot child came running across the dusty tiles near the dry fountain shouting, "They caught another priest! They caught another priest!"

"Virgen Santa," the *padrona* said, and crossed herself with the cold bottle of beer in her hand. She held it to her forehead and let the cool condensation trickle down her brow. Then she shuffled across the speckled shade and placed the bottle on the table before a woman with a face as white as porcelain. The *padrona* watched her with pity. She stuck out in the shade like a white ghost in the night. Her broad white cheekbones and tall forehead glowed below a lace shawl that covered her head. She must have had very short hair, because nothing showed or lumped below the shawl. Her white blouse with turned-up collar had dust in the creases, and her long travel skirt was too heavy for this climate as were the lace-up boots that too showed their age. When she heard the sound of the horse hooves thudding, her face went tight and she

pulled her white lace shawl low over her eyes.

High above the plaza the bell began to toll, a dull and shallow sound like someone banging with a hammer on a pot. The soldiers had tried all week to lower the bell to melt it down and cast into a cannon. But to no avail. The bell now perched on planks, half out of the steeple, half in, tilting over the roof of the jailhouse far below, lashed by ropes to the great oak beams from which it once hung. The porcelain-faced woman glanced at her watch, but the *padrona* touched her arm.

"Not by that bell, senorita," the *padrona* said. "It only rings to warn the *generale* to stop riding the lieutenant's wife." She backed away but couldn't keep her eyes off the strange woman. She's much too beautiful, she thought. Too beautiful and too delicate to survive here. Then, seeing her own callused and knobby hands, she thought, It's good to be robust and ugly; good for a longer life.

As the first horses broke into view, the *padrona* saw the dead man slung across the saddle. His arms and head bounced playfully in the sun. *"Dios Santo,"* she whispered. "They did kill another."

"It's time for a revolution," a big man near her murmured.

"Why not?" the *padrona* retorted. "We haven't had one all week."

The horse soldiers turned into the plaza. Their dust cloud billowed over the cantina and the fountain, and over the man stringing lanterns between the fountain and the walls. They halted in the meager shadow of the church. The lieutenant gave quiet orders. Two soldiers lifted the dead priest, carried him to the church door, laid him down. They looked around for his cassock, but they couldn't find it and the boy who'd been using it as a flag was gone.

Dusting himself off with his gloves, the lieutenant tried to stride firmly toward the cantina, but he had to duck under the dangling lanterns and step over piñatas lying on the ground. The pale-faced woman lowered her head, cast down her eyes.

The lieutenant looked around and raised his cap. *"Buenos días,* visitors to our hospitable town," he said, trying to hide his disdain. "I apologize for the delayed arrival of your ship. While you wait, may I see your *documentos?"*

As he began checking papers, he noticed the pale woman in the shadows. From then on he glanced her way every chance he got. She sat there beautiful and rigid, like the pale painted wood statue of the Virgin he used to stare at in church. That was before the order had come to exile the priests and nuns and ransack the churches, nail the doors shut, and burn the Virgin in the plaza on a pyre. He remembered feeling a deep sadness as he watched the flames make the paint bubble on her face.

When there were no other papers left to check, he approached the pale woman without looking her in the eye. Taking her papers, he also took her hand. He lifted it halfway to his lips and clicked his heels. She looked up. The lieutenant stopped, riveted. Her eyes were dark blue, mesmerizing. They shone fearful, yet inviting and irresistibly warm. Something in him stirred, something he thought had died so long ago—the feeling that he could love boundlessly, and be loved in return.

He looked at her documents and regained his composure. "Madame is French?"

"Madame is Irish," the woman countered, her eyes now edged with a trace of defiance. "Just born in France."

As she drew back her hand, he noted no wedding ring.

With forced indifference, she looked down at her watch. "What time is it here, really?" she asked with a thin smile. "The bell seems to ring anytime it chooses."

The lieutenant stiffened. "With that priest still in charge, it is difficult to tell."

"Perhaps you should kill him too," the porcelain woman challenged.

"Excuse me, madame," the lieutenant said, offended, "his death was an accident. And it's not the nuns and priests we're driving out but the stupidity they teach."

"And him?" She nodded toward an old priest who had come out of the church and now stood praying over the body.

"He runs the orphanage; no harm in that. He has stopped saying Mass in that hocus-pocus language, and stopped threatening us with hell if we don't give him the few pesos we've earned." Then, while looking over her papers, he added, "We are also hunting a French spy, who seems to be buying guns and stirring the rebellious." He eyed her. "Madame, are you here to start a revolution?"

"I can try, if you like."

The lieutenant forgot his life long enough to laugh.

"I am waiting for the boat to Panama," she offered.

"And what awaits you in Panama?"

"A boat to Tahiti."

"Oh," he said, surprised and sad that she was going so very far away. "The captain of the sailboat out there is sailing for Tahiti," and he looked around the plaza but saw him in the distance coming in the skiff. When she didn't comment, he added, "And what do you expect to find in Tahiti?"

She looked into the lieutenant's earnest eyes, seemingly so anxious to peer into other lives. "I have learned to *expect* nothing from life, *Teniente,"* she said with a sigh. "That way I'll be spared the disappointment."

"Oh, yes." He smiled. "Disappointment . . . I've heard of that. Are you going, then, just to find adventure?"

Her face turned hard, her eyes cold. "No," she said, her tone completely changed. "To find my brother. A painter. He last wrote from the island of Fatu Hiva, near Tahiti, over a year ago."

Startled by her gaze, the lieutenant looked away. He handed back her papers. Unable to think of anything else to say, he saluted.

He turned and stepped out of the shade of the cantina and, taking off his cap, welcomed the blast of sun.

Chapter 4

Nello was dreaming. He was five years old. It was a cool summer sunset in his village perched in a crescent cove below mountains capped with snow. With the salmon run now finished, the beach was a maze of sticks with fish stretched open on them drying in the sun, or on racks over smoldering chips of alder. The smoke drifted across the sunset waters, still except for the slow swirling of the tide. With the tide, the wind was turning. It came cool and smelled of snow.

The boy on the horse looked down at the sleeping man in the shadow of the dying tree. He lowered his rifle at him, wrapped a nervous finger around the trigger, and whistled.

Nello awoke. The horse loomed big and dark against the sky. With the sun behind the rider, the face was obscured, but Nello could clearly see the rider's finger on the rifle and the strange black flag dangling limply over it. *"Buenos días,"* Nello said, as welcoming as if he'd been waiting for him all day. The boy didn't move. Only the rifle shook a little. Jesus, Nello thought. He's so edgy he might shoot.

"Eres un espía," the boy said. You're a spy.

Nello laughed out loud. He propped himself on an elbow and

held the binoculars in offer toward him. "I'm hunting wild goat," he said. And let the reflection from the glass dance on the boy's hand.

"With a pistol?" the boy said with disdain.

Nello gave a cold smile. "If you're very good, there's nothing to it." Meanwhile, with his left hand, he felt the pouch of gold coins buried in the sand.

"You're a liar," the boy said with a sneer. "You are the French spy trying to start a revolution."

"Me? No. I'm part Indian, part Italian. And I'm going to Tahiti. On that," he said, nodding toward the ketch. "Thirty days at sea. Maybe forty. We need all the meat I can get."

"Pull out your pistol slowly and lay it in on the ground."

"Come on," Nello coaxed.

"You're a spy," the boy repeated.

"What the hell is there to spy on here?"

"You're here to help the rebels." His voice rose in anger and at the prospect of success. "The pistol," he said firmly.

Nello sat up to pull his left hand out from under him. With the right, he aimed the reflection from the binocular lens onto the horse's muzzle. I hope I can shoot straight with my left hand, he thought. And in one move he raised the gun and fired, while driving the blinding reflection into the horse's eye. The horse went mad.

The gunshot rang out, deafening in the silence.

The squat, puffy-faced general rode into the plaza on a horse too small for him. He dangled his legs merrily, happy to be this close to the ground and even happier to be this close to lunch. He saw the soldiers in a confused group near the church, and sighed. This will not be good for my digestion.

He guided his horse carefully around the piñatas on the ground and waited until the whole group saluted before dismounting. The dead man lay as if sunbathing on the steps. The general turned away. "Who is he?" he asked, but didn't want to know.

"A priest," a soldier offered.

The general took a few steps toward the sea and, hoping no one saw, crossed himself using his bent thumb on his forehead, nose, and eyes. He disliked strife. What he liked was glowing there before him, a pale young beauty, long-limbed, with skin white as porcelain, striding from the shade of the cantina toward the hotel while looking wistfully out at the blinding sea. It's not my fault, he thought, that God made me love women. If it were wrong, he wouldn't have given me eyes. Pity she walks as stiff as a nun; and such a fine ass, at that. Good God, what a waste! When he heard horseshoes thudding on the hard-packed dirt, he turned.

A lone horseman rode into the plaza, with a man he didn't recognize walking before the horse. From the horseman's rifle a priest's black cassock dangled. Not another, the general thought. Not before lunch.

The boy rode anxiously straight to the general, jumped off his horse, and saluted with fervor.

"Another priest?" The general sighed.

"No, Señor General. A spy."

The boy rattled off the whole story about the hoof marks and the boot marks, and the bright reflection in the hills above the sea. Then he waved the binoculars and described his attack, and how only his great horsemanship kept him in the saddle. He concluded with how, when he visited the great city of Guadalajara, he had seen them shoot a spy in the Plaza de Toros just before the fights.

The general listened and pretended to care, but wished all the while that God would strike the boy dead. "Good work, soldier," he muttered. "Lock him up; you can shoot him tomorrow."

)ía de los Muertos, he thought. The living have to

ɪᴋ another beer.

He had watched two soldiers lead Nello to the squat jailhouse below the steeple, and watched all three vanish through a doorway darkened by the shadow of the bell above. The afternoon grew hotter. The air was thick and heavy as before a storm, but there wasn't a single cloud in the sky—only the sea fog crept in through the entrance of the bay.

The lieutenant came from the jailhouse with his head down in the sun. He talked to the *padrona,* who handed him a beer. Holding it against his temple, he stopped at Dugger's table.

"Buenos días, Capitán" he said. "I wish you a happy Day of the Dead."

"Likewise, *Teniente,"* Dugger said.

"May I, *Capitán?"* the lieutenant said, pointing at a chair.

"I was about to offer," Dugger said.

The lieutenant sat but kept his chair turned slightly from the table. "You said you were staying three days. I thought by now you'd have sailed off to Tahiti. I wish you had." He sighed. "Now your friend is in jail. Why is life like that?"

"We are waiting for supplies," Dugger said. "The coaster is late. I can't set to sea for thirty days without good supplies. Now, can I ask you *why* you put my first mate in jail?"

The lieutenant took a long swig of the beer and snorted a quiet laugh. "Why?" he repeated, and raised his eyebrows until his eyes shone white. *"Why."*

With the nail of his thumb, he drew careful lines in the condensation on his bottle, as if it were the most important venture in his life. "May I confide in you, *Capitán?"* he said with a note of apprehension. "That is the question I ask myself each day: Why? When I awaken, I ask, Why bother to get up? And the last thing at night I ask, Why bother going to bed?" He drank, then returned the bottle to his temple. "Why? Always, why? *That* is the question." He laughed sadly and took a slug of beer. "The boy found him hiding in the arroyo with binoculars," he said. "He convinced the general that he had found a famous spy. Are you a famous spy too, *Capitán?"*

"Oh, sure," Dugger said, and waved his beer. "We're all famous spies."

"I wish I were," the lieutenant said. "Then I might find out what the hell is going on around here." He took a slug of beer, then he cheered up. "There was a beautiful young woman here, Irish, she said, going to Tahiti to find her lost brother."

"Couldn't he get lost closer to home?"

"It's not easy to get lost," the lieutenant said pensively. "Why, for example, you, dear *Capitán.* Why are you sailing all that way?"

"To get lost." Dugger smiled.

"There." The lieutenant slapped his knees. "Get lost from what?"

"From ever being found."

They raised their bottles, clanked them, and drank.

"The other day you said you're looking for a French spy," Dugger said. "My mate is half Italian, half Indian."

"The general won't mind. Having someone shot is good for the morale. Can I buy you a beer, *Capitán?"*

"You already shot the priest."

"Oh, him," the lieutenant said, as if he'd forgotten long ago. "I let him go. He drowned. We watched him swim the inlet—stupid man—too stupid to allow for the outgoing tide. He drowned in the undertow."

The sun had fallen. Long shadows filled the plaza.

"Do you ever let spies go?" Dugger queried.

"I let everyone go." The lieutenant frowned. "But the general doesn't. And that boy. That horrible boy. I wouldn't be surprised if he chained himself to your friend."

With his face distressed, he held up his empty bottle to the *padrona.* When the fresh beer came, he took a long slug, and waited until the heat carried it to his brain. With renewed confidence, he went on.

"He's a horrible boy, you know. Completely crazy. But not stupid. I saw the footprints too, *Capitán.* Boot prints. From the sea. Deep-sunk boot prints coming up; much shallower going back. Many times. Carrying something. What would anyone in good boots carry from the sea? A herd of mermaids? One by one?"

Dugger laughed a warm laugh. He eyed the lieutenant and thought, He's all right. The fellow is all right.

The lieutenant leaned forward as if to be closer to his beer.

"If not mermaids," he said, "what?"

The cur got tired of the noise above him, struggled onto his haunches, and dragged himself away to another table.

"Guns, perhaps?" the lieutenant offered. "Lots of guns? There are always lots of guns for poor people to kill each other."

"Guns for dreamers," Dugger said.

They sat silent and drank.

"It's nice up in those hills." The lieutenant sighed. "And so dark at night, you can't help but dream."

The man in the plaza struggled with the lanterns, trying to get the arc of the strings equal in length, as if anyone would notice once it had gotten dark.

"We're all dreamers," Dugger said quietly. "And probably all crazy."

"We should all be shot at sunrise." The lieutenant smiled.

"Who is sane enough to shoot us?" Dugger retorted.

They began to laugh, softly at first, then they couldn't stop themselves.

"You mind if I visit him?" Dugger finally asked.

"Be my guest," the lieutenant said. "But you might not get out alive. The crazy boy would love to shoot two spies."

"I could kill him," Dugger offered.

The lieutenant fell silent and looked him in the eye. Then, with much care, he drew more lines on his bottle.

"You're right," he said quietly. "We're probably all crazy."

Chapter 5

Kate waited.

The sun had sunk into the mist over the sea and the air around the ketch was soon drained of light. The bay flared a sudden emerald-green, then grew dark, and the hills, the town, the sky were swallowed by the night. She held the wheel of the anchored boat. In the dark, where the town had been, flames flared, some high, others tiny and faint like flickering, guttering candles. Overhead the first star glowed.

She had often taken a turn at the helm these past weeks, usually at night, and she held the wheel now with deep affection, wondering how it would be to sail off all alone, out of the bay into the unlit sea, out of the lives behind her. The thought calmed her. It contained no fear, no shape or face. She closed her eyes and wondered if the darkness had a sound. When she opened them again, the sky was thick with stars.

Throughout the afternoon the stranded passengers had drifted out of the cantina, ambled in the shade, come back, turned their chairs to face a new direction, and now sat and watched the plaza being set up for the fiesta.

The sun turned blood-red, then sank into the sea. The plaza filled with people streaming from the cemetery. Some carried flaming candles, others sleeping children, and some were empty-handed but full of memories of the dead. The dangling lights glowed over them and over tables loaded with plantains, red peppers, limes, dried lima beans and coffee beans strung into necklaces, hardened cane sugar cut into cubes and carefully piled, and bottles of colorful juices in tidy rows. The air was sated with the steam of boiling corn, the smell of roasting fish, charred meat, and the sickly sweet smell of burnt sugar for candy floss. A mariachi band played on the church steps, their shadows from the firelight bobbing on the wall. People milled about, eating, drinking, and eyeing the woven chains of orange marigolds. Children danced, the soldiers grew drunk, and the passengers of the promised coaster mingled timidly with the crowd.

Dugger wove his way through the revelers, as unhurriedly as he could manage, toward the dark alley that led behind the jail. He stopped for a bite of *pan de muertos,* followed by a slug of tequila from a thick glass, checking each time to see if someone followed. A little girl sat on the ground beside her pyramids of limes. She wouldn't look up, not even when he cajoled her, not even when he put a peso down beside the neat green piles. She stared at his boots as if they were warning enough not to look their owner in the eye.

He had nearly made it to the alley when a woman's anxious voice stopped him. "Good evening, Captain."

Dugger turned his head. This must be the Irish one, he thought. "Good evening," he said, and wished she'd go away.

She glanced over her shoulder. "I have heard you're headed for Tahiti."

"I'm headed for the loo," Dugger said, slurring.

Her face changed. A flame sparked in her blue eyes and she halted a nervous smile to purse her lips. "Excuse me," she said.

Maybe it was her eyes, or the firelight on her cheeks, or just the many glasses of tequila, but she seemed to him the most intriguing woman alive.

"I'm sorry," he said. "I have to get . . ."

She grabbed his arm. "Don't leave me," she said, as firmly as an order. "He's coming."

The general came toward them weaving through the crowd. He slowed often, turning here, smiling there, like a benevolent godfather exchanging pleasantries.

The woman squeezed Dugger's arm. "Take me with you."

"To the loo?"

"To Tahiti." When she saw no sympathy in his eyes, she pushed the hem of her shawl off her forehead to reveal her shorn blond hair, so short it almost stood on end. Then she whispered, "I'm a nun."

The general now walked a direct path toward them.

Dugger pulled his arm away.

"They shoot nuns," she said, with a plea in her voice.

"And hang gringos who help them. So let's not let him get two birds with—"

Someone fired a pistol into the air and people laughed and the mariachis played louder.

"You won't help me then," she said, her voice suddenly hard.

Dugger couldn't stop looking in her eyes. There was something wrong about her. Those eyes had turned cold. Icy. Almost eerie. Something frightening that he remembered having seen before. You're just drunk, he thought.

The crowd gave a cheer.

Dugger saw the general, with a saggy drunken stare, glaring right at them only steps away.

"Slap me," he told the nun.

Her eyes widened at him.

"Slap me, then walk away angry toward the sea. Then he

won't think you're running. And no man in his right mind would follow an angry woman."

She slapped him so loud that the people around them turned. Then she strode away.

Dugger waded back into the crowd and made his way to the general. "Oh, *Generale,"* he slurred, flinging an arm over his shoulder. "I have a gift for you. A pirate's ring. I won it at cards from a genuine pirate. Name your price."

"You need to sleep," the general said, watching the pale woman walk toward the water. Just as well, he thought, she's too stiff anyway. But such a perfect . . . ah, never mind. He turned and resigned himself to the flowing crowd.

Chapter 6

One more tequila, Dugger thought. It's always that last one that enlightens. Shows the way. To God only knows where. *"Hola,"* he said loudly to an old man with bonitos stacked before him in the dirt of the plaza. He raised his glass of tequila and drank it down. As best as he could, he strode down the dark alley that circled the church. A dozen steps past the steeple, where a dull glow came through the bars of the jailhouse window, he stopped. "Hey, sailor boy," he called softly.

Nello's head rose behind the bars. "Jesus, Cappy," he said. "I can smell your breath from here."

Dugger laughed. "Liquid courage."

"Go get some sleep."

"Can't." Dugger snickered. "We're sailing soon."

"You're dead drunk."

"That may be so. However, when you hear the church bell toll three times, hide under your bunk. You got a bunk to hide under?"

"Sure. Nice wooden bunk with no mattress."

"Fuck the mattress. Hide under the bunk until the walls crumble."

"You gonna blow up the jail?"

"I'm gonna blow it down."

Snorting with drunken smugness, he vanished in the dark.

He broke into the church through the narrow side door reserved for bringing out the dead. A lone candle flame hovered somewhere in the darkness and, from high in the steeple, the mariachis' music and singing tumbled down as if falling from the sky. He closed his eyes to adjust to the dark, but the world started spinning, so he opened them again. He felt his way along. At the bottom of a wooden ladder fixed to the steeple wall, he looked up. The bell, lit by firelight, seemed a hundred feet above.

"Jeezus," he growled. "Why so high?" He put his hands on a rung. Climb, he thought, one rung at a time. It's like walking, except you have to use your hands. He managed a dozen rungs, then his arms began to shake. Don't look down. Don't look up. Don't look anywhere. Just climb. But his hands wouldn't let go.

When he was five years old he had climbed an old cherry tree in his grandfather's yard, to look over the houses and see what mysteries lay beyond. He did well until the last branch. It was dry. It broke off in his hand. He fell through the dense old bower, its tangled branches slowing his fall. And all the way down—seemed such a long time—all he could think of was how sad his grandfather would be if he died.

He didn't break a bone, but his dread of heights remained—he was convinced the next fall would be his last. It was a strange dread, not that of falling, but that something he depended on—a handle, a grip, a footing—would somehow give way. But soldiers have been working here for days, he told himself—same ladder, same rungs—so what are you afraid of?

Think of something more scary than falling, he chided. Cover a fear with a worse fear. He tested the next rung, and when it held, he went on.

He climbed without looking down, but he felt the ladder and steeple sway, and not to the same degree each time, nor even the same direction.

He was wheezing, out of breath. If only I weren't so drunk, he thought. If I weren't so drunk, I wouldn't be bloody up here. Whoever invented steeples? And ladders? And thinking? He concentrated on a vision of the pallid woman. Her face turning suddenly into a death mask. Now, that was scary. Those eyes turning icy. That steely mouth. Keep climbing, keep climbing. That padlock of a mouth holding everything inside. "Almost there," he muttered. "Almost there."

Hanging sixty feet above the ground, with every muscle clenched, he suddenly remembered where he'd seen her face before. In nightmares. He'd read about her in a poem in grade school. Later that night he'd dreamed she came into his room and sat on his bed. Touched him with hands of ice.

Her *lips were red,* her *looks were free,*
Her locks were yellow as gold;
Her skin was white as leprosy,
The Nightmare Life in Death *was she,*
Who thicks men's blood with cold.

An opium-smoker wrote that about a sailor who had sinned, and was doomed to sail forever with the half-dead woman as his only companion. And here she was. That's why she wanted to sail with him to Tahiti. Death for a crew. Death at the helm in the middle of the sea.

He reached the top rung, out of breath, his heart pounding with fear. He flopped onto a plank and clutched it. "Aya yaya ayee," the mariachis sang. He pulled himself up to the opening in the belfry. Breathe deep. Just breathe deep. Then he forced himself to look down.

Behind the church, the cemetery shimmered with the flames of a thousand candles. Women were still polishing headstones with rags. Glowing skeleton costumes swayed among the graves draped with flowers; sugar skulls littered the grass.

In the plaza before the church, bonfires flickered and colored lanterns dangled, and people danced languidly as if swimming through darkness among islands of light. The scene started spinning, so he looked away to the dark sea and the ketch lit by stars.

He pulled his knife from its sheath. Gripping the familiar handle cleared his head. He crawled along the plank toward the bell, climbing under and over the timbers that had been used to slide it from the steeple. He wove himself through the web of ropes that lashed the bell to the beams above. The music swelled and children shrieked in delight. He waited until the song ended in a long boisterous trill, then he reached up, grabbed the bell rope just below the tongue, and slammed the tongue with all his might against the bell. A thunderous echo shook the steeple. He thought he'd go deaf. He slammed the tongue again. Then for the third time. When the sound died off, someone in the plaza cried out, *"Es uno milagro! Mira! Mira!* Look at the bell rope hanging still against the wall. How can the bell ring by itself, if not by miracle?"

Dugger crawled along the plank to the ropes that tethered the bell.

Then he reached up and cut them.

The ropes recoiled with fury, slicing the air. They struck his face and chest. He grabbed for the plank, but everything was sliding, falling—the beams, the timbers—and the great bronze bell slid sideways and slammed the steeple. It broke the wall. Beams swung and bricks poured down, and bats and ropes zigzagged through the dust. The bell teetered; then toppled. With its tongue clanging a last toll, it tumbled toward the plaza through the firelight.

Kate sat near the cockpit with her legs over the side, watching the lights and the flames of the plaza on the shore. She longed to be there, among the crowd, the smells, the music and laughter, and it struck her then that she couldn't remember when she last laughed out loud. And to dance. Oh, to dance. Close to him, with her head on his shoulder, arms wrapped around each other. She stood and started swaying to the rhythm of the music that came in waves with the breeze over the sea. Maybe if you don't look, she thought, the yearning might go away. She picked up the tail of the mainsheet from the coil and trailed it over the side, back and forth in the sea, creating a stream of phosphorescence behind it. Seeing the sea sparkle, she smiled. I can make my own lights.

The church bell tolled three times. She turned and saw it catch the firelight as it fell. It hit the roof of the low building beside the steeple, and a moment later there rose a tumult of crashing, breaking, shouts, and cries. Gunshots rang and a great cloud of dust rose and billowed over the plaza in tall glowing streams. Kate rushed to the mast. She grabbed the main halyard and began to hoist the sail.

Dugger fell backward into the abyss. The plank he had been on was flung into the air and he was catapulted through waves of dust, hitting walls and rungs, beaten from all sides on his way down. So she *was* Death, he thought, and waited for the last blow, the ground against his head, when he felt a rope wind tight around his upper arm. The rope yanked his arm from the socket of his shoulder, inflicting a pain he had never known.

He dangled in blinding agony.

He groped with his foot and found the ladder, then wove his good arm around a rung. He unwound the rope. His bad arm hung like a rag doll's. He eased himself down. Once on the ground, he sat against the wall and let the wave of nausea subside. He spit out some blood. Slowly, from the elbow up, he felt along the arm. No break. But it was out. Dislocated. He had seen it happen enough aboard big ships, when winches or windlasses grabbed sleeves; or when nets being fed out with lead balls snagged an arm. And he had seen old Morrison pop them back in, but first he would give the man a thick stiff rope to bite so as not to break his teeth. Then he put his fist into the man's armpit, took a firm hold of the elbow, and with a quick but ferocious jolt drove the elbow into his side. Levered, the arm would pop back in. But old Morrison was dead. There was no one to help. If he didn't do something quickly, he'd soon pass out from pain.

He stood up and put the bad arm gently against the wall. He edged the fist of the good arm slowly into his armpit. Then gritted his teeth. He waited until the music hit a crescendo, then, with a lunge, drove his elbow hard against the wall. His body shook with pain. But he had felt the pop. And his arm hung better. Useless and aching like hell, but it hung better.

Chapter 7

When the dust cloud hit him, the lieutenant's laughter turned into a cough. He was still coughing when the boy came running, waving his pistol, his dust-caked face streaked with tears. He kicked a crowing rooster from his path and ran at the lieutenant, shouting, "He got away! He got away!"

"Who?" The lieutenant wheezed.

"The spy," the boy roared. "My spy!" The rooster crowed. The boy spun, and with a quick shot reduced it to swirling feathers. He turned and ran back into the dust cloud of the plaza.

The lieutenant strolled through the bedlam of the crowd and, stopping by a fire, sat on a box of fireworks guarded by a soldier. For a while he watched and listened to the madness, then—and he could never explain why—he rose and calmly threw the box of fireworks into the flames.

The night exploded with light.

Sparks spewed, rockets shot up in a chaos of angles, fire wheels spun and rolled away, hissing cones sizzled, and arcs of fire burst among the stalls, against the fountain, the church, the steeple, and the sky. Children shrieked and slapped the sparks and one yelled, "This is better than Christmas!" In a boisterous mass, people pushed toward the sea. "This is a revolution!" a man shouted. "It's the end of the world," an old woman cried. A braying donkey kicked down a fruit stall and the mariachis played with added fervor. An old Indian woman turned a skewered fish over the coals.

The pale woman forced her gait under the dust cloud aglow with light. She tried to escape toward the safety of the darkness, but the voice of Mother Superior rang out in her head. "We do not swing our arms. We place our weight on the entire foot. We float." And she hurried stiffly along the sand where the sea left bubbling foam.

Someone grabbed her arm from behind and spun her. It was a firm grip, but it didn't stop her; instead it propelled her in the opposite direction, toward the crumpled pier. She smelled the tequila before she saw the lieutenant's face. He pushed her hard and fast and she stumbled, but he held her arm and quickened his stride.

They were almost at the pier when she saw the skiff of the ketch. He yanked her to a halt. She tried to run, but he lunged for her and tore the buttons off her blouse. She froze. The curves of her breasts shone pale in the night. He came nearer. Trapped between him and the skiff, she said in cold defiance, "Go ahead. I don't care about that."

He stopped, and pulled her to him instead. "The general thinks you're a nun."

She laughed out insolently. "I'm the opposite, " she blurted. "My name is Darina. Remember, *Teniente?* Do you know what that means?"

The lieutenant didn't know and didn't want to. He yanked her into the skiff of the ketch and pushed her under the foredeck. "Tell the *capitán,* he'd better leave tonight." He pulled a crumpled canvas from the floorboards and covered her with it. Then he lifted the stern and dragged the skiff into the sea but left the bow still wedged in the sand. He leaned on the gunwale and caught his breath, then he straightened, turned, and walked slowly back toward the plaza and the light.

Chapter 8

Dugger cradled his aching arm and staggered out the side door. He stopped at the ruins of the jail, the walls fallen outward, bars twisted, a fire smoldering somewhere in the rubble. "Nello!" he called, but nobody replied. He walked over the pile of rubble but found nothing but splintered planks.

At the stables the boy saddled his horse, cursing, and Dugger ducked his head and hurried on with rockets and sparks shooting over him.

He stumbled along the surf until he could see the ruined pier and the skiff.

He stuck the bad arm into his shirt, leaving the good one free to lift the bow and shove it into the sea. He was surprised at its weight. With the skiff afloat, he waded in and glanced along the shore. There was no Nello. Through the shouts, music, and explosions now came the sound of horseshoes clattering on stone. Dugger clambered in, grabbed an oar, and turned the bow seaward.

The horse broke darkly through the illuminated dust, the rider's elbows flapping like short wings. Dugger plunged the oar off the stern and poled the skiff with one arm, fiercely, through the shoals. The horse charged down the narrow street. Dugger, now on his knees, plunged the oar, but even bent double he could no longer touch bottom. The skiff drifted. The horse neared.

With his one good arm, he tried wrestling the oars into their locks. He had them. But when he tried to row with one hand, an oar fell into the sea. He cursed and retrieved it when he heard a voice nearby, weak but determined. "I can row."

She was on one knee, holding her blouse closed. She got onto the thwart and took an oar, then reached out to him for the other. Wedging the handle of one oar beneath her thigh, she slipped the other smartly into the lock, then braced her feet and pulled with every muscle in her body. She rowed with long hard strokes. "I'm from Inishturk," she blurted between pulls. "An island. We row before we walk."

Through the dark, the sails of the ketch billowed toward them.

Thank God for Kate, Dugger thought.

Over the distant blast of fireworks now came gunfire from the shore. The boy bridled his horse but it jittered in agitation and the shots went wild.

"There's a man running on the pier," she said.

A bent figure ran down the fallen pier, waded through waist-deep water, then climbed up its seaward end.

"My first mate," Dugger said, smiling deep inside.

She began to turn the skiff, but Dugger stopped her. "Not yet."

The horse had settled and the boy now saw the hopelessness of his shots from that distance, so he holstered his pistol. Better this way, he thought. Now I can kill them all. And he spurred the horse and rode off at full gallop on the long curve of beach that ended at the narrow rock-lined pass.

Behind the stump of the broken steeple, like an eye in wide amazement, rose the moon.

Nello reached the end of the pier and he eased himself down a plank, leaned on a piling, and awaited the coming skiff. He jumped in and, seeing the bare-shouldered woman, lost his balance in surprise.

"She's a nun," Dugger said.

"Good disguise, Sister . . . "

"Agnes," Darina said.

Nello looked down at Dugger's arm.

"Dislocated," Dugger said. "But I popped it back in."

Nello pulled out the pouch of coins and dropped it in Dugger's lap, "No more beans and rice," he said. "Is Kate sailing alone?" Then he added, "I'll row, Sister." He took the oars and turned the skiff toward the ketch, which was now sailing parallel to the shore. They edged near. He tried to match the speed of the ketch, but the skiff still bumped hard amidships and Darina had to reach quickly for the gunwales and hold on.

Kate was bracing the wheel with her knee, pulling hard on the sheet to avoid the pier, and only when Dugger was aboard did she see the woman. She was climbing loose-limbed over the lifelines, her long skirt cumbersome. The moon shone on her pretty face and white flesh under the torn blouse. Kate felt a pang of jealousy like a blow to the stomach. She turned away and waited for it to pass.

When Dugger neared, she saw his face welted and bloodied and her jealousy turned to fear. "Are you all right?"

"It's nothing," Dugger said. "Shoulder came out, but it's back in."

The pier was near. Kate said, "We have to tack." As the men tended the sheets, she spun the wheel with one hand and with the other tied her hair.

The jib slatted and the winch whirred as Nello hauled it to port. The bow swung, the ketch stood upright, then with an easy motion heeled and pointed past the pier. Dugger stood near Kate. "She's a nun." He nodded toward Darina.

"I could tell from her habit," Kate said.

"They shoot priests and nuns here," Dugger went on. "She stowed away in the skiff. Then she rowed. Saved my life."

"You should pin a medal on her chest. She has it ready for you." Then she looked down at his limp arm.

She kissed his face. "I'll make you a sling."

The moon threw long shadows as sharply edged as daylight.

Holding in her hands a small cotton bag, Darina sat with her shoulders slightly hunched. Kate checked the sails before she looked at her again. She envied her feminine clothes, the lace shawl, the skirt, the lace-up boots, but felt good about them being out of place on the ketch. Then she saw her full mouth and eyes big and dark in the moonlight. Pretty but defenseless, she thought. "You'll get less spray on the port side," she said sternly, and was surprised when the woman got up and crossed the deck.

"Thank you," Darina said.

"You stow away often?" Kate queried.

Darina listened for a hint of humor but heard none. She smiled nervously. "This is my first time," she said.

"You climbed aboard like you do it all the time."

Darina blushed. "I'm from Inishturk," she said. "An island. We grow up on boats."

Kate turned the wheel a notch, then looked up at the sails. "I can mend that blouse for you," she said.

The current was washing the ketch toward the pier. "We need more sail," Dugger said.

He took the wheel, Nello hoisted the yankee, and Kate sheeted it in. The ketch heeled more and the bow pointed just past the pier when a tirade of shots rang out from the shore.

"Get down! Get down!" Dugger yelled.

At the bottom of the alley, two soldiers—one leaning against a wall, the other sitting on a crate—were firing with little interest toward the land end of the pier. A lanky figure struggled up the fallen pilings, then ran out on the teetering pier toward its end. The bow of the ketch passed the first piling. The soldiers reloaded without haste, then fired again. The runner slipped and stumbled but came on. As the mast pulled abeam the pier, he came in full flight, then, with an enormous leap, landed in the mainsail well above the boom. The sail collapsed and he slid down, spilling onto the deck.

Dugger grabbed his knife. "This is an infestation," he muttered.

"We have to tack," Kate said.

The sails shook as the ketch came fast about and then, with everything sheeted tight, headed out of the bay. The lanky man huddled on the side deck to keep out of their way.

"Capitaine Dugger," the man said in a heavy French accent. *"Je m'excuse d'arriver comme ça* . . . not the way for a gentleman to board."

"Jesus," Nello said, surprised. "It's him!"

"Who?'

"The one that bought the rifles."

The man dusted off his pants; a faint smile creased his face. "One helps where one can." Then he added politely, "Robert Guillaume, at your service."

"I don't need service," Dugger said.

"I will of course pay for my passage," Guillaume said.

"Passage to where?" Dugger said.

"To Tahiti, *naturellement."*

"We're full up." And he put his good hand back on his knife.

"Please, I am happy to sleep on deck."

"It's over three-thousand miles, a month's voyage. We haven't the food. You'll have to swim back." Dugger nodded at the shore.

"I am an expert fisherman. I can catch my own meals."

"And when we run out of water, can you make your own rain? Get overboard now or you'll have to swim too far."

Guillaume looked around. "The army will kill me ashore." Then he flatly said, "I will pay in gold." And he drew from his pocket a small handful of coins.

"Even a pound of gold can't buy fresh water in the doldrums."

Guillaume looked at the ragged crew: Dugger's slinged arm, Kate in cast-off clothing, the shorn woman holding rags, Nello covered in dust and blood and kneeling from fatigue. "How about *fourteen* pounds, *Capitaine*?"

Dugger looked at Nello, who signaled nothing. He stiffened the grip on his knife.

"Or if not fourteen pounds," the Frenchmen softly said, "then how about fourteen . . . *tons.*"

Guillaume looked around. No one moved.

"Fourteen tons of gold, *Capitaine.* Would that induce you to ration your drinking water?"

The sails shook. With a nudge of the wheel, Dugger dropped the bow and filled them. Against the dark of night, he could see the boy dismount in the pass.

Guillaume clutched his small side pack and spoke hurriedly. "Inca gold stolen by the Spaniards and hidden in a church's catacombs in Pisco, Peru."

Dugger saw the boy draw his gun and sit on a rock, waiting.

"For centuries monks guarded the gold in secret," Guillaume went on, "until one of them fell in love and ran off with a sailor. Now it's in a lagoon near Tahiti. Fourteen tons. I have the map." He held out his bag. "A fair price for a first-class ticket, *non, mon capitaine?*"

The bow of the ketch rose over swells that squeezed into the bay. The sea fog came in long plumes from the darkness. Dugger saw the boy settle behind a rock, and rest his forearm across it, his gun glinting in the moonlight. From that distance he couldn't miss. Not with his hand steadied. Dugger tried to edge farther to the shoals. The ketch rolled wildly in the cross-waves from the point and they all grabbed for something to keep their balance. If only the fog would come, Dugger thought.

"Everyone below," he finally said.

Nobody moved.

"Now," he said.

THE BOY WATCHED THE KETCH sail into the pass. He set the sight of his gun on the helmsman's chest. Don't waste a bullet now, he thought, wait until they're so close you can see fear in their eyes. He saw them walk past the helmsman and go below. Good, he thought. They are scared. Less confusion. I will kill the helmsman with one shot and the ketch will hit the shoals, then, as they come out, I will kill them one by one.

He watched the ketch roll toward the long tendrils of fog. He aimed at the helmsman just below his hat and slowly squeezed. Then the ketch sailed between him and the rising moon. His finger froze.

He knelt in the still-warm sand and gazed in childlike wonder as the billowing sails of the ketch slowly filled with moonlight, as if the moonlight itself were pushing it out to sea. He gazed as the helmsman drove the ketch through the glitter toward the open ocean, where the fog closed in like giant wings and hid it in the swirling, silver mist.

Book Two

The Voyage

Chapter 9

The wind stiffened and they sailed straight out to sea so that by midnight they were well clear of the bank of coastal fog. By four bells, the last mountain had sunk below the east horizon, leaving nothing around them but endless, heaving water.

Darina had felt seasick trying to sleep down below—hadn't said so, didn't complain—but Nello saw her with shoulders hunched forward, staring blankly at the floor, so he told her to go above, where she'd feel better in fresh air. Later, when they were well offshore, out of reach of the heat of land, he came up for his turn at the wheel and without a word put a blanket in her lap. She thanked him with her eyes cast down, and wrapped it around herself.

Through the two hours of his watch, they sat in silence.

When Kate came to take the helm, Nello bade good night and turned in, and the two women remained alone under the billowing sails. With the sails balanced, the ketch held course on her own, so Kate touched the wheel only now and then to keep the bow from swinging in the odd cross-swell that pushed against the keel. In the chill dawn she buried her face in Dugger's sweater and let its sleeves slip down over her hands.

Darina watched the horizon.

"Do you feel better out here, Sister?" Kate finally asked.

"Much. Thank you," Darina gratefully replied, and felt even better for Kate having asked.

"Where is this Inish . . . "

". . . turk," Darina offered. "Inishturk. Just off the Irish coast. A small island. So beautiful. So wild." Her memories came flooding back and her throat tightened. "We saw the stars only once in a while. Mostly on winter nights." Then, to avoid being asked more questions, she added, "Where are you from?"

Kate tried hard to recall her childhood, but there were only fragments, and none that fit together. "Vienna. The river froze around broken reeds . . . there was music in restaurants; violins . . . And a big Ferris wheel that . . ." She couldn't remember the rest, so she added, "That touched the stars." To hide her lack of memory, she blurted, "Is your convent on Inishturk?"

Darina turned back to the sea. Her mouth went tight. "No," she finally said. "In Galway."

"Is that nearby?"

"You have to cross all Connemara if you go by land. Or sail by Slyne Head and inside Aran if by sea."

"I read about a convent. It was peaceful, with big gardens. Is yours like that?"

Darina made a small sound, sarcastic and sad. Then she took a deep breath. Her eyes drawn hard now, she looked up at Kate. "Do you know the Magdalenes?"

Kate shook her head.

"Or the Magdalene Penitents?" When Kate's face showed no recognition, she said, "Mary Magdalene?"

Kate clutched the spokes, feeling exposed. The name sounded familiar . . . but she shook her head.

Darina spoke softly in short phrases with stumbling pauses, as if reciting something she had to memorize for school. "Jesus cleansed her of seven demons. She witnessed his crucifixion and his burial . . . She was first to see his resurrection . . . An apostle to apostles . . . Loved by Jesus more than the others."

Kate stared at her, fixated. It all sounded incomprehensible, like a foreign tongue she recognized but couldn't understand. She had forgotten the wheel. The ketch wandered off course, the sails luffed. When they filled, the booms slammed with a bang. Almost at once, the hatch slipped back and Nello's tousled head popped out into the night. He squinted sleepily at them. "Everything all right?" he asked.

"I slipped," Kate said. "Everything is fine."

Nello came up, walked the moonlit decks to the bow, looked up to check the rigging, then came back. "Just call if you need anything," he said, and dropped below. The hatch slid shut.

Grateful for the interruption, Darina had drawn back against the cockpit coamings, the blanket pulled up high around her neck.

They remained silent. At long last Darina said, "Forgive me. I've lived the life of Mary Magdalene since I was fifteen."

"How long ago was that?"

"Seven years." She paused. "And you? How long have you been at sea? You look awfully young to be such a good sailor."

Kate blushed in the darkness. She looked away. What could she say? That she couldn't remember? That she didn't even know her own age? When she felt the blush drain off, she leaned down to hold her face in the binnacle's glow. "How old do you think I am?" she asked.

Darina moved closer for a better look. Kate's face looked wiser than she expected, more worldly. "Twenty-seven?" she said. When Kate turned back to the wheel without comment, Darina asked, "Am I close?"

"You're dead on," Kate said. She looked down at Darina. The wind and the damp sea air had mussed up her short hair, and her big round cheeks glowed fresh from the wind. With her face now softened, her mouth had grown wider, full. Her head slowly tilted. She seemed at peace.

The cross-waves came more frequently now and Kate had to hold the wheel with both hands and brace her feet to keep the ketch on course. I'm being pushed too far west, she thought. The ketch is struggling. I wish Dugger were here to ease the sails. "An inch at a time," she could still hear him say. "Let out an inch of sheet at a time." She unwound the jib sheet from the cleat but held it tight around the horn; she could feel the power of the sail and had to brace herself against it. "An inch at a time." But when he first showed me in the dinghy it was easy. There was never much wind in that closed bay, not with those cedars shielding it. Beautiful tall cedars. He kissed me in their shadow for the first time.

My God! She thought, and held her breath. I remember *all* that.

A small rogue wave hit. The ketch lurched. Darina sat up.

"Was she a saint, this Mary . . . ?" Kate uttered. The moon touched the west horizon and dissolved in the mist.

"Magdalene," Darina said. "Yes. But first she was a penitent." Then she quoted distantly, "Cometh Mary Magdalene early, when it was yet dark, unto the sepulcher, and seeth the stone taken away." She spoke dryly, as if confessing some often-mentioned shame. "In the house of Simon the Leper, Jesus sat at meat. There came a woman with long hair and an alabaster box of ointment of spikenard, very precious, and she broke the box and poured it on his head." Kate held her breath, because all of a sudden she recognized the words. Darina went on, "And Jesus said, 'She hath done what she could; she's come to anoint my body . . .'"

And Kate heard herself murmur, "'. . . for the burying.'"

"You *do* know Mary Magdalene," Darina said in surprise.

"It seems so," Kate whispered.

"Jesus cleansed her of her demons and she repented. The Magdalenes were like her: full of demons." She looked far to the west, where the last of the moon now sank. "Fallen women," she said.

The ship's bell tolled eight times. There was stirring down below. The new watch was coming up the ladder with heavy steps. The hatch slid back.

Darina whispered, "I'm a Magdalene."

Chapter 10

As if sliced by a knife, the dark dawn split with light. A pink glow poured out of the black clouds and splashed along the curve of the horizon.

With sunlight slanting into the galley through the hatch, Guillaume threw sizzling pork bits into the iron skillet, then sliced peppers and diced onions. He sang softly an old melody he had learned as a boy, about a shepherd whose true love had died, and who was begging a low cloud to carry him to heaven to find her. He emptied the skillet and poured in the whipped eggs.

Dugger pulled the blanket over his head and pressed against the hull so the sound of the rushing sea would drown out the Frenchman's singing, but the rattling of the skillet and Nello's thudding on the deck above broke into his dreams. Morning, he thought, why does it always have to be bloody morning?

They sat in the cockpit eating Guillaume's cooking.

"This is very good," Kate said.

"Merci, Madame," Guillaume said. "Thirty days at sea is a long time. It is best to divide it up with succulent meals. *N'est-ce pas?"*

Dugger lowered his fork and took his first good look at the

man. His blond hair was slightly graying at the temples. His eyebrows, slightly raised, gave him an air of pleasant bewilderment. Creases flanked his mouth and one meandered above his chin, but his forehead was smooth, as was the skin beside his eyes, which were mostly twinkling as if he never ceased to find something amusing in life. He wore a canvas jacket that looked like it had taken long journeys before. He's too tall and gangly, Dugger thought. His damned limbs will get tangled in the rigging.

Within three days they had settled into a routine. In daylight everyone but Dugger took four-hour turns at the helm, and Nello, Kate, and Guillaume took two-hour turns at night. Kate had sewn a sling for Dugger's arm, so he felt comfortable enough to steer for short spells during the day when the others were around to trim sheets or shorten sail. The rest of the time he moved around listlessly trying to do chores with one hand that required two.

Nello took sextant readings morning, noon, and night, then, with the new coordinates, corrected their dead-reckoned progress on the chart. He stayed busy keeping the taffrail log free of sea grass, patched sails, and whipped the ends of lines with waxed string.

Kate seemed to be all over the ship wiping dried salt from varnished cap rails and hatches using the morning dew, then taking over the galley to bake saltwater bread in a pot. She mended Darina's blouse and Dugger's clothes, soaped his hair and poured seawater over him as he sat on the cockpit sole. Then she went to wash his clothes in a wooden bucket on the aft deck. Darina saw her begin to scrub the clothes laid on the wood. She stood and watched as if unable to look away. Then she came and knelt beside her. "Let me do that," she offered, and took the pail. "I'm a good scrubber. I'm a Magdalene, remember? For seven years I worked in their laundry. They made us scrub clothes every day from dawn till dusk."

Kate looked down at her hands. Underwater in the pail, her knuckles looked enormous, the joints of her fingers gnarled, the creases deep and wide—the hands of an old woman.

After meals, Darina knelt on the aft deck, scrubbing the dirty dishes in a pot. She seemed most comfortable when working; at other times she was nearly invisible on the ketch. With her lace shawl over her head to fend off the sun, the speckled light shimmering across her face, she would unfold a small bundle of letters and read them over, but the boat's movement soon made her queasy, so she spent long hours huddled on the aft deck watching the stern wave spread over the empty sea. She spoke only when spoken to and even then in a quiet and unassuming fashion, and always ending in such a way as to invite no reply.

When alone, she gazed often at her hands, surprised to find no wet clothing in them. She could still feel the burn of steaming water of the laundry, as she dragged the boiling clothes out of the cauldron and readied them for a beating on the stone. And she could smell the acrid stench of the bar of lye, feel her hands cramp from fatigue at day's end, hear herself scream out when her fingers jammed in the rollers and the girl cranking the handle just kept cranking because she was too afraid to stop. And she remembered how she learned to stand the pain when coals from the iron spilled onto her feet and burned through the flimsy slippers to her flesh. She stood there in silence.

That was the worst: their enforced silence. Some sixty girls and women of all ages, facing each other in two rows, scrubbing, in endless silence. The slosh of water, slapping of hands, and silence. Day after day; dawn till dusk. The same face across from you. And you weren't allowed to even ask her name. You spoke only three times a day, to utter prayers—whose power faded the longer you scrubbed in the steam.

You scrubbed for the nuns, for the priests, for the wealthy of the town, and all you got was a bowl of porridge twice a day, and Sister Phyllis yelling, "You'll wash the filth out of your own lives when you wash the honest dirt from people's clothes."

"Morally unfit for Irish society" was their crime. Women of the night, unwed mothers, or victims of fathers' or brothers' or uncles' passions, or girls from orphanages deemed too pretty to be let out. They had been committed by priests, or doctors, or relatives, sentenced to the Magdalene laundry behind twenty-foot-high walls with broken glass cemented at their top, without mention of how long they would be kept there. It often turned out to be all their lives. And when they died, the word PENITENT was chiseled in their tombstones, to remind them for eternity that they'd fallen.

The Magdalenes and their demons.

But she wouldn't mention all of that to Kate. Why sadden her? Let her live in her innocence. In the immaculate bliss of long-lost memories.

Under Nello's direction, Kate and Guillaume had been sewing an awning from an old sail to be rigged between the mizzenmast and main shrouds to shade the cockpit. Kate finished stitching an eye for a hook when she looked up at Guillaume pushing through the big three-sided needle with a sail-maker's palm. "You sew well," she said. "And you're an excellent cook."

Guillaume smiled broadly but didn't reply.

"You'll make someone a good wife," she said with a laugh.

Guillaume pulled the waxed line through tight and snug. His smile waned and he said without a hint of irony, "I hope so."

At the rare times he wasn't cooking, Guillaume fished. He fabricated fanciful lures out of tin cans, strings, and wire, and had caught a small bonito the first day, which he served up in thick steaks with fried onions, beans, and rice. The head and spine of the fish he tied off the stern and trailed behind the ketch as bait.

One day, with the sun high and the view into the sea still deep, he saw a fish he didn't recognize follow behind, and swim around the bait. Hello, fish, he thought. Do you like the shiny lure? Come close. Closer. Then, repenting, he added, Sorry, fish. Being hooked is no joke. Believe me, I know what it's like being hooked. And be dragged along. To want to swim free but be forever dragged along. If we weren't hungry, I promise you . . . So I'll hook you, but in my heart of hearts, I hope you shake yourself free.

He watched the lure flash back and forth underwater and thought, All my life I've been dragged along. By traditions; expectations. Everyone wanted me to be something I wasn't. My father said, "What the hell is it you want?" I didn't know. But I knew what I didn't want: his life. I just wanted to be happy. To look for someone to be happy with. To dream with. To look for someone who's been looking for me.

Chapter 11

Twilight shrouded the ketch in somber hues and the air was heavy before nightfall. Darina came up the companionway ladder and quietly slid the hatch closed behind her. "Good evening," she said to the lone figure at the helm.

"Evening, Sister," Nello said.

The ketch rolled softly over low, long swells, and the ropes creaked a gentle chorus in their blocks.

"I hope I'm not disturbing you," Darina said.

"No," he said. Then he added more reassuringly, "No."

A strip of blazing light clung to the horizon. It lit the sprinkling of rain that fell over the ketch, so fine the drops dried as soon as they fell. A benediction, Darina thought. "It's so beautiful out here," she said. The drops made her skin tingle and she ran her hand up, then down her arm. The movement caught Nello's eye.

He turned his head slightly as if to say something, but upon seeing her stayed silent. Even with the constant motion of the ketch, she bore herself stiffly and upright as if held up by gimbals. She sat now with her palms flat on the raw wood beside her thighs, drawing in the warmth remaining from the day. Behind her the evening star burned a small hole in the sky.

"Do you believe that our fate is in the stars?" Nello mused.

"In the stars?" Darina absently repeated. "I would say it's in our hands." She laughed softly. "Unless we let others grab it."

"Not in God's hands?" Nello asked, genuinely surprised.

"I think he has his hands full; must be a lot of work moving those stars around every night."

Nello felt his throat tighten with attraction. He turned away.

When he didn't answer, she crossed her arms against the chill. The twilight thickened. All around her, colors deepened: the varnished wood, the greened bronze port lights, his white shirt luminous below the canvas sails, and a thread of brilliant red—the telltale on the portside shroud—a length of yarn to indicate the wind, blood-red against the now-indigo sky.

"The stillness is lovely," she said, barely louder than a whisper.

Nello pocketed his pipe, then checked the compass. He waited for a while before asking, "Aren't you cold?"

"I'm from Inishturk." She laughed. "That's cold."

As suddenly as they had come, the blazing colors faded. When the darkness was complete, Nello stuffed his pipe and struck a match. Seeing in the light of the flame that she was still awake, he killed the flame. "And what is it like, this Inishturk?"

She hesitated. "It's small. Maybe a mile long. The cliffs are . . . enormous. The waves so cruel they carve holes through the rock." Then she smiled. "Sorry. It's an island. North of Aran."

It came suddenly over her with the clarity of a dream and an intensity she hadn't known in years: the bursts of sunlight through clouds onto green moors, the scattered houses by the harbor, the lone creek where sheep drink; and the great waves crashing against the cliff, making a sound deeper than thunder. Green water climbed halfway up the bluff, and the spray flew skyward like upward-driven rain. And she remembered how, at the first light of dawn after summer storms, she and her twin brother Michael would run across the island down to the raging ocean, to where it had carved a big hole, leaving a graceful bridge. And they would stand hand in hand in mortal terror close to the coming waves, and watch the next giant breaker bulge under the bridge and come roaring through the hole and up the chute. Then they would turn and run, escaping, howling in delight—her brother laughing so loud it rang over the roar—with the spray engulfing them and the wave towering behind.

And how in later years Maeve Flynn, two years older and the wild beauty of the island, would insist on coming along. In her red dress, her favorite, tight at the bosom and flowing from the waist, she stood beside them, but, when they ran, always ended up a bit behind even though with her long legs she could outrun them in a heartbeat. But she lagged behind and cried out for Michael to help her, and when he stopped and turned, she'd run into his arms.

Until one day she cried out but they just kept on running. And when they finally turned, Maeve Flynn wasn't there. And forever thereafter, Maeve Flynn wasn't anywhere. Only her red dress rode the current around the island and came into the harbor one evening on the tide.

Darina stood up suddenly, as if she meant to run. She seemed startled to see Nello there in the binnacle's faint light. He leaned heavily on the wheel, the bulk of his stout shoulders and arms pressing his shirt and vest. His crumpled black hat was pulled low on his eyes, and the short curved pipe hung like an upturned question mark at his chin.

She sat back down and turned toward the darkness.

Her brother went silent after that for weeks. He would climb to the highest, windiest point of the cliff to sit and watch the sea. And he wouldn't let her go with him to watch storm waves anymore. He stopped her at Connally's cottage, whose windows, even though well back from the cliff, were caked with salt that glittered in the sun. From there he would go alone down to the murderous hole.

Once she snuck after him and watched from behind a shepherd's windbreak on the hill. He stayed back from the bridge, sat against a windbreak but on the windward side. Embracing his knees, he watched the waves roar in, watched as if expecting one to bring Maeve Flynn back from the sea.

Nello saw her fingers reach out in the dark, as if to beckon someone or push something away. He sucked on his pipe and the embers lit his eyes. "They say no man's an island," he said gently. "Or woman."

She tried to say something, to break the vise of memory of her brother at Connally's window drawing in the caked salt with a sharpened twig. Always the same thing, storm after storm: Maeve Flynn in her dress.

"I'm sorry," she said. "I get caught in memories."

But she didn't mention how Mr. Connally, who had no children, came back one day from Galway on the boat, bringing a flat tin box of colored pencils and a pad of paper that was nice to touch. Her brother drew on the pad after that. He kept it under his pillow because it was full of Maeve Flynn, but now without a stitch of her red dress on her.

Darina looked up. Nello, lit by the compass, was staring at her hard.

She shuddered. "Sorry," she said again. "Something I thought I had forgotten long ago."

He watched her shudder become a shiver. That must have been some memory, he thought.

"Take the wheel," he ordered gently.

She didn't rise.

"Come on," he said. "Take the wheel."

He changed course five degrees to allow her latitude for mistakes without disturbing the setting of the sails, and waited until she had her hands on the spokes. "Steer two hundred degrees."

He left her at the wheel and went below.

She did her best, but felt a strange crosscurrent tugging at the rudder and the bow would swing and she would overcorrect in the other direction. He came up carrying a blanket, but instead of handing it to her, he unfolded it and wrapped it around her as she peered down at the compass. He got the ketch tracking back on course, then pulled a silver flask from his pocket.

"Here," he said. "Have a drink. It's not the blood of Christ, but it does the trick."

She held the flask to her lips and took a drink of the rum and coughed. "It's very strong," she said, and felt a rush of heat surge through her deep inside.

"Take another," he offered.

She did, then held out the flask.

He took back the flask but held her hand with it. "Come here," he said gently.

She hesitated, then took a small step closer and he wrapped his arm around her and pulled her near. He rubbed his hand on her back until the blanket was warm. She was rigid, holding her breath.

"It's all right," he said. "Sailors do this after cold gales to put the heat back in."

Her shivering slowly eased.

"Fishermen too," she said. "When they're pulled from the cold sea."

The ketch flew south by southwest in the sun. The trade winds blew without gusts or lulls and the needle of the log pointed fixed at eight knots. The air seemed to grow hotter by the hour and Nello calculated six more days to the equator. That night, when the first flying fish sparkled in the moonlight, Guillaume sprang to action. With Dugger's permission, he stitched two small fishnets into one and draped it from the main boom to catch the fish that flew across the deck.

"Are you a fisherman, then, *Monsieur*?" Kate inquired. "Or a treasure hunter? Or a sea-cook?"

Guillaume laughed as he attached the net. "None of those, madame. I'm happy to be whatever the moment calls for."

The next afternoon, Guillaume asked if he could bring the chart of French Polynesia out to the brightness of the cockpit because his eyes had become somewhat weak with age.

He studied the chart, made measurements with dividers, pulled out a small black notebook held closed by knotted string, read, scribbled some notes, then, without looking up, said, "Some of the gold is still in Inca jewelry, some was melted into Spanish coins. All of it is sunk off a small coral island in the Tuamotus."

Nello, sitting near him whittling a bung for a seacock, looked down at the chart and smiled. "Can't be more than a few hundred of those, spread over, what? A few hundred square miles?"

"No, *Monsieur,*" Guillaume corrected politely. "Spread over a few thousand. Fortunately, I have the map that reduces the search to just three islands, and just one tiny atoll," and here he read from the notebook, "with a steep, coral pinnacle on its eastern shore. Behind it lies a deep, pear-shaped pool."

Nello stopped whittling. They all looked up at each other, then at the chart—all but Darina, who sat nearby, oblivious to the world.

"At the bottom of the pool," Guillaume continued, "in a grotto, the gold." He closed his notebook but kept a finger in it as a marker. "The runaway monk told his lover, Alvarez, about the gold guarded by the priests in the catacombs. Alvarez, the monk and three shipmates sailed back to Pisco. But they killed the monk at sea before they reached port. Alvarez and the ship's captain, Killorain, were good Catholics, so they impressed the priests of Pisco with their love of God. Then they warned the priests that the runaway monk was coming with a shipful of cutthroats the next day for the gold. The priests, of course, were frightened. It was too late to send for soldiers from Lima, but Alvarez had a plan: they could load the treasure on his ship and sail it to Lima—guarded by the priests, of course. At dusk, when the fog rolled in, they began to load. It took all night, using five donkeys; over twenty trips each down the steep steps to the harbor. That was how I calculated about fourteen tons.

"They set sail before dawn. By the next day, all the priests were dead. Their bodies were kept aboard for days until they were well clear of the coast. The sail to the Tuamotus is normally easy with the trades, but the big schooner, overloaded and short-handed, struggled, and the four grew exhausted and failed to watch the currents that carried them into the doldrums. They drifted there for weeks and ran out of water. One man became so deranged they had to kill him.

"A storm finally brought rain but it also blew them onto a reef near Raraka. They hauled the treasure from the wreck for nights on end, and rowed it, nearly a half mile to the pool. A lone Chinaman lived on the island diving for pearls. They got him to hide the gold in the underwater cave. Then killed him. During the next storm, they burned the ship to leave no trace. They sailed their skiff and some gold to Tahiti to buy a schooner, but there were none for sale, so they booked passage to Australia to find one. Within days two of them were killed in a drunken brawl. Killorain went to jail for twenty years for manslaughter. He emerged a tramp. I met him a few weeks before he died."

The wind eased; the ocean smoothed. The sky was blue and cloudless all around, and the ketch seemed to glide atop a blue sphere in clear space.

"Gold." Guillaume sighed. "Fourteen cursed tons, *mon capitaine*. All yours."

"And you?" Dugger asked from the helm.

Guillaume smiled. "Me? I'll be happy with a small *pourboire*. A tip." When they all looked skeptically at him, he added, smiling, "I will celebrate my fifty-third birthday next month. At a certain time in life, things such as gold seem, how you say? Silly."

"But it does buy a roof over your head."

"Oh, I have a small roof in the Jura. With two rows of vines, even a pond for geese for fois gras and six plum trees for *eau-de-vie*. And I have a pension when I retire."

"From cooking?"

"No, *Capitaine,*" Guillaume said firmly. And he took a deep breath before he added, "From being a spy."

As if a sudden gust of wind had weather-cocked their heads, they gazed at him, amazed. First Dugger, then Nello, then Kate, imperceptibly drew in arms and legs, as if leaving them extended would reveal things best kept hidden. Only Darina stared at Guillaume with a spiteful gaze.

Guillaume noticed her malice. He straightened up, offended. "I imagine being a spy is a bit like being a nun," he said. "No one knows who we are, what we think, what we want."

Dugger felt a strange unease run through him.

"Was it you who tried to start the revolution in Mexico?" he asked.

"The poor people of Mexico, especially the natives, needed a helping hand. France is on the side of the oppressed," Guillaume said without apology.

Dugger remembered the lieutenant but said nothing.

"Especially if it might give them a stepping-stone to French Polynesia," Nello said.

"Are you planning to start a revolution in Tahiti?" Kate inquired.

"No, madame. This time I'm hoping to stop one." Then he added, "I'm hoping to find the man who *is*."

Darina turned away, as if she had suddenly found something to hide.

The trade winds were steady now, with whitecaps night and day. Rare gusts blew salt spray across the bow and cabin, and it dried to shiny crystals on the varnish and the sails.

"So, tell me, Guillaume." Nello smiled, as they sat after dinner in the cockpit, Nello steering, Darina washing up, Guillaume smoking a short, thin cigar. "In Tahiti, is it the rich French colonialists rising up against the oppressed poor?"

"We are not colonialists, *Monsieur,"* Guillaume replied, offended. "At least I hope not. The French have never been like the English or the Spanish—we have no desire to 'rule the waves,' or to exterminate *les indigènes,* or put them in open prisons that they euphemistically call 'reservations.' We try to insert ourselves into the existing culture, to learn from it; learn their customs, how to cook, how to dance. It is true that we try to bring peace among warring tribes. The Tahitians—the Marquesans even more so—have been forever at war. And not just island against island but village against village, valley against valley."

"It is a harsh and brutal land, islands of old volcanoes eroded into canyons, with isolated tribes. When the harvest is poor and food in short supply . . . All we want is for them to live in peace."

"As long as they live the French way, right?"

"Whatever way they choose, but without the wars, without the cannibalism, without the infanticide."

"And without their dances?" Darina looked up at him from the aft deck. "My brother wrote that you even outlawed their feasts and dances."

"Ma chère soeur, it was not the French government that forbade them to dance, but your Catholic Church. And you would sympathize if you had seen the dances. They start out so beautifully, romantically. But as the night wears on, they become—and

I don't say this disparagingly—savage. Their wild nature overcomes them. The whole tribe. Women have been known to die from the ecstasy. And I don't mean *le petit mort,* I mean *le mort finale.* Sorry to be so frank, Sister. I'm sure this kind of physicality is not something you . . ."

Guillaume watched her blush deeply. She clasped her hands. He looked at them for the first time: they were not the pale, limp, soft hands of a nun. Between the thumb and forefinger the muscle bulged round, as did the heel of her hand. The knuckles were large, worked; the hands creased, the fingernails worn. And underneath the thin shirt he saw strength in her arms.

You do know physicality, Guillaume thought. About flesh and bone. Maybe you would understand the way they danced, in the firelit steamy night. Their wild smiling eyes. The sweat running down naked limbs, their chests. Their flowing movements; then their violent movements. Exuberant, uncontrollable joy. Your God must look with pride at the bodies he had created. So perfect. So perfect for that moment which he made them for: for the power and the beauty. Not to bend or kneel in limp supplication, but to dance. To dance with utter abandon, under the moon, the stars, to the rhythm of the drums, the roar of the waves; up to that supreme moment, that fleeting, everlasting moment of ecstasy. The ecstasy.

Chapter 12

The last trace of light drained out of the sky and the ketch sailed suspended in an enormous darkness. Kate was at the helm softly humming, then she fell silent and there was only the sound of the stern wake folding behind them like a sigh.

Darina sat near her in the cockpit, wrapped in her blanket, with eyes open wide staring at the stars. She was afraid to go below and sleep, for now, when she closed her eyes, Maeve Flynn's mother stood before her, holding out her arms. "Go away," Darina whispered to the darkness.

She and her brother had turned fifteen that day, more than a year after Maeve Flynn drowned. She was running home on the path with a stringful of shiners from the harbor when Maeve Flynn's mother stepped out of her little yard. She held out a flimsy package wrapped in brown paper. "It's Maeve's favorite dress," she said. "I bought it for her on her fifteenth birthday." She had taken extra work combing wool on the mainland to afford it. Maeve had no father. Some people said he had been lost at sea, others said he was lost in a pub in Galway, but they all said it was his blood that made Maeve so wild.

The mother held out the package: "It will fit you now, now

that you've filled out. How nice you'll look. You'll add color to the island. And what a joy it will be to see you bounding up the hill."

She was afraid to tell anyone at first. Their father said never to accept anything. "Every man must look after his own," he said. Not that anyone on that poor island had anything to spare. Maybe he had said it because he had nothing to give.

The first summer storm blew all through the night. She couldn't sleep. She heard her brother get up at first light, heard him pick up his boots, walk in his bare feet, and softly shut the door. She just lay there. You can't do it, she told herself. You just can't. But she rose and watched him walk over the hill. Then she slipped off her nightgown and pulled the package from under the bed.

She put on Maeve's red dress; it clung to her every curve. She looked in the mirror while tying her hair to one side, like Maeve. Then she softly shut the door and went out into the dawn. "Such a pretty dress," she mumbled.

Kate glanced back. "Pardon?"

Darina shook herself from reverie. "Just remembering," she blurted. To avoid being asked more, she added quickly, "Where did you wear your first nice dress?"

"In church," Kate said, surprised at the sudden memory, "walking with my father, with everyone looking at me. I was wearing a long white dress, holding flowers."

"Your wedding?"

Kate hesitated. She could only see isolated faces and the slanting light. "I don't know . . ." she said finally. "I can't remember."

"You can't remember your wedding?"

Kate concentrated on keeping the ketch on course. "No," she said, "I can't remember very much beyond the past four weeks."

Darina wasn't sure she had heard right. "What do you mean you can't remember?" she said.

"Not clearly. My oldest whole memory is one night, four weeks ago now." She gazed at the compass as if at a crystal ball. "We fled from a snowy village in a cove. Dugger, Nello, and I. There were big mountains, a full moon, tall trees, deep snow. And terrifying carvings of beasts. But I can't remember things clearly before that. Just pieces. I only know my name because Dugger kept saying it."

Darina looked away in confusion. Mother of God, she thought. How can this be? All my life I have been trying to forget. Pretend things never happened. With hard work, and prayer, and Sister Claire's help, I nearly managed. Inside the Magdalenes' walls, it was easy. Everything was in order like the beads of a rosary. But out here, on this ocean . . . in this darkness . . . if only the dawn would come. Hail Mary, blessed be thy name . . . And she instead, poor child, blessed with no memory. When she turned back, Kate was staring at her.

"It's not so bad, really," Kate assured her.

"Amnesia," Darina blurted. "Did you hit your head? Or have some kind of shock? Sometimes it comes when you are trying to forget."

Kate stared at the faint glow of the candle flame flickering in the binnacle. "Sometimes I get a glimpse," she whispered.

"Can't Dugger tell you what happened?"

Kate hesitated. "He doesn't know how bad it is. I don't want him to worry. He worries enough about everything already."

Darina moved her fingers along the stitching of the blanket's hem as if over a rosary.

"Here," Kate said. "Let's have some liquid courage." She held out the flask Nello had left her. Darina took a sip, then gave it back.

"To your health," Kate said, and took a long draught.

"And yours."

Down below, the ship's bell struck eight times. The watch had ended.

The moonglow spread above the eastern horizon as if the dark of night had begun cautiously to bloom.

Chapter 13

The trade winds strengthened throughout the dawn and there were whitecaps when the sun scorched the circle of the sea. The companionway hatch slid open, the smell of fried bacon filled the salty air, and Dugger climbed up, squinting into the searing light. He looked around the vast emptiness as if there could possibly be something new to see, walked without a word past Nello at the wheel, lowered the canvas bucket over the side, and scooped the top off a wave. Awkwardly, with one arm, he pulled the bucket onto the deck, washed his face and neck, hung the bucket back in its place, then, staring with yearning far ahead, he came and sat down beside Nello.

"You're a half hour early for your watch," Nello said.

"Too many people down there," Dugger muttered.

"We could throw some overboard."

"Should have done that in Mexico. You want me to steer?"

"No. But you could stop grumbling." He was gauging the latitude of the rising sun. "We'll cross ten degrees north by noon," he said. "That's nearly two hundred miles a day. Not bad for ship with a one-armed captain, eh, Cappy?"

"Wonderful," Dugger said.

In the white haze that masked the curve of the horizon, a short black line drifted north into the sun.

"Did you see it?" Nello said, his voice full of excitement.

"Oh, good," Dugger said, blocking the sun with his hand. "More company."

"Come on, Cappy. A month is a long time on this raft. There's nothing wrong with fresh faces."

"You really like her, don't you?" Dugger said.

"Who?"

"The death mask with blue eyes."

"She's a nun," Nello said.

"Like no nun I've ever seen."

"It's still coming," Nello said, fixing his gaze on the horizon.

The dark curve showed clearly now, rising, falling, thickening in the sky. It dropped at great speed until it nearly touched the water, then as it neared the ship it banked sharply north, its drooping wings stretching across the sun.

"It is beautiful," Dugger murmured.

"We're a blessed ship, Cappy," Nello said. Then he slipped open the hatch and called below, "Ladies and gentleman, we have an albatross."

Kate's tousled head was first out of the hatch, followed by Darina, with dark shadows under her eyes from lack of sleep, and a moment later Guillaume, excited, holding in each hand a gutted flying fish.

The albatross reached the top of its rise, then, dropping its head, came downwind at speed. Its enormous black wings, as wide as the stern, drooped in a curve from its white body, and swept gently upward at the tips. Its long, gull-like beak yellowed in the sun, and its dark, knowing eyes seemed to glance with calm amusement over the ketch and crew.

Darina murmured, "They say it's a lost soul."

Guillaume raised the flying fish so they glittered in the sunlight, then he threw them in an arc behind the ship. The albatross let them fall, then plucked them from the sea.

"We must already be at ten degrees north," Nello said. "There's an island east of us."

"Will we see it?" Kate asked anxiously.

"It's more than five hundred miles away," Nello said.

"Good God. How can it fly so far?"

"It doesn't fly," Nello said. "It glides. Watch. It rarely flaps its wings."

Guillaume waited until he was sure Nello would say no more then he politely added. "Their wings lock, I believe. Isn't that so, Mr. Nello?"

"I didn't know that," Nello said.

"There is a sheet of tendon," Guillaume went on, "that locks their shoulders with the wings extended so they remain outstretched without using a muscle. In fact its heartrate is no more in flight than at rest. See how it catches the vertical air off the face of a wave, then it glides to the next one? For every foot of height, it can glide twenty feet. Sort of sails on the wind. Like us."

"Just more quiet," Dugger said.

"And less grumpy," Nello said.

After the albatross arrived, life changed on the ketch.

They all moved about less, spent time watching the bird as it followed, watched it soar in gusts, then dive deep and come up with small squid, or come close in when Guillaume waved his hands full of galley scraps. And they spoke less, searching the sky silently when the bird glided away, and breathing sighs of relief when, an hour later, it returned.

Watching the bird, they began watching the sea and sky: the movement of clouds, their changing colors of pinks and grays and whites, the narrow curtain of rain falling far away slanted by the wind, the way the waves curled, then broke, the way their long, smooth backs flowed like liquid silk.

And that night they began at length to watch the stars.

Darina had gone below at four bells, shut the door of her small cabin, and, without lighting the lantern, sat on her berth with her feet flat on the floor. Then she closed her eyes and prayed. Watching the bird, she had missed her prayers at vespers, so first she begged for God's forgiveness, then said the Lord's Prayer, but said it all by rote, not hearing a single word until "Forever and ever. Amen."

When she opened her eyes, the moonlight was dancing on the bulkhead through the port light. She went to the small mirror bolted to the bulkhead. With no mirrors in the convent, she had to steal a glance in the shop windows in Galway on those days before Christmas when the Magdalane Penitents took their yearly outing. But those were fleeting glances and all she ever saw were her big cheeks reddened by the cold.

Now she looked pale and ghastly in the moonlight. With her high forehead, jutting cheekbones, and the moonlight leaving dark shadows in the hollows, if she had no eyes and lips, she could have passed for a skull. She ran her hand over her shorn hair. It was growing out; felt silky to the touch. She had been used to her bristly shaven head. She rubbed her cheeks softly until she gained a blush. You look almost alive, she thought.

She clasped her hands and mumbled a childlike rhyme that she'd first heard Sister Claire say alone in the chapel behind the Ortus Conclusus, the walled garden near the pond. It was a small, secluded chapel where she liked to go and pray, until that winter evening when she found the thick door locked and the window shuttered. She heard a man's voice inside murmur a prayer against demons. Then another voice, impossible to say whether from man or beast, bellowed, howling, in utter agony. Sister

Claire said it was an exorcism. She never returned.

She crossed herself, climbed into her berth, and lay against the hull. The water rushed noisily close to her head. She felt the wind through the port light ruffling her blouse. As she drifted off, she whispered, "And give eternal rest to the soul of Maeve Flynn." She was nearly asleep when she heard herself say, "And the child."

Chapter 14

Kate's watch was to begin at midnight, so Darina was surprised to find Nello at the wheel. "Good evening," she said, trying to hide her confusion.

The moon burst from the clouds so bright it hurt their eyes. The ketch came alive—the sails, the deck, the lines all glowed. The stern wake etched white curves into the night, and a boat length behind, yawing left, then right, were the white breast and dark wings of the gliding albatross.

"Like a guardian angel," Darina said.

"But half white angel, half dark," Nello said.

"So silent," Darina said. "It suits the night."

"My favorite time of day." Nello smiled.

The hatch slid back and Kate's head slowly rose. "Sorry I'm late," she said.

"I'll take your watch if you want," Nello offered.

"I'll be fine," Kate insisted, covering a yawn.

"I'll make sure she stays awake," Darina said.

Nello looked at her. Her mouth was tight again. Except for the dark veins at her temple, the moon lit a face as cold as alabaster. Maybe Dugger's right, he thought. "Good night," he said, and, passing the silver flask to Kate, he went below.

"This is for you," Darina said, and handed Kate an empty book. "Perhaps if you were to write . . . things might come back as you write."

"That's awfully kind," Kate said. "Or I can draw. I love to draw."

"Yes," she said, but her lips went even tighter. "Drawing is good too."

Kate raised the flask. "To unexpected friends." She smiled. She took a quick drink and passed it to Darina.

Darina raised the flask. "To friends," she said, and the silver glittered as she drank. Then she sat down near the wheel.

The ketch veered off course and Kate moved quickly to bring it back. "If I could just steer my brain like I can steer this ship," she mused. "I'm always trying. One day, hoping to ignite some memories, I asked Dugger if he remembered our first kiss. 'Sure,' he said. 'Oh, yeah?' I said. 'Let me hear some details.'"

Darina sat up. In the darkness she saw Maeve Flynn in her brother's arms.

"Did he tell you?" she urged Kate.

"Yes. He said I started crying. Not a very romantic thing to do, was it? And that I held him so hard, I almost cracked his ribs."

Darina watched the albatross come abeam the ketch. It stared at her, then raised its wings and leaned against the wind like Maeve Flynn under the bridge. "Did it help?" Darina said.

"Oh, yes. As he went on, everything came back. My dinghy. Last summer. I sailed it alone after midnight to his ketch. He'd been sleeping on the aft deck and when I bumped the ketch he woke up. He didn't say anything, just reached down, and held my face in his hand. I couldn't imagine anything nicer. Then he got into the dinghy and we sailed to where tall cedars blocked the moonlight. I was aching for him to touch me again. He kissed me. My temple, my cheeks, my lips. We were so in love."

The albatross banked, flew off north, and vanished as if swallowed by the night.

Darina saw herself in the red dress following her brother on that stormy night. "My brother was in love," she blurted. "With Maeve Flynn." It had been years since she'd said her name aloud.

"Who's Maeve Flynn?" Kate asked, utterly surprised.

"She drowned. He loved her. My brother loved her. And she drowned." She looked up, her face calm, but her blue eyes shone with tears. "And after every storm, he would sit and watch the waves. Watched them roar up the chute. Where she drowned. Waiting for the next wave to bring her back from the sea."

Dear God, Kate thought. The compass, she thought. Watch where you're steering. South. Two-o-five. Without a word she reached out and took the flask. She drank, then handed it back to Darina.

Darina gazed down at the tops of her sunburned feet. She felt the rum rush to her head, and the words and images boil inside her, as if they just couldn't wait to be let out. She began telling Kate all about Inishturk: the harbor, the houses, the sheep, the bluffs, and the raging sea. She told Kate about Michael, and how they were inseparable since the day they could crawl. How they'd played with dolls for years and he'd pretend to be a girl, then later they'd play soldiers with swords and she'd pretend to be a boy. And how after a battle they drank water with molasses and pretended it was ale. Then she told her about the storms, the waves. And Maeve.

Kate stood spellbound at the wheel.

Then Darina told her every detail of the day that Maeve Flynn died: the sound of round stones grinding in the waves, the smell of kelp that hung in wreaths from rocks. And Maeve, oh, Maeve, with her laughing eyes.

Then she told her all about the brother's year-long grief, his silence, and the pictures he drew. And about Maeve's mother and the red dress in brown paper. And the night of the next storm when her brother got up in the dark and headed toward the sea.

"I unwrapped the paper and pulled out the dress," Darina said, and swallowed hard.

"You don't have to say any more," Kate whispered. But Darina kept looking down as if she hadn't heard.

"I tied my hair to one side just like Maeve. Then I took off my nightgown and slipped the red dress on. I felt as if I had entered a new life.

"I went out and ran past Connally's cottage, circled past the bridge, then doubled back and ran down a cleft to the shore. The waves were as big as hills. The island shook from their pounding. I could barely catch my breath. I hid behind a rock. The water swirled around my knees. It felt like ice. My legs cramped, then grew numb, but still I waited. He finally came, and sat down. And, like a statue, watched the sea. I prayed to God to forgive me; I swore on my eternal soul that I meant no harm. I meant to help him.

"As a long wave receded, I stepped out into view. The dawn lit us both. He stood up. He was far away, up the slope. Then he started down toward me. I panicked. I held out an arm like I'd seen Jesus do in prayer books, and he stopped. I waved to him—waved goodbye—then, when the next wave rose around me, I sank into it and swam under, and hid back behind the rock. He came down to the shore yelling, "Maeve." He ran into a wave. Almost drowned. I crept up the cleft and ran away through the dawn."

She looked pleadingly at Kate. "I thought I could help him, don't you see?"

"Yes," Kate whispered. "Of course."

"I never told anyone. Not even in confession."

Tears filled Kate's eyes. She reached out and touched her arm.

"It's all right," she whispered. "It's all right . . ."

Darina looked away. "Hours passed before he came home. When he stepped into the house he was shaking from the cold. His lips were blue. But worse were his eyes. It broke my heart to see his eyes. They weren't just sad, but pleading, pleading for something. Or for something to end. I don't know. Our mother heated water on the stove, but by evening he was trembling with fever. For three days he burnt.

"The storm raged on, so the doctor couldn't come. Our father tried to sail to Galway for him, but when he launched the skiff, the storm threw it back on shore. He got Father O'Malley for last rites. My brother looked at him with such relief, as if this was what he had longed for all his life. Father O'Malley left after midnight.

"I went to bed but didn't sleep. Just lay there in the dark with the rain pounding like pebbles on the slate. My brother tossed, and whispered Maeve Flynn's name.

"I lay facedown on my bed and promised God I'd do anything he wanted if only he would please let my brother live. I touched the worn paper of the package under the bed. Then I slipped on the red dress.

"I went out into the rain and walked around the house to my brother's window. The moon came and went among the clouds. I put my face against the pane to see inside; he barely made a lump under the sheet. Then he turned. And saw me. His eyes came alive. He sat up, then came toward me as lightly as a ghost. His face abeam, with an infinite tenderness in his eyes. He raised his hand and put it against the pane. Against my face. Then he slowly drew. Across my forehead, down my temple, around my chin, my neck, then down where there was no moonlight. His hand stopped moving . . . It stopped at my heart."

Darina fell silent. She lowered her head into her hands. She kept her face down for a while, then looked up and stared off into the night. "Then suddenly he was gone from the window. I heard the door. I didn't dare look up, but I felt him there beside me. The rain poured down. He took me in his arms. 'We can't,' I whispered. 'You know we can't.' 'It's you,' he whispered back, his voice full of life. His eyes blazed with fever. I pushed him, pulled him, nearly had to drag him back inside. He was drenched. 'You'll catch your death,' I whispered. He had his face against my neck. He kissed my neck, my shoulder. His face was so warm. Then he pulled my dress down, all wet, he peeled one arm at a time. I felt his hot tears. 'I love you,' he whispered.

"I said, 'I love you too.' It felt so good to say it. 'I love you too.'"

Darina bit her lip; her chest heaved with gasping sighs. "My heart was breaking . . . I loved him."

Kate wrapped an arm around her. "Of course you loved him," she whispered. "He's your brother."

But Darina pulled back, her face contorted, "You don't understand; I *loved* him. Maeve Flynn died because I *loved* him. That day in the storm, I grabbed his arm. When Maeve yelled, *he* turned, but *I grabbed his arm* and pulled him up the shore. I loved him. God forgive me; I *loved* him. And that night . . . that night . . ." She sobbed. "I loved his hands that night . . ." She whimpered softly, then gave a great sigh as if swallowing her pain.

Kate clutched her, their faces touching, mingling their tears.

Chapter 15

By noon the air had densed into a haze. The sun grew sickly pale, and the restless sea, sallow and without luster, heaved as if exhausted. The wind blew in fits and starts, the ketch slowed, surged, then slowed and surged again, the sails straining, then luffing with a lift and bang of the boom. The albatross gained height, fell, pitched, and yawed unable to find a constant line of lift. After a while it gave up, landed on the waves, pulled its head under a wing, and slept.

Nello leaned heavily against the port shrouds and spread his feet for steadiness. He held the sextant perpendicular with one hand and with the other swung the sextant's index bar, then yelled down through the open skylight, "Cappy! Time?"

"One minute," came the reply.

Through the clear half of the fixed mirror he could just make out the horizon, and he swung the angle-measuring arm until its mirror reflected the sun onto the fixed mirror below. Then he rotated the fine adjustment, bringing the rim of the sun down to the edge of the sea, and yelled out, "Ready. Mark!" Down below, Dugger entered the time into the log just as the ship's clock tolled the first of eight bells. It was noon. He went up for his turn at the helm.

"Where's the bird?" Dugger asked, looking around, surprised.

"I didn't see him fly off," Guillaume replied, letting go of the wheel. "He might just be sleeping."

He sat down in the shade and watched Dugger settle the ketch on course with one arm. It's always there, Guillaume thought. No matter how friendly he tries to be, there's always that sadness in his eyes.

Nello, holding the sextant, stopped and looked around at the thickening sky. "Nasty, and getting worse." He went below to do his calculations.

"Will it rain, *Capitaine?*" Guillaume asked.

"It will do something," Dugger said. "With this dismal a light."

Thunder rolled across the heavens as if someone were rolling an empty barrel in the attic. Guillaume wiped the sweat from his eyes. "If you don't mind my saying so, it would be advisable to be moving your arm or the shoulder will lock."

"Like the wings of an albatross."

"But only one wing."

"Then I'll go forever in circles." Dugger smiled.

"Like most of us," Guillaume said.

Dugger eased his arm out of the sling. It felt stiff, but without pain. At first, he rested it on the wheel, then little by little, he used it to steer. "Good idea. Thank you," he said.

Guillaume didn't reply. From the locker below the seat, he pulled out a wooden box of fishing gear and, with a honing stone, began sharpening a hook. He had not fished since the albatross arrived, afraid that the hooked fish might attract and hook the bird, but while the bird was gone or sleeping he could give it a quick try.

"Is it the male that comes so far alone?" Dugger asked.

"Male, female, in between. I don't really know. I guess whoever gets the wanderlust." He set the tip of the hook in his fingernail to see if it was sharp enough to catch, but it just slid off. "They mate for life, you know. Funny; when they court—preen, stare at each other, dance, even point their bills at the sky and utter a kind of howl—it's all so exciting. So new. Each pair invents a language all its own. But once it's over—the courting, I mean—they never use it again. Maybe it's like falling in love: once the fire goes out . . ."

The haze darkened and a louder rumble rolled. The light dimmed and the air became heavier to breathe.

"Guillaume," Dugger said. "Isn't it odd for a spy to tell everyone he's a spy?"

"You don't believe I'm a spy?"

"No," Dugger said.

"There, you see? It worked!" And he gave a quiet self-congratulatory laughter. "Had I told you I was a buyer of pearls, or a copra trader, or that I had a thriving pineapple plantation, and then made just one little error, a slip, you would say, *Aha! Caught in a lie. Must be a spy!* As it is, you don't believe me, plus you probably think I'm crazy, and that allows me to spy to my heart's content. *N'est-ce pas?"*

He tried the hook again, and this time it stuck. "Anyway, aren't we all spies? Don't we watch each other constantly wondering, What does he think? What does he feel? What does he really want? And if we can't figure it out, we remain miserable."

"What's wrong with miserable?"

Guillaume studied Dugger's face, the drawn cheeks, stubborn cleft chin, the furrows on his forehead, the deep creases beside his lips that now beamed with a broad smile. And his eyes, a child's defenseless eyes that couldn't for a moment hide what he felt.

"Rien du tout!" Guillaume said. "Nothing at all. Being miserable keeps one young. Keeps one *amusé.* In fact, I can't imagine what 'happy' people do for fun."

"Fall in love?"

Holding a flying fish over the gunwale, he sliced open its underside, releasing a flow of blood, then slid the hook into its mouth and out its eye.

"Fall in love? *D'accord,* but why? I propose to you that they fall in love to have their hearts broken so they can join *les misérables. Les misérables* can dream. Dream of a touch, an embrace. A night of flesh to flesh; the long hours in the moonlight. But what's there for a happy man to dream of? A new pair of pants? A tie?"

"You might have something there."

"Oh. I *do* have something there. I was taught two vital things about spying: One is trust no one, not even your mother. And two, they will always, always, always try to make you fail. Not the enemy but your own people. Your comrades, your *commandant,* your friends. *Vraiment.* They are set on you failing. And you know why? Because failure will torment you, make you miserable, and that will bring improvement. Innovation. I hate to guess what they have waiting for me in Tahiti."

He dropped the fish and fed out just enough line to have it alternately skim and dive, but kept it short in case the albatross returned. "Anyway, if misery pushes spies, it will surely push most people. Take you, for instance, *Capitaine.* Take your life. What a life! *Merveilleuse!* Danger. Glamour. Adventure. Your own ship; une *femme ravissante.* And how did it come about? What triggered it? Happiness? I'd bet on misery. You were miserable enough to throw away all, to become a man without a home, without a country, without bounds—what could be more romantic?—all because you had been truly miserable. Had you been happy, you'd still be there, buried in some dismal warehouse, grinding through a dismal day with your dismal wife and dismal children awaiting you in your dismal house. No, *mon ami,* God blessed you with his greatest gift: misery. To have and to hold, forever and ever, amen."

Dugger looked back at him, then broke into laughter. When he stopped, he shook his head. "Maybe we really *are* all crazy," he said.

"It's this air." Guillaume sighed and wiped his forehead with his sleeve. "It's like breathing steam: boils your brain from inside. Anyway, I'm not so much a spy as what I believe you call a secret agent."

"What's the difference?'

"Not sure. I guess a spy tries to find out what's going on; instead, a secret agent tries to stop it."

"The rebellion?"

"The rebellion."

"The glass dropped two more millibars," Nello said grimly, standing in the companionway with a book in his hand, looking at the sky. "With this haze I can't get a true horizon. We might be near the equator, but I'm not sure if we're above or below it."

"Two millibars since when?" Dugger asked.

"Since yesterday. And two the day before."

"Damn," Dugger said in an undertone.

"Short notice, soon past. Long foretold, long last," Guillaume recited.

Dugger spun around to look at him. Guillaume smiled.

"You know too much," Dugger said. "You really are a spy."

He shrugged. "I keep trying to tell you that."

"And her." Dugger nodded toward below decks and the cabin. "Is she really a nun?"

"Don't you think she is?"

"Is that what spies do? Answer a question with a question?"

"It's the best way to learn without giving yourself away. As for the sister, I'd wager fifty-fifty."

"Well, if she's not a nun, she's the dullest woman alive."

"Or the most intriguing," Nello said irritably. "Now can we

get back to the problem at hand before we die here of gossiping?" He opened the book of the Hydrographic Department of the Royal Navy and read aloud. "If the corrected barometer reading is five millibars or more below normal, it's time to consider avoiding action for there can be little doubt that a tropical revolving storm—the most violent of storms at sea—is in the vicinity." Then he looked around to catch the direction of the wind. "But how do we take avoiding action if we don't know what we're supposed to avoid? Look," and he spread the open book on the cockpit seat. There were two diagrams of tropical storms. Storms in the northern hemisphere, where the winds spun counterclockwise around the eye, had their most destructive part, 'the dangerous quadrant,' north of the storms path. In the southern hemisphere, where the winds spun clockwise, the "dangerous quadrant" lay south.

"I think we're still in the north," Nello said. "The swells are coming from the southeast. That means, to escape the eye, we have to keep running south."

He went to the aft deck to check the direction of the wind, before it was deflected by the sails. Facing dead into the wind, he spread his right arm slightly more than ninety degrees and pointed. "The storm is somewhere there. It's blowing less than force six, so the worst must still be a couple of hundred miles off. At least ten hours before it hits us."

"Well," Guillaume said, "if you have no objections—I have a feast in mind."

"Sure," Dugger grumbled. "Why not a last supper?"

Kate sat at the desk under the deck prism, writing in the notebook she had received from Darina. *I think there'll be a storm,* she began. Through the skylight she heard voices, mingling with rustling from the galley. She didn't really listen to what was being said, until she heard a strange voice from above. It was low and agitated and stirred unease in her. It was Nello. She wrote, *Something is wrong. I have never heard Nello sound worried before. The day feels strange, the light is so gloomy, and the wind is blowing harder but in spasms. The sky looks awful. Even the bird has gone away. It feels lonely now. Having him here was almost like seeing land.* The writing stirred her and she wrote quickly, with passion.

We have been gone eleven days. Dugger said the voyage might take thirty; it scares me to think that we have . . . She stared blankly at the paper, trying to do her sums. For God's sake, Kate, common arithmetic, she snapped in frustration. How can you forget something so simple? Are you doing this on purpose? Act dumb so they'll look after you? But they don't even know. So what's it all about? Think. Sums. You were good at sums, remember? Jesus. How can you remember you were good at sums and not remember how to do them? Are you insane? You start with thirty open fingers, you close eleven. How many are left? Use your head. Use your fingers. I don't have thirty fingers. Damn, damn, damn!

The door of the cabin opened. She slammed the book shut. Dugger came in.

"Sorry," he said. "We need you at the wheel for a bit. The weather's changing and we have to batten down the ship. A great excuse for Guillaume to cook a feast." And he stood before her chair and touched her head. "You look tired. Is it the motion?" and he held her head gently in his hand. "I miss you like crazy," he said. Then he gently wedged her legs apart with his knee and smiled. "Mostly your thighs."

She held his hand. "You don't like so many people aboard, do you?" she said.

"It's all right."

"We're lucky they're so nice."

"Nello thinks she's intriguing. Do you?"

Kate tied the string around the book and said, "She's the most intriguing woman I can remember."

A rogue wave slammed the bow, the ketch veered, and they grabbed for handholds. They headed up the ladder.

"Dugger," she began, then fell silent as she climbed. "If the storm comes . . . How far is the nearest land?"

Dugger tickled her bare foot. "About two miles," he said.

"Two miles?" she exclaimed. "Why didn't you tell me?" And she stuck her head out the hatch and spun around, looking but seeing nothing. "Where?"

"Under us," he said.

"Oh, sweet Mary," Kate whispered. "Two miles of water?"

"Don't worry." He smiled. "After six feet it's all the same."

Book Three

The Storm

Chapter 16

They prepared for the storm. First they lightened the bow, so when hurtling down a wave, the ketch wouldn't bury her bowsprit and foredeck in a trough and pitch-pole, surely shredding sails, breaking masts. Dugger slipped the anchor from its chocks and Nello reached down, grabbed the fluke, and hauled it onto the deck. He drove his marlinspike into the eye of the shackle pin, then beat it with a winch handle to turn it. With the anchor freed, they hauled it aft and lashed it in the lazarette.

The overturned skiff they put behind the mainmast and secured it with a crosslash to the grab rails on the house. Below decks they hauled the anchor chain from the forepeak and coiled it behind the mast step in the bilge. Then they dogged down the hatches, skylights, all the ports, so only the two cowl vents now piped the tepid air below. Anything loose they stuffed into drawers or lockers; cabin doors were hooked open, books tied in, only Guillaume's galley where he whirled among pots and pans remained an untouched mess.

The wind gained force. They dragged out the storm jib and storm trysail, leaving them in their canvas bags, pulled out the head of each, and lashed it to the mast, ready for the track.

Guillaume hurried. "Five minutes," he called. Darina set the table in the cockpit with tin plates and cups. Kate steered. With the sails straining, she tired fast. Nello came aft, smiling, looking calmer now with the ship battened down. "We might just outrun the bugger," he said, and took the wheel.

Kate tried to sound calm. "Will it be like the storm off Oregon?"

"It'll be a lot warmer," he assured her. "A warm rain. In a blow, that makes all the difference."

"And we could use a bath," Kate said.

"Dinner is served!" Guillaume called out, and came up with a mound of chopped tuna garnished with sliced mangoes.

Dugger poured rum in the cups and raised his. "To the equator," he said.

"Wherever it may be," Nello said.

"Le bienvenu!" Guillaume offered. And the tin cups clanged.

Dugger slipped the sling over his head and stretched his arm with care.

"To a two-armed captain," Kate toasted.

Darina said a quiet prayer, then picked up her fork. "Oh, my, this is good."

"Heaven," Kate said.

Guillaume's next plate was covered with small rolls. "Bonito wrapped in bacon," he said proudly.

"My God," Dugger exclaimed. "And what is this?"

"Pommes frites. French fries," Guillaume said apologetically. "Made of sweet potatoes. It was all we had."

"To *pommes frites,"* Dugger toasted.

"To the chef," Kate said.

"To good company," Darina said softly, and everyone murmured, "To good company."

"Eat hearty," Dugger advised. "With a full stomach, you

won't feel queasy."

The ketch caught a wave and surged across the face. Nello hung on with force, but tried to hide his straining from Darina. Thrilled with the fresh speed, he said, "At this rate we'll be in Tahiti before cognacs."

Dugger took the helm. Nello ate.

Guillaume returned with a plate of fried plantains. "May I waste some rum?" he asked, then doused the plantains and set them aflame. They ate and drank and chatted like excited children about the food, the bird, even the coming storm. Only Dugger eyed the sky and steered the ketch.

Nello pulled out his harmonica and began playing an Irish air. For the first time since they had known her, Darina blushed. Then she began softly to sing.

There's a tear in your eye,

And I'm wondering why . . .

Guillaume rose and bowed before Kate. "Madame, may I have this dance?" he asked.

They danced with fluid steps, and twirled around the cockpit. Darina sang with more heart and the others joined in.

When Irish eyes are smiling,

Sure, 'tis like a morn in Spring,

In the lilt of Irish laughter

You can hear the angels sing . . .

When she got to the refrain they all joined in; their voices drowned out the wind.

And when Irish eyes are smiling,

Sure they steal your heart away.

A hard wave slammed the ketch. Cups leapt. Plates slid. Kate and Guillaume lost their balance. They stopped singing.

A gust hit, and the boat heeled.

They washed up in a silent hurry.

Nello helped Darina carry down the dishes. She thanked him

with a smile that vanished quickly behind worry. "You must have seen bigger storms on Inishturk," he said.

"Many," she replied.

"If you begin to feel queasy, it helps to sing."

She glanced at him with gratitude.

"And remember," he went on, "all storms end. And when it's over, you'll have had the time of your life. You'll want to go and do it again."

"Especially if you're crazy," Dugger added.

"We wouldn't be out here if we weren't," Kate said.

"I'll drink to that," Darina replied, emptying her cup, then finished washing.

"Sister," Dugger said, "you'd be safer wearing pants." When he saw her hesitate, he added, "Captain's orders. We might need you at the helm."

"I'll get you something," Kate offered, and they went below.

She pulled out a pair of threadbare cotton pants of Nello's. Darina went in her cabin and came back tying a stiff rope as a belt.

Kate beamed. "Now you're a real sailor."

"Still feel like a washer woman," Darina said, and her face went dark. "It's as if the nuns took everything: my hair, my name, my youth." Then, with a defiant smile, she said, "But I kept my demons."

The ketch lurched hard and there were confused footsteps above. Grabbing for handholds, they hurried out on deck.

The east grew dark with gnarled black clouds, a great clenched fist hurtling at them through the sky. Lightning flashed straight down. Thunder shook the sails.

"Let's drop the mizzen staysail," Dugger said quietly to Nello right beside him. Then he grumbled, "What the hell kind of cloud is that anyway?"

"If we were up north, I'd say hail. I'm not sure where we are, Cappy, but it sure isn't up north."

"If it's not hail, what is it?"

"I'd guess cats and dogs."

"Maybe we should leave the sail and try and outrun it." He steered with one hand and rolled the injured shoulder.

Kate came out, with Darina following. She headed past the helm for the calm of the aft deck. The ketch lurched hard and Darina lost her balance and began, with a jolt, to fall over the side. She reached for the mizzen shroud but missed and went on falling. Nello grabbed the shroud with one hand and, with the other, her arm. Then, all in the same motion, he swung her back aboard. She fell against him. He held her there. Their faces almost touched, and, out of breath, stiff with fright, she wanted to whisper, *Thank you,* but her throat was so tight, her lips moved without a sound.

"I like those pants," he said. "Didn't want to lose them."

"So you want the sail up or down?" he said to Dugger, stepping down into the cockpit.

Dugger just looked at him as he tried to hide the blush. The black cloud grew taller, its dark ribs more dark.

"Let's run," Dugger said. "I don't want to know what's in there."

Guillaume popped out of the hatch. He followed their gaze to the darkness in the sky. *"Mon Dieu,"* he exclaimed. "The devil's angry today."

"Pull in your hook and line," Dugger told him. "A fish will slow us down."

Guillaume hauled in the line. The day went dim like twilight. "I've never played Beat the Devil before," he said. "This is even more fun than spying."

The seas gained height with steeper faces. Their tops curled dark. The spume glowed eerie white against the somber sky.

Dugger called everyone back to the cockpit. "We're going to double the watches," he began. He tried to sound unconcerned, but his voice was flat and hard. "We'll have two people on deck at all times, one to steer, one to give a hand. The others rest. Kate will start with me. Then Nello with Sister Agnes. After that, I'll back up Monsieur Guillaume, that way Nello or I will always be on deck." When he saw them stand in silent apprehension, he added, "These things always look worse then they really are. We just have to think ahead, that's all. We'll reduce sail little by little. Always early. Always in plenty of time. If we need to, we'll run with just a jib. If you see something odd in the sails and rigging, or even if you just feel that something is straining too hard, tell us. The boat can take anything if we treat her right . . . After all, a storm is just air and water."

In the stifling gloom of the salon, Nello and Darina headed to their cabins for a rest. As he hooked the gimbaled table to keep it from swinging wildly, she leaned close and planted a fleeting kiss on his stubbly cheek.

Then she stepped into her cabin and closed the door.

The air was steam. It clung to her skin in drops and streamed down her face like tears.

Chapter 17

The storm closed in. They tried to escape with all sails flying, but by early evening the low black clouds had caught them, swirling like molten lead, fusing with the darkness. As the wind grew, they reduced sail piece by piece, dousing the mizzen staysail, then replacing the yankee with a jib half its size, but the ketch still yawed wildly as she sailed down twisting slopes. They dropped the mizzen.

With his shoulder strong again, Dugger took extra turns at the helm, tirelessly fighting the rising wind and seas. He feared the steepening waves but relished the exhilarating power of the ketch. Cleating the empty mizzen halyard, he glanced at the sea behind them. There were only waves and clouds—the bird wasn't there. His heart sank, then he thought, Would you be here if you didn't have to be?

Night fell without the soothing lull of dusk. The light vanished suddenly from the sky leaving only the suffocating dark and the hiss of breaking seas. Now and then a pale smear flared up in the gloom as a wave convulsed into churning pools of foam.

Dugger steered, with Kate close beside him. He followed no compass course, steered only by the angle of the wind that blasted across the deck, pressing on in the doomed attempt to outrun the storm. Belowdecks the others were wedged into their berths, Guillaume trying to read, Nello staring at the deck beams near his face, and Darina watching the gimbaled lantern steady on the bulkhead while the ketch rolled and heaved.

Then the first gust hit.

An atrocious blast of wind knocked the ketch onto her rails and covered her with flying sheets of water. She lay with port deck under in the stunning darkness, but even half submerged, she persevered and sailed.

Dugger and Kate fell into a cockpit corner, but with an iron grip he held on to the wheel. The ketch righted herself, shedding the sea in streams. Dugger clutched Kate, but the feel of her wasn't enough; he had to hear her voice. "Are you all right?" he shouted, but the wind and crashing seas blew his words apart.

"Yes!" Kate shouted back. "Fine. Really."

The main hatch flew back and a glow shot into the sky. "Cappy! Kate!" Nello roared. "You still there?"

He burst out of the hatch, the storm lantern in hand, his face strained with worry. He hooked the lantern onto a boom-bail and it swung with each lurch of the ketch, lighting the vaporous air and their faces.

"Storm trysail!" Dugger shouted, and Nello went and crept toward the mast. Dugger slid Kate's hands onto the spokes of the wheel. "Steer one hundred degrees! Then when I wave like this"—and he swung his arm back and forth as if shooing away a fly—"head up to two hundred so we can drop the main! Understand?"

Kate repeated, "One hundred. Two hundred."

Dugger took the doubled mainsheet, wrapped it around her waist, and knotted it. "In case you decide on a swim," he shouted. With his knees braced against the cabin, he inched forward to the mast to uncleat the halyard and wrestle down the main. Another gust hit and through the trembling light, streams of brine flew at him like hail.

Just wind and water, he thought, but a bit too much of both.

The halyard wouldn't give. The salt spray had soaked the hemp, each tug of the sails had pulled the knot tighter around the cleat, and the sun baked the salt hard in the braiding, so he had to use the marlinspike to loosen it.

Kate put all her weight against the wheel, clutching the spokes, repeating, "One hundred. Two hundred."

Nello had the lash-downs ready and Dugger finished prying open the knot. Holding the halyard in one hand, he waved the other toward Kate. But with her eyes filled with brine, Kate didn't move. "Two hundred!" Dugger bellowed. "Two hundred!"

The next gust hit and the ketch went on her side into the churning sea. She struggled to right herself, but the gusts detonated one behind the other. A wave burst over Kate and forced her to her knees, but she clung to the spokes, gasping in the foamy air.

The wave smashed Nello into the sail, his face into the canvas, and he swore if they made land alive, he'd never look at the goddamn sea again.

Dugger slid overboard. He had been standing beside the mainmast waving to Kate to head the bow into the wind, when suddenly the ketch went over. He grabbed the rigging, but a surge of water lifted him and he was swept into the sea. The wind drove the ketch into him, and all he could do was hold his breath and wait. The sails were above him, so he knew the ketch hadn't gone turtle but just lay on her side, and with the keel levering her, she was bound to right. Sooner or later.

Down below, Darina and Guillaume were hurled across the salon. The world turned on its side, the bulkhead lamp went out, and they crashed into each other. They lay next to the port light that was now buried in the sea.

In a lull, the drowned ketch began lethargically to rise. She rose slowly, held down by the water in her sails, whose weight, as she righted, began to tear the seams. Stitching parted and distended panels burst. The ketch stood upright and dumped Dugger on deck. The clouds cleaved, the moon shone down, the torn slabs of canvas fluttered like great laundry.

Nello helped Kate up, and turned the wheel. Dugger knelt on the foredeck and with resolute calmness wrapped the sheets around the jib and staysail, then tied them to the lifelines to keep them from flying overboard. Then he uncleated the mainsail halyard to drop the main, but it wouldn't fall. Its lower panels rippled freely, but an upper panel, still one with the bolt rope, had wrapped itself around a shroud and held the halyard tight.

"It's stuck!" Dugger shouted, yanking at the rope to show Nello. "Need the bosun's chair!"

Nello came forward through the buffeting wind.

"I have to go up and free it," Dugger yelled, his voice shaking with worry. "Or we'll lose it."

"So we lose it!"

"And sail with what? If we save the pieces . . ."

"We have a storm sail!"

"The size of a handkerchief! It'll take us a year to reach Tahiti!"

"It'll take you longer if you drown!"

"How can I drown? I'll be tied in! For Chrissake, get the chair!"

Nello considered ignoring him, but Dugger's face remained unrelenting. He turned and headed below to find the chair.

"Get Guillaume to tail!" he heard Dugger call.

The ketch slid down a wave rolling from side to side, the masts drawing fierce arcs across the ragged clouds.

Guillaume tailed the jib-halyard as Nello cranked the winch.

Dugger, his feet dangling from the narrow plank of the bosun's chair, his hands clutching its canvas sides, was pulled slowly up the mast. Don't look down, he told himself. You're tied in, you can't fall. And if you do, what the hell? With the ketch rolling, you'd be pitched overboard. It's only water.

With no sails to dampen the roll, the masts swung like a metronome. He was thrown against the shrouds on one side, then flung through the air into the shrouds on the other. He grabbed the halyard with both hands. Tatters of the sail thrashed him like bullwhips and the rain slashed through the moonlight in silver streaks.

He was past the spreaders. From up so high, the ketch seemed in another world, struggling in immense seas that besieged her from every side. The lantern's yellow glow wandered in confused circles, now lighting the flooded cockpit, now the tangled ropes near the mast.

Darina had come up and gripped the mizzen shrouds. This is no Inishturk storm, she thought. There, you stood on solid granite. This is the violence of heaven sent to destroy the ketch. And crew. Who can it be after but me? Me. The sisters warned you there was no escape. You can escape the Magdalenes, but heaven will always find you. She closed her eyes and clasped her hands and prayed. Forgive me Father, your worst sinner. *Mea culpa, mea culpa.* I deserve all your wrath. But please, Lord Father, let them live.

Kate steered. She could barely make out Dugger near the top of the mast, swaying from side to side, and she mumbled, "Dear God, bring him down safely." As the mast swung, he flew from starboard, kicked the head-stay, and, forty feet above the deck, was pitched toward the mast. He hit hard but hung on. The rain poured down his face, into his eyes, but he began to unwrap the sail. Calmly, Cappy, he told himself. Don't yank or tug, or you'll just make it tighter. It's just a piece of canvas, an old lady could do this. Like untying a shawl. He managed to ignore the height and wind, but his heart was pounding and he had to force a breath. He unwound the tangled canvas from the shroud, then rolled it up and knotted it so it wouldn't tangle again.

Nello roared, "Well done, Cappy!" and Guillaume shouted too, and Kate was so thrilled that for a second she closed her eyes. A wave caught the rudder and the ketch spun to port. The next wave knocked her down.

Guillaume was thrown against a stanchion. He lost his grip on the halyard he'd been tailing and it fed quickly out over the winch. With the halyard now free, the bosun's chair was loose—Dugger fell. The fierce swing of the ketch catapulted him away from the mast, out over the waves. He plunged in a deadfall with the rope trailing behind, and vanished in the abyss of wildly heaving seas.

He surfaced. The seas loomed like cliffs around him. Far up among them, the lantern glowed, then grew faltering and faint, until it vanished in the darkness.

Chapter 18

Dugger floated on his back and tried to catch his breath. Breaking crests and dangling clouds loomed high over him. A wave lifted him, and his hopes rose too that from the top of the wave he might see the ketch, already turned, coming in the moonlight, but once on the crest he glanced around and saw only foaming seas.

He made a brief attempt at swimming, but his bad shoulder ached when he raised his arm too high. Besides, he was unsure of the direction, so he stopped. His head hit something hard—it was a piece of wood; the seat of the bosun's chair. With the halyard still attached, trailing behind. He clutched it. The sound of rushing seas came at him through the dark, passed by, then crashed, as if on unseen reefs. Once in a while there was silence; the wind dropped, the seas fell, and the world became so peaceful he thought the storm could not return.

Then it did.

A savage gust churned up the sea and he closed his eyes and tried to forget where he was. He let his head fall back into the sea. Think of something else, he told himself, something good. In the darkness behind his lids, Kate's face came alive. She looked sad;

holding back tears.

He felt immeasuarble warmth flowing from her; from her arms that clutched him in need, or in passion; from her mouth that clamped over his with urgency; from her whisper, "This is another world."

A black wave broke over him; he swallowed water and coughed. He kept his eyes shut and summoned more visions—one at a time—always close enough to touch. Why her? After so many years, so many women, why suddenly her? Maybe because she loved with such fervor, as if there were only that moment, murmuring, "I never imagined life could be so exciting."

HE SHOOK HIS HEAD. If these are your last hours, he thought, at least put up a fight. He took a deep breath and began swimming. I'm not dying until I see her again. If they can't find me, I'll find them. Or land. It can be done. Remember the Burmese who fell overboard off West Africa a hundred miles from land, and all he did was follow the rising sun, swimming no more than maybe fifteen miles a day—drank rain, even caught a fish that came close out of curiosity. He knew that as long as he kept on, endured, and sang—yes, that was a big thing, wasn't it, he sang, sea songs and folk songs, even lullabies his mother used to sing. Over and over, songs without a break, for hours on end. He sang and swam for six days; the ship's log bore him witness. By then he had no strength for singing, not even humming, but he kept thinking the songs. And on the evening of the sixth day, he *heard* a song. A new song. And he saw, with swollen eyes, a sand spit of the shore. His eyes were much too dry for even a single tear.

So Dugger swam. The clouds were riddled with moonlight and he marked that as east, and swam. And sang. It was a song about an aging highwayman, his hair turning like winter's early frost, his face lined by love and loss and laughter, but even though his eyes still blazed bright, the young and fickle women no longer looked his way. It was a melancholy melody, and he swam slowly, crawling up the waves and sliding like a child in a sled down their shiny backs. Fifteen miles a day, he thought, and one day you'll reach the coast of Chile or Peru. He wasn't sure which, but he was sure of the distance—he would be there by Easter.

"And those fickle women never even look my way."

He swam with his eyes closed and saw Kate in the shadows of that long-ago moonlit night, only the white of her breasts and her eyes, and he felt her flesh against his mouth, then tasted the sweet damp of her thighs and heard her gentle voice and his head filled with her fragrance of a jungle flower and smoke. And he felt his head in her caress.

Then later, when they were wound around each other, he whispered, "I love your taste."

"You can taste me forever," she whispered back. After a long while she said, sighing, "I wish time would stop."

And he remembered feeling a great calm and thinking, This is where life begins.

She kissed away a tear from the corner of his eye and whispered, "You will always have my love."

He swam until his arms shook from exhaustion. He lay out of breath in the storm-torn sea. "I'm sorry," he murmured, "I would have died for you." It's such a waste to die saving a torn sail. But maybe it will help. Maybe Nello can pull the sail down now, and when the storm is over and the sun warm again, you can sit in the shade of the awning with needle and sailmaker's palm and sew up the pieces. And maybe you can sing to pass the time; a good song, a cheery song . . . any song except "My Bonnie Lies Over the Ocean," because by then your Bonnie might be miles under the sea.

He swam.

Chapter 19

An ominous stillness fell upon the ship. The wind ebbed and the only sound was the lantern squeaking, swinging in the bale. They all stood in disbelief, staring at the darkness where Dugger had vanished.

Nello moved first. With all the force he could muster, he hurled the life ring far into the gloom. It splashed on the wave behind which Dugger had sunk. Yanking his shirt over his head, he yelled, "Throw in anything. We need markers!" He bundled it up and threw it after the ring. Then he dove down the companionway to crank the engine, shouting at Kate, "Turn back! Turn back!" He groped for the flywheel handle in the dark.

Kate spun the wheel. "Dugger, don't leave me," she murmured. The ketch headed upwind and, degree by degree, kept turning in the dark. But where is *back?* Kate thought. Where on earth is, *back?* She looked for the life ring but it had vanished among the waves. She wanted to call Nello to help, but he was down below.

With a pummeling gust the wind returned. The ketch struggled. Kate turned aimlessly into the seas that loomed as high as bluffs. She watched the compass spinning. One hundred. Two hundred, a voice rang in her head. "Yes!" she hissed. "That's it!" I was steering one hundred. The opposite of one hundred . . . No! No, idiot! The *inverse* of one hundred *degrees* is . . . Then, in a luminous rush, she remembered it *all.* She saw the long blackboard at school, the severe face of Frau Kleine, and the numbers, the circles, the neat columns of sums, all of it came back—a long, continuous, crystal-clear memory. There are three hundred and sixty degrees in a circle. So the *inverse* of a number is the number minus *half* the circle, hence minus one-eighty. One hundred degrees *minus* one-eighty leaves *minus* eighty. Three-sixty minus eighty is two hundred and eighty. "That's back! Dammit!" she hissed, "Two-eighty is *back!* Thank you, Frau Kleine.!" She spun the wheel. She heard the engine sputter, then start up with a roar. She felt the propeller bite. The compass card wobbled. She watched and stopped it at two hundred and eighty.

NELLO CLAMBERED OUT onto the bridge deck. "I'm holding two-eighty!" Kate shouted through the roar. A wave broke over the bow and swept the deck so only the masts and the skiff remained above the surface. Nello unclipped the lantern from the bale and waded through the boarding sea onto the bowsprit. Clutching the forestay, he held the lantern high, and with the bow pitching wildly he was flung waist-deep into the sea. Then the bow swung high and he stood above the waves, throwing a feeble patch of light into the night.

Kate thought she saw the bosun's chair float by and ran at the rail, forgetting that Dugger had tied the rope around her waist. She fought the knot with one hand, the other on the wheel. Darina saw her struggle and grabbed on to her arms.

"I can swim!" Kate shouted. "I saw him!"

"It was just Nello's shirt!" Darina shouted back, and she held her in her grip as tightly as a vise.

Nello stumbled aft with the lantern.

"I saw him!" Kate yelled.

"It was the shirt," Darina countered. "But I did see the rope."

They were down in a trough with a wave hiding the moon, and only as the wave moved on and they climbed did they see the jib halyard on the smooth face of the wave, snaking like a serpent, slowly in the moonlight, up the face of the wave, into the foaming crest.

Kate pointed the ketch at the middle of the rope, held that course, then searched the waters as the ketch crabbed sideways, rolling across the seas. Nello clipped in the lantern and untied the boathook, and with a knee braced on the cabin side, he scanned the sea. They neared the rope.

Dugger felt no fear. Lying on his back, turned away from the wind, he breathed well, taking a bit of salt splash now and then, the rest of the time feeling the rain falling softly on his forehead. He felt a deep sorrow that he would never touch her face again. It isn't fair, he thought. I'd give anything to touch her a last time. His mind drifted. He smiled. Anything? Like what? You haven't much to give. The bosun's chair? Your shirt?

He shook his head. Stop it! If you drift, you're dead. Look for the tip of the mast. Or even the lantern's glow bouncing off a cloud.

He swam fifty hard strokes toward what he judged to be a glow, but when he stopped, the glow was gone. He treaded water and rested. The night hung thick over him. The wind fell, and for a moment the only sound was the rain hissing on the sea. He felt an overwhelming thirst; opened his mouth and drank the rain.

The ketch climbed a wave slowly into moonlight. Nello lay on his stomach on the port deck and slid as far as he could out over the gunwale, reaching with the boathook out toward the rope.

Darina came and knelt beside him, holding down his calves to keep him from teetering and slipping overboard. Twice he lunged too soon and the bronze tip splashed short, churning phosphorescence in the black water.

On the third try, he reached the rope. He held the boathook firmly and twisted it with care to get the rope to cinch around the bronze tip of the hook.

With riveted concentration, Kate steered. She could see the rope bulge over the hook and adjusted the wheel to the slightest gust of wind, each nudge of sea, to keep the bow from falling away and pulling the hook loose from the rope.

Then she looked at the top of the wave where the rope vanished in the foam. She convinced herself that she saw Dugger there, now swimming hard toward them, now treading water, sometimes still, sometimes waving, but always smiling, so happy to see her. But when she blinked he was gone, leaving only the foamy crest or, when the wave moved on, the sloping, hollow darkness.

Nello had the rope twisted around the hook and he felt the weight of the rope now as it was cinching, and he hauled in the hook inch by inch, as if playing a fickle fish. The rope was coming slowly when the rogue wave hit.

DUGGER SWAM HARD, pushing the board of the bosun's chair with his shoulder. When he tired, he draped an arm around the board and rested. He rested looking sideways at the clouds, black with ragged edges lit by feeble moonlight, and he tried to be systematic searching cloud by cloud for the lantern's glow, working the sky a quadrant at a time.

He remembered falling into the water west of the ketch, so he concentrated on the two eastern quadrants, forcing his eyes to move slowly back and forth across the moon, forcing his brain to think hard and not miss a single cloud. Next, next, next, he told himself, the ketch can't be too far. Nello is running the ship. If anyone can find you in this hell, it's Nello. He figured he had been in the water almost an hour, but the water was warm and so full of salt he floated well, especially with the board.

His heart almost stopped when he saw the glow. It was a dim yellow speck, as faint as a candle flame through thickly falling snow, but no amount of blinking could wash it from the sky. Take a calm breath, he told himself, but it was no use, he was already thrashing and shouting as he swam, drinking, choking, spitting, and tangling in the rope. Near the glow, white in the pale moonlight, was the tip of the mainmast with the tattered sail. Swim! Goddamn you! Swim!

Then, with a brutal blast of wind, the mast vanished from sight.

The rogue wave fell like an avalanche on the ketch. Its black wall had loomed, rising higher in the moonlight, then collapsing with a deafening boom onto the deck. It threw Nello against the cabin. When it passed, the boathook was gone, its handle bobbing and sinking off to starboard. He lunged for the skiff and struggled with the lashings. Darina grabbed his hand. "You can't row in this wind!" she shouted.

"I can't leave him there!"

"You can swim to get the hook!"

"I can't swim!" Nello snapped.

Darina straightened up. "I can."

She stepped over the lifeline and, with a headlong leap, plunged into the sea. The first thing she felt was the warmth of the water.

She swam with even strokes and when she got to the boathook, she heaved it as hard as she could toward the ketch. It banged the hull and Nello hoisted it on deck.

She continued with angular strokes toward the rope at the

edge of the lantern's light. Grabbing it, she caught her breath. She tied a loop in the end and pulled the rest of it until it gave resistance. She then slung the loop over her shoulder, turned toward the ketch, and with steady, powerful strokes, she swam. She was less than a boat-length away when unexpectedly the rope went tight. She went under. Nello hung from a lifeline and reached the pole toward her, but she was too far out. She was coughing up water and struggling awkwardly to swim again.

Nello coiled up the mainsheet and with a wide swing threw the coil right at her. She draped a tired arm over it. Treading water, she took the loop from her shoulder and tied the mainsheet through the loop. She waved to Nello and he pulled the mainsheet tight. She was too worn out to hang on; the rope slipped from her hand.

Nello hauled the rope in and Guillaume came to help. They saw the bosun's chair bobbing on a wave, and pulled and pulled until they saw Dugger, with an arm over the chair, bobbing behind. A unanimous shout cut into the night. Dugger raised his head. He looked half dead, and as he neared they saw his eyes just white slits, but in the corner of his mouth curled a little smile.

Guillaume rang the bell in exultation, and Nello and Kate reached down over the side and hauled the helpless Dugger, by the arms, over the rail. He lay on the deck as limp as a wet doll.

Guillaume stopped ringing the bell when he noticed the empty sea. The nun was gone. The water was a lifeless sheen that melted into darkness.

Chapter 20

With no strength left even to shout, Darina floated and watched the ketch sail slowly away. She closed her eyes. There was only the wind moaning between the waves. She took comfort in the warmth of the sea. All her life the sea had been icy water on her skin, even in the summer, even in the stony shallows at the north end of the bay, where the sun warmed the stones and they in turn the tide as it came in slowly around the point. She always jumped in dreaming of warm water, and now here she was in the warm water of her dreams. She felt a languid pleasure, as comforting as Nello's arms when he had warmed her that night.

She let her head fall back and heard the engine of the ketch thudding through the water like a giant heart. Then it stopped. No matter how hard she tried, she could no longer hear the sound. She looked up. Among ragged clouds shone a lone bright star. She treaded water and stirred swirls of phosphorescence. In its light, she saw her legs move through the sea, and below them the water dark and darker still, down into the yawning, beckoning deep. In a fearful rush she sensed the miles of sea below her. She treaded harder. "Thank you, Lord," she whispered. "For the warm water of my dreams." Then she recalled the prayer she had uttered an hour ago, begging God to bring back Dugger and take her in his stead. "Thank you for hearing my prayer," she said.

She heard a bell. It was a sweet, rolling, reassuring sound, of whose direction she could not be sure. When she rose atop a wave it seemed to be below her, when she sank into a trough it tumbled from the sky. Her first day as a Penitent flooded over her, the bell calling to mass, the long echoing halls with the sun slanting inside, and the sound coming toward her as if floating on the light. She remembered the sad pride she felt in her new clothes and her new shoes squeaking softly on the stone. She had felt she was on her way to an audience with God. But later, sitting in the scrubbed pine pew, she remembered her brother, and through that long first mass she could not look at the man hanging on the cross.

She stopped treading water and for a moment sank. Maybe God is sending me straight down into hell, she thought. Too late, I've been there. Among the loving sisters. With their awful smiles. She recalled the damp horrors of the laundry with the girls and women lined up along both sides of the long trough like shorn sheep. The sisters forbade them to help each other. Or make friends. They used to line us up naked, she remembered, and laugh at our pubic hair. They bound our breasts so we were no longer women, and beat us, and made us stick things into ourselves, and said that's your lover: Satan. And tore up any letters ever sent to us. Except for Sister Claire, who must have been there to remind us we were human. But the others, my God, the others. Demons who would not even tell our parents we were there. And especially Sister Phyllis, who told poor Mary she would help her escape. One night she put the gardener's ladder against the wall, and Mary climbed up, and when she was at the top, Sister Phyllis yanked the ladder away. And there was Mary, twenty feet in the air, wildly wailing, impaled on shards of glass.

Sister Phyllis said that should teach us all a lesson.

Then there was the morning when Sister Phyllis came to talk to the short girl who used to cry endlessly because she wanted to find her mother. Sister Phyllis stopped beside her at the steaming trough. She told her in a flat, bored voice that her mother had died. The short girl replied that she'd never known her mother. And Sister Phyllis said yes, you did; you've been washing clothes across from her every day for thirteen years. And she pointed at the empty post across the rising steam. That was the night Sister Claire brought her Michael's letters, and whispered that, with the next shipment of laundry, she would help her flee. She fled.

From hell. *That* was hell. So you can sink me all you want; it won't hurt a bit. Then she struggled to the surface and thought, Don't abandon me now, Lord, not when I'm so alone.

She heard the bell again. She thought she saw the ketch rising among the waves, with Nello at the helm rushing to her rescue. She kicked hard and a wave slapped her face, and when the water had run from her eyes the ketch was gone. She lay back on the sea and looked up at the stars. She used to dream about a small stone house, its walls whitewashed bright, on an island with warm waters and countless trees. And there she was with a tiny baby at her breast, and a good wood fire blazing in the hearth. And the sound of his footsteps coming to the door, and in he would come and hold them both in his arms.

Oh, how she had dreamed of having that baby. Weeks after her brother's fever, her monthlies didn't come. The first two days she had been terrified. Then little by little she began to love her child. She planned to hide her belly when it grew, with a big shawl into winter, then spend much time in Connally's barn, warm among the sheep. She could deliver it as she had done with the lambs. She would build a little nest in the warmest manger, of curly wool she'd combed out of the sheep. Then one night they would carry it, wool-lined nest and all, down to the harbor shore, and set off in a curragh across the starlit sea; the three of them, alone, for a beautiful, distant place, where the water was so warm.

But then one day, running home, she felt wetness on her thighs, and with a rush of blood the loving dream had ended.

Too late to dream now, she thought. There comes a time when it's too late to dream. Then you have to make do with your memories.

The clouds parted, and stars spilled out, but they were strangers to her, as strange as the warm sea in which she'd soon be dying. She said a Hail Mary. Then, calmly treading water, she began to give thanks, to her parents for her life, Sister Claire for her brave kindness, Maeve Flynn's mother for the dress, and her brother for all his love. And then she thanked God for a breath of peace in the last moments of her life.

Chapter 21

They sailed all night in ever-expanding circles from one tattered patch of moonlight to the next, through foaming crests that exploded into spindrift, in long dark troughs that seemed to never end.

When Guillaume had stopped ringing the bell, he held the braided bell rope frozen in his hand and said in a voice so low the others barely heard him, "I can't see her anymore."

No one looked up. They were propping Dugger against the cabin side. "We got him back, didn't we?" Nello said with a laugh, and Kate embraced him, kissed his face, embraced him again. Then she knelt and, with a mother's love, she cradled Dugger's head.

Guillaume stared at the empty sea in disbelief. "She's gone," he repeated louder, until Nello turned his head. As if jolted by a shock, he leapt to the rail. He searched the layer of foam along the ketch, then, finding nothing, looked at the empty sea. *"Porco Dio,"* he whispered. "How can you do this?"

He ran below and shut off the engine. Back on deck, he ordered everyone to silence. They listened. There was only the wind in the rigging and the sea rushing against the hull. He roared, "Sister!"

There was no reply.

He sliced the lashings on the skiff, flipped it right-side up, and stuck the boathook handle down into the hole made for the mast. He unclipped the lantern from the main boom and hung it on the hook. Holding the stern, he slid the skiff over the rail and lowered it into the sea. The lantern swung wildly as the skiff tripped over a wave. He jumped in and stood on the starboard gunwale, tipping the skiff and letting the dark water rush in and fill it. When it was so swamped only the gunwales and boathook stuck out of the sea, he grabbed the lifeline of the ketch and pulled himself back aboard.

The ketch sailed off. The skiff stood like a fixed buoy in the dark, the lantern a tiny beacon in the vast gloom of the night.

They began their search by sailing around the skiff. They pulled down the torn main, raised the storm trysail in its place, and sailed steadily in ragged but ever-widening circles. The first one was tight—a boat-length from the skiff—and they watched, yelled, and listened for her. Halfway around the first circle Nello rang the bell. No response came from the night. When he closed the first circle he rang the bell again. Dejected, he eased the helm and widened the circle to more than two boat-lengths. At times he lost sight of the lantern and had to wait until a wave lifted the ketch before finding its glow.

He steered watching the compass, counted to ten, then changed course five degrees. But it was impossible to sail any reliable circles. With the erratic wind the ketch sped up, slowed, then sped up again. When heading into the wind they made little headway, then downwind they rode the waves at well over ten knots.

Hours passed.

The last cloud had receded from the sky and Darina floated in a sea of flickering stars. She heard no wind or breaking seas, only the sound of a distant bell. I must get to vespers, she thought, or I'll disappoint Sister Claire. She hurried toward a yellow glow distant in the darkness, where, in the humid chapel, the candle at the foot of the cross was lit for prayer. She felt the candle pulling her, pulling her into its light.

It struck her that she wasn't running but swimming in the sea. I do have to swim, she thought, I have to try or I'd be committing the greatest sin of all. She swam with the jerky, choppy strokes of exhaustion, murmuring, "for thine is the Kingdom, the power, and the glory . . ." and she slowed because the glow was gone and she was no longer sure whether she was swimming straight or swimming up or down, down toward the bottom of the inky sea. All of her felt limp, incapable of motion—but she swam.

She swam gasping for air, praying for an ounce of strength to lift once more an arm, once more move a leg, then again and again. She tried to turn her head to breathe but she was too tired and inhaled water.

She was out of air. The stars dimmed. She flailed feebly and felt wind on her face but had no strength left to breathe it in.

Then right before her burst a gleaming light that seemed to come nearer and nearer among the stars. She felt herself moving slowly toward it, so close she could almost touch it, and she reached up for it, up out of the dark. She raised her arm, but it fell back lifeless into the sea.

Far away, she heard her own voice say, "Amen."

They stared with wine-dried eyes into the night, changing posts each half hour to stay alert. By the eighth circle, the lantern seldom showed. By the ninth, it vanished. Dugger thought it had run out of oil, but Nello was sure he had made an error at the helm.

She's drifting at the same speed as the flooded skiff, he told himself. Just remember that. She has to be nearby. If she's not in this circle, she'll be in the next. If she's not in the next, she'll be in the one after.

But by the next circle he lost all concentration. He couldn't recall at what heading he'd started, and couldn't decide whether it was best to keep widening the circles or to start tightening them now, or perhaps to sail right back to the skiff and begin the search again. But the skiff was gone.

He hauled up a bucket of water and poured it on his head. She'll be all right, he told himself. She's from Inishturk. Tough as a rock. You saw her swim, saw her row.

Tighten the circle. Tighten the circle and you'll find her as sure as . . . Nothing is sure. It's all a guess. Except for her big white forehead. That was for sure. And the veins at her temples. He had felt them against his cheek when he held her that night. He had felt them pulse. He had felt her heart. That's not crazy, he thought, I felt her heart. And she leaned hard against me with her whole body. And what did you do? Instead of holding her with all your strength and never letting go—haven't you learned that nothing else counts?—you let her go. You pushed her away, told yourself she can't love you because she's a nun, told yourself a lie. You just couldn't believe that someone might really love you.

Now find her.

He tightened the circle, rang the bell, and sailed on. He leaned close to the compass, whose candle flame lit his eyes, and the madness etched by shadows in the creases.

Dugger stood at the helm, staring at the compass for no reason. The ship's bell chimed. Six hours in the sea, he thought. I almost died after one. Her secretiveness gone, her mystery gone.

Kate was so exhausted she slept where she stood. She held on to a shroud and her head drooped as she dreamed. In her dream she heard a chime ring out three times. It was the doorbell—an odd time for the postman so late in the day—and she knew right away it was news from the war. She looked down at the official letter and she knew: her father.

She walked past her sleeping mother to her room, pushing her finger under the envelope's flap. She opened it at the window without turning on the light, so the words would look less harsh. She read long phrases, and then her father's name. Near it the words that almost stopped her heart: *in the line of duty.*

The lamp man lit the gas lamps on the street. Kate watched him. Everything has ended, she thought. There's no reason to do anything now. She put the letter back in the envelope and went to bed. The envelope she placed on the pillow beside her. She put her hand over it gently and closed her eyes. She didn't cry. She remembered a day her father swept her up and held her on his arm. She stroked his dark mustache down toward his mouth. He pretended to eat her fingers with a growl. He was hers. All hers. Then she felt her tears between the pillow and her cheek.

She woke with her tears running down Dugger's arm. He cradled her head. For the first time since her father died, she cried for him. Dugger held her gently and let her cry.

"The postman came," Kate whispered.

"It will be dawn soon," Dugger said.

Kate looked up and realized where she was. "She'll be easy to find then. Right?" her voice thin, without hope.

"Yes. With the seas down and the light."

Dugger held her and watched the horizon for first light. He stayed silent after that, afraid he might blurt out that the skiff was lost, that she was lost, that they had circled too often, confused by fatigue and turns—too many turns—and by the waves that grew more chaotic with the wind change in the storm. He didn't want to blurt out that after a few hours in the water your mind begins to go. Especially so far from land, especially at night. Especially alone with all that water below you.

Dawn came with painful brightness. It lit the crumpled sail, the tangled ropes, the cut lanyards of the skiff, and the haggard crew squinting at the tumultuous seas. The worst of the storm had passed, but great swells still remained.

With shaky hands and his eyes burning, Nello put the binoculars to his face. But he looked without seeing, without hope, sometimes forgetting what he was looking for. The ship's clock chimed four times.

The sun exploded over the horizon, throwing a blinding shaft of light onto the sea. To the west it sparkled on the waves and seared their eyes. The only place of rest was in the shadow of the sail. He had never felt seasick in his life, but now a wave of nausea ran through him, and he had to lower the binoculars and look hard at the boom gallows and feel the screwheads in them: something solid, unmoving, with a clear purpose, a reason.

bird shot back at them hard and dark, swept clear around the ketch, then flew away again.

"It's just hungry," Dugger said.

Guillaume went below to get some flying fish. The bird came and Guillaume flung one high, but the bird let it fall. It gave a cry, then turned away and flew back into the sun.

"Not hungry," Nello said.

"It wants us to follow," Kate said.

"It's just shaken from the storm," Dugger said.

No one disagreed.

"Stupid bird," Dugger muttered. But he took the mainsheet and slowly winched it tight and turned the wheel back until the ketch pointed again toward the blinding light.

They shielded their eyes with hats and hands.

Nello held the binoculars rigidly against his eyes, focusing, readjusting.

"Don't look at the sun," Dugger ordered.

The bird flew alongside, its wing touching the sail, and then rose. Up ahead, like a small scar across the sun, weaving slowly just a boat-length ahead, was the bobbing boathook and the lantern. And the skiff.

Dugger eased the sheets and slowed the ketch, and now saw the lantern glisten in the sun, the painter of the skiff trailing in the water. Slumped over the stern with her head on the thwart and arms spread on the gunwales, facedown, was the nun.

Kate buried her face in Dugger's arms. Nello turned away. Guillaume crossed himself for the first time in eighteen years.

The albatross banked and flew off, back to where Guillaume's fish silvered on the water.

"I told you it was hungry," Dugger hoarsely said.

Chapter 23

By midday there was no trace of the storm. The sky had cleared, the wind fallen, the sea shone smooth and blue, and only long swells gently lulled the ketch. Nello had dropped the sails, and everyone fell exhausted in the shade of the awning or the coddling comfort of their dark berths below, and soon the only sound was of long, soft breaths.

The albatross played the light air just off the port bow, then settled on the sea and tucked its head under its wing. The last cloud vanished over the horizon, and in the blue circle of the sea, under the clear dome of the sky, there was only the sun, and the bird, and the ketch.

At twilight, Nello awoke from a slumber so deep that for a moment he wasn't sure whether it was sunset or dawn. He lay facedown on the crumpled staysail, his arm under his head, with the smell of the warm wood and the tar of the seams confounding his dreams. Men were pouring hot tar between paving stones on the quay of Rangoon, and in a forest in Ceylon fresh-sawn teak boards were piled under the palms. And in both places there was the nun, walking near him.

One by one the others stirred, all except Darina, who slept

motionless in her cabin with the covers over her head to drown out even the soft whoosh of the sea.

Guillaume stoked the galley stove and soon the fragrance of fried garlic and salt cod filled the air. By the time Darina came on deck, they all huddled around the cockpit table under the dangling lantern. They ate and drank, passing with few pauses the second bottle of rum. They talked at first quietly, then ever louder, recalling the barbarous storm, their paralyzing fears, and the gloom that had seeped like a poison through their hearts at the prospect of an unsuccessful search. And only at long last that strange matter of the bird.

They drank until they laughed and clutched each other's arms.

In the midst of it all, Guillaume vanished. He rattled about the galley and soon came up the ladder with a cake barely higher than a waffle but in its middle a fluttering candle.

He stopped and bowed before the still sleepy Darina. "Happy first day back, Sister," he said.

"To a hell of a nun." Dugger raised his cup, then added bashfully, "You know what I mean."

Darina blushed. Her cheeks glowed in the candle light.

"A wish. You have to make a wish," Kate said.

Darina looked down. They all stood still. For a moment there was silence, then she said, "I wish you would call me Darina."

"Call you what?" Nello asked.

"Darina," she repeated. "That's my name."

"To Sister Darina," Dugger offered.

"No," Darina said. "Just Darina. I was with the sisters in Galway, but not as a nun. I scrubbed laundry for seven years. I was committed for my sins." When she saw everyone in rapt attention, she went on. "I said I was a nun so you'd bring me with you." Then, looking away, she added, "I'm a Magdalene Penitent."

Guillaume's cup froze midair in surprise.

"You know what that is, don't you, *Monsieur?"* Darina said with a sad smile.

Guillaume didn't respond. He glanced at the others and saw that only Kate knew. He raised his cup. "To Darina," he said warmly, "the most intrepid lady of them all."

They clanged their cups. She blew out the candle.

For the next five days they were as spirited as children. The trade winds returned steady and reassuring, and with the yankee and the storm trysail and the mizzen all balanced, the ketch sailed her course as if on a rail. Nello and Kate stitched and patched the main. Dugger sometimes steered, sometimes let the ketch go on her own to take sextant sights of the sun or stars.

Guillaume fished and cooked without respite. From a steel washer and shredded ribbon he devised a fancy lure, which, dragged behind the ketch, dove and skimmed like a livid squid. He caught a big bonito and two smaller fish they didn't recognize, which he gutted, sliced, and marinated.

Darina took a piece of dry sharkskin and feathered the old varnish, then spread fresh varnish on the wood, never spilling a drop. She hummed a hymn but soon switched to shanties.

Her skin had grown tanned and her eyes seemed to have become an even deeper blue, and they smiled more often now. Late one afternoon, when they were alone in the cockpit with the falling sun glaring on the ripples of the sea, Dugger spoke to her directly for the first time since the storm.

"There is an old tradition among seamen," he began without looking at her. "When someone saves a life, he is not thanked for it no matter how brave the gesture." He paused. "But everyone knows that the gratitude is there." He glanced at her, caught her eye, and then glanced away. "And if the need arose, the other would, without hesitation, do the same." Then he said more softly,

"Without hesitation." When she said nothing, he took a deep breath and asked, "Do fishermen on Inishturk do that?"

She thought for a while before she replied, "I don't know. But I do know that that's the most I've heard you speak since I met you."

Her forwardness made him blush and he turned his head to check the mizzen. "I'm not the chatty type."

"Never have been?"

He turned back and shook his head.

She laughed out loud. "Did you just use up your last word for today?"

He couldn't help but laugh. For a moment they held each other's gaze, then he said, "You shouldn't let the glare of the sea hit your face in late afternoon. It can burn you worse than the noonday sun."

She shifted about. With the glare now behind her, he could no longer see her eyes.

That night, after the last of Guillaume's rum-drenched tart was gone and the long rounds of compliments ended, Guillaume finished his third glass of rum, leaned back against the cockpit coaming, and stared up at the stars. "If you had all the choice in the world," he mused, slurring the words slightly, "where would you like to wake up in the morning?"

For a while nobody answered. Dugger lit his pipe and blew a cloud of smoke at the chimney of the lantern. Nello held the sextant to his eye and shot a star. Finally Kate spoke. "In my lover's arms."

The wind blew the smoke into the darkness over the sea.

"I had geography in mind," Guillaume said. "But I must admit, I prefer your response."

Something like a breath of wind stirred beside the ship. Then Dugger said, "My lover's arms sound good to me too." And under the cockpit table he wove his toes into Kate's.

"Me too," Nello added. "Especially if I had a lover."

"Tout a fait, I can think of no better place," Guillaume said with a wistful sigh.

Then they looked up at Darina, but her face gave away nothing and she said, "I hope you don't all have the same lover, for it could get awfully crowded in here."

The whooshing sound rose again beside the ship and they saw the albatross. It ghosted on the air that swept over the swells, and with the white of its eyes and its underwings glowing in the lantern light, it hung motionless as if fastened to the darkness.

"Okay, I have another one." Guillaume brightened. "Can you remember the best day of your life?"

Darina glanced worriedly at Kate, but she was still riveted on the bird against the night. "You first this time, Monsieur Guillaume," Darina said quickly.

Guillaume sighed. "One night in the Dordogne, in a small *pension* over a noisy cataract, *une gorge.* Owned by a lovely woman who cooked like an angel. I rewarded myself with foie gras laced with truffles and washed it down with a bottle of Sauternes."

"I knew it was going to be food," Nello said. When no one else volunteered to speak, he said quietly, "When I was five, my granddad took me climbing in the Dolomites. It was all pink crags. I was scared to death. We climbed a peak, not steep, but high. The whole world lay below us. Even the clouds. And my granddad said, 'If you ever doubt yourself, just remember you were up here when you were five.' "

A tin cup clicked against the bottle in the silence.

"And you, Captain," Darina gently nudged.

Dugger emptied his glass before replying. "Well. I have to say my best day was a night. The night I got the ketch. Blind luck . . ."

"Oh, sure," Nello injected, aiming the sextant at a small, bright constellation. "The fool owner cut her anchor lines in a gale to collect the insurance. He fell in and drowned. The ketch was heading for a cliff with no one aboard her. Cappy rowed out in hellish seas and saved her. He was nearly killed but managed to raise the sails. He salvaged her."

"You never told me that," Kate said, astonished.

Dugger shrugged. "Not much to tell."

Guillaume clapped, and the others clapped with him. *"Capitaine,* my esteem for you rises every day."

"Mine too," Kate said in open admiration. She looked far out to sea where the stars touched the horizon. Then she said softly, "My best day was a night too. When Cappy salvaged *me."*

No one stirred. Kate looked up and saw their tipsy, expectant faces.

"It was twilight, Cappy. Remember?" Kate beamed like one flush from a night of love. "The twenty-ninth of May; three days after my birthday. We had sat down to dinner—me and my husband—a dour and vicious man to say the least. Our big motor yacht, over eighty feet, was anchored in a cove near Vancouver. Cappy's ketch was anchored near us, in the shadows of the woods. Mr. Tippins, the captain of our yacht, had asked Cappy for advice on how to rig a sailing dinghy my husband bought me for my birthday. A big birthday; I was turning twenty-five.

"Cappy rowed over alone—he lived alone. When I saw him, my breath stopped. We had met two weeks before, you see, in passing, on a street corner. I smiled. He frowned and we fell . . . Hopelessly, stupidly—like children do. The kind of falling that leaves you staring at the ceiling at night, dreaming.

"Two weeks later he found me. That twilight. The cabin boy and butler were serving dinner, and the bosun went around the decks lighting lanterns. There I was, surrounded by crystal, lace curtains, and silver, and there was Cappy, barefoot and on one knee, out on the aft deck in the dusk with our captain, showing him how to align blocks and chain plates, fairleads and cleats. I saw his eyes, ablaze with that intensity as if every moment of his life were the best. Oh, God, how I fell. I almost swallowed my fork with the roast duck. He saw me. A bolt of lightning is but a glimmer to that feeling."

"You're drunk," Dugger said, embarrassed.

Kate smiled. "No more than you."

"Oh, love," Guillaume said with a sigh. "How it dwarfs them all. Fame . . . fortune . . . conquest? Sad jokes. Toys, for those afraid to fall into its ecstasy. Its catastrophe." He laughed and shook his head. "Love. Blind love. Without it life is . . ." then, catching himself, he said, "*Tais-toi,* Guillaume. You're sounding like a girl."

Nello moved away and held the sextant to his eye.

"What? *Monsieur*," Darina pressed, "what is life without it?"

Guillaume swished his cup and stared into its depth. "It seems—to me—but a slow march to the grave."

"Oh, yes!" Nello cried out. Then, smiling broadly, he lowered the sextant and announced, "Ladies and gentlemen, we have crossed the equator."

When the others went to bed, Kate remained with Dugger on his watch. He sat in the cockpit and she lay in his arms. "There's nothing wrong with your memory, is there?" he said, holding her face.

"Why should there be?"

"You said there were things you couldn't remember."

She laughed. "I don't remember saying that."

He bit her neck. "You know, they say that on a long sea voyage you have to exercise. To stay limber. Gymnastics are good. Or stretching. I once saw a yogi in Madras who could wrap his legs around his neck. Can you do that?"

"No, darling," she purred. "But I can wrap them around yours."

Chapter 24

The seventh day after the storm, the ketch stood in the doldrums as if it had run aground. The air hung damp and stagnant, and the sea lay without a swell or ripple. The calm of the first two nights had been a blessing; they dropped the sails, tied off the wheel, and all slept strewn on the deck bathed in starlight. But at sunrise the haze was so bright it hurt their eyes, and the air was a smothering wet rag on their faces. The sails hung damp and limp like forgotten flags.

By midmorning, nerves were frayed. Making a pot of coffee, Guillaume called up in agitation that he couldn't cook without water and there wasn't a drop coming through the pump. Nello swung below in disbelief. He unscrewed the bronze lid of the main tank on the port side, and with a long stick gauged its depth. The stick came up dry. He shut off the valve to the tank, then unscrewed the lid of the small spare tank to starboard. He expected to see water to the lid, but there was only dark air. He gauged it. Two inches of water showed where there should have been ten. He checked the valve and found it open. He went above. "The last five gallons," he said flatly to Dugger.

"Where the hell did it go?" Dugger snapped, slamming down

the canvas bucket.

"I guess the storm," Nello lied. "We were on our side so much. Maybe the lid was loose." He didn't mention that someone had opened the valve.

"That's bloody great," Dugger grumbled. "At a quart per person per day, it will last four days. Three days after that, we start to die."

They abandoned the course for Tahiti and headed for the Marquesas, closer by nine hundred miles. Dugger tightened the water rations to half a cup at dawn, another at noon, and a last one at sunset. Using salt water to cook, the fresh water might last ten days, by which time they should hit Nuku Hiva. If not, then some other island in the northern Marquesas group. To make sure they hit something, Nello worked a heading between Nuku Hiva and Ua Huka, less than thirty miles apart. In almost any weather, they'd spot one or the other. Unless, of course, they sailed by both in the middle of the night. But in that case they would run into Ua Pou.

With the awnings stretched between the masts, a decent downpour could fill the tanks in half an hour, even a steady rain could fill them all by noon. But there was no rain, only the sun's flame on the mirror of the sea.

"Won't it be lovely to step onto solid ground?" Kate mused. She shifted uncomfortably in the stifling shade.

"As long as they don't eat us," Darina replied, then began reading aloud from her book by Segalen. "The major reason for conflict in the Marquesas, over the centuries, was drought. It dried up their main staple: the breadfruit in the valleys. Mangoes so shriveled even birds wouldn't peck them and the coconut-robber crab had no fallen coconuts to eat. Whole villages were reduced to sharing a few birds—pigeons, fruit doves, rails and parrots—whose meager flesh barely replaced the amount of effort expanded upon their capture. It pushed those starving inland toward the sea. Those living on the sea pushed back. It was village against village; hunger against hunger. When the breadfruit dried, the wild pigs died, and 'long pig' caught in battle took their place. And yet the tribes of the islands never thought themselves eaters of human flesh."

Kate shuddered and Guillaume turned away.

Darina went on. "Segalen once asked a chief if he were a practicing cannibal. The chief roared in anger as if he'd just been stripped of his last bit of pride. 'Never have I eaten anyone from my village.'"

"What a relief," Nello said with a sigh.

The ketch had no steerage. Without wind she made no headway, so the rudder couldn't bite, yet she seemed to hold her bow on course—south by southwest—maintaining the illusion of progress. Every few hours, a rogue wave came and went, a remnant of some distant storm that disrupted their slumber.

The ketch rolled violently, the masts whipping, the sails emptying, then filling with a bang; cups tumbled and pots slid and the crew grabbed sea rails or grab rails, stanchions or the gunwales. Then the ketch returned to its motionless heading.

They shifted uneasily under the awning. When the sun made the deck too hot for bare feet, they sloshed the decks down every hour, then sat and suffered in the slowly rising steam.

Dugger raised sails, attempting to capture wind that wasn't there. Darina was buried in Segalen; Kate wrote in her diary with the deliberation of an engraver etching into metal; Nello fixed things that didn't need fixing, and Guillaume read, for the hundredth time, his curled sheaf of notes.

"We should swim often," he suggested. "The Polynesians say you need much less water if you swim. Cools your body. Or wets your pores. I'm not sure which, but it works."

"You know a lot about the Polynesians," Nello said almost in accusation. "Is it all written there in your stack of papers?"

"No," Guillaume said flatly. "I spent three months on Nuku Hiva a few years back."

"You never mentioned that," Dugger said.

Guillaume shrugged. "You never asked."

The albatross, sitting nearby on the smooth water, raised its head from the shadow of its wing. A breath of air stirred all around the ketch, and near the curve of the horizon a veil of rain drifted under meager clouds.

"On Inishturk," Darina said wistfully, "it drizzled every day."

The cloud came near and brought its thickened veil. A few drops fell. They splattered on the deck and tickled their skin. Then stopped. The veil moved on. The hot, wet air engulfed them once again.

"Were you snuffing out a revolution on Nuku Hiva or starting one?" Nello asked Guillaume.

He didn't reply right away, just stared off past the bow far into the distance. "No." He smiled. "I was snuffing out candles on the captain's table. I was in the navy. A petty officer, I think you English call it."

"No one here is English," Darina snapped.

"I meant *'in* English.' Never cared for the sea much. Just wanted to go somewhere far away."

"Who doesn't?" Dugger grumbled.

"Those contented in their lover's arms," Guillaume replied. "On Nuku Hiva, I learned how to be a secret agent, how to deceive, how to lie. That's when I realized I'd been playacting all my life. So, I figured, why not get paid for it? So I signed up for the Secret Service."

"To turn people against each other?" Darina said, her voice brittle. "You French did that to us. Told the poor Irish to rise up against the Brits, and you'd be there to help. Well, we rose, didn't we? Then we died. And the rest of us ended up worse than before."

"We meant well," Guillaume said. "You just misread what we told you."

"My brother went to Dublin to fight with the Brotherhood. He was shot and beaten and driven from Ireland because he received a shipment of pistols from the French and mistook that for the first of more to come. Well, nothing came; not even bloody bullets. Except the ones the Black and Tans pumped into his back."

"Five thousand Frenchman died on Irish soil fighting for you at Bayonne," Guillaume rebuked her. "And we helped Wolfe Tone in 1798. We just tried to give a helping hand again."

"It was bullets we needed, not your helping hand."

She was gripping the edge of the seat with both hands, her face flushed with anger. Dugger and Nello stared at her. Kate watched the men watching her.

Guillaume went to the canvas bucket and poured what seawater was left in it onto his head. "Revolutions," he said with a sigh. "come from deep inside. You can't start them. And can't stop them. They just explode. You can tinker with them, fool yourself into thinking you have an effect. But . . ."

Darina didn't answer. She walked out into the sun and climbed down the rope ladder into the sea that felt no cooler than the air.

Kate followed, and they swam away from the ketch. Dugger and Nello climbed down too, floating near the stern, while Guillaume swam slow circles around them, with long, patient strokes. The sun sank suddenly and the world went red: the clouds, the water, the murky and misty air, and they all stayed in the water until the sun was gone and a quick green flame flashed across the sea.

FROM THAT DAY ON, Guillaume kept his notes in the drawer of his berth and spent all his spare time poring over charts. Kate was the first to note the change in him. The smile, the eyes, the floating eyebrows remained, but he kept his gangly limbs close to his body, tucked in tight as if afraid of injury. He became more vertical.

After lunch, with his sheaf of papers, he withdrew into the shade, read without looking up and made notes in the margins. When he rose, near sunset, he walked aft and gave a weary smile to Darina, alone at the helm. "To defeat your enemy," Guillaume said, holding up the pages, "you have to know him better than you know yourself."

"And if you don't know yourself at all?" Darina ventured.

"Then you'd be the world's worst secret agent." He laughed an honest laughter. "Which I might just be."

"And your enemy . . . ?" she said, pointing at the papers.

A moment of confusion clouded his eyes. Then he said with genuine admiration, "Magnificent." He began to open the papers but at once caught himself. "Fascinating. Imagine a handsome man, a European, living as a savage. Loving as a savage. Shedding his civilized affectations for the jungle, the bush, the sea. And shedding his clothes, and covering himself instead from head to foot with pictures. Tattoos. Like Marquesan chiefs and warriors did decades ago. After each battle they told the story of their conquest, or defeat, in pictures; on their flesh. That was how they remembered, that was their history. But that was long ago. The custom vanished."

"Along with the dances . . ." Darina said.

"And for good reason. Tattooing was a big thing, you see, a special house was built for each event. These places were *tabu,* sacred, for tattoos also protected you from evil." He fell silent, leaving out the part about how evil could penetrate through ears, mouth, nose, vagina, any hole, and all those places for men and women alike were patiently tattooed with a bone needle or mother-of-pearl needle with a handle. And he left out how the people were held down so they wouldn't writhe with the pain of the needle being hit with a hammer to make the wound, and how the wound was filled with the soot of burned *ama* nuts, mixing with the blood and forever turning blue. Thousands of holes punched in the skin. Then the house was burned and a great feast began, with dancing and coupling and human sacrifice. So the priests stopped it. "Too brutal," he simply said. "But now it's back. And not on a Marquesan but on a white man. Imagine. Why? Why would anyone suffer so much? For some pictures? And pictures of what? For who to see? What does this strange, strange man have in mind?"

"Maybe he was just a painter without a canvas."

"Maybe," Guillaume said, unconvinced. "But now he wants all the islands as his canvas. To be painted in blood. Not his, of course. The poor island devils . . . Him and his revolution. *Un homme bizarre.*"

From his sheaf of papers, he handed one to Darina. It was a copy of an old etching. It showed a man, naked but for a twisted loincloth, of good musculature, standing, holding a tall, carved war club, staring into the distance. His head was shaved but for two twisted tufts near the temples, and his whole body, save his hands and feet but including the top of his head, was covered with tattoos. They seemed to be arranged in a couple of dozen zones, framed with clear skin. Like pictures. There were fine lines crossed that looked like nets, and there were pointed teeth and fishtails and faces.

"Weeks of pain," Guillaume said. "At first I thought, how could he be so crazy? A cultured European. What vile madness drove him? And you know, at first, the very question gave me a sense of calm, a sense of sanity. I was grateful I wasn't him. But as days passed, that sense of superiority ebbed. And the questions changed: What great passion drove him? I asked. What visions ruled him? In the night? At twilight?

And I found myself overcome with sorrow—oh, not for him, he's fine, but for myself, for living with the lid shut so tight on my emotions. Barely a notable pulse. Barely a breath. I sometimes wonder, if you put a feather under my nose, would even the finest of down near its stem give a flutter?"

He smiled a distant smile and put the etching back into the sheaf and tied it with a string. "So that is the enemy I have to get to know. If I don't know him, I can't find him. And if I can't find him, how can I kill him?

"I had an old teacher in Neuilly. He said, if you know what makes a man laugh, you know him. And if you can make him laugh, you got him." Then he tapped his papers with his forefinger. "I wonder what it takes to make him laugh."

THE AIR WAS STEAM. It has to rain, Dugger thought. It just has to rain. The sun, the haze, the sea all glowed like coals. When the twilight changed to darkness, not a star came out, and the night had an eerie luster. At eight bells, lightning flared. At first in wide flat horizontal sheets, then straight down like blades slashing through the dark.

The squall slammed the ketch, tipping her hard and taking everyone's breath. Then they were happily drowning in a great downpour of rain. They shouted and laughed with joy; Kate tossed her hair to rinse it in the rain; Guillaume thrust his face skyward, tongue out, mouth ajar; and Nello ran to check the canvas trough that led down to the tanks, and dragged his salt-caked clothes to slap them on the deck, which was ankle-deep in freshwater.

When the squall passed, a breeze remained and, by morning, grew into steady trades. The ketch was making eight knots under a brilliant sun.

That night, alone on watch, Guillaume waited until the lamp below guttered out. He moved silently, tightening the sails, trusting the rush of water to cover the noises. He went back to the wheel and changed course twenty degrees. The ketch obeyed and turned a bit eastward. Just before his watch ended, he eased the sails again and edged the ketch back more westward.

After the squall, Kate saw Dugger bloom. He had not shaved since Mexico, and his look of brooding sadness was compounded by his stubble. But now in the crisp sunlight the creases smoothed near his eyes, and in the corners of his mouth there often lurked a smile. The morning after the rain, with the water tanks both full, he had heated some water and shaved. He looked to her many years younger, and the smile, though barely perceptible, became permanent.

During Nello's night watch, Dugger came on deck. They didn't speak. Nello steered by keeping the forestay pointed at a star. After a long while Nello asked softly, "Do you trust him?"

Dugger said, "He has honest eyes."

"But did you notice how suddenly they harden? Turn suspicious? Follow you? Just for a second or two, then he catches himself."

"He is a spy. Must be a habit."

"And the gold? Do you believe him about the gold?"

"I don't know. Why not? It's as good a thing as any to believe in. Besides, he has so many details. Who would invent all that make-believe?"

"He's a spy. His life *is* make-believe."

"But why make up so much? I mean, fourteen tons . . ."

"If he had said fourteen ounces, who'd care? Who'd go that far for a pound of gold? But if the lie is big enough . . ."

"Why are you so suspicious now?"

"Because my dead reckoning has been strangely off for days."

A feeble light filtered on the east horizon. Nello looked over the side to check their speed. He smiled. "Two hundred more miles, Cappy. Tomorrow we'll be basking in paradise."

"Palm trees and sand."

"And beautiful women,"

"And ferocious men."

"And the most alluring in-betweens," Guillaume added. He had come up silently, unnoticed in the dark. "All through the islands firstborn boys of chiefs were brought up as girls, to spare them in case of war, when all the men might be killed off or taken away. Intriguing, don't you think?"

Neither of them answered. They were counting the miles. "I'll start getting the anchor ready," Dugger said.

Chapter 25

They spent the day in a restless, seldom-broken silence, staring often ahead at the bare horizon.

On the last watch of the night, Darina, with her eyelids drooping, steered the ketch as best she could, holding course by pointing the bowsprit at a curved constellation that sank lower and lower in the southern sky. Halfway through her watch, she saw a shape rise from the foredeck and amble haltingly toward her but not until it was close enough to touch did she recognize Dugger. She had seen him in the moonlight sleeping on a sail bag, but once the moon had set, she had forgotten he was there.

"Segalen wrote," she now blurted to cover her surprise, "that the natives paddled out half naked in canoes to greet boats sailing into their harbors. They sang and brought gifts of fruit and flowers. Do you think they'll do that for us?"

The sound of flapping wings shuddered the air beside them. The albatross had abandoned its customary post and now flew past them, dark against the stars, then banked toward the east and vanished.

"I'm the wrong one to ask, "Dugger replied, his voice coarse with sleep. "I always expect the best."

Darina lost the constellation and had to swing the bow to find it again.

"Are you ever disappointed?"

"Always," he blurted. "But I get over it. Like a kid who doesn't get the present he'd hoped for. He just dreams about the next time."

She looked at him warmly. "You do have this air of . . . a big kid."

"Thank you. Just what every man wants to be: an overgrown child."

"I just mean you're uncomplicated. It makes people comfortable."

The compass light was just enough that he could see her eyes. They seemed direct and defenseless in the pale light.

There was movement overhead right above the mizzen, and the silhouette of a frigate bird—fine-tipped V-shaped wings and long split tail—circled against the stars.

"Jesus," Dugger whispered. "We must be near . . ."

"Oh, good," Darina said, but her eyes drew tight with dread.

A good breeze blew, the sea heaved low, and the distant billowing clouds grew brighter against the dawn. Near their center two looming peaks stayed dark, and between them, like a beacon, hung the morning star.

Dugger reached for the bell-rope and gently rang the bell. He paused, then rang it louder once again. One by one sleepy faces came blinking into the dawn. Without a word he pointed past the bow toward the peaks, then said softly, "Land."

They sheeted in the sails, the ketch heeled, and they headed into the wind directly toward the peaks.

"Land," Kate said a whisper. "I'd forgotten what it looked like."

"I love land," Darina said.

"You'll love this land more than you can imagine," Guillaume said. "The natives call it Te Henua Enana, Land of Man."

"And the women?"

"They don't have to call it anything. It's theirs."

For almost an hour no one said a word, gazing at the land that seemed to grow more inhospitable the nearer they came.

Dugger had the helm. Nello stood beside him with the chart partially unrolled in his hands, glancing nervously down, then up, then all around them at the empty sea as if expecting something to pop up out of the darkness. "I would guess Nuku Hiva," he said without conviction.

"Then you'd be wrong," Guillaume said, with a tinge of hardness they hadn't heard before. "Nuku Hiva's mountains have more crags."

"What, then? Ua Pou?"

"That's too small. It looks like Hiva Oa. The current must have set us to the east.

Dugger searched the chart until he found it. "So is that good or bad?" he asked testily.

Guillaume smiled. "It's very good." But his smile faded quickly.

Passing a headland as serrated as cracked crystal, they sailed near black rocks that lined the shadowed shore. Waves climbed lazily, foaming white over them. As day came, the steep slopes showed tangled greenery, and from a saddle between the peaks, a waterfall cascaded down onto the black-sand beach five hundred feet below. The clouds pinked but never left the island, scattering only enough to reveal farther sharp-edged ridges, like bent and twisted blades. Around the tallest peak, to the west, a ring of a cloud hung slightly askew. Like a wreath on a tombstone, Darina thought. The clouds whitened, the sea shone bright; it was morning. "Look," Darina exclaimed, and pointed at the headland in surprise.

There must have been a shoal beyond the headland, because where she pointed the waves rose high, curled, then ran in a lazy arc into the next bay; and, ducking in a perfect curl, riding on a board, a slim, dark figure weaved and swerved alone.

"La planche," Guillaume uttered. "A surfing board." The surfer's naked body shimmered wet and dark, and only when a boat-length off did the curves of her hips and breasts become plain to see. She bent at the knees and dropped a shoulder, dragging her left hand in the water to turn back into the wave, her long hair falling in wet clumps around her neck.

"A girl," Darina remarked, awed.

"Must be from Inishturk," Nello said without lowering the binoculars.

The girl swung near the ketch, and seeing her audience, she broke into a smile. He watched in helpless fascination. Beyond her alluring nakedness and unaffected smile, there was a kind of instinctive grace in her fluid, sensuous movements; the grace of the curling waves.

Now she leaned forward, shifted her weight, then cut hard to her right and vanished behind the point.

They entered the bay.

What seemed from afar like gnarled scrub now showed a tall, lush jungle on the slopes. A narrow strip of palms surrounded the bay, and just behind them, dark and steep, ran a broad curve of black rock hundreds of feet high, some freestanding in spires, forming a fortress-like wall between the land and sea. Near the middle, between towering formations, a narrow crack cut through the steep black stone and led into a shadowed canyon.

From the jungle slopes, a mist slid seaward, confounding shapes and distance. The ketch inched toward land. Flanking a peak, the sun rose blazing, and on a crest, a single palm stood black against the sky. A low swell broke with a murmur on the sand. There was no sign of life ashore: no movement, smoke, or fire.

Around the bay, the slopes fell with unwelcoming steepness into the sea.

"Too deep to anchor," Nello murmured, looking over the side.

They edged toward the falls, where the sand formed a delta. When Nello saw bottom, he lifted the anchor shaft, raised his arm in a signal for Dugger to luff the sails, then, letting the anchor slide, fed the chain over the roller. He fed the chain out slowly so as not to disturb the stillness that hung over the land.

The anchor touched bottom and sent up a puff of sand.

The sails filled, the ketch crabbed. He let out chain until it hung in a lazy curve, then he wrapped it around the Samson post, and it snubbed as the anchor bit. The flukes dug in. The ketch stood still.

Kate, gazing at the waterfall, clung hard to Dugger's arm. "My God," she whispered. "Eden."

A gentle land breeze tumbled from the canyon full of bird cries and fragrances: sweet, bitter, of ripe fruit and fresh flowers, and damp decay. A pack of wild horses broke out of a grove and trotted unhurriedly to the falls to drink. Then, one by one, they bolted along the shore, racing a cloud's shadow that flew over the sea.

Dugger uncleated the halyards, and the sails slid with a flutter to the deck.

Aft of the ketch the sea swelled then curled, translucent and alive in the morning light. It broke in a low murmur along the rocky shore, a swoosh, then a thud, as if an enormous door were shutting behind them. To starboard a bird shrieked. They turned to look.

That's when they saw that Guillaume had disappeared.

Book Four

The Land of Men

Chapter 26

Father Murphy opened one eye so that if anyone looked in he would seem wide awake while, with the other closed, he let himself believe he was still asleep. The sun gleamed between the bamboo sticks that served as his window and the sea breeze surged in through his open door, rippling the mosquito netting dangling from the fronds of the roof. Something rustled overhead and dry bits of frond drifted down and stuck to his sweaty face.

"Watch ye for ye know not when the master of the house cometh," he quoted the Gospel of Saint Mark. "At even, or at midnight, or at the cock-crowing, or in the morning; lest coming suddenly He find you sleeping." But the cock didn't crow because weeks ago the villagers had, in a show of defiance, abandoned their village on the curved shore weeks ago, dragging in hasty anger their goods, pigs, cocks, and chickens past the *gendarmerie,* where Testard, Le Sous Gouverneur des Îsles Sud-Est stood pouring sweat, in his cap and crisp white tunic, ordering them to stay. They went on as if deaf, past the little fort, past the palm trunk painted white whose top had been hacked off and replaced by a sun-bleached flag of France, and they snaked in single file through the crack in the mountains inland, to who knows what shadow-filled deep valley in the jungle.

Father Murphy stayed behind, his flock reduced to two Chinamen, the Finn, and Testard and his eight French marines, but a week ago even the marines left the island for fear of an attack, and would only return once they mustered reinforcements. So there remained only Testard, who refused to leave his post; the listless beachcomber from Lapland they called the Finn, who had lost half a hand either to a shark or a sword fight, depending on how drunk he was when telling the story; and a couple of Chinamen who looked like death warmed over from holding their breaths while diving on the sunken reef for black pearls all day, and smoking opium in their hammocks under the banyan tree at night. Only one native stayed, Hapa, the old half-blind carver who had come down from Nuku Hiva to trade a bag of lead type he'd salvaged from a printing press at Taipevai to melt down into bullets. He traded it for the tall, straight trunk of a *hau*, which he now chiseled from sunrise to sunset, hollowing it out for his pirogue.

When he heard a voice he had never heard before, Father Murphy opened his other eye. The voice was a clear, school-learned French, but in such an urgent whisper that he could only be sure of two words, *otage* and *dangereux*. He heard Testard indignantly reply, *Je suis tout seul. Qu'est-ce qu'on peut faire tout seul?* At which the voice turned angry and called him a *salaud,* a weak wretch.

Father Murphy, straightening his nightshirt, hurried stealthily to the window. Under the shade of a drooping mango he saw the back of Testard, but the other man was hidden behind the trunk; only his white hand swung out once in exasperation. Then he must have left because Testard fell silent and, holding his black beard in search of comfort, turned and looked with apprehension out at the empty sea.

"This is the day which the Lord hath made," Father Murphy called out piously from his door. "We will rejoice and be glad for it. Won't we, Testard, you decrepit Frog heathen, who are without doubt the first in line for hell?"

"Memai. A haakoi!"—Come here. Hurry!—the *sous gouverneur* barked, trying to speak in English, but it came out Marquesan.

His eyes darted along the beach and he ran a hand through his beard, which he wore thick despite the heat to give some strength to his unassertive chin. "Do you see a boat out there? My eyes are inflamed today."

"Your eyes are hung over today." Father Murphy yawned. "No boat. Just old Hapa hacking at his log."

"They must be anchored past the falls," Testard said, regaining his composure.

"Who?"

"The pirates."

"Pirates?"

"Yankee pirates. And an Irish woman pirate with them," he said, poking a finger of accusation into Father Murphy's chest.

"You still drunk, Testard?"

"Some respect please, *mon cher père,"* he retorted with authority. "I have received solid information. There is a ship of pirates anchored off this coast. Why did that crazy Baudichon take the platoon to Nuku Hiva when he should be here minding the garrison?"

"Because the governor ordered him to."

"Quelle charogne," Testard muttered. "He sends orders from Tahiti to a place he's never seen a thousand kilometers away. And I'm left here alone to defend the fortress against a ship of cutthroats."

Suddenly that notion appealed to him as heroic, and with firm, purposeful steps he marched along the beach toward the "fortress," a stonewall flanking a courtyard, with a squat block-house set into the bluff. But as he walked past the abandoned village with its teetering poles, torn woven mats, sticks of bamboo, and palm fronds, his heart sank. What a place to die for, he thought. "He died defending nothing, in the middle of nowhere," he quoted aloud his own tombstone. Then he added bitterly, "Died defending France, even though bloody France is a million kilometers away." And he spat with disgust toward a big land crab patiently gnawing a fallen coconut. But prudence of habit overcame him. He picked up a stone, approached the crab, and crushed its shell. Then, with the long legs sawing madly, he carried it home for dinner.

The bluff loomed dark over the ketch. They stood silent, gazing in disbelief at the empty sea, where there was no trace of Guillaume either alive or dead. In an attempt he knew to be futile from the start, Dugger went below and checked Guillaume's cabin. It was empty. His bundle of notes was gone, as was his canvas pack. The cabin itself was left neat and tidy; even the bedding was folded thoughtfully on the bunk, as if a grateful houseguest wanted to leave as little trouble for his host as he could.

Dugger was saddened, though not by the loss of the gold, nor the loss of a protector in these alien islands; it was, rather, the fact that Guillaume had left no note, no goodbye, no explanation. As if the last three weeks at sea had meant nothing at all.

On deck, Kate was folding the sails in even slabs, Nello hung in the ratlines with binoculars in hand, studying the shore, and Darina stood on the aft deck finishing her morning prayers.

Nello climbed down and came aft.

"Better this way," Dugger said. "All that gold would have sunk us."

"Even half," Nello added.

"Even one ton," Dugger said.

"There's nothing I want to buy here anyway," Kate said, and she punched the folded sail.

"What good is gold anyway?" Darina said, but her voice bore no conviction.

"Did he leave a note?" Kate asked, adding, "Of course he didn't," before Dugger could reply.

"What would he have said?" Darina asked. *"I betray and lie. Goodbye?"*

"There's a kind of fortress beyond the knoll," Nello said. "I could only see the roof." Then he looked at them one by one and said, "You look like you just found out there's no Easter Bunny."

"Bloody Guillaume," Dugger growled.

"We'll find him," Nello said. "Where can he go? It's an island."

"But he knows it and we don't."

"But we do know he's a secret agent. That puts everyone on this island on our side."

"Except those in the fortress. The ones with all the guns. "

"Come on, Cappy. Where's your optimism?"

Dugger climbed the ratlines. "Guillaume took it," he said.

Father Murphy went down to the creek to wash himself of night sweat. Pirates, he mused, wouldn't that be just the sight for sore eyes? New faces. White faces. And an Irish lass, at that. Oh, to have her here in the shade of a banyan tree tipping a pint, reminiscing about the fine bays of County Cork or the lovely views around the Ring of Kerry. Or talk about how John Redmond fought the Brits. Or even Synge, who'll burn in hell for a Protestant, but was nevertheless a fair-to-middling poet. Then they would have another pint and sing, "I'll take you home again, Kathleen, /Across the ocean wide . . ." Oh, a pint.

then, looking around, sure that no one could see, he stepped out of his nightshirt and sat in a pool to his waist. Feeling more awake, he thought, Calm thyself, Murphy. Just say your morning prayers and forget about Irish lasses. Remember what Father McWhir taught you in seminary: "If you have a roving eye, it's no use having the other fixed on heaven." And forget about the pints. Heed your father who always said, "Drink is the curse of the land. It makes you fight with your friends and shoot at your neighbor." Then he stood up, dried himself, and, looking toward the fortress, murmured, "And it makes you miss him."

On the way to his hut, he crossed himself, poked at a ripe mango with a stick, cut it open with a sharp stone, and ate the fibrous pulp while saying softly, '"I believe in God, the Father Almighty, Creator of heaven and earth." Then he pulled two bananas off a stalk below the fortress and ate as he prayed and banged on the door. He called loudly, "Testard . . ." but there came no reply. He banged again. "Did the pirates get you?"

He went around the back. Inside the walled yard some hens pecked the dust in the shade of what the locals called the "peeping palm." Rooted in the bluff, the curved coconut palm leaned over the wall and into the fortress yard, its enormous fronds hanging high overhead. Before the marines came, Father Murphy recalled kids jumping off the cliff and swinging on a rope tied just below the fronds. They swung in great circles and long figure eights while those on the ground ran for their lives, screaming.

"Testard!"

No reply.

He turned and walked home, disappointed.

Chapter 27

There was smoothness in the man's movements over the rough terrain as he edged under the shadows toward the waterfall and the ketch. He kept to the inside of the ledge where the runoff had deposited silt more gentle on his bare feet. Where the slope was too steep for trees, leaving the path exposed to the sun, he stopped. In the flickering shadow of a *toa,* his body, intricately tattooed from ankles to forehead, glowed a deep blue-green; only his pants, which came to mid-calf, set him off from the undergrowth. He leaned with both hands on his rifle, squatted, and watched the ketch.

Confusion filled his eyes, which, even squinting at the sea, were inviting and a rich blue. He thought the ketch beautiful and a sudden yearning came over him for a life from long ago. But as fast as it had come it was washed away by the knowledge that the ketch had doomed his plans. He saw the crew under the falls and thought, why did they have to arrive just now, when he could sense—with good reason—that victory was near; or if not a clear victory, at least a blow the French would fine, he thought; either would be better than this slow and silent death.

But now the ketch and its crew stumbled into his way, with what powerful weapons he could not even guess. Whose side they would take, he had little doubt. The good thing was they seemed few, and one of them was a woman, and another as slight as one. Maybe they could be scared off before the frigate came. With a terrifying scheme.

Maybe we should do what the French did to us, he thought. So brilliant, so heartless: that torture of the cliff.

He studied the cliff, as high as ten men, its sheer, bulging face, and the fortress with its walled yard etched into its base. A single palm grew from a ledge just above the fortress walls, its curved trunk towering over the yard, its great fronds giving shade. And he remembered the day the French marines dragged Kiko, with his hands tied behind his back, up the goat trail to the cliff's top.

They had rounded up the whole village in the twilight and made them stand along the shore and watch Kiko on the bluff. They stood him at the very edge and tied his feet with rope so he couldn't even struggle. Then the commandant shouted so everyone could hear, "Who is the leader of the revolution? His name! Give me his name!"

But Kiko just smiled and stood as silent as a tiki. Two marines grabbed him, one on either side, lifted him up, held him horizontal, then swung him back and forth counting, *Un . . . deux . . . trois,* and then they threw him, headfirst, into the abyss. The women covered their eyes. Some screamed. The men stood in silent shame. Kiko flew without a sound and disappeared behind the fortress wall.

Then they led the next man, Karim, to the top. And he wouldn't speak either, not even when they tied his hands, not even when they tied his feet, not even when they lifted him up, not until they counted, *Un*. He blurted a name then, just loud enough for the

French to hear. But they threw him off the cliff anyway. And laughed out loud. And Karim screamed all the way down, even long after he vanished behind the wall, because the French had measured the length of rope around his ankles with precision, the rope whose other end they had tied to the great palm. So Karim screamed, dangling headfirst, swinging like a pendulum but in wild figure eights, his long hair sweeping the dirt floor of the yard.

So brilliant. So heartless. *Diabolique.*

Maybe we should do the thing with the rope, he thought. But something slightly different; a nasty little twist.

His gaze softened; his blue eyes filled with mischief. The viciousness of it completely slipped his mind.

ÉMILE TESTARD WAS BORN IN 1894, to a well-to-do family of antique dealers in Touraine. His father believed in hard work. During Émile's early school years, he had him cleaning bronze and silver with cyanide in a small back room kept closed to save on coal. The cyanide weakened his lungs for good. During his school years he was often ill and in bed. He read about fearless adventurers in exotic places and he dreamed. His mother gave him a book by Professor Ernest Darling, who, after two bouts with pneumonia, weighing only 80 pounds, too weak even to speak, was declared incurable. Tired of futile treatment, Darling sailed for Tahiti and withdrew into the wilderness, naked. He emerged after four months, in perfect health and weighing 160 pounds—and wrote a book.

Through his mother's connections with the Colonial Department, Émile was accepted into the marines as a scribe second class with the idea of sending him to recover in the South Seas.

governor's assistant. Within two years he was named *sous administrateur* to the Marquesas Southern Group, made up of the lush volcanic islands of Hiva Oa, Tahuata, and Fatu Hiva, home to seventeen tribes with a total population of nine hundred. At Atuona on Hiva Oa, he was given a house made of planks with a kitchen and a bed. He spent his days acting as gendarme, and his nights drinking rum with Father Murphy and the Finn. And late at night by the light of smoldering candlenuts, Émile Testard wrote long letters of observation and advice to the governor in Papeete, fourteen hundred kilometers away. The letters were well thought out, beautifully written, and never mailed.

The first one began, *Respected Governor and Kind Patron,* and went on with unbridled gratitude, giving thanks for the unique opportunity. A passionate outburst followed. *"I will never forget the evening you gathered us new arrivals to the Colonial Service in your garden, and had us, as a sort of warning, take turns reading aloud about Conrad's Kurtz, the ivory trader of good intentions deranged by the jungle. By the middle of that night, we were all under its spell. My voice went dry as toward the end I read, "But his soul was mad. Being alone in the wilderness, it had looked within itself and, by Heavens I tell you, it had gone mad."*

I didn't sleep that night. Or for some nights to come. I wanted to be Kurtz. But completely unlike him: I would hold on to my eternal soul. I promised myself that my last words on earth would not be, "The horror! The horror," but, with all conviction, and deep satisfaction, "The beauty! The beauty."

His last letter, begun weeks ago, was somber, but still optimistic. It lay unfinished on his table. It spoke of attracting responsible settlers with land grants, to increase the trade in copra, and fruit, and maybe even pearls; of better health and medicine for the natives decimated by disease and infertility brought on by that gift from beyond the sea, syphilis; of restoring the islands to their glorious and vibrant precolonial Garden-of-Eden splendor. By the time he wrote that letter, the population of the Southern Group had declined to below six hundred.

The letter concluded, *We must not judge the Marquesans by our European ideals. At this moment they are in a period of transformation; abandoning little by little their savage morals and habits, to step onto the path of civilization. During this complete evolution, the* indigènes *must be watched very closely, like children. It would be advisable to employ, in their management,* un mélange de douceur et de force, *sweetness and power; to visit them often, to listen to their complaints and pleas, to punish them without abuse but also without weakness, and at last to protect them—like children.* My children.

At the end of a sleepless night, as the darkness of the palms broke away from the darkness of the night, when the wet air sat heavy on his chest, he smiled to himself, full of the fatigue of disillusion, and was on the verge of rising from his bunk and adding to his letter, *"The beauty. The beauty,"* but fell asleep. He awoke to the solitary sound of Hapa's adze thudding into the wood of the *hau.*

FROM BELOW THE EVES, Father Murphy unhooked a short fishnet, pulled a small basket from under his bed, and walked along the beach, sticking to the shade, toward the waterfall. During the downpours of October, the great cascade hollowed a pool that for months remained a pond where fish came in from the sea to feed. He didn't like fishing there because it meant fishing alone. He preferred to work the open shoals with one of his native flock or the Finn or Testard on the other end of the net, wading in waist-deep, chest-deep, looping the net, circling slowly, chatting, laughing, herding the fish until they wound up in the net, then reaching in calmly and scooping the ones they wanted into a basket.

But there was no one to fish with in the shoals today. So halfway to the falls he stepped into the woods to gather leaves of the bluff, caught the steel of the shaft against the dark sand.

Darina sat in the bow, staring at the shore.

From the rocks below the southern bluff, Testard saw the skiff emerge. Sweat poured down his sides. He laid down the last rifle and pulled out the small spyglass with the crack across the lens. *"Mon Dieu,"* he whispered, spying Kate. *Quelle belle pirate.* He could only see the back of Nello's hat, but looking ahead to Darina with her short blond hair thought, And that boy is pretty too. Then he suddenly remembered the word that had echoed daily through the fortress—how could he have forgotten?—*otages.* Hostages.

That was the solution. Hostages. If he could take those three as prisoners, he could stay alive. He could keep the rest of the pirates from attacking until the frigate came.

Hostages had kept the French alive for years on these islands. Since the day of annexation by Dupetit-Thouars in 1842, every native Marquesan living on the coast was a hostage—undeclared. Whole villages were undeclared hostages. That's what kept the garrisons safe: natives close at hand, easy to round up, easy to punish, imprison, kill. Safety assured through instant revenge. That's why, once the villagers moved inland, the garrison was defenseless. With no hostages at hand, the marines were prisoners in their own fortress. No match for even a small group of rebels. That's why, last week, the governor ordered them to leave: to prevent being overwhelmed like garrisons often had been over the years. To prevent what would incite the natives to rise and kill them all: a victory, as in 1880 when an admiral had to come from Tahiti with a flotilla and, with cannon fire, wiped whole villages off the map—the flimsy shacks, the frail canoes, and the people.

Testard hurriedly donned his official white tunic, slapped the visored cap onto his head, slung a loaded rifle across his back, grabbed two others, one in each hand, and, cutting a swath through the flock of chickens in the yard, ran with heavy footsteps under the cover of the jungle to the far end of the beach to get the Finn and the Chinamen.

Through his binoculars, Dugger watched the shore. He saw something white running behind the scrub, then lost sight. He went below, loaded the Winchester, clambered up the rope ladder again, and, with one arm around the mast, sat with the rifle in his lap. Maybe I can shoot a goat for lunch, he thought.

The ketch rolled gently on the long swells from the sea.

Chapter 28

Nello held the oars hard in the water to keep the skiff from catching a breaker and crashing onto the hard black sand. He waited for a lull, then told Darina to jump before they hit, grab the rail, and hold the skiff back until he could ship the oars and jump in to help her.

Dugger sat on the spreaders, and watched them pull the skiff up through the sand. He leveled his binoculars on the deserted village spread among the trees: the poles with a few mats still dangling, the odd thatched roof, a clearing with no one in it but an ambling dog, which, reaching the middle of the clearing, sat down in the sun as if lord and master of it all.

That was when Dugger noticed the flowers. They seemed to rain down from bushes and trees, and pop up low like carpets from the ground. Near the beach were dense thickets of yellow hibiscus and pink morning glory; farther back, bushes of gardenia, red ginger, waves of bougainvillea, and clumps of flowers and fruits he had never seen.

An immense calm had settled over him and he didn't know why. He watched Nello and the women with a strange detachment, as if they would get along just fine without him and everything would somehow turn out as it should. The only emotion he felt was a vague envy, for not having been born on this wild island, for not being native to the village and the mountains—for not being able to call this place home.

He saw Kate run on the hard sand, stomping with both feet, and the breeze brought her cries: "Land! Solid land!" Then she stood and beckoned with a wide swing toward the ketch, and Dugger could hear over the murmur of the surf, "Come on, Cappy! Come on!" He saw the three of them now running like children, the women awash knee-deep in the surf, and Nello at first cautious looking into the woods, but then freely wading in among the trees, holding out his shirt, filling it with fruit.

Dugger lowered the binoculars and with unwavering concentration began checking the blocks and tangs and the jackstay on the mast.

Father Murphy shaved quickly, then tried to clean his house. He had seen the skiff push off from the ketch, so he flung a few fish in his basket and, with his nightshirt still tied between his legs, ran for the trees and home. Now he hung the basket of fish from the beams, flung remnants of fruit out the back door, straightened his only chair, swept burned-down candlenuts from his windowsill and opened his Bible randomly on the table. His eye leapt over "Woe onto you . . . hypocrites!" One dreary wet blanket, that Matthew, he thought, and flipped the pages. "We also should walk in the newness of life," he read from the Romans. My very thought. He smiled, and pressed the page down flat, then reached outside and plucked a handful of gardenias and sprinkled them, as if the wind had brought them, just inside the door.

He glanced into the mirror and pulled back, a little startled. His fleshy face seemed sallow and unhealthy. It's the heat, he thought. No Irishman can ever get used to it and keep his sanity. He was not yet forty, but he felt suddenly old. Perplexed, he poured coconut oil onto his hands, then rubbed it furiously into his hair to darken the streaks of gray.

He put on his only cassock, worn out from use, faded by the sun, and much too heavy a weave for the tropics, and headed down the beach hoisting up its hem, when he suddenly and haltingly thought of the flowers. He swerved into the woods to gather a bouquet.

The Finn sat on the flat rock that jutted into the pond shrouded by the jungle. He had come down from his hut on the hillock because he thought he had seen the pink glimmer of crayfish in a corner of the pond under an enormous fern that formed an umbrella over it. He could either wade in with barely perceptible movements and reach down to fling the crayfish one by one ashore, or to go back to his hut for the small net he'd fashioned from old mosquito netting and the branch of a hibiscus he'd soaked and bent into a loop.

Testard's unwelcome voice rose nearby, but the Finn made no reply. He heard Testard in his cabin, opening and shutting the plank door in a hurry, finally appearing, out of breath, on the hillock above.

"Pirates," Testard gasped. "A shipload of pirates. Three of them just landed by the falls." And he waved his two rifles, then rested their butts on the ground.

"Crayfish," the Finn said. "If you bring down the net from behind the door, I'll give you half."

"Pirates," Testard insisted. "We can take three hostage to keep ourselves alive."

"Are you still drunk, Testard?"

"For God's sake, man! A shipload of pirates!"

"Pirates."

"Yes, pirates. They're after the Pisco gold."

"Well, they have the wrong island by five hundred miles."

"I'll get the Chinamen," Testard blurted, tipping the rifles. "The four of us can surround them. Put them in the fortress. They're our ticket to safety."

"Like the villagers?"

"Come on, Finn."

"What would pirates want from us?"

"Why don't you ask them that while they cut your throat?"

The Finn smiled. "Maybe we can sell them crayfish."

"I'm making you a temporary gendarme. Ten francs a day."

"You don't have ten francs."

"I will when the frigate gets here."

"And if it doesn't come?"

The anger of helplessness flashed in Testard's eyes. "Get up, Finn. That's an order. Get up or I'll shoot you."

With little conviction and much effort, the Finn rose from the rock and started up the path. "You couldn't swat a fly," the Finn said, and took one of the rifles out of Testard's hands.

Testard turned. His hand shook from excitement and he stepped quickly to his right and looked down at the clearing and the dog. He whistled softly. The dog raised its head, got up, and ambled toward the shade. Testard raised his rifle and, in mid-motion, shot. The dog spun as if doing a little dance, then collapsed in the sand.

Without looking up, Testard was off with firm strides toward the shoals to get the Chinamen.

The Finn watched him go. "Not a trace of sanity left," he murmured. He ambled down into the clearing, sliced off a vine, tied the dead dog's hind legs together, and hung it from a branch. He would skin and dress it later, then gather some banana leaves and roast it in a pit.

Chapter 29

A Fairy tern glided gracefully over them, its wings and fan-shaped tail glowing white against the sky. From the dense bush along shore, yellow reed warblers with long red beaks darted into the sun, then turned in jagged arcs back into the shadows. White-capped fruit doves with dark green wings, and flocks of noisy Lorikeets, as blue as the sea, flashed among the palms, and mynahs gurgled and whistled while pecking at rotting fruit along the ground.

"Paradise." Kate laughed and plowed her toes through the soaked black sand. "I never knew the world could be so beautiful."

Darina stood half in shadow, lowered her head, and said a quiet prayer of thanks, for their safe arrival, for all the beauty, for her brother, amen.

Nello had left them behind, crossed the shallow pool, and stood under the waterfall. He pulled off his shirt and washed and drank, and made himself promise never to set foot in salt water again.

Then he heard the shot. It was dull and muffled, and with the splashing of the water on his head and the breaking surf and the grating noise of the mynahs, he couldn't be sure at all. He convinced himself that it had been the thud of a coconut hitting the ground, until he looked seaward and saw Dugger standing frozen on the foredeck, the binoculars fixed just beyond them in the palms. He waded out onto the sand, wrung out his shirt and wiped his face, and wished like hell Dugger would yell or signal. Then, deciding it had been but a coconut, he strode up the sand and sat down in the shade. He heard footfalls behind him, but before he could turn a voice called out, "Ye are no more strangers and foreigners, but fellow citizens with the saints in the household of God."

THE WOMEN HAD GONE UNDER THE FALLS and were standing close to each other, letting the water cascade over them. "How can people live anywhere else?" Kate said, the water running into her mouth.

"Turn. I'll wash your hair," Darina said. She gently teased out the tangles from Kate's hair and rinsed out the salt.

FATHER MURPHY STEPPED INTO THE SUN and headed toward the laughing bathers, calling out, *"Mave mai. Me mai a nuku mai.* Welcome to Paradise." Kate was first to emerge from the spray and walk toward him, wringing out her hair and pushing it from her face.

"You must be the beautiful lady pirate." He smiled broadly and, seeing her breasts through her dripping shirt, tried to fix his gaze on just her eyes. "Silver and gold I have none, but such as I have I give to thee," and handed her the bouquet of yellow and red flowers. To clarify his intentions, he added somewhat nervously, "Apostles, chapter three, verse six. I'm Father Murphy. Welcome to Hiva Oa." Then he raised his voice and called toward Darina, who had stepped from the falls and pushed back her short hair. "Welcome, young man, and may the Lord be with you."

"What beautiful flowers," Kate said, and turned to show them to Darina when she saw three armed men, with rifles leveled at them, step out of the bush.

Nello leaned back. "Some paradise," he grumbled, sliding his hand closer to his gun.

Like some giant in a tattered straw hat, the big Finn stood over the two slight Zuo brothers beside him. They had been getting ready to row out to the reef and dive, wearing only faded printed cloth wrapped around their loins, but Testard had insisted that they get dressed, so one had put on a small black vest, the other a collarless wool shirt he saved for winter, and they now stood thin-legged, straining under the weight of the leveled rifles.

The Finn, even armed, had the air of a bystander. His pants, which ended vaguely at his calf, were torn and holed, his shirt cuffs had worn away long ago, and his shirt pockets sagged with what he'd beachcombed that day: a coin, the stem of a pipe, a spike, an empty rifle shell. He was tired. Tired of the heat, the bugs, the endless sun, the sea; tired of Testard and the Chinamen, and even of Father Murphy. All he wanted from life was to be cold again and see the countryside covered in deep snow, and hear words that he remembered from his childhood, words that stirred his heart even in his sleep.

Testard had stopped, shocked at the effect the beautiful white woman with her wet clothes had on him. He had seen the most lascivious native women in beastly naked debauch, but that was different, that somehow didn't stir something deep inside. He stood pouring sweat, trying to think of the proper salutation. He put his pistol away, then took it out again. At last he decided it was best in his hand but held behind his back, so he seemed a petty official going for a stroll. *"Madame, messieurs, bonjour. Je suis Émile Testard, sous gouverneur des Groupes Sud-Est."*

When Kate turned to him and began to reply, Nello suddenly

stood and replied in English, "Good morning, Governor, I'm Nello Cerriaci, the first mate of the ketch anchored beyond. I apologize, but we do not speak French."

When Kate looked at him questioningly, he just glared.

"For heaven's sake, Testard," Father Murphy chided. "Why the guns?"

"A precaution, Father," Testard said containing his anxiety. "We have, I'm sorry to say, information that these are . . . adventurers . . . pirates to be plain. My duty is to protect the people of these islands." Then, turning to Kate, he said gently, "I shall have to ask you to be my, let us say houseguest, until we find out otherwise. How many more of you on board?"

"Ten," Nello said.

That's a lot, Testard thought, and he stepped back slightly out of the line of fire.

"My dear governor," Nello said with as much charm as he could muster, "the lady here has come all the way from Ireland in search of her brother, from whom she has not heard in a year. He's a painter. Well respected in his own land."

Testard was barely listening. He stared at the ketch aglow in the bay without signs of life aboard her, and wondered if the other pirates had come ashore below the bluffs to attack.

A dark cloud came on a hard, cool wind, luminous around the edges, with its center black. It hid the peaks and its blackness seemed to tumble down the falls. Darkness fell over the ketch and the shore and Dugger could no longer see clearly the movements of the little group standing on the beach.

He could do nothing to help. He couldn't even go ashore without the skiff. He thought of getting the Winchester and picking off in quick succession the three bastards with the rifles and that idiot in the white uniform who, judging by his pompous stance, was commanding the show.

He ran below, but instead of the rifle he took his pistol, wrapped it tightly in oilcloth, tied it in a bundle with his boots behind his neck, then went above and slipped over the side. He swam with breaststrokes, to keep the gun dry, to the bluffs.

The goat path was too narrow for his feet. He crabbed along it sideways, toes to the rock. The trees and vines behind him hid the shore. He didn't want to see his shipmates anyway, telling himself that as long as he wasn't watching, nothing bad could happen. He clung to ferns and creepers and edged along. Without warning the wind became a squall. It swept along the bluff, buffeting him with gusts, whipping him with fronds and branches. Then it began to rain. Heavy raindrops pelted his face, and poured into his eyes until he could barely see. The bluff became a waterfall, hiding all but a few feet of green around him. The goat trail was a stream.

When it led steeply to a ledge below, he lowered himself on a vine and ran on, head down. In the scrub, just short of the big falls, he stopped. The stream of the falls was a cascade of mud. It was raining too hard to see clearly the beach beyond, but the closer he got, the emptier it looked. He cut inland under palms.

Light poured down ahead. He saw a clearing awash with water in the pelting rain, encircled by abandoned huts, the fronds of their roofs lifted by the wind, the mats of the walls fluttering like flags. When he saw no movement, he circled the houses. He was staring at a drenched parrot taking refuge in a ruined hut when he bumped into the dead dog hanging by its legs. It swung lightly in the wind, its ragged fur washed backward by the downpour.

Something moved across the clearing. A lanky blue-green figure came through the jungle, barely distinguishable from the downpour that covered him. He stood vague and immobile like some vaporous apparition between two bamboo huts tilting on their stilts. Dugger untied the bundle from his neck and pulled out the gun. The apparition faded. It must have stepped back, because its outlines softened, then dissolved in the rain.

"Guillaume?" Dugger called softly, but the downpour washed it away. The rain hardened and there was nothing left but the whipping fronds and raindrops thundering like a drumroll in the palms.

THEY WALKED SINGLE FILE, silent and drenched, through the rain, past the village, with the Finn leading the way, followed by the crew of the ketch, the Zuos, then Testard, with Father Murphy straggling well behind. His water-laden cassock hung like a lead cape on his shoulders, and he cursed under his breath, then uttered, "Forgive me, Father," and crossed himself to calm his rage.

Dugger crouched in the thicket and let them pass. They were so close he could smell the wet wool of the cassock. Then he stepped out, with three strides caught the priest, wrapped his arm around his neck, and covered his mouth. He held the pistol barrel across his own lips to signal him to silence. The priest stared into a sunburned face, the green eyes hard but not unkind, and could have sworn he saw a quick smile. He blinked in agreement. "Welcome, my son," he whispered into Dugger's palm.

Dugger released his hold, and when he saw the priest remain silent, he mouthed, *Thank you,* then went, with noiseless strides, to catch up to the column. When right behind Testard, he raised his pistol and put it against the nape of his neck just above the uniform's white collar.

"Tell them to drop their rifles," he ordered quietly.

There was no reply. Then he heard a quick yelp from the priest behind him and in the same moment felt a blow to his head and everything went black. His knees folded and he fell, face-down, into the rain-pelted mud.

Flush with excitement, Father Murphy had been leaning against a palm tree, running his hand across his face in a futile attempt to dry it, when he saw the lanky tattooed shape emerge from the thicket, raise his rifle, and swing its butt into the back of the green-eyed man's head. He saw the man crumple to the ground, and the tattooed man step back into the scrub and vanish in the rain.

He watched Testard, utterly bewildered, lean over the crumpled body in the rain.

Chapter 30

The rain blew out of the bay as abruptly as it had come. The clouds, still towering, were swept out into the sunset, and the wind kept shaking water from the palms. Birds ruffled their feathers, trying to dry out.

From where they sat in the courtyard of the barracks, they saw only the lofty clouds and sky, and the top of the peeping palm. There were two iron loops embedded knee-high in the stone wall, and the Finn and the Zuos had run a chain through them and put leg irons on the men—Dugger, Nello, and Darina—and let them sit on a bench next to the wall. Kate they allowed to roam.

In the last color-drenched light, their white shirts glowed, the leaves turned a poisonous green, the bougainvillea blood-red. The air was dense with the odor of wet earth, gardenias, and the smell of roast meat rising from the pit. One of the Zuos sat on his haunches beside the pit, occasionally lifting the banana leaves from the roast and pouring coconut milk and crushed mangoes down between the hot stones that lined the bottom of the pit.

Testard had changed into a dry shirt that already hung limp from the humid air. He moved efficiently through the yard and barracks, filling the roles of jailer, good host, and defender of the fortress. He had the big table brought out into the yard, below the bower of the leaning palm, but close to his chained guests so they too could partake in the festive dinner. He set out a tablecloth and china, with Kate's bouquet of flowers in a pot, before scurrying inside to ready more ammunition for the rifles. Next, he prepared a bowl of rum with slices of papaya, bitter grapefruit, vanilla sticks, and bananas, and smilingly served his guests while carefully staying beyond the length of their chains. And all the while he remained vigilant, glancing often through the open gate at the beach and bay, or at the gloomy bluffs that loomed behind the fortress, unsure which attack to prepare for: that of the natives by land or of the pirates by sea.

The Finn leaned on one side of the gate and rested his rifle against the other. He surveyed the darkening shore, where the other Chinaman was doing as he was told: keeping an eye on the clearing, the groves, and the bay for any movement.

Father Murphy sat at the head of the table with his damp cassock still steaming, distractedly fishing in his cup of rum for a bit of fruit. For once in his life he was speechless, overwhelmed by the new faces. Sure, the *Aranui,* the old steamer, came six times a year to drop off supplies and pick up sacks of copra; and the small French frigate came to show off its cannon each July, and once in a while a trading schooner would happen upon the bay, but none of them was anything like this ketch or its crew. The others were all Malay or Thai, and the few white faces among them had the same life-hardened stare that neither wanted nor expected anything from life. The crew of the ketch was different. There was a spirit in their eyes, a vigor in their movement, and, yes, beauty.

He had not seen a white woman since he couldn't remember when. This must surely be a sign. Now he had trouble keeping his eyes off Kate. He could not get enough of her hair streaked by the sun, her pretty, honest face, her hazel eyes. As she moved around the yard arranging cutlery and plates, there seemed an unconcerned ease about her, as if she could imagine only the brightest of tomorrows.

And that pretty blond boy. So fragile-looking, with transparent skin, and that full mouth—and big blue eyes that seemed to hide something. All afternoon the boy remained silent, seemed to watch the enigmatic mate and the captain for signs of what to do. That enigmatic mate—gruff, unshaven, all sinew and bone, big jaw set—with his right eyebrow rising and falling as his left eye squinted intensely, darting here, riveting there, evaluating every move, every word, every reaction. He seemed more quick and able than the younger captain he served, who often appeared sunken deep in melancholy, until he suddenly burst out with a curt sarcasm, or anger.

You're judging him too harshly, Murphy, he chided himself. You might not be all that cheery yourself if you'd just gotten a good solid whack on the head like him, then ended up in chains. For all you know, he might be a barrel of laughs another day. And who are you to be judging anyway: a priest without a flock looking for salvation in a cup, droning in his empty chapel to himself, hearing his own confessions; assigning his own penance; converting no one but himself to insobriety?

I'll drink to that, he thought, and raised his cup.

You're not such a bad priest, the rush of rum assured him. You cared for your flock body and soul when they were still around; stitched their wounds; cooled their fevers. Maybe they ignored you and remained savages, but then God must have made them savage for a reason. Maybe he just wants you to serve blindly. To test your faith. Or maybe he wants you to learn something from *them*. After all, he gave them a Garden of Eden; maybe they are God's most innocent children. Just look at their eyes. Look at their ready smiles. Look at them share their last bite with whoever passes by. Is there a more truly Christian soul than in a savage? Sure they have bad habits—they take their neighbor's wife; sometimes they kill their infants; and instead of loving their neighbors, they eat them roasted in an *uma* now and then—but overall, overall . . .

Father Murphy raised his glass. "Welcome to paradise," he toasted. "And if it's not quite that at the moment, we'll certainly make it so."

With the roasting meat not yet done, Testard sat down at the far end of the table, opened his ledger, its pages wavy from dampness, and like some polite hotelier asked for information of his prisoners. He felt too embarrassed to begin with the woman, so he started with Nello, whom he didn't like.

"Your full name, please," he said with quiet courtesy, not wanting show his anxiety.

"Nello Cerriaci."

"Place of birth?"

"Beware Cove."

"And where is that?"

"Where it rains even more than it does here," Dugger snapped.

"The west coast of Canada," Nello said, then whispered, "Come on, Cappy, let's stay on the man's good side."

"Date of birth?"

"Eighteen eighty-one,"

"Profession?"

"First mate."

"Of a pirate ship," Father Murphy blurted, and had a little laugh.

"Your domicile?"

"The ship."

Testard moved on quickly to the boy. "And you, *jeune*

homme?"

Darina looked at Dugger for help, but he didn't look back.

"Go ahead, son," Nello pointedly said. "The gentleman is the governor of these islands. We are under his protection, so go ahead."

"Darin," she mumbled. "Born 1899, County Galway, Ireland. Cabin boy."

"Domicile?"

"The pirate ship, Testard," Father Murphy mocked. "Can't you tell the boy's a murderous pirate? Have you ever seen a more vicious face? Why don't you ask him how many throats he's cut? Use your eyes, man. Trust your judgment. Hang the beggar before it's too late."

"Père Murphy, je vous en prie," Testard said softly, and went on speaking in French but so quietly that Kate heard only *"Il a les mêmes yeux que Peintures.* The same eyes as Pictures. Only when Father Murphy replied bitterly in French did she clearly understand his every word.

Darina leaned over to Nello. "Do you ever tell the truth?" she asked nervously.

"Not on dry land," he said.

"Why do you want me to be a boy?"

"You ever play poker?"

"Oh, sure. Every night. We used the host as chips."

Nello felt a sudden rush and he had to look away. He could stand her eyes, but her humor left him helpless. Stop it, he told himself. There's no time for this.

"In poker," he murmured, "there is only one aim: to hide from your opponent what you have. The more confused he gets, the more likely you'll beat him."

"I'm the one that's confused."

"That's all right; you're not playing this hand."

"Father Murphy," Testard said now in English, forcing a perfect calm, "could I ask you to cut up the roast meat for our guests?"

The priest fell silent. He stared in confusion at the Chinaman by the pit, and said something to Testard half in French, half patois. Nello looked questioningly at Kate for a translation, but her gaze was fixed firmly on the pit.

The Chinaman began folding back the leaves, and cursing when he burned his hand. Then he took two poles and slipped them, like long chopsticks, on an angle into the pit. He pushed deep, then pressed down, raising the mass, covered with leaves, out of the ground. Father Murphy, endlessly chiding, grabbed the other ends, and they carried the mass, like a corpse on a stretcher, through the clouds of rising steam into the barracks. They dropped it somewhere out of sight with a thud.

Testard had moved on to questioning Dugger, and as Nello started listening, he heard, "And your last port of call?

"San Lucas," Dugger responded. "Mexico."

"But you weren't there very long."

"Is that so?" Dugger said, surprised. "Did you have a spy aboard?"

"No, Captain. I have eyes. San Lucas is a hot desert town. Had you stopped a long time, you would have surely bought yourselves hats of straw instead of the hot felt ones you wear."

"Perhaps we're as attached to them as Father Murphy is to his cassock."

There were sounds of reprimand from the barracks and a cleaver thumping. The sky had lost its light; only the clouds far to the west still held in them the remnants of the day. The other Zuo had come up from the shore and said something to the Finn, who stood dark against the last light on the sea.

Father Murphy came out with a candle, cupping his hand around the flame. "The last real candle we have," he said sheepishly, and began lighting the strings of candlenuts dangling from wires across half shells of coconut. They smoldered, flared, and smoked, mingling bitterness into the sweet fragrant air.

Testard had run out of questions. He had to turn to Kate.

She was standing, leaning heavily on a chair, her eyes distant, reflecting the flames. The courtyard was filled with shadows dancing to the rhythm of the fronds against the stars.

"Chère Madame," Tetstard began, "and where were you born?"

The Zuos came out with a wooden tray ringed by steaming yams and roasted bananas. At its center, piled high, were fragrant slabs of meat.

Chapter 31

Their chains rattled as they pulled the bench close to the table. "Wild goats are most difficult to hunt," Testard began, forking a piece of meat into his mouth, while staring Father Murphy into silence. "They put themselves between you and the sun, then stand there and watch you being blinded. You have to outsmart them. You put a shard of mirror in a place they frequent, and while they're bewildered by it . . . an easy shot."

"A little deception goes a long way," Nello said.

"Even with goats," Dugger added.

"It works with flocks of sheep," Father Murphy added. "Until one day they head for the hills and leave you behind for good."

"But the Patient Shepherd finds them all," Darina said gently. "I remember the Bible saying that."

"Excellent, my boy," Father Murphy chimed. "Every last one of them."

They ate with the ferocity of the nearly starved, the fragrant plantains, the rich, sweet yams. The meat—their first in almost three weeks—was succulent and toothsome, so good to gnaw and chew.

"Best goat I ever ate," Nello said.

Testard passed around the bowl of rum. The last daylight had gone; only a towering cloud rose beyond the bay, a pillar to the dome of stars. The sound of clacking mah-jongg pieces came from inside the barracks and, with it, the tangy fragrance of smoldering opium.

As he filled Kate's glass, Testard said, "So you are here in search of your brother?"

"Yes," Kate blurted. "A painter. He was living in Tahiti but wanted something wilder. He was headed to . . ." and she looked pleadingly at Darina.

"Fatu Hiva, you said," Darina added.

"Yes. Fatu Hiva. The last letter he sent was from aboard the tramp steamer."

"The *Aranui,"* Testard interjected.

"Yes. They were sailing at dawn into Nuku Oa,"

"Nuku Hiva," Testard corrected.

"Yes, of course," Kate said.

"I have heard of him," Testard said. "I have heard he painted well. With passion."

"Why do you say paint*ed?"* Darina butted in. "Did something happen to him?"

"Not as far as I know. They found his things in his shack not long ago. Everything in order, all his things, his brushes, paints. But he was gone. And hasn't been back since."

"How long?" Kate asked.

"I'm not sure. Some months. But do not worry yourself, madame. Around here men vanish for a bit all the time. They fall in love in some canyon in the mountains, or get drunk on a ship and wake up islands away, or simply decide to go native on some tiny *motu* and beachcomb. It's normal. And perfectly safe. There are no dangerous animals, not even snakes. I'm sure he'll show up soon. Especially once I send out word that you have come."

"Thank you, Governor. You are very kind."

"My pleasure," and he raised his glass in her direction and drank. "And you, dear Captain Dugger. What are you searching for in this far corner of the world?"

"Peace and quiet," Dugger snarled. "I must have taken a wrong turn somewhere."

"Oh, there's peace and quiet here," Father Murphy interjected. "Another ounce of peace and quiet and we'll be certifiably deceased."

"It's a fine place for contemplation," Testard objected. "It brings out one's true character; both weaknesses and strengths. 'Solitude sometimes is best society.' I believe Milton wrote that."

Darina grinned. "He wrote it in a pub."

Testard laughed too generously. "And you, Monsieur First Mate. What is it you seek?"

Nello put a large bite in his mouth and, raising his fork for emphasis, said, "Revenge."

"Ah, fascinating," Testard said in admiration. "What kind of revenge?"

"Haven't decided yet."

"May I ask upon whom?"

"Don't know yet."

"But for what offense?"

"Don't know that either. But I have read that revenge keeps the mind sharp and the heart pumping, so I've decided to take revenge for something, somehow, on someone. It's something to look forward to. Like Christmas."

Father Murphy laughed a hearty laughter. "A ship of madmen," he said. "Thank you, heavenly Father, for sending us such delightful company."

"Yes." Testard smiled. "To good company."

They raised their cups and drank. Forks clanged against plates, when on the fragrant breeze oozing from the canyon the deep rumble of drums stirred the air. Thudding and forceful, it mingled with the endless crashing of the waves. They all looked up into the flickering light.

The large from of the Finn stepped into the light of the barracks doorway. The rifle dangled from one hand, an opium pipe from the other, and he stopped in the doorway, perfectly still. The mah-jongg pieces clacked behind him; he threw a quick word over his shoulder and the clacking stopped. He walked across the courtyard to the gate and stood, massive against the starlit foam, and listened.

Testard got up and started after him.

"Shhh," the Finn said.

Testard stood still.

Darina heard Nello shifting in the chains.

"Shhh," the Finn commanded.

A wave thudded hard and the ground under them trembled. A new sound came in the night, distant voices of women singing.

"So beautiful," Kate whispered.

"They're coming," the Finn said. He took a deep draft from the pipe. Another wave crashed, hissed, then died away. "The singers are standing still," he said. "But the drums are coming."

Testard sobered in an instant. He strode into the barracks and snuffed the candlenuts. The barracks went dark. He came out with the Zuos, all three carrying rifles. One by one, they blew out the candlenuts in the courtyard, leaving only Father Murphy's candle fluttering in the breeze. The wind had blown the wax off to one side and it hung stiff and white, refusing to fall.

"Maybe they just want to talk," Father Murphy suggested.

Dugger snorted. "Or ask us to dance."

"How about some quiet?" the Finn said, and took a few more steps into the darkness.

A fluttering moth with dark wings touched the flame. It

threw a giant shadow on the wall until one wing flared. The smell of it burning filled the night. "They're coming faster," the Finn said, and in agitation took a long drag on the pipe.

"So what if they're coming?" Nello asked.

"They're coming to attack us," Testard said. "I have feared this since the day I arrived. While they lived here in the village, peace was guaranteed. We could take hostages."

"You and the Chinamen?"

"Me and the platoon. But the platoon left for Nuku Hiva. It was just a question of time before . . ."

"How many are there?" Nello asked.

"Fifty men. Maybe twenty rifles."

"Why would they attack?" Darina asked.

The Finn had come back in through the gate, pulled it shut behind him, and slipped the bar in place. "Because they want us dead," he said flatly.

"It *is* their island," Father Murphy said. "They just want it back. I know exactly how they feel."

"We could all get the hell out of here on the ketch," Dugger said.

"And how do we get to the ketch?" the Finn said.

"We have a skiff," Dugger said.

The Finn, in a low voice, said, "There is no skiff."

No one moved. Testard looked hesitantly at the chains, then at the Zuos, then beyond the wall at the heavy darkness.

"There is no skiff," the Finn repeated. "The Chinamen saw someone take it in the twilight."

In a sudden burst of anger, Dugger yanked the chains. The drums thudded louder, more frantic, then went silent. "You need our help, Testard," Dugger snapped. "Undo the damned chains or we'll just sit here and watch you die like a dog."

"Like a dog," the Finn repeated. "Then they can roast you with the plantains in the pit."

"We can swim to the ketch," Darina suggested.

"The undertow and the currents would take us to China," the Finn countered.

A shrill cry ripped the night. Then another voice, formidable and cold, uttered guttural sounds. Testard reached into his pocket and pulled out the key. He knelt beside Darina and felt around for the lock.

"Raouti," Father Murphy's voice murmured in the night.

"Who's Raouti?" Nello asked.

"The one who shouts," the priest said. "Leads the battle. Incites them to bravery. And hatred."

The voice roared longer sounds, audible words, phrases.

"What did he say?" Nello asked.

"He's telling them to rage," the Finn said. "Rage like wild dogs. Tear them apart. Tear apart their will and flesh."

The *raouti* roared on, his voice rising, riding on the wind.

"How long does he keep this up?" Dugger asked, annoyed.

"Just until we're dead," the Finn said. "Not long. Because some of them are climbing the hill behind us now."

Testard fumbled urgently with the lock.

"Don't look up," the Finn whispered. "There is someone right above us in the palm."

Nello lunged and snuffed the candle. The yard went dark.

As silently as they could, they slipped off the leg irons. The Finn took a last drag, then put the pipe on the ground. Over the singing and the drums and the yelling of the *raouti* came the metallic sound of a rifle bolt sliding back.

There was rustling in the fronds high above. Lit by the meager starlight, the Finn slowly raised his gun. The opium colored his vision and he saw the palm outlined in shimmering yellow, the fronds black against the stars with silver pulsing in between, and he saw something moving, something with arms and legs.

"Shoot him," Testard whispered.

The Finn aimed but held his fire.

"Shoot him," Testard repeated.

The chants and drumming grew; the voice of the *raouti* repeated a single word.

The Finn aimed, but the palm trunk was in the way. Then the figure up there stopped moving and the Finn held his breath, and while the *raouti* shrieked, "Rage!" again, he fired.

A frightful scream filled the air. The figure fell from the palm at their feet in the sand.

"It's a goddamn kid," the Finn said.

The kid, frightened but unhurt, ran for the gate. Testard pushed him out into the night, then slid the bar back in place. The *raouti* fell silent and the drums ebbed.

"That was some attack," Dugger said, and, with his eyes used to the starlight, reached for his cup. "A miracle we survived it." He took a long sip. "Can you still see someone on the bluff?"

"Never could," the Finn said. "There's a steep rock slope right above it; we can't see them and they can't shoot us. But I heard movement."

"And now?"

"Not now."

Testard pulled the snuffed candle from the cup and lit it again. The faces around him glowed anxious in the candlelight. "Well," he said, and reached for a wooden bowl that had been set beside him, "would anyone like some *poisson cru?"* and lifted a ladleful of a mushy pink concoction that smelled of fish, lime, and coconuts. "Finely chopped wahoo, from beyond the reef." He smiled wearily.

The Finn spoke quietly to the Zuos and one of them climbed onto the wall by the gate and straddled it, looking toward the canyon. The other Zuo sat at the base of the wall and watched the cliff. The bowl was passed around and they scooped a bit of pink mush onto their plates.

Darina took a bite, then whispered, "I smell fish."

"You're eating fish," Nello said.

"No. I mean live fish. A lot of it. Coming from there." And she pointed up the bluff. "I really do."

"I believe it's just the sea," Father Murphy assured her.

"Perhaps," Darina said, but thought, The sea is below us and the fish smell is from above.

"I smell it too," Kate said. And stood up and walked into the middle of the yard.

Testard finished his *poisson cru* and wiped his mouth. "And for dessert, *Messieurs et Madame,"* he said with a sigh. "Courtesy of our—" but a small stone rolled down the cliff, bounced with a clang on a tin plate, and came to rest before him. They looked up. Nothing moved.

"I can't hear a thing," the Finn said softly.

With a sudden burst the drums rolled loud, then stopped. The *raouti* shrieked once. Then silence. Another stone came and landed in the sand.

They all remained frozen in the flickering candlelight. "Shh," the Finn said. He backed toward the gate and raised his rifle, pointing vaguely upward at the palm. He stopped. Something up there shimmered.

Then it plunged.

Dark and enormous, it plunged from above—tied by the tail, its jaws open wide, swinging on a long rope from the top of the palm—a wriggling, dying, but still ferocious shark. It swung in a long arc away from the cliff, then it swung back, writhing, lurching directly at the table. Twisting in fury, it swept cups, plates, and pots, its merciless eyes dull in the feeble light, its great jaws gaping with rows of teeth deathly white.

The drums and a shriek cut into the night. Like a murderous pendulum, the shark swung from the palm, back and forth in jagged figure eights, its eyes dripping blood, its gleaming teeth like blades, biting plates, chairs, chunks of meat, a corner of the table, wrenching itself with rage.

It knocked over the Finn, and toppled half the chairs. Kate stumbled across the yard trying to get away. Dugger grabbed a chair and hurled it at the shark. "Shoot it!" he roared, but the Finn was down on the ground. Nello grabbed Darina and pushed her against the bluff. Testard dove across the yard for the rifle by the door. Enraged by the confusion and the smell of its own blood, the shark snapped from side to side, plowed along the table through the fruit and glasses, flinging the clump of flowers high into the air. It doubled on itself, and red foam flew from its mouth past the glittering wire that once held its jaws tight. It opened its jaws now like some enormous trap and with a distorted twist swung and lunged at Kate.

Kate ran but tripped as the shark swung toward her. Its teeth caught her hip. Its nose pushed her forward and she slammed against the wall. The shark hit too, shuddered, and let her fall. She crumpled to the ground. The shark began to swing back across the yard.

Testard had retrieved his rifle, slid the bolt, and swung to fire, but the shark came fast, and its jaws locked on his arm and chest. It lifted him like a rag doll, and didn't let go of him until they were back over Kate and slammed with a great shudder against the barracks wall.

Dugger covered Kate with his body, but the shark now swung away. Nello crawled on his elbows, picked up Testard's rifle, and, lying on his back as the shark flew over him, put a bullet through its eye. The shark shook. It stopped writhing. But swung on. Its blood ran down its nose in streams and drew long lazy spirals on the ground.

From the bluff above came a singular, fervent laugh. Darina froze, then pushed herself out of Nello's arms.

Chapter 32

The drums fell silent and singing rose, nearby, from the water. The Finn picked up his rifle, cocked it, and pushed open the gate. Dark forms emerged from the scrub along the shore and moved, slow and graceful, toward the white foam of the sea. A torch was lit. Stocky naked men carried small pirogues down to the shore, their outriggers fine and delicate in the starlight. They launched them but held on to prevent them from flipping in the surf, then, one by one, they pushed through the breakers, with the torch in the lead and the others spreading wide. The women stayed behind, standing knee-deep in the foam, singing and slowly weaving their hips and shoulders in undulating cadence with the movement of the sea. Their wet flesh glimmered. The men knelt in the pirogues, all paddling in rhythm. They glided unhurried over the somber waters.

The Finn found the pipe, took a long hit. "They're going fishing," he said with a sigh.

The shark hung still. Father Murphy had relit the candlenuts, and the shark, lit like some pagan offering, dangled over the devastated table.

"I'm all right," Kate said, hobbling across the yard, when Dugger and Darina grabbed her arms to help, but she was glad to reach the chair and sit down. The shark had hooked her belt but its teeth had sliced her hip. She held her hand over the gash, holding the cut closed. Dugger lifted her hand. The cut was long but shallow, "Nello can stitch you up," he said.

"Sure," Nello said, trying to hide his worry, while helping Father Murphy drag Testard to the table. "If I can stitch a storm sail, I can stitch that scratch."

"We have needle and iodine," Father Murphy offered, and took a coconut full of candlenuts and vanished in the dark.

"You better drink a lot more rum," Dugger said to Kate. "Needles sting."

"I'm all right," Kate insisted. "But could someone cut down the shark?"

The fleet spread in a wide half-moon across the bay, the torch glowing and swaying in rhythm to the song. Then, like a hundred silver flames shimmering in the night, schools of flying fish flew past the torch, dazzled by the curious, unaccustomed glow. The pirogue with the torch headed back to land; the others fell in behind, herding the fish to shore.

As the circle tightened, the sea boiled silver, then the dark sand of shore was filled with silver light.

Nello pulled out his knife. The shark was taller than him, and he went around it to the side Kate couldn't see. The shark's jaw hung open. Putting his boot on the teeth for footing, he grabbed its dorsal fin and climbed. The next foothold was the gills, but there were no handholds past the fin, so he drove the blade of his knife through the coarse skin, between dark stripes. He reached up and grabbed a small fin near the tail, yanked out his knife, and reached up to slice the rope. But the blood and slime of the shark made the handle slick, and the knife fell with a soft thud to the ground. He cursed. From the bluff far above, a shot rang out and the rope split and they fell, Nello clutching the shark.

The lone laughter rang out again from the bluff. Darina glared at where it came from, but the darkness yielded nothing.

DUGGER KEPT KATE UPRIGHT and held the wound closed tight. He made her gulp rum. Nello went down to the sea to wash off the blood and slime of the shark. When he came back, Father Murphy was already at the table, pulling closer the candle and candlenuts, laying out a tincture of iodine and a thread and needle.

"I'll do it if you like," he said to Nello. "I've sewn up half the island after shark bites and knife fights. Sometimes I'm not sure whether I'm priest or seamstress."

Kate smiled. "Sew away, Father," she said. "A stitch in time . . ." But she winced from the pain.

"Take a few deep puffs of this," the Finn offered, and handed her the pipe.

Kate puffed. Dugger held her in his arms and Father Murphy knelt on the ground, and while Nello held the candle close, Father Murphy began to sew with small, tidy stitches.

The Finn and Darina were working on Testard. A pool of blood was darkening at his side.

"How is he?" Nello asked.

"He'll take some sewing," the Finn said.

When the iodine was poured in, Kate hissed through gritted teeth, then let out a soft yelp when the needle pierced her skin. "I could use more light," Father Murphy said. The Finn picked up two coconut shells and held them near his hands.

Father Murphy worked silently. When he was done, he rinsed the gash with iodine again.

The Finn laid candlenuts out around Testard. When Nello came and put the candle beside him, the Finn looked up and said under his breath, "She's gone."

"Who?" Nello said.

"The girl who's not a boy."

Nello turned. Darina was nowhere. The yard was empty except for the shark. He went to the gate and looked out at the long curve of the shore, now deserted in the moonlight. After a while, the singing rose again but distant now and fading somewhere in the canyon. It echoed until it melded with the wind and waves, and the muffled murmurs and soft groans of the night.

Chapter 33

The ground under her feet was soft with rain, and the great leaves brushed against her and drenched her with rivulets. The near-full moon had come over the crest, but it seemed to throw more shadows than light. She told herself not to be afraid because this was like Inishturk except for trees and bushes, and actually better without drunken fishermen staggering at you in the moonlight. There are no dangers here, she told herself, except for the odd shark swinging from a tree. If these people wanted to kill you, they could have killed you in the fortress. They could have killed all of you, but instead they played a joke; to humiliate you with laughter.

The sound of that bubbling, boisterous laughter still rang in her head. A laughter like Michael's. He used to call it chortling. She had never heard anyone else chortle in her life.

The path at the bottom of the canyon narrowed and steepened. It became a creek bed with water around her feet, then swung uphill. She stopped. She closed her eyes and listened. She could no longer hear the sea behind her or the singing up ahead, only soft growls and screeches. She forced herself to concentrate, to drown out the night sounds and listen for voices. There were none. She went on.

At first she had watched her every step, but now she was propelled by yearning. Once in a while she stopped and whispered, "Michael?" Then she pushed on, full of hope. The bushes slapped her hard, and big roots tripped her, and she stumbled but kept from falling, and felt stronger for it.

Judging by the moon, she had been gone an hour, and she began to tire from struggling in the dark. She thought she'd have caught the singers by now—they moved at such languid ease when working on the beach—and it struck her that she might have completely lost the path. She stopped and looked up.

Crenellated spires towered all around her, some cracked, some splintered, but beyond them the mountains stood solid in the moonlight. Another half hour brought her to a saddle. Uphill, toward the moon, was a ridge of mountains, but to her right a slope of grass fell into the sea, where a narrow bay silvered in the moonlight. On one side of the bay, where black rocks backed the shore, a low house huddled, no bigger than a hut. Scatterings of palms fringed its sandy beach, a pond glowed behind it, and she could hear running water gurgling below. Its own world, she thought. Oh, Michael.

She saw movement. Off the point of land, the dark shape of a canoe swept across the sea. It came at great speed straight into the bay, and when it made a sharp turn she could make out the girl riding on her board.

Down a winding goat trail, Darina began the descent.

NELLO WALKED, FULL OF RUM, to the deserted village. He stopped and called out, "Darina," but there was no reply. He circled to the waterfall, saw no one, then headed back to the fortress.

The Finn sat by the gate. "She wouldn't have gone that way," he said. "There's nothing past the village but the Chinamen's shack, and mine. Then a cliff. The only way out of here is the canyon. There is a single narrow path on the island, the rest is jungle."

"And sea."

"There's no one on the sea."

Maybe she went to find the skiff, Nello thought. Those blue eyes were capable of anything. "She likes to be alone," Nello said.

"Who doesn't?" the Finn said.

"How are things inside?"

"The father is stitching Testard like a stuffed goose."

"Will he live?"

"The Father? I doubt it. He drank enough rum to kill the average horse."

"I mean Testard."

"Who knows?"

"I'd better go try to find her," Nello said.

The Finn didn't answer. He held the opium pipe out to Nello. "You can take this if you like. Helps you see in the dark. Helps you see things clearly that aren't even there."

Nello took the pipe, inhaled its smoke deeply, then handed it back.

"And you better take this for company," the Finn said, handing him the rifle.

"Good company," Nello said. He headed for the canyon.

"And if she comes back?" the Finn called.

There was no response.

Darina stopped near the shore behind the palms. The moon lit the hut perched against the bluff, surrounded by low shrubs like a tiny cottage with a garden. The girl rode her board right onto the sand and stopped below Darina. The moonlight streamed off her graceful limbs and upturned breasts. She pushed her long drenched hair over one shoulder, and reached down into the foam and pulled out the tapered board. *"Bonsoir,"* her soft voice said.

Exhausted, Darina leaned back against a palm. "I don't speak French," she said hoarsely. "Do you speak English?"

The other hesitated, "A lil'bit," she said. Then, with languid movements, she dragged her board up the beach into the shadow of the palms.

Darina sat heavily in the still warm sand. The salty breeze felt good against her face. She closed her eyes. The sounds faded, then blurred into one.

"Does everyone go crazy here?" Dugger grumbled tiredly. "What the hell do you mean, they went off into the night?"

"I didn't say *they,*" the Finn objected. "I said *she* vanished, then *he* went to find her."

Jesus, Dugger thought. After a bloody month at sea, all I wanted was a good night's sleep with no sails or waves to worry about. He thought of the ketch unattended in the swells.

"Will the natives be back?"

"Ah, the natives." The Finn sighed and took a deep puff on his pipe but it had burned down. Patiently he stuffed it, lit it, puffed away, then handed it to Dugger. "Have some of this. It helps you understand the natives."

Dugger puffed. The more he puffed, the more distant the Finn seemed, until, with his drawn face and deep-set eyes, he looked like someone from the world beyond. "The natives," the Finn repeated. "The Kanakas. The brutes. The savages." He raised his eyebrows as if in a shrug. "Who knows? They're fickle. Sometimes as happy as children, then they get insulted and want war."

"And now?"

"Now? They're fed up now. Fed up with us all. The French marines, the Irish priest, the Portuguese sailors who come and shanghai them to dig bird shit for fertilizer in Peru, then send them back with smallpox; the Yankee whalers who come and have their way with the women, paying a nail a go. Sometimes there are no nails left in a whaling ship even to hang a hammock." He went to the table and dug around in the rubble for something to gnaw. "And with the nails they leave their diseases: tuberculosis, scarlet fever, measles, the clap; you name it, they leave it. Half the women here are barren from the clap, the other half sick with it. Except for the pretty ones they hide in the valleys. They're slowly dying out. There used to be some fifty thousand Kanakas in these islands. Now there's a few hundred."

There was a gurgling sound from inside the barracks, like someone trying to breathe through water.

"Poor dumb Testard," the Finn went on. "He thinks all will be well when the Kanakas are like Frenchmen. With maybe a dance hall and a sidewalk café. So he had the poor buggers start building a sidewalk; from nowhere to nowhere." He laughed a quiet laughter and shook his head. "And Father Murphy had them start on a cathedral made of coral. Can you imagine? In the middle of bloody nowhere. What minds! No wonder the Kanakas are fed up. Wouldn't you be? They spend their strength on these imbecile creations, and have little left for fishing or making *poi poi*. So they weaken. Then the disease gets them . . . Fed up."

He passed the pipe to Dugger.

"And the whites?" Dugger murmured.

"What whites? We're it. Oh, there were a few dozen at one time: mutineers, ship-jumpers, some convicts who escaped from the prison on Eiao and made it across a hundred miles of currents and sharks. And a few dreamers. Some went crazy, the rest died."

"Died how?"

"Knifed. Shot. Clubbed in the dark. Pushed off a cliff by a Kanaka or another white. Shark food."

After a while Dugger asked, "And you?"

"Well, I don't seem to be dead yet. Guess I might be crazy. Do you think I'm crazy?"

"You seem okay to me."

"Pity. That must mean that I'm about to die."

Dugger got up bracing himself against the wall, and pushed himself off toward the barracks. "You're all right, Finn," he said. He stopped beside the dead shark, watched its dead eye in the moonlight, then turned back to the Finn. "Will they attack?"

"I suppose so. They've been told the marines will come with the frigate. With a cannon. I doubt they'll wait for that."

Too tired to walk around, Dugger stepped over the shark and into the bunkhouse. The place reeked of blood and iodine and rum. Testard, pale except for patches of caked blood, lay in the candlelight. Kate was in a bunk, turned to the wall asleep, and Father Murphy sat snoring in a chair, an empty cup dangling from his hand. When Dugger passed, he stopped snoring and mumbled, ". . . and delivered them into chains of darkness, to be reserved unto judgment . . ."

Dugger sat down beside Kate and leaned against the headboard. He closed his eyes. Go crazy or die, he thought. It's nice to have a choice.

Chapter 34

Guillaume lay high on a cone-shaped crag, looking down at the hillside village in the moonlight. Only a lone old man, graying but unbent, wearing a *pareu,* shuffled among the huts with a torch of woven *pandanus* flaming in his hand. The huts were on terraces encircling a clearing, with a creek running through it. The village was smaller than he remembered; the terraces seemed the same, but there were fewer huts, with wide gaps between them where old huts had collapsed and were never replaced.

From seaward came women's voices, ringing off the canyon walls. He pulled his notebook from his pack, drew a quick sketch of the village, the creek, the biggest house atop a *pae pae,* a raised platform of stones that he remembered to be the chief's, and the towering crags that surrounded the village—the high positions from which you could get clear shots. The French called this place La Vallée des Verges, the Valley of Phalluses.

Then he waited. He flipped to the back of the book to refresh his memory of the Marquesan phrases he'd scribbled there years ago: *Did you miss me? You look as beautiful as ever. Did you wait for me?* but the pages had gotten wet, the words were washed away.

He stirred nervously, remembering what else he was here for, so he pulled his pistol from his bag, checked the chamber, wiped the barrel dry, and set it out where the wind could blow over it. Madness, he thought. You'll go mad trying to do both: kill *and* find love. Love is madness enough alone. Especially after all these years. All this time of trying to forget. Yet how the memories still flood over you: the dreams you dreamt together, the passion, the frantic lust. And those beautiful enigmatic eyes that left you helpless and defenseless. In love. Maybe they're gone forever, those eyes. Perhaps dead. Buried, with all the others that died here whose huts collapsed and were not built again. Or maybe they're back there with the singers in the canyon. Coming.

The old man hurried across the clearing and vanished in the jungle. A minute later Guillaume saw his torch on the rising path that wound between sheer cliffs.

He stashed the notebook in his pack but held on to his pistol and pushed his way through the bush and followed. With his arm extended to guard his face from branches, he clambered quickly through the patch of jungle to the mouth of the canyon.

How quickly you abandon the passion of the heart for the passion of the chase, he thought. Or maybe they're the same? Or maybe the chase is better: once you get your prey, the struggle is over; with love it just begins.

The walls closed in so tight only one man could pass. The torch popped up far ahead and climbed steeply toward the moon. When it reached the crest it vanished. He climbed. He was out of breath when he reached the top. The wind blew harder here. He crouched and looked over the edge. *Mon Dieu,* he thought. This can't be. They said it hasn't existed for centuries.

A narrow grassy plateau hung between two peaks. Below one edge was the dark and sullen jungle; far below the other, the glittering swells of the sea. Great stone platforms lined the plateau—aglow in the flame of torches lit now by the old man every dozen steps. At the far end, a high altar loomed under a great banyan, and a long stone platform with a round black pit from which rose a whimpering plea; a cry. The wind brought the odor of decaying flesh. A place of sacrifice.

The old man lit the last torch near the banyan, came back to the altar, stuck his torch between two stones, and from a niche pulled a long white festive gown and slipped it over his head. He walked with slow grace to the plateau's edge, stopped, and looked up into the dome of stars.

From the beach aglow in the moonlight, Father Murphy came up and stopped beside the Finn at the fortress gate.

"What do we do now, Finn?"

"About what?"

"Jesus, Finn. About anything." A wave crashed in a long thunder on the sand, and he didn't speak again until there was silence. "About what to do when the frigate comes? It has to come. If they lose this island, they will lose them all."

"So they lose them."

"Then what will happen to us?"

"Oh, I'm pretty sure they'll kill us; you know that, don't you, Padre? The frigate will come and blow up a few shacks, slaughter some poor devils, and sail off; a job well done. Then the Kanakas will wait for the right time to take revenge; then we're dead."

"Jesus, Finn, you should get some sleep."

The Finn sucked some cold smoke out of the pipe. "Have you ever eaten shark, Padre? They say eating a shark is in fact eating a man, because a shark will have eaten a man in its time."

"It's the opium, Finn. It's turning your brain to mush."

"To each his own savior, Padre."

"I'm shutting the gate," Father Murphy said in helpless anger. "Are you coming in or staying out?"

"Oh," the Finn said, "I'll come in. I miss that old dead shark."

With a swing of his cassock, Father Murphy went toward the dark stench of the barracks. "I believe in God, the Father Almighty, maker of heaven and earth," he mumbled.

"And the pipe," the Finn added. "Don't forget the maker of the pipe."

Darina shuddered awake, unsure whether she'd slept for minutes or for days. The moon lit the little world on whose edge she slept. She was leaning against the base of a palm, the moon overhead slashed by swaying fronds. The girl stood in the pond below her hut, naked, humming softly, distractedly washing her shoulders and long arms.

Darina kept looking at her in helpless fascination. The girl finished washing but remained in the pond, massaging her small breasts as she did every day, pumping gently just as the older women had showed her, when they were teaching her how to make them larger and more firm. After a while she reached for a broken coconut, crushed some of the white meat in her hands, spread her legs, and slowly rubbed the pulp in her shadowed regions, around and around, slightly up and down, to whiten the dark flesh, a cherished sign of beauty. She rubbed patiently until she breathed hard, her thighs and buttocks writhed, and her head fell forward as she gave a gentle moan.

She stood motionless awhile, then she rinsed off, dried herself, turned, and softly humming, walked into her shack. She lay down just beyond the opening of the door, brought an arm over her head to shade her eyes, and lay still, only her back heaving with long, even breaths.

Nello hurried along the path. The growth overhead made strange patterns against the moon, and left torn and tangled shadows on his arms. He cursed, mixing saints with hogs and dogs. You are completely crazy, he told himself, chasing a madwoman in the land of madmen at night.

He stopped and smelled the rum on his own breath and the stench of the shark still on his arms. You should be back there looking after Kate and helping Dugger, not chasing some chimera in the night.

But he walked on and didn't stop until he reached the saddle.

Below him were the small bay and the hut and the pointed board lying under the palms. Through the open door he could see a naked form lying in pale light. He felt a rush of the heart.

Chapter 35

He had heard of these ancient sites. There were tales of sacred rites for warriors who had showed bravery in battle, for virgins initiated into womanhood by warriors, for the births of new chiefs, and for old chiefs when they died. And he had heard of human sacrifice, and the gruesome feasts that followed, heard Kanakas talk about it like fairytales from the past. At those times there were the dances and the "long pig" was still eaten. But the sites were said to have been overrun by jungle; no one knew where they were, or if they had been at all. But this *was* here: the grass of the plateau worn, the torches ablaze, readied for something.

Guillaume steadied his elbows on a rock and looked through the binoculars at the flat boulder before the altar and the banyan tree towering in the torchlight.

Something in the banyan's roots caught his eye. The long roots of the banyan hung in cascades from the branches, some thick as a thigh, some so fine they danced in the wind. But on the thick roots there were lumps; rounded, bulging. At first he thought they were only an anomaly of nature, but when he refocused the binoculars, he saw the eyes. Most of the lumps were grown over by root bark, but some were not yet completely enclosed and showed yellowed foreheads, cheeks, the dark holes of the eyes. And off to one side was a fresh head with swarming bugs.

He felt a wave of nausea at the thought that under that swarm might be the head he loved.

In a sleep no deep enough for dreams, Darina leaned against the tree. When she heard someone yell out, she looked up but saw only the gloomy jungle and the sea, and the girl asleep in her doorway.

Then she heard a loud curse and behind her the jungle parted, and, limping through the trees, holding his thigh with blood seeping between his fingers, came Nello.

When he saw her he stopped. "Are you all right?" he asked, then walked into the sea. "Lava rock," Nello hissed. "Cuts like coral." He rolled the leg of his pants above his knee, then washed the wound. The gash was short but deep. "Do you know how to sew?"

The girl had awakened in her hut, and now sat looking at the blood coloring the man's leg.

She slid from her doorway, tying her *pareu* around her waist, but instead of coming toward them, she went to a thicket of leathery, heart-shaped leaves. She picked their yellow flowers, then came and stopped in front of Nello. The flowers were mostly closed, but some showed a ring of red deep in the crumpled petals.

"C'est trés bon pour la blessure," she said softly, pointing at the wound.

Nello smiled. "You are a doctor?"

"A lil'bit," she replied.

She knelt before him and, with great concentration, dabbed the wound dry with a corner of her skirt. Then, one by one, she laid the flowers across the gash. She squeezed them down with the palm of her hand. Nello watched her. The girl couldn't have been more than twenty, her face unlined, sincere, brown but light enough to show freckles bloom. Her eyebrows almost touched, her lower lip a gentle pout, and her large dark eyes watched his to make sure she was causing no discomfort. What a beautiful child, he thought. *Ravissante,* the French say. No wonder sailors were bewitched in these islands.

She worked with a great calm, her long fingers gently placing the petals, pushing hair from her eyes, her hair shiny, black, and wavy like the sea. Her skin was smooth, with pearls of sweat, and rising from her body was the smell of coconut oil and spices. Nello couldn't take his eyes off the muscles above her breasts. And her scent filled his head. In all those weeks at sea, in that confined closeness, he couldn't remember smelling Darina at all.

The girl finished laying the flowers, then she tore a long strip from the bottom of her *pareu* and wrapped it around his leg, tying a perfect figure-eight knot at the end.

"You're a sailor too," Nello said.

She looked up; her freckles shifted as she smiled. "A lil'bit . . ." she laughed.

From far away came the roll of drums and her smile vanished as quickly as it had come.

"Why did you come here?" she asked, turning to Darina, but stopped suddenly when she saw Darina's eyes glowing deep blue in the pale light.

"What is it?" Darina asked.

"Nothing," the girl lied, and looked away.

Darina told her about searching for her brother, his age, how he liked to draw, how he had painted pictures in Tahiti, his laughter and his blue eyes just like hers.

"Many blue-eye men come," the girl said, looking off. "Then

they go away."

She got up and dragged her board into the sea, floated it along the shore, her *pareu* swirling in the foam. When she was far away, she unwrapped her *pareu* and left it on the sand, lay on the board on her stomach, and, keeping her toes in the air so as not to tempt the sharks, she paddled with strong, long strokes out to the point, where there was nothing but rocks, long waves, and surf. She sang a soft melody that rose and fell with the heaving of the sea.

Chapter 36

Escape to the side, Guillaume heard his sergeant yelling, never ahead. He rolled just far enough off the path to have the foliage cover him. The first naked feet, those of a child, walked by near his face, followed by the flattened, toes-sticking-sideways of old women who had spent long days walking in the sand and long nights dancing wildly in the grass. Next came the feet of many young women, and he wondered if he could recognize the ones that had walked with him so many times along the shore.

The women sang a cheerful hymn, and men's gruff bellows answered from afar with the thunderous sounds of the *pahu anaana,* the great hollow rosewood-covered-with-sharkskin drum. The voices were unguarded, exuberant, and he thought, I love these people, I even love their feet. How could I have left?

The heavy feet of men moved past him now, and the smell of fresh fish from a net slung on poles between dark shoulders, followed by clumps of plantains and sheaves of banana leaves, and the sour and sweet smell of *poi poi.* Then a new sound arose, a sailor's ukulele, and pair of white man's feet passed by, covered from the ankles up with tattoos. They stopped a moment, then went on. That must be him, Guillaume thought. I could kill him now. I *should* kill him now. The drums beat beside his head and the ground shook under him. But what about her? What if I lose her. Lose her for good.

When there were no more feet, he moved to the ledge and looked below. The procession wound down the slope, the torches on the plateau catching them as they went. With his binoculars he searched the crowd for her face.

The men unloaded the *poi poi* and the fish and banana leaves near a pit. The old man in the white gown came with a long-bladed knife, sliced a big fish open and held it up to the crowd, then dropped it into the pit.

Drums thudded.

The crowd encircled the *meae*, women toward the land, men toward the sea. A fleshy young girl, wound in tapa cloth, now climbed the *meae*, where two stone tikis threw shadows at her feet. She danced on her toes, slow and sensuous, and her hips rolled and she swayed. As she raised a bird-of-paradise above her head, she seemed to float.

Guillaume stuffed his white shirt it his bag, and rubbed handfuls of mud onto his face and chest. Crouching low, he began his descent.

The girl danced with more fervor, rolling her hips, thrusting her pelvis, and swung her torso wildly, her long hair making circles in the torchlight. Three men in long leaf skirts leapt up beside her. The biggest one grabbed the edge of the tapa cloth. She spun. Reams of the tapa cloth floated to the stone until she spun naked, her oiled and sweaty flesh glittering in the torchlight.

She danced leaning back with knees bent and parted toward one man, but, as they touched, she danced away. The biggest of the three men moved in and grabbed her thighs. He slid them up his own. She wrapped her legs around him and threw back her head and arms.

"Mon Dieu," Guillaume said softly, staring through the binoculars, because, near a corner of the *meae*, he found the face he longed for: the dark eyes glowing with excitement, the smiling mouth warm and wide, the graceful long chin and the thick black hair with a wreath of gardenias askew on the brows.

The man lowered the fleshy girl onto a hollowed stone lined with banana leaves. She writhed slowly. The big man danced over her, then with great care and gentleness he eased himself into her. The girl's hips pulled back and the man let her. Then he entered her again, gently but deeper. The drums grew softer; women sang. Some cried. Guillaume ran.

He was halfway down the slope, with his eye on the gardenias. The crowd swayed. When the first man rose from the girl, the youngest of the men went and wiped her brow. Then he held her in his arms.

GUILLAUME BACKED INTO A THICKET at the edge of the plateau; the dark pit near him stank of fresh decay, but the wreath of gardenias was less than fifty steps away. After all these years.

Across the plateau, beside the giant drums, the tattooed man's ukulele fell out of rhythm. Seeing the tall white figure in the thicket, his face turned solemn under the tattoos. He strummed distractedly. Then he began to move.

THE OLD MAN IN THE LONG WHITE ROBE put on a priest's parrot-feather crown, and, with his long knife pointing down, stepped from the altar and came through the thicket toward the pit. Guillaume withdrew into the woods. The drums grew louder, faster. The second man lowered himself onto the girl. She gripped his waist.

Guillaume watched the priest kneel over the pit, reach down, and pull out a small, screeching black pig. He held it by its hind legs; it wriggled in the air. He pushed the pig down onto its stomach, held back its head, and, holding its snout, thrust the long blade through its throat.

But the pig wouldn't die. It flung its head from side to side, the blade whirling wildly in the light. The old priest held it down as best he could, but the pig thrashed with all its might and the long blade swung and struck the priest below his heart. He gave a cry. Then, still holding the pig, he fell back against the stone.

Guillaume forgot the crowd and the gardenias, forgot every restraint he'd learned as a spy, and ran to the old man and knelt down by his side. The pig still fought. Guillaume pulled out the knife and with a ferocious blow pinned the pig to the ground.

The old man's breathing was ragged; he looked up at Guillaume. "Strong pig," he said in French, and pushed out a weak smile. Guillaume didn't respond. He opened the old man's robe and saw the blood flow with each beat of the heart. He placed his palm gently over it. "Poor pig," the old man said. "He deserved stronger hands."

"You are strong," Guillaume said.

"Who are you?" the old man asked.

"A fool," Guillaume said.

"I know you, yes?"

"Peut-être," Guillaume said. "Years ago. When I was young."

"Mon Dieu!" the old man answered. "You are the one that Joya loved."

"Joya was love-struck," Guillaume said.

"Who isn't?" the old man said. "Why did you come back?"

"For Joya."

The old man smiled. "Good," he said.

The drumming and the singing softened.

"How is she?" the old man asked.

"Who?"

"La vierge."

The girl was sitting up on the *meae,* with one arm around the boy who had come before to wipe her brow. Her hair had stuck in tangles to her face, but through it Guillaume could see an exhausted smile. The boy was shy. She wrapped him with her body as best she could and she moved for him as much as she could. The boy buried his face into her shoulder.

"She's fine," Guillaume said.

"A silly custom." The old man sighed and winced with pain. Then whispered, "I'm so tired."

"We're all tired."

The old man smiled. "The song is nice."

Guillaume watched his eyes turn unseeing in the moonlight. They stared past him at the darkness flickering with stars.

The tattooed man backed off the *meae.* He circled the crowd, strumming his ukulele but never taking his eyes off the bushes where he had seen the white man disappear. Why would a white man come up here? he thought. Who would dare follow, after the shark? Who'd take such a risk? To do what? To whom?

Guillaume saw a shadow coming through the woods. He lowered the old man's head gently to the ground and wiped the caking blood on his hands in the grass. Bent low, behind the rocks, he headed toward the altar, where the crown of gardenias swayed. He headed toward Joya.

The tattooed man followed.

Chapter 37

The stench of the room awoke Dugger with a start. The dead air hung suffocating, dark. He went out. The Finn sat on the bench against the bluff, the rifle on the table before him pointed over the dead shark near the gate. He was picking bits of meat off a plate and chewing them, less out of hunger than boredom. *"E aha te hakatu?"* he said. "That's Kanaka for 'How are you?'"

"Never better," Dugger said, and wondered how far he'd have to go to get away from the stench. "Anybody back?" he asked hopelessly.

"Not a soul."

Dugger looked at the bluff above and the shark, which had collapsed as if deflated. "Look. We're trapped like rats in this courtyard," he said, only loud enough for the Finn to hear. "One man can pick off the lot of us from up there."

"I told you the rock curves," the Finn said with a sigh. "They can't shoot into the yard."

"They shot the rope."

"That was up high."

"The kid could have shot us from the tree."

"He's just their climber. He's much too small to carry a rifle, never mind fire it."

"So you're just going to sit here?"

"You have a better idea?"

"I'm taking her back to the ketch at first light."

"And your friends?"

My friends? Dugger thought. They can go to hell. One's more crazy than the other; just crazy about different things. "They know where the ketch is."

"And if they need help?"

"What help?"

"Help, help. If the Kanakas capture them." He chewed on a dry hard-cooked piece. "You ever eat dog before?"

"Why would they capture them?"

"I already told you. They want us gone." He tore a piece of meat from a leg bone with his teeth. "Dog is very good as long as you cook it the native way in the *uma*. Otherwise you can't chew it and it stinks." He got up and took his rifle. "Look. If you want to stay awake, I'll go home and get some sleep." And he headed for the gate.

"Can't you sleep here?"

The Finn laughed. "And be trapped like a rat?" He shouldered his rifle and headed out into the night.

THE DRUMS BOOMED AND THE CROWD DANCED, SWIRLING. The wind swept across the plateau, whipping the torch flames. At a hollowed stone people stopped and with half shells of coconut scooped *kawa* and drank, with the *kawa* running down through the sweat on their bare chests.

A woman, naked but for some *pandanus* leaves between her legs, picked up a flaming torch. The dancers pulled back to give her room. She swayed, undulating, rising and falling. She leaned back; the torch lit her thighs.

Guillaume crouched low on the edge of the clearing, then

turned toward the altar. The drums thudded so loud Guillaume felt the thudding vibrate in his bones. The stench of rotting flesh from the dark pit made him gag. He stayed low and went on to get upwind of the pit.

Five men closed in on the woman with the torch. She leaned back, bent her legs, and offered herself.

Guillaume turned the corner of the altar. Joya's head bobbed in the crowd just steps away. He wanted just to grab her and vanish with her in the night, off this damned plateau, off this island, sail south, in anything—a skiff, a pirogue, a raft—to some small *motu* where the lagoon was smooth and the breakers thundered far away. He pushed on. He had lost all instinct for caution and stood at full height, as nervous as a child playing hide-and-seek, trying to reach home.

Across the way, behind the tiki, the tattooed man knelt beside the old man on the ground. The old man's eyes reflected the cold moonlight. Then he raised his hand to the old man's eyes and closed them. Still on one knee, he lifted the old man in his arms. He was surprised at how little the old man weighed. Holding him in one arm, he picked up the dead pig, leaving the long knife embedded in its neck.

Guillaume waded into the crowd of swaying bodies, into the scent of scorched leaves, smoke, and *kawa*. Dancers leaned against him smelling of coconut oil and fish; all he wanted was a whiff of gardenias.

The five men engulfed the woman and their limbs entwined. Her cries of delight cut through the thud of drums.

Guillaume stopped. Just beyond his reach, but so close he could smell them, the crown of gardenias glowed. With her head down, she was dancing slower than the others. He pushed aside a sweating back, and reached out and said, "Joya."

The tattooed man hauled the dead pig and the old man through the bush. He had come to the stream and brushed against great ferns. He picked his way over the wet stones of the stream and marveled at everything so gigantic in the moonlight, and wondered why he never noticed their enormity all these years. And then he wondered if, by magic, he had suddenly grown small.

He passed a man lying facedown in the stream, drinking and smelling of *kawa*. Beyond the stream he turned toward the torches and the crowd.

Joya stopped dancing and turned slowly. She looked confused staring into the mudded face, searching for a hint of who stood there. Her eyes and gardenias glowed white in the torchlight. She was smaller than Guillaume remembered her to be, her brow higher, but below the thick eyebrows shone those dark, mesmerizing pupils, enormous and shining like black pearls. Behind her right ear was a wilting hibiscus. She stared, trying to understand this mudded apparition. After a while she asked with all her heart, *"Meitai tupapau?"* Are you a ghost?

Guillaume tried to wipe the mud from around his eyes. A smile broke in the corners of her mouth. "You're too dirty to be a ghost," she said. Then she reached out and touched his face. Her fingers made a slow, curved line from his cheek down to his lips. Her face relaxed, her mouth softened, her eyes became inviting.

Neither of them noticed the drums slowing, voices falling.

Looking at the flower behind her right ear, he uttered, "You're not taken."

Instead of a reply, she said without reprimand, "You went so far."

She ran the tip of her finger through a long crease in his face. "This is new," she said. Then he saw the dead priest.

The dancers eased their limbs and turned toward where, through the ring of torches, the tattooed man now came. From one arm trailed the bloodstained gown of the priest, from the other the black hide of the bleeding pig.

Between two torches, he stopped. Tears so filled his eyes that he looked completely blind. He seemed to wait for guidance from the crowd. The drums fell silent except for a hesitant one that went on slow, then fast, as if trying to find a rhythm it had lost. From all that silence rose a woman's voice, melodic and mournful, singing, *"Mara mara manue."* One by one, more voices followed, softly, like the endless murmur of the sea.

The tattooed man laid the priest gently on the altar, keeping the knifed pig in his other hand. He looked around for the white face in the crowd. People followed his gaze. Deep in thought, he moved toward Guillaume. The crowd opened to make way, then closed in. Guillaume stepped back. The precipice yawned behind him and, in the updraft, he could smell the sea.

Joya moved protectively before him. The tattooed man stopped, looked at one, then the other; then he raised the pig. "Why?" he said in English, and furled his tattooed brow. "Why?"

"It was an accident," Guillaume said.

With a startling movement, the tattooed man wrenched the knife out of the pig. Then held the animal by the scruff, its limp legs dangling. "Why?"

Without comprehension, the crowd took up the cry. *"Vy! Vy! Vy!"* The lone drum now beat with resolve. Other drums followed, and men made guttural cries and, shoulder to shoulder, began to stomp their feet, and moved in a mass from the torches toward the dark. The tattooed man felt the surge behind him and, with pig and knife in hand, stepped toward Guillaume.

Guillaume grabbed Joya and pushed her out of the way, then took a last step back. In the updraft from the sea, he tasted salt.

The tattooed man yelled something, but the cries and singing and the drums now drowned it out.

Guillaume spoke too, in rapid French and English, explaining, pleading but not being heard, all the while glancing around for a way out. But the crowd had spread in a wide crescent to the bluff, blocking all escape. The only way open was the precipice behind them. Joya shouted something and her face flushed and she grabbed Guillaume's hand and pulled him, running along the edge. *"A haakoi!"* she shouted. Hurry!

Guillaume stopped in confusion. *"Ua hei,"* Joya said. It's all right.

She turned toward the spur of land that stuck out like some narrow altar. Without looking back, she ran toward its end. Beyond her the sea silvered with moonlight, and her slight form stood out magnificent against it. She ran in full flight, then, with an enormous leap, she jumped, her arms outstretched, all of her dark against the glitter of the sea.

She fell.

The drums thundered wildly. Hands grabbed Guillaume. With a violent shudder that seemed to tear him to pieces, he struggled free and ran. Halfway along the spur, he looked back. No one followed. With long, loose strides he ran toward the tip, toward the moon, the stars, the immense, silvering sea.

The tattooed man lay the dead pig on the ground. He walked, head bowed, to the platform of the drums, picked up his rifle, and without hurry went to the cliff's edge. On the glittering sea, he saw two dark spots bobbing. He watched them as they touched. When they parted and headed for shore, he raised his rifle, aimed at the one without the fan of dark hair, then fired. Until the gun was empty.

Book Five

Ki'i

Chapter 38

With his eyes half open, Dugger leaned against the warm bluff. *"Aux armes, citoyens,"* he heard sung. *"Formez vos bataillons."*

And he dreamed of that spring in the Rue du Bac, after that endless war of mustard gas and mud, and the soul-breaking wheezing of the lungless dying in the night. Her voice was more beguiling than the anthem, and he watched her fervor boil as she passed by the tables of the café that spilled onto the roadway, calling all Parisians to arms, against what no one quite knew, with what results no one quite cared. He watched her hair come loose around the temples as if stirred by a storm, and she and a small following grew to many behind her, and two nights later in the mansard under the tin roof, she wrapped her legs around him, and kept growling through her moment of elation, *"les maîtres de nos destinées, les maîtres de nos destinées,"* the masters of our destinies. He couldn't for the life of him understand what she meant then, and was terrified by the words just now. He snapped awake.

Testard stumbled out of the barracks into the courtyard,

caked from head to foot with patchy blood. Carrying what was left of the depleted bottle of rum, he tripped over the shark, gave it a kick that was absorbed by its deflated, infinite softness of death, then his eyes rolled happily on to Dugger by the wall.

"Oh, Cappy," Testard chimed drunkenly. "Captain of the vile pirates, *marchons, marchons,"* he sang. *"Qu'un sang impur,/ Abreuve nos sillons!"*

He sat down on the jaw of the shark, which still held its rigidity, took a slug of his rum, and smiled. "When I left here, there was a *soirée,"* he slurred. "What did you, Cappy, do to my grand *soirée?"*

"Stay calm," Dugger cautioned. "You have fifty stitches in you. The father advised you to stay calm."

"The father?" Testard slurred. "He's Irish. They eat nothing but potatoes and on Sunday a bite of mutton. Would you allow a man fed like that to give you advice?" He took a long slug and sang, *"Contre vous tout prêts à se battre! Aux armes, citoyens."*

"Calm down or you'll bleed to death."

"'Devoured by a shark at the dinner table,' will read my tombstone, Cappy, captain of the cutthroats. What a noble way to die for an *officier de la Republique, n'est-ce pas?"*

They sat silent for a moment while a wave crashed. In the brief stillness afterward, they heard distant voices and the drums.

"They will come, Cappy. *Mon cher capitaine.* They have threatened to kill us all ever since we dangled some of them from the cliff. So they'll come, all marvelous, magnificent, muscular, and drunk. And they will shoot us down like dogs, and perhaps if we're lucky we will have the honor of being thrown into the *uma* with the yams. And they will pass bits of us around the fire, and pray to their gods to make them as strong as us. And as wise as us. And as fearless as us in battle. Or in bottle." And he raised the bottle and took another pull. "The problem with you English is that you don't drink enough. Or when you do, you drink until you crawl with your asses in the air and your muzzles on the ground. Are you English, Cappy? One of those jolly good chaps?"

Dugger grabbed the bottle and took a big slug. The rum hit him suddenly and hard.

"Marchons, marchons," Testard sang with quiet venom. *"Qu'un sang impur / Abreuve nos sillons!"*

"You ever think of those words, Testard? 'May an impure blood water our furrows?'"

"How come you know our anthem, Captain Limey? Or Savonian, or whatever you are."

"My German teacher was French," Dugger snapped. "So whose impure blood are we talking about here, Testard? Everyone who ain't pure French? You inbred Frogs. What are you doing here at the end of the world anyway? Did your mother hate you? Or your father think you not quite a man? So off you sail to Bunga-Bunga-land to show them what a tough little fellow you really are."

"Oh, Cappy. How angry you are with life."

"It's not life, Testard! It's you!"

"You're angry with *me?"*

"Oh, no. I'm practically in love with you. You arrest me, chain me, have my woman half-killed by a shark, my friends are who knows where. My skiff? Forget it. My ketch? Hell, for all I know the natives may be using it for firewood. Why on earth should I be angry with you?"

As if a wave of clarity had just washed over him, Testard sat upright and listened to the distant drums. Then his shoulders dropped and he sat as deflated as the shark. When he spoke, his voice was full of sorrow. "You know, Cappy, those poor bastards will come. Then they will die. Because the marines will come back in a day or two and surely bring the frigate with its cannon. And on it will be Admiral Thouars, who will sail into this bay with his cannon and give the Kanakas maybe an hour to abandon their village inland and move back here and be good little hostages." And he took the bottle back from Dugger, raised it in the air, said, *"Santé."* Then put it to his lips and drank until he coughed the dregs. "Admiral Dupetit Thouars," he hissed straightening up and saluting the dead shark. "The current pride of France, whose grandfather forced Queen Pomare, the queen of Tahiti, a gentle woman about to give birth, to sign her country over to the French or have his fleet raze Papeete to the ground.

"It was just eighty years ago, Cappy, when he accused the queen of insulting two missionaries. He demanded an apology, ten thousand U.S. dollars, and that the French flag be raised over Papeete with a twenty-one-gun salute or, as he so sweetly wrote, 'Lack of compliance on your part, will force this servant of France, to fire with all cannons upon your town.'"

"Charmant . . . Un vrai homme. A real man. And you know what his ship was called, dear Cappy? Thouar's ship that was going to murder and maim women and children? *Venus.* I swear. *Venus.* The goddess of love. Is there no shame left in the world, Cappy? Or a sense of sorrow left in any heart?"

He stood and staggered to the gate and opened it and let the sound of the surf roar loud into the yard. "My children," he lamented. "My poor cursed children. What can I do for you now?"

He came back and sat down on the shark. "It's a long time until dawn." He sighed. "And that's bad. But what's worse is we're out of rum. And worse still is that I'm too drunk to go and find another bottle." Then he sang softly, *"Marchons. Marchons. Mes petits cochons."* And he laughed at his joke. "You like that version better, Cappy? *Marchons marchons,* my little swine?"

He fell silent. Then he lay down exhausted on the shark and slept. The candlenuts had burned down. Their dying flames cast softer shadows than the moon.

Chapter 39

Something moved in the roof of the hut above. The Finn jumped up. He had been sleeping fitfully in his hammock, one arm dangling with the rifle in it, the other holding the opium pipe across his chest. He heard the rest of the gunshots, one close after another like a barrage or a firing squad. "Goddamn!" he growled. "Goddamn, goddamn, goddamn!"

He took a long drink of water from a bottle to clear his head, but still nothing made sense. All he felt was a violent unease, and something as bitter as bile in his mouth. He stumbled to the water's edge, checking the rim of dark mountains against the sky, but the sky showed no sign of early light. When he reached the barracks gate, he threw it open, and only in the last second did he think to yell out, "Don't shoot! It's me!" Dugger took his finger off the trigger of his gun.

"Jesus, Finn," Dugger snapped.

"Get your woman," the Finn replied. "Can she walk? She'll have to. Go along the shore and find a pirogue. Get it down to the water and wait for us."

Dugger listened, barely comprehending. "What about the dark?" he quizzed.

"To hell with the dark!"

"Why are you so upset?"

"I'm not upset. They are." And he nodded toward the canyon while he strode across the yard. "You hear the shots?"

"Sure."

"They have almost no bullets. Last week they made some out of old type from a printing press. Believe me, they don't waste them. Something's up."

Dugger followed him into the barracks. The stench was even heavier than before.

Only one candlenut smoldered, and its smoke filled the air. The Finn kicked the chair under the priest. "Wake up, Padre," he said. "It's time to pray."

"An hour ago you were ready to die," Dugger said.

"I still am; but not today. Come on, Padre," and he dumped a pitcher of water on Father Murphy's head. Then he leaned down to him. "Listen. Can we carry Testard, or will he fall apart?"

"What are you talking about?" Father Murphy slurred.

"We have to carry Testard. Will that kill him? Will he open up and bleed himself to death?"

"Carry him where? What's going on? It's still dark."

"Padre. There was a volley of gunfire up the canyon. Maybe a dozen shots. Fast. Like an execution. They've stopped singing. They've stopped the drums. So they either fell asleep or something serious is up. Yes or no?"

"Yes or no what?"

"Testard."

"I don't know. I sewed him as best—"

"I'm sure you did. But I don't want to move him if it'll kill him."

"Move him where?"

"The ketch." But he didn't even bother to await an answer; he just started to take apart one of the beds. It had a good plank maybe two feet wide, and he yanked it up—no nails—and threw it on the floor so loud Kate stirred awake.

"Can you walk?" Dugger asked her.

"Of course I can," she snapped, and got up, but instantly sat back down again.

"What hurts?"

She winced. "What doesn't?" Then she straightened up and said, "Of course I can walk."

"Let's put this plank under him," the Finn directed. "Give me a hand, Captain."

Dugger laid the plank on the ground beside Testard, then, lifting him from the shark, slipped the plank under him.

"You'd better tie him," Father Murphy said.

"Sure. Get a rope," the Finn said, struggling with Testard's deadweight.

"Marchons, petits cochons," Testard softly sang.

The Finn had found a new bottle of rum, uncorked it, and poured some into Testard so fast that half of it ran down his face. *"Marchons."* Testard gurgled and coughed.

They ran a rope under the board and tied him to it, crossing his legs and arms. They walked the makeshift stretcher across the courtyard, the Finn ahead, Dugger behind. Kate stepped fearfully past the shark and leaned on Father Murphy.

"Goddammit," the Finn hissed as they went out through the gate. "Put him down." And he put his end of the board down so hard that Testard's head bounced. He ran back across the yard and inside, and threw the smoldering candlenut on the ground and snuffed it with his boot. Then he came back through the darkness. "We don't want them to know we're gone. Let them lay siege to an empty place." He shut the gate from inside, bolted it, then he scrambled up over the wall. "You got a French flag aboard?" he asked.

"You want to bury him at sea?"

"We need a French flag so the frigate won't fire on us."

"I don't have one," Dugger said.

The Finn climbed back the way he had come, lowered the flag from the hacked palm, and tied it around his waist.

The moon, nearly touching the horizon, hung pale over the sea. They picked up Testard, who started singing, but the Finn shook the board so hard Testard's head rattled. "Shut the hell up or I'll drop you for good." They shuffled silently along the shore, sinking into the sand softened by the waves. Crossing a shallow creek, the Finn made for the palms, and when they reached dry sand he put his burden down. "Come on," he said, and vanished in the scrub. Dugger followed. He could barely make out the Finn in the dreary light, pulling fronds of palms apart, moving on to a pirogue. "Here," he said finally. "It's heavy as hell but stable." He grabbed the bow and Dugger the stern. They struggled in the sand. The pirogue budged.

"I didn't know you were such a charitable Christian," Dugger panted.

"You think I'm doing this to save his life? Hell! I hope he dies. But not yet." Out of breath, they stopped and rested. "The marines left here to get help a week ago. With good winds they can sail there in four days. Once they find the frigate, they can make it back in one. So they might be back by morning. With the cannon. And an admiral who loves to hear it roar. Last year he leveled a village for stealing his laundry. He might just blow your ketch apart, then ask you who you are. Having Testard aboard might stop him firing on you. Although I wouldn't bet on it." He grabbed the bow and leaned into it again. "Hey, Padre!" he hissed, "Come give us a hand."

With Father Murphy lifting the outrigger, they dragged the pirogue into the water and waited for the wave that would float it.

"Hold her," the Finn said to Father Murphy, and went to get Testard. They slung the board across the hull, and Dugger went back to help Kate. He lifted her into the stern and told her to stay low. They pushed out. "Get in, Padre," Dugger ordered, and pushed the priest headfirst over the side. They were up to their waists, then their chests, in the sea; after a last push, they pulled themselves aboard. They had started paddling when Father Murphy, without a word, stood up and jumped overboard. He caught a wave and with a few strokes made the shore.

"My flock," he shouted back. "I can't leave my flock."

"Keep paddling!" the Finn shouted. "He's crazy. Let him die."

The moon touched the sea, dissolving in the mist. The ketch with its raked masts lay resolute against it.

Chapter 40

A pearly dawn light filled the sea and sky. Darina swam out through the surf into the smooth sea, the freshness of the water and the effort of swimming distracting her from thoughts of her brother. Past the southern point of the bay an islet jutted, sloping to a flat rock over which rolled the sea. She swam, wishing she had taken off her clothes—she had wanted to after she'd seen the naked girl—but the voice of Mother Superior rang in her ear about indecency, immodesty, and another word that began with an 'i', which she now forgot. She scrambled barefoot up onto the rock, peeled off her clothes, wrung them, and hung them on a shrub to dry. She sat on the rock and pulled up her knees so she'd feel less naked.

The girl rode her board and sang softly to herself to keep rhythm, and her hips swayed and her limbs hung loose, and her knees stayed soft and felt the motion of the sea. Just sing and feel the sea, her uncle Nataro had taught her. Your body is a feather, all your weight is in your feet. And he taught her to shift her weight with joy just as when she danced. Or made love, he'd said. She snickered when he said that, but he didn't. It's all the same, he said, you do one thing well and everything else follows.

But now her lips kept forgetting the song, and her knees were set hard, because she kept seeing that injured man with one eye squinting, and the woman with eyes enormous and blue. She wished they hadn't come. This was her place. Just her and the rocks and the sea, and the long-tailed *tevake* and *toake,* and sometimes *faufee* and even *mokohe* that would come and watch her in fascination, and sometimes fly very close beside her, along with her, and listen to her sing. She could sing with them, but not with these people with the strange eyes. Especially the woman with eyes like lagoons. Just like the eyes of that man who once loved her, who had wanted her forever. For his wife.

The girl paddled her board toward Darina, glancing over her shoulder, keeping an eye on the shark feeding near the point, the black tip of its fin dark against the glitter. *What are you doing on the surface, shark?* she said silently. *You're a reef shark who should be feeding on the bottom.* Then she thought, What a strange woman. She's in the wrong place, like the shark. And how strange she looks, with her body all white but her face brown; as if someone had given her the wrong head.

Just below Darina, the girl slowed.

"Could you teach me how to do that?" Darina asked.

"Sure," the girl said, sitting up, looking at the shark.

After a while Darina said, "Do you live here alone?"

"Sometimes. Sometimes I go up to the village and find a man," the girl said with no emotion. "Is that yours?" She nodded toward Nello under the palms.

"No," Darina said. "He's nobody's man."

"And your brother? Is he somebody's?"

"Yes," Darina said, and felt her body tense. "I don't know. In his last letter he said he was in love."

"L'amour," the girl said, shrugging her shoulders. Then she laughed.

"He said he was madly in love. *Fou* in French; no?"

All the *étrangers* go crazy for love, the girl thought. Worse than drinking *kawa*. Especially for the love of that stupid *demi,* with her half-white skin, her straight nose, and her small pink lips. And the small pink between her legs. Not fleshy and dark like ours. She must have rubbed herself with coconut milk all her life. Just to drive men crazy. So crazy they will do anything to please her—even scary things, even kill others. One even stood the pain for weeks of having himself tattooed from head to foot like warriors of old times. Sad. All that for the small pink of that damned *demi.* Then she thought, I'm a *demi* too. So why are they all so crazy for her? And for me only a lil'bit?

"Then what happened?" the girl asked.

"Then? He stopped writing," Darina replied.

"Did he say what she was like? This woman he loved so *fou?"*

"Oh yes. He said she was the most beautiful woman he'd seen in his life."

The girl looked down at her reflection in the sea. "They all say that," she mused.

"They must say it to you."

She laughed. She had forgotten to paddle and the current had pushed her landward, so she lay on her stomach now and, with both hands, paddled hard. Darina watched. From far away, came the sound of her brother's laughter. Startled, she looked around. There was no one in sight. "Did you hear that?" she asked.

"Pardon?" the girl said.

"That laughter."

The girl listened. "It's only water," she said. "Under the rock. There is a big hole."

Distracted, Darina stood bolt upright, forgetting her nakedness, and searched the bluff.

"It's only the water," the girl insisted.

"How much farther is the village?" Darina asked, pulling on

her pants, stumbling on one foot.

"Not far," the girl said, surprised.

"Can I find it?"

"There's only one path. The one you came on."

"Look after him," Darina said, pulling her shirt over her head, nodding toward Nello. "He's a good man. " She picked her way over the rock, waded across the shallow pass, and disappeared in the shadows of the scrub.

Une femme bizarre, the girl thought. She sat up and, still sitting, caught a small wave, and laughing at the thrill, crossed her legs and rode the wave until it burst on the sand and set her on the shore.

Nello watched her drag her board up the sand. She walked unhurriedly past him to retrieve her *pareu,* and on her way back stopped before him unabashed, unteasing, for a semblance of modesty letting the *pareu* dangle between her thighs. "I will bring you something," she said, and walked to the pond, waded in, and, standing in water up to her thighs, washed the salt from her hair and skin.

She disappeared for a while and returned with her *pareu* tied around her hips, carrying mangoes, and on a banana leaf some raw fish chopped fine with bits of lime. She laid it before him and went and got a coconut with its end chopped off, to drink.

Nello thanked her. While he ate, she went and gathered more hibiscus flowers, stuck one behind her right ear, and gently pressed the rest. When he finished eating, she came and knelt beside him. She pushed up his pants leg, untied the piece of cloth, took the old hibiscus petals from the wound, and put on new ones. Nello watched her, her hair falling forward, her dark eyebrows that almost touched, her soft mouth that moved slightly as she worked. "Thank you," he said.

She didn't answer, just worked the petals gently on his thigh.

Embarrassed by his stirring, he squeezed his legs together, but it didn't help. She saw it and sat up, her wide shoulders slacked, and she smiled an open smile. Then she took half a mango and ate the yellow pulp, some of the juice running down her chin, dripping onto her breasts and her stomach. She wiped her mouth with the back of her hand.

"Your friend go away," she said.

"I saw. She does that."

"You not go after her?"

"Not anymore."

"She's beautiful."

"So are you."

Her lips smiled, but her eyes stayed serious.

"Are you still hungry?"

"No."

"Thirsty?"

"No."

She stood up and brushed the sand from her knees. "Can you walk?" And she held out her hand to help him up.

Cascades of bougainvillea tumbled from the roof of her hut, and hibiscus crowded around the stilts, and gardenias bloomed velvet-white against the rock. Once inside, she reached a hand back to help Nello up. His legs ached as he climbed, he winced, and when she saw it, her face reflected his pain. Then she drew back to let him in.

It was a tiny place full of shadows, and a mat of long banana leaves piled low against the back wall. She moved aside in the small space to give him way.

"Sleep," she whispered, in that loving voice mothers use with sleepy children.

He lay down on his side to keep the pressure off his hurt leg. She sat in the doorway with her feet dangling out. The sky grew dark. A black cloud slithered down between the crags. With his eyes half closed, he watched her naked back shimmering in the light. She reached back with both hands to the muscles above her shoulders and massaged with her fingers just above the bone.

"They hurt?" Nello asked.

"Sleep," the girl replied, then, sensing him still watching, turned. "I paddle too much."

With the darkening sky, the day turned into twilight.

Nello got up. "Here," he said, and got down on his good knee behind her and gently pushed her hands away. She let him. First with his thumbs, then with all his fingers, he began kneading softly the muscles of her shoulders. At first her muscles stayed hard. He slid his hands lower to the round muscles of her arms. And pressed. He rolled his fingers as on the keys of a piano, but firmly, slow and deep into her flesh. Her flesh grew soft. He went back to massaging the stiff muscles near her neck. He pressed and rolled and kneaded a long time. Her head drooped. Her breathing deepened.

"So nice," she said.

"Shhh," Nello said. "Sleep."

She took a deep long breath, as if drifting in a dream. He sat down behind her with his legs on either side of her. "So nice," she whispered.

His fingers reached past her collarbone to just above her breasts. There were muscles there, firm and vertical. "I didn't know these existed," he said.

She gave a small laugh no louder than a sigh. Her head sank low and gently to one side.

The sky grew black. The sea as black below it. The first big raindrops rattled on the fronds. Then the rain came. It poured. Deep curtains of rain covered up the sea. The warm rain fell, caressing her shoulders, and ran in long rivulets down her ribs and thighs. She sighed deeply. Then she reached up with both hands onto his and pulled them, through the rivulets, down onto her breasts. He felt them, firm and warm, and she pressed his fingers and moved them around against them. She leaned her head against his. Her wavy hair smelled of mint and *tiare* and sandalwood. He touched his face against it, kissed her neck, kissed her hair.

She reached back to touch his head, and his mouth found her fingers. He kissed them with a tenderness he had never felt before.

The rain thundered on the roof. She pulled one of his hands against the softness of her mouth, and ran her lips, caressing, over his rough fingers. He bit her neck. She turned, and in the stubble of his craggy face, her lips found his mouth. The rain ran over them.

She pushed him gently onto his back. "Don't move," she whispered, and helped with his wounded leg. She unbuckled his belt. "Sleep." He felt her hands around him. Then she squatted over him and slowly lowered herself. Her eyes closed. Her head fell forward, her thick hair tumbling down.

As if kneeling on her board, paddling out to sea, she rose and fell and moaned softly a long time. Her lips parted slightly, the rain dripped from her hair, the fragrance of flowers and spices now melded by the rain. He took her head in both hands and pulled her mouth to his. Her smell, like an opiate, tumbled over him. He held her. And hoped the rain would never stop.

Chapter 41

The pirogue bumped the ketch riding over a swell. "Shouldn't we bring him aboard?" Kate said, looking down at Testard lying in the pirogue, drunk and lost in another world.

"I'd leave him," the Finn suggested. "Cooler in the shade of the hull."

Lashed to the board, Testard stirred. Then he rattled on to no one in particular, "The king of France has sent me to enforce immediate reparation due to a great nation, which was gravely insulted when our two apostolic missionaries were ridiculed . . ."

"Jesus." The Finn grunted. "If I have to hear this again, I'll drown the son of a whore."

"What's he saying?"

"The letter from the French admiral to the queen of Tahiti."

Testard rambled on. No one listened. Dugger motioned to the Finn to follow him to the foredeck. He spoke softly with his back to Kate.

"Can you sail?"

"Sure," the Finn said.

". . . will force this servant of France to fire with all cannons," Testard grumbled.

"Could you handle this boat with just her? She's quite apt."

"You going on vacation?"

"I'm going to find the mate."

"And the blondie?"

"To hell with the blondie. Can you handle the boat?"

"The boat? Sure. But why the worry about your mate?"

"We're friends," Dugger said.

Testard cried out. Next to the pirogue, rubbing its gray back against the wood, cruised a small reef shark.

"Mother of God," the Finn growled. "He must be bleeding."

He scrambled down and kicked the shark hard in the back. It turned up an evil eye but swam quickly to the depths.

"We better haul him aboard," Dugger said.

"Tirez!" Testard yelled. "All cannons at once. Reduce the place to dust! *Tirez!"*

"Where do you think they ended up?" Dugger asked as they pushed Testard aboard the ketch. His stitches were holding, but blood seeped everywhere, rivulets trickling down his legs and arms.

The Finn looked up at Dugger and slightly shook his head. "There's only one path out of here, and that's the canyon. It leads to a village. The rest of the island is deserted, except for a hut or two.

A rustling came from behind them in the cockpit. Kate was leaning down, feeling Testard's pulse. When she looked up, her eyes were full of tears. "He's dying," she whispered.

"We're all dying," the Finn murmured.

"He's dying *now,"* Kate blurted.

"Some people have all the luck," the Finn said.

Dugger came, knelt beside her, and took her hand. It felt hot even here in the shade. A shudder of fear shot through him. "You're looking better," he lied. She smiled. He kissed her on the forehead to check her fever. "The sun has turned your hair blond," he said.

She laughed. "You're terrible at small talk," she said. "Your face looks in pain when you try."

Dugger went sullen, couldn't look her in the eye so he looked at her forehead. "I'm going to find Nello," he said. "The Finn's here. Seems a good man. Will you be all right?"

She held his hand tight. "I'll be fine," she said, then added, "Where's Darina?"

"Nello went to find her."

"And the father?"

Dugger looked toward shore, where the black frock of the priest stood like a statue in the sand. "He went to find his flock."

"There's a lot of 'finding' going on." She smiled.

"There are a lot of people lost," the Finn said.

Dugger kissed her forehead. "I'll be back soon."

"Or we'll have to come and find *you,"* the Finn said.

Dugger climbed down into the pirogue, sat astride a hull, and took the paddle.

"I'll drop you off," the Finn said, and climbed down beside him. "You never know, we might need it here."

With the sea running across their bow, they paddled awkwardly toward the bluff, where goats grazed high above.

At the rocks, Dugger leapt ashore and pushed the pirogue hard back out to sea. The Finn paddled away with long firm strokes. He turned his head and called, "Captain!" Dugger stopped.

"Don't be long," The Finn said.

The sun had made good progress in the sky. It shone straight down and the sea was a deep blue.

"If I'm not back by dark . . ." Dugger called.

But the Finn wasn't listening. He had turned the pirogue and was heading toward the ketch.

Dugger hurried along the sand toward the priest, who was standing bareheaded in the sun. Son of bitch, Dugger thought. Another idiot. Was I put on this earth to be a nanny to idiots? Thank God for Kate. The only sane person within a thousand miles.

He charged up behind the priest, grabbed his shoulder, and spun him around. "You have three choices," he blurted. "The French can bomb you, or the Kanakas can eat you; or you can get the hell onto the ketch." And he pushed the priest with so much force that he stumbled onto one knee in the sea. The priest rose, his cassock soaked, stood there like a wet crow.

"Thank you for your generous offer," he said, and tried to wring the water from his sleeves.

"I'm not making it again," Dugger snapped.

The priest looked longingly toward the village. "Heavenly Father," he mumbled.

"To hell with heaven," Dugger growled, and turned and marched along the beach to the barracks. He kicked in the courtyard door. The shark was still there, reinflated with heat and rot, but much of it had been butchered off: the jaw, the fins, the eyes, and great slabs of the jowls. A puddle of blood stretched across the courtyard. The air stank. Calm down, Dugger, he told himself, or you'll wear yourself out. He went into the barracks and took two rifles and his pistol, stuffed his pockets with ammunition, grabbed a machete from a nail on the wall, and marched across the courtyard through the blood. The priest stood where he'd left him. Near him were the two Chinamen, their arms loaded with pieces of the shark. Dugger marched to the path in the steamy shadows of the canyon.

Father Murphy crossed his hands and hung his head. "Heavenly Father," he whispered again, "have mercy on our souls. Do not lead us into darkness. Do not lead us to a place of no return. Dear Lord," he said, and looked up at the sky. "Please make it rain hard, to keep away the frigate. And guard my poor flock. For thine is the kingdom and the power and the glory." He went to the open courtyard. "And mine is the dead shark, and the leftover cold dog."

Chapter 42

When Guillaume broke through the surface, there were gardenias on the sea. The bullets hissed softly in the water around him. Joya floated nearby, her eyes filled with terror and glee. With firm strokes she swam into his arms.

She smiled. "I haven't done that since I was little."

They huddled under the overhanging rock with the sea at their feet, cold in the shadowed grotto. They had been lying silently in each other's arms watching the sunrise. There is so much to say, Guillaume thought, maybe it's best to say nothing, in case you say too little and leave out the best. Or say too much and have the best lost in the muddle. In her arms he felt at home. As if he'd never left.

"I'm thirsty," Joya said. She broke out of Guillaume's embrace and walked deeper into the gloom, where water streaked the dark slabs of stone. She cupped her hands, moving them back and forth until she felt a trickle. "Come. Drink," she said.

Guillaume came slowly limping, every joint stiff and aching, legs and chest blue from slamming into the sea.

They filled their hands and drank.

"Was he dead? The Atua," Joya finally asked.

Guillaume shuddered. He was surprised at the question because it was about someone other than them. He had forgotten that there were others. Not only on the island, but in the whole world. "It was an accident," he said distantly, with as much effort as if he were pushing uphill a block of stone. "He was killing the pig. It fought. The knife . . ."

"They will want revenge. That is our way."

"I'd forgotten," Guillaume said, and felt a sudden distance between her and his life.

"On anyone white," Joya said.

"Yes. I remember now."

"Especially with Ki'i leading them."

"The man with the tattoos?" Guillaume asked.

"Yes."

"Who is he?"

"A man who fell in love."

"With becoming king of Fatu Hiva?"

"No. A *demi.*"

She offered her hands full of water to Guillaume. He drank, and when he was done, he kissed her wrist. She pulled them away gently and filled her hands again. "This Ki'i," Guillaume said pensively. "What color are his eyes?"

"Blue," Joya said. "Big and dark and blue." And added in the same breath, "You have to leave the island. They know you're alive. Kids jump here all the time."

"I'm certainly no kid. It almost killed me."

"Ki'i will hunt you. He hates the French. He wants war."

"The frigate is coming with the cannon."

"And the French will kill us all."

"I know," Guillaume said. "That is why I'm here."

"To kill us?"

"No. Just the one who wants the war."

"Sometimes I want war."

"Sometimes so do I."

She drank, tipping her hands, pouring the cool water down her throat. Then she said, wiping her mouth, "Sometimes I forget that you are a French soldier."

"I'm worse now." Guillaume sighed. "Now I'm a secret agent."

"What is a secret agent?" Joya asked.

"He's a man who . . ." But his voice trailed off as he picked up a stone and threw it into the sea. The rings spread quickly, then vanished. "He's a man who no one knows."

Joya smiled sadly. "I'm a man who no one knows."

Guillaume reached out and touched the gentle face. "I know you," he said. It struck him then, that he had seldom thought of Joya as a man. To him, she had always just been Joya, the one he loved. As delicate and graceful as any island woman, but more gentle and more kind. He loved her for that. He loved him for that.

This heat can kill you, Darina thought. She had left the path to find the running water she heard deep in the shadows, but the sound now seemed far off and she stopped, confused. She had climbed hard, hurrying, pushing herself up the rocks, sure-footed on the rough ground, pouring sweat so her shirt stuck to her skin and her short hair hung drenched. The sun kept climbing. Birds stopped singing. Nothing moved. But her.

She went on, her heart pounding in her head. She pushed through the stifling undergrowth toward the faint sound and thought, Maybe it's just a mirage of the ears. Come on, Darina, she chided herself, don't lose your mind now. There is no mirage of ears. Your brother's laughter was no mirage. Neither is the sound of running water.

The thick growth scratched her face and arms and tore her shirt, but the sound of water grew louder, and a breath of cool air came through the vines. Then, through the dark green growth, she saw water cascade into a pool among boulders. She pushed through and waded in, peeling off her shirt and pushing it under to rinse out the sweat. She pulled it out and held it above her head so the water ran over her hot skin in rivulets.

Joya came back from the deep shadows of the grotto with her cupped hands full of water and held them out to Guillaume.

"It's hot," she said. "You have to drink."

"Yes," he said distractedly. "This Ki'i, how did he get to be . . . ?"

"I'm not sure," Joya said. "He was the man of Lil'bit. She's called that because that's what she answers no matter what you ask her. She lives in a cove because she likes the waves.

"One day the *Aranui* sailed in with supplies. You remember the *Aranui?* Old steamer of Mr. Chan. He can take you to Tahiti or the Tuamotus. You'll be safe there."

"And you?" Guillaume asked, looking away, not wanting to see her face when she replied.

She stepped to the water's edge and delicately fished out the remnants of her crown of gardenias from the swell. "One day the *Aranui* brought this *demi.* A bit Kanaka, bit Chinese, bit something else, who knows . . . from Tahiti. She looked down on us. Savages, she called us. Eaters of men. She had golden skin and hair the color of white sand; nice and straight, not like our hair of wild horses. My father took her as his daughter. Then she was princess of Hiva Oa."

"Ki'i fell in love with this *demi,* but he wasn't Ki'i then. He was just pale and white, with those big blue eyes. He fell in love and he couldn't sleep, couldn't eat. Finally, one night, the *demi* let him in her bed. For just one night. She wanted to try him out. She promised to marry him, but she wouldn't give him her bed again until then. She said to Ki'i, 'I am the princess of Hiva Oa. I cannot marry a man without tattoos. Real tattoos that show what wars he has fought, pictures of battles he has won.'

"So Ki'i went to war. Against the French. All alone. He knew how to work those sticks that go *boom.* He stole them in Tahiti where they build roads. He blew up a bridge at Papeete and a tunnel in the mountains. And some shacks. Each blowup was a story for tattoos. When he was covered, he came back to the *demi.* By then she was like this," and she drew a bloated dome around her belly. "With his child."

"At first the *demi* looked at the tattoos. She looked fascinated at each picture. But then she looked at all of him covered from head to toe—even his ears. And she laughed. She couldn't stop laughing. The next day she told him she couldn't marry a man who looked so very silly.

"Ki'i went away for a long time. He came back on the *Aranui* one moon ago to get his son. And every day he plans the war against the French."

A breeze came up and the sea shone, rippled and blinding in the sunlight.

"And his son?" Guillaume asked.

"Not born yet. Maybe born tonight. Maybe tomorrow."

"But you said it was a son."

"No. He came to get it *if* it was a son."

"And if it's a girl?"

"I don't know. Maybe he'll kill it. Sometimes we do that."

Guillaume felt a chill.

"And the *demi?"*

"She's in seclusion at the lagoon to have her child."

The sun beat down hot now. Guillaume drew back into the gentleness of the shade. This will be easy, he told himself. This should be very easy. Find the *demi* with child and you'll find the man.

"I have to go talk to him," he said. "But I'll be back for you."

Chapter 43

Dugger ran up the slope of red earth, with a rifle slung on straps over each shoulder, the butts of the rifles banging against his hips, and the sweat pouring in streams into his eyes. Some goddamn paradise, he hissed, where the natives welcome you with open arms.

His mouth was dry from thirst. He wished something would move in the bush: a goat or a wild boar or even a parakeet that he could blast with a shot. Then he'd feel better. Just to have someone feel worse than him.

He had given himself an hour to find Nello, but the hour had passed long ago. Another half hour, he said to himself, and not a minute more, because then he was turning back and getting on the ketch and hauling anchor and hoisting sail and getting the hell out of here to some island where . . . Where what? Where there was nothing, that's what. A few palms for shade and some birds for color. And maybe a turtle. He'd like to have a turtle. Calm, slow, couldn't give a damn about the bloody world. When he's fed up, he just draws his head into his shell to get some sleep. What he'd give right now for a bit of sleep. And water. He could do without sleep, but he needed water.

Kate moved slowly across the deck, holding on to rigging at every step so as not to stretch her stitches.

The Finn had found the hook and line, and sat with his legs over the rail, fishing off the stern. "You should keep moving," he suggested. "Or you'll stiffen up."

"It doesn't hurt much," she said.

"You're one tough lady, lady." the Finn smiled.

Kate glanced at the stump of his hand, then moved on. "Cappy said that if he's not back by dark, we should sail out of here. To go where?"

"Oh, he'll be back," the Finn said. "He's too mean not to be back."

"Does he seem very mean?" Kate asked.

"Mean enough to make it back."

Kate stopped and caught her breath. She had moved to where she could see and hear Testard softly raving in the shade. The color had left his features long ago. His face looked like wax, his lips open with dryness.

"He needs water," Kate said.

"He needs a lot more than water," the Finn replied.

Testard took no notice. "We French are kind and sensitive, not like the English who crush those they conquer . . ."

The Finn wrapped his fishing line on the head of a stanchion and went below. He came back with a tin cup dripping water, knelt, held up Testard's head, and poured it in his mouth. Testard drank. And raved. Then he stopped. "Finn," he whispered. "Where is the frigate? This is no frigate. It's a silly boat with sails."

"It's coming," the Finn said.

"Yes . . ." Testard whispered. He turned his head and looked down at his stitches and the blood caked hard and black along and among them. His eyes came alive with fright. "Finn," he whispered, "I don't want to die . . ."

"Who does?"

"No. No!" Testard objected. "I don't want to die on this silly ship. I want to go home."

"The frigate will take you."

"No. I mean *home,"* he said, now panicked. "There. The island. That's where I want to die." A faint smile twitched his lips. "With the stupid shark."

"Fine," the Finn said.

"Will you help me?"

"Sure."

Testard tried to rise.

"Not yet," the Finn said. "It's too early yet."

"You promise?" Testard pleaded.

"Sure," the Finn said. But to practice his skills at sailing, he tried to loop a rope around a cleat with his stump.

Chapter 44

The girl lay on her back asleep on the mat beside Nello. Her arms were spread like a child's above her head, open and unprotected, and she breathed long deep breaths of someone unconscious to the world. He got up. His leg had stiffened, but he saw no fresh blood, so he eased himself out of the hut onto the rocks, found his rifle, and began to climb. He used the rifle as a walking stick and scrambled up the slope to the path, changing his mind every few steps about what to do once he found it—whether to keep climbing or head down to the ketch.

Dugger worried him. Dugger's temper worried him, his headlong dives into mires with no way out, especially with Kate injured and him edgy and no help on the ketch.

He felt bad about Darina. He worried about her innocence that let her go into the night jungle. And he had to admit he missed her. Missed watching her small moves, her simple gestures that said so much more than words. Then he hoped maybe she had somehow come to her senses and had gone back to the ketch. But not likely. She must have gone on. Too goddamn stubborn not to have gone on. Too obsessed. Too Irish.

He scrambled ever upward, his leg aching, his lungs wheezing. He should have brought a coconut to drink. He remembered the gentleness of the girl when she gave him the coconut. That serene face. An honest, caring face. Unprotected, naked, like the rest of her. He stopped and leaned against a rock. The sun was high, the sea the deepest blue, the clouds on the horizon bursting, rising. And down below him the cove, the warm sand, the hut. And her arms. Maybe he should just go back to her arms. Maybe her arms are all you can ask of life, he thought. The barrel of the rifle was slippery in his hand. Which do you chose? And how do you decide? *Perchè la vita oggi è veramente troia?* Why is life truly a whore today?

They left the high-priest on the plateau where he died. The woman finished washing him, poured coconut oil scented with *tiare* blossoms onto her hands, then rubbed it gently into his hair. She sealed the gash in his chest with flowers held in place by wrappings of banana leaves, then wrapped him in a piece of tapa. She laid much food around him, in case the spirit got hungry, then angry in the night.

Some people had sobered. Women came and sat around the body and wailed, sometimes dreadful and deafening, sometimes soft and melodious. Men came and took turns recounting stories, mostly invented, of the old man's bravery, his kindness, his virtues, his wisdom in reading entrails, his skills at sacrifice. Some told funny stories and the women interrupted their wailing and laughed. Then wailed on.

The tattooed man walked slowly around the plateau, talking softly to one man then another, until he had around him four of the biggest and strongest of them all. The fifth one they left behind to dig the grave.

West of the plateau they descended on a serpentine path to the shore. They got into two canoes. The third vessel—a pair of canoes tied together with a platform, like a raft—they dragged behind. They paddled close to the island in the shadow of the bluffs, in the cove where the girl's hut lay, where they beat away with paddles a school of feeding sharks. They paddled into a low grotto and landed on a tongue of rock. From the shadows, they hauled out a short, knee-high schooner's cannon. It was wrapped in cloth soaked in pig's fat, and with two men at each end, and the tattooed man directing, they dragged and lifted the cannon up onto the raft. It sank down to its gunwales. Then they waited, watching a dark smudge grow on the horizon.

Guillaume climbed the rock face, often resting, all the while glancing up to see if someone was watching. The climb was long. He ended up in a thicket near the saddle and lay in the bush to get back his strength. Below him the women wailed on the plateau.

He circled the *maeve* with care, keeping in the cover of the scrub, searching for the place where he'd hidden his pack, while glancing down at the people coming and going on the plateau. He looked for the man with tattoos, but he was nowhere.

Dugger stopped to rest. His mouth was so dry his lips stuck to his teeth and he couldn't swallow. Hearing water cascading in the jungle's shadows, he pushed toward it. He found the pool's flicker between the leaves, and he knelt and drank. Then he heard thrashing somewhere in the shadows behind him. It was haphazard, as if some large animal were tangled in the vines.

The thrashing became frantic. He splashed water on his face, filled his hat, and poured water over his back and shoulders. He got up and shouldered the rifles. The water made sucking sounds in his boots. The thrashing had slowed as if the animal were tiring, and now over the burble of the water, and the sounds in his boots, he thought he heard someone gasping for air.

SHE HEARD HIM COMING, but she pushed on without looking back, trying to get away from the cliff to find the path.

Dugger kept yelling at her to stop, beat the jungle with a rifle butt to cut his way toward her, and finally got close enough to grab her. He spun her in anger. "Why the hell didn't . . ." Then he saw her face. She was scratched and bleeding on her arms and chest, holding her tangled shirt between her breasts, but her face was calm, the eyes cool, her gaze defiant, holding. She caught her breath.

"Why did you run?" he wheezed.

"To find my brother."

"Alone?" When she didn't answer, he snapped at her. "What the hell makes you think he's on this island?"

"When someone shot the rope I heard a chortle."

"A what?"

"A chortle. It's a laugh you can't stop. So you snort. It was my brother."

"No one else in the world laughs, right?"

"Not like my brother."

"So why didn't you yell out to him?"

"I don't know. I was too shocked. I don't know."

"So why are you thrashing through the jungle? Why not use the path?"

"I was thirsty," she said without any emotion. "I lost the path."

"And?"

"I'm not thirsty anymore."

Dugger felt an urge to turn and leave her there. "You're cut everywhere," he said. "Put that shirt on. The fewer germs in those cuts, the better. Go back to the sea and wash them out."

"No!" she said firmly. "I'll be fine."

"This is not Galway," he barked. "You're not strolling through some goddamn glen! This is hell, where everyone is crazy. Do you think normal people attack others with a shark?"

"Please don't give me orders. I'm not on your boat anymore."

He let go of her arm. She had always been distant, but not hard or stupid. Her eyes looked more glazed.

She glanced at his arm, where under the rolled-up sleeve trickled a stream of blood. "You're cut," she said. "You should go back and wash it out."

He grabbed her shoulders and pulled her so close he could feel her breath. She didn't even blink. "I'm not risking my boat for you," he growled. "As soon as I find Nello, I'm hoisting sail and we're gone. Do you understand? You'll be stuck on this rock alone with that crazy priest. " He pushed her away and gathered up his rifles.

"He's back there in that cove you passed. With a native girl."

Dugger stopped, amazed. "The priest?"

"Nello. He fell and hurt his leg. The girl is taking care of him."

She stared at him without emotion.

Dugger shouldered his rifles. "Look. I don't know what you're hiding, but one day you'll find out that no one gives a damn."

He took a bearing off the cliff, and as he vanished among the great leaves and specks of flickering light, he called back, "You have half an hour."

She didn't follow.

Father Murphy clasped his hands and looked worriedly out to sea, past the ketch and past the point, where the curve of the sea shone a deep blue against the sky. He thought he saw a puff of dark smoke rising, the kind of smoke a steamer leaves when running on full boilers. It might be the old freighter, the *Aranui,* he lied to himself, coming at the end of the month like clockwork. But it's not the end of the month; the moon has not yet eaten all the stars. He smiled. "Eating the stars." That's how the natives thought the moon filled up each month. They saw the young moon thin and frail with its mouth open wide, then each night they watched it get bigger and brighter as it ate the stars around it until it grew fat and round—as round as the belly of a woman full of child. And having eaten them all, it glowed bright with all their light, and there wasn't a star left near it in the sky.

He caught himself at once: It's not the *Aranui* and you know it. It comes but once a month, exactly on the same day. The *Aranui* has four more days to go. And if that's not the *Aranui* on the horizon, it can only be the frigate. But it's best not to think of that; get on with your life. "Which is exactly what?" he asked himself aloud. Then he heard the ship's bell ringing thrice, the same way he used to ring the bell when he called his flock to mass. He thought he was dreaming until he looked back at the ketch.

The Finn stood in the cockpit ringing the ship's bell, waving his arm broadly, beckoning.

Father Murphy thought he heard some words, but the only one he could make out he thought was "hard."

What is "hard"? he thought. Life is "hard." Every bloody thing in bleeding life is hard. That's no bloody news. Certainly not news enough to ring the bloody bell. But he waded into the sea up to his knees with his black cassock flowing around him in the foam, as if coming a few feet closer would help to solve the puzzle of what's "hard."

The Finn had climbed into the pirogue and with mighty strokes paddled toward him. Father Murphy wished he hadn't drunk so much the night before.

When the Finn closed in, his hoarse voice came clearly. "Testard," it was saying, "Testard." Then, "Last rites."

Father Murphy became suddenly sober, but couldn't for the life of him remember the last rites. He hadn't given one for years, the natives never let him go near their dying, and now he fumbled about in his memory for the words. "Dearly beloved," he rushed in a murmur, "we have come together in the presence of Almighty God . . ." No, that wasn't it. He waded toward the pirogue. "Maybe it's with penitent and obedient hearts, that we confess our sins . . ." No, that wasn't it either. He slipped and sank up to his neck in a wave.

The Finn steered hard to keep the pirogue headfirst through the sea. Father Murphy clambered in and they paddled back.

The stream of black smoke grew darker on the horizon.

Guillaume found his bag and slung it over a shoulder. He turned and followed the creek down through the village to a hillock of voluptuous mangoes. He saw the crumbling *meae* where Joya said he should turn down a thin path to the sea and the *demi.* He neared. I'm here to help, he kept telling himself. I'm here for the common good. He moved down the path until he saw the sea and the hut on stilts in the shallow lagoon.

You should have stayed with Joya, he thought. Just a few days until the *Aranui* comes, then if you asked her—no, if you insisted—she would have gone with you. Where? Anywhere.

There was no movement below him at the hut, but to be sure, he sat and waited. He didn't know how much time had passed when he heard a muffled cry. Startled, he jumped to his feet. The cry came again, of pain, but held in. He hurried down the slope to the shore.

At a thicket of bamboo, he stopped. A yellow flickering light shone down through the leaves. Before him was the hut. An old woman came out of the hut, a basket on her arm, and waded ashore. She walked along the forest, reaching up now and then for fruit. Guillaume circled, keeping the hut between the old woman and himself, then he waded, without a sound, into the lagoon.

In the shadow of the palms he put his face against the hut's slats. The *demi* lay on her side next to the doorway. She lay with her head resting on her arm, with only a tapa draped across her thighs, and she ran her hand over her swollen belly, lit by the sunlight tumbling through the door. There was something majestic about her—the repose, the straight nose, the perfect mouth and noble chin. Guillaume understood how she could bewitch a man. And for an instant a jealousy ran through him, one he could not recall having felt before; he felt jealous of all men who lusted after women.

He heard the old woman returning and he ducked below the floor of the hut into the darkness. Then, without a ripple, he eased himself underwater and swam along the bottom toward shore, stirring up sand with his fingers as he went.

Slinging his bag over his shoulder, he scrambled up the slope, up to an outcropping with a clear view of the hut. No one could come or go without him getting a clear shot. He pulled out his revolver, checked it, cleaned it. Drawing back into the shadows, he waited. With the warm breeze over him he must have dozed off, or surely he would have heard something before he felt, on his neck, the cool, gentle touch of the muzzle of a gun.

Chapter 45

Nello had turned uphill. He hadn't really meant to, but when he reached the path using the rifle as a crutch, the last push of the rifle made him bear right, so he turned uphill, away from the ketch, away from where everything in him said he should have gone.

He wasn't sure what he'd say to Darina when he saw her, if he ever found her, or to Dugger when he returned—if he was still there, if the ketch was still there—he just pushed on uphill, into the gloomy canyon, until he heard footsteps grind on broken rock ahead. He stepped off the path deep among the ferns, and let the great fronds of the ferns shroud thickly over him. The steps grew louder, closer, and he pumped the lever of the Winchester gently, but it made a metallic click no matter how he tried. The steps abruptly stopped.

Goddammit, Nello thought, whoever that is knows the sound of guns. He pointed the barrel at where he had last heard the steps. Then he heard the thud of rifle butts knock together. Good, he thought. As long as they're moving, they're not ready to shoot. But he felt the sweat break quickly over him. He saw slow movement through the ferns. He leaned his shoulder against a tree trunk to steady his aim, somewhere about chest-height. He was looking forward to the invigorating thunder of the gun. He slid his finger down the trigger for more leverage, when he heard grunts and sighs louder than the pounding of his heart. The rifle butts banged again, and he wondered if he could get two men with one shot, when he heard an angry grumble: "If you want to ambush someone, smoke a less putrid cigar."

"Goddammit, Cappy!" Nello hissed. "I bloody nearly shot you!"

"Well, you didn't, so quit yelling. You ever been to a Turkish Bath? This place is steamier than a Turkish bath. Darina said you were hurt."

"Is she all right?"

"Was she ever all right?"

He pushed through the last frond and stood pouring sweat, his hat crushed in his hand, his eyes rings of fatigue.

"How's Kate?"

"Kate's okay. She's better."

"One hell of a lady."

"So is Blue Eyes. She's up there. Maybe a quarter mile." He reset the rifle straps on his shoulders so the rifle butts sat snugly on his hips.

The sound of gasping breaths rose behind them on the trail. Nello aimed. Dugger ducked to give him a clear shot.

Father Murphy clutched the bible between his knees and paddled with all his might, with the Finn straining right behind him, and thought, Blessed are they that do his commandments, that they may have right to the tree of life, and may enter through the gates into the city. For without are dogs, and sorcerers and whoremongers, and murderers and idolaters, not to mention the French frigate with a great big cannon that can blow this island into kingdom come.

He pulled hard and they rammed into the ketch with a thud. He stood up quickly and crossed himself. "And the grace of our Lord be with you. Amen."

"Move, Padre," the Finn said, pushing him aboard in one quick motion. "Because the grace of your Lord won't be with *him* much longer."

Testard lay in the shade of the awning, with Kate beside him holding his hand. He mumbled in a near-whisper, ". . . We're a benevolent nation. We are men of good will . . ." Father Murphy knelt beside him, but Testard just raved on as if the priest weren't there. "To inspire the joy of hard labor. Murder and theft will disappear, and marriage will create, in the end, the true and only—" He coughed with convulsion but without strength.

"For God's sake, man," the Finn hissed at the priest, "say what you have to say and let him die in peace."

Father Murphy trembled with uncontrollable fear. "I can't remember," he mumbled. "I can't remember the last rites . . . It's been so long . . ."

"You damned old drunk," the Finn growled. "Tell him anything. Tell him a bedtime story. Here." And he grabbed the Bible from the priest, whipped it open, and threw it in his lap. "Read any damned thing."

With shaking hands, Father Murphy held the book and his eyes fell on the page and he read with trembling voice, "And Jesus said unto him, This day is salvation come to this house, For the Son of man is come to seek . . ."

Testard had risen. With his last vestige of strength and the Finn's help, he sat halfway up. ". . . *les indigènes doivent être surveillés de très près, comme des enfants. Mes enfants. Mes chers, chers, chers enfants.*"

"May the Lord Jesus Christ protect you," the priest rattled. Then he touched Testard's forehead with his thumb, but, not remembering the phrase, stopped himself and turned red.

"We'll need oil, won't we?" Kate prompted in a whisper.

The priest looked at her, astonished. *"I anoint thee,"* it suddenly came to him, and he gave Testard the sign of the cross. He looked pleadingly at them. "I have no oil," he said.

Kate rose slowly, protecting her wounds, and went below. She came back at once with a greasy puddle in her palm. The priest dipped his finger in it but grimaced with doubt.

"It's lard," Kate whispered. "It's all we have."

The priest ran his finger over Testard's feverish forehead. "I anoint thee with the . . . oil of sanctification in the name of the Trinity that thou mayest be saved for ever and ever."

Testard smiled. His gaze went inward. *"Mes enfants,"* he whispered for the last time.

"You are not dying alone," Kate prompted in a whisper.

"You are not dying alone," the priest repeated. "You die with Christ, who promises and brings you your eternal life."

Testard went limp, seemingly content. He looked with immense gratitude at Kate's loving gaze. Tears filled his eyes and he raised a hand toward her face and whispered barely audibly, "The beauty . . . The beauty."

The Finn let him down gently to the deck. "Son of a bitch," he murmured. "So much for our ticket with the French." He stood and looked above the awning, past the masts, beyond the cabin, where the dark smoke, like some filthy rag, dangled in the sky. I wonder who'll be next, he thought, to get smeared with holy lard.

NELLO HELF HIS FIRE as the figure rushed passed them, then recognizing the long limbs, the smooth strides. He called out, "Lil'bit."

The girl stopped and turned. She pushed toward them through the scrub and, catching her breath, said, "The frigate is coming. There is smoke on the sea."

"When will it get here?" Dugger blurted.

For a second she was startled by the new voice, then she looked up through the bowers at the sun. "Near dark," she said. Then, with a movement like a deer taking flight, she was off running hard over the broken ground, uphill toward the plateau.

Dugger froze in sudden helplessness, then, pushing toward the path, he growled, "If they catch us . . ."

"We have done no wrong."

"If Testard arrested us, why wouldn't they?"

"Testard can vouch we helped him."

"I'd rather run."

"Outrun a frigate?"

Dugger stopped. "You've got half an hour," he said. "If you're not back, I'm sailing without you." And he turned and headed downhill toward the ketch.

Nello took the rifle and hobbled up the hill.

With the gun to his head, Guillaume sat, unmoving. You're finished, he thought. The second time in two days you have dropped your guard. Whoever it is came silently, but that's no excuse. And there was no love to distract you this time. No passion. No Joya. Just you. Careless you.

He began to turn his head, but the gun pressed harder and he froze. "I have money," he said in French, and repeated it in English when there was no reply. When there was still no sound, he added, "I have fourteen tons of gold."

The holder of the gun made a nasal sound, a snicker. Then silence. Minutes passed.

Nothing moved anywhere and Guillaume started thinking that perhaps there was no gun, just a branch he was leaning against, and maybe he had just imagined the snicker, until he heard feet shifting slightly. He began to calculate the distance between his elbow and the gunman's thigh. He had to be there standing upright; he couldn't be leaning forward and holding that position for such a long time. If Guillaume spun fast enough to drive his elbow in the man's knee, the side of his knee to knock him off balance, then roll while with his other hand he raised and fired his gun . . . Unless, of course, it was a rifle and the man was out of reach. But then you can roll, grab the rifle barrel, and fire at the same time. His concentration must be broken by now. He must be tiring standing there. But why doesn't he speak? Or do something? What is he waiting for?

"What is it you want?" he asked. And was surprised when the gunman whispered, "Shhh."

Then came the cry.

It was shrill but from a great depth as if from the deepest part of a soul, not of fear but pain, and not pain without pleasure. The old woman he had been watching jumped. She swung her feet up over the sill of the hut and disappeared inside. There were words and calming sounds, then another cry, longer than the last. Across the cove, in the low steep scrub, someone began to move. The scrub shook and Guillaume looked but saw only movement without a shape, and not until it burst out onto the sand did he see the tattooed man, his tattoos glowing dark blue in the sun. He moved with hurried strides along the shore, slowing only when he was near the hut. He waded in and pushed on toward the door.

Guillaume squeezed the grip of his pistol and began imperceptibly to raise it along his leg. The gunman must have been distracted watching the hut, because there was no change in the pressure of the barrel of the gun. The tattooed man was looking into the hut, and Guillaume was aching to raise his pistol aim and fire; he would never again get such a close and easy shot, easy except for the gun against his head. That was when he first smelled the gardenias.

IN SILENT AWE the tattooed man watched the *demi* in the hut roll her head from side to side. She had her knees up, legs apart, and the old woman was massaging her legs to keep the muscles loose, prevent them from cramping, and sometimes with a wet tapa cloth she wiped the *demi*'s brow. The *demi* looked elated, in pain, and beautiful, and a deep ache and sharp bitterness filled the tattooed man. He tried to concentrate on the shadow between her thighs, waiting to see a small head appear, tried to share the *demi*'s expectation, but all he could feel was envy of the unborn child upon whose birth the *demi* now focused her life.

The old woman began to hum, a slow soothing melody, and she gently rocked the *demi* where she lay, until her limbs slackened and she closed her eyes and smiled. "Sleep a while, child," the old woman said. "It will not be born while the sun is high."

The tattooed man drew back from the wall and moved pensively through the water to the shore. Once there, he looked out to sea at the vast blue water and sky, then he walked unhurriedly back along the shore.

Like shooting fish in a barrel, Guillaume thought, watching him. But you have to shoot him now; ten more steps and he'll be gone for good, safe in the thick scrub along the shore.

He squeezed the handle of his pistol, coiled his leg muscles, then as violently as he could he moved. He whipped his head to the side and down, rolled to his left, swinging back his arm, and as it hit the rifle barrel, he swung his pistol up, and without aiming, without looking, with his head still down, he fired. He was facedown in the dirt when the body fell beside him. And on the ground rolled a crown of fresh gardenias.

Chapter 46

The day went suddenly dark, with only a slit of sunlight cutting through the clouds. Exhausted, Darina sat on a stone. Folds of hibiscus bushes shrouded over her. A quick rain came, slanting through the sunlight pattering on the leaves, making the flowers tremble. The world oozed color: hibiscus petals glowed against the dark green like hot coals, red and white, with pink-ringed centers.

Her eyes burned from fatigue. She turned her face up to the sky and let the rain wash over them. She was holding her face up when Lil'bit ran by. She saw her fleetingly through the trees, a bit of her here, an angle of her there.

The rain drenched Darina, awakened her. She pushed herself to her feet and fought through the undergrowth to the path turning uphill. She had gone some distance when someone called her name. She stopped. The voice called again, hesitant but urgent. Recognizing Nello's voice, she calmed. He came through the speckled light, hobbling, toward her, stopping only when they stood face-to-face.

"Are you all right?" he asked, out of breath, and his gaze raced over her.

"I'm fine," she said as strongly as she could manage, but seeing his concern, she felt her eyes tear up. "And you?" she said looking at his leg.

"It's nothing." Then he said, "The frigate is coming. It would be best to go."

"Go where?"

"I'm not sure. Out to sea. Another island. Anywhere." When he saw she remained unconvinced he added, "We can come back when it's all over. When things quiet down."

"When my brother is dead."

"Are you so sure he's here?"

"I'm not sure of anything."

For a moment she seemed to him frailer than before, seemed to tremble slightly as if the ground shook under her.

Darina leaned slightly forward, sure that if he moved toward her, gave even a nod, she would just keep leaning and fall into his arms. She would wrap her arms around his neck and hope that he would hold her, hard, comforting, protecting her from all harm. But he didn't.

He stood there watching the veins throb on her temples, watching her eyelids sag, waiting for a sign of yearning or wanting that would encourage him to move, to sweep her up like one does a tired child, into his arms, and carry her with long strides down to the harbor, the ketch, out to sea; out into the enormous safety of the empty sea.

But she gave no sign.

He leaned on the rifle awkwardly and waited.

"It's such a burden," she said, and said no more.

Far ahead, in the canyon, voices began to shout.

"It's all such a burden," she repeated, and reached out and touched the wrinkled petals of a hibiscus, which at her touch began to shed raindrops like tears.

"If I'm not back in half an hour," Nello said quietly, "he said he'll sail without me."

"Then you must go now," she said.

"And you?"

I'll go with you, she thought. I'll go with you as long as you hold me, as long as I'm close to you, touching you, because I'm so tired of being alone, alone every night, alone in the world. And I won't be a burden, I'll stand on my own, I'll have all the strength I need as long as you are near.

But she didn't say anything. She let the hibiscus petal slip away, and pushed the raindrops from her eyes.

"I had better go," she said, her voice now full of strength. And she turned away and walked with much effort uphill, on the path full of shadows.

"Can't we leave the awning up to give him some shade?" Kate asked.

He's dead, Dugger thought. The least of his worries now is shade. "It will foul the sheets," he said. "I want to be ready to set sail." But he stood there watching the shore, waiting for Nello.

"I'm sure he won't mind getting a last bit of sun, miss," the Finn added, and kept untying the awning's knotted lines.

"I'll cover him with his flag," Dugger said. "That way, if the French catch us, we'll say we were simply giving him last honors. We'll say he asked for a burial at sea."

"I promised him I would bury him on the island," the Finn said.

"Let's keep him a while," Dugger said. "For insurance."

Father Murphy sat on the cabin top, his eyes fixed on the horizon where the column of black smoke suddenly paled, then all but disappeared. The sun fell. "I think they've slowed," he said. "Perhaps even stopped."

"Maybe they blew up the boiler," Dugger said hopefully.

"That would be a blessing," the priest said. Then he rose and went to the gunwale near the pirogue. "I think I'll head home," he said, looking at the empty village, its walls turning pink with the falling sun.

"Why don't you stay for supper, Father?" Kate said, and looked hard at Dugger.

"Yes, Father," Dugger said. "The more, the merrier."

"It's safer here," Kate insisted.

"Sure," Dugger said. "At least no flying sharks."

The Finn stood holding a shroud, staring into the distance at the darkening horizon. The bloody French, he thought. They're out there waiting. Circling. *Exactly* like the sharks.

Chapter 47

It was a small, battered, single-cannon frigate that had been abandoned on the banks of the Chao Phraya River, downstream from Bangkok. When the Great War came and ships were scarce, they fastened steel plates over the worn planks of her bow, replaced the rings of her enormous pistons, and put the old frigate back in service.

Then they found Pétard, a sea captain who'd sailed a two-masted brigantine all his life chasing pirates in the South China Sea, and they put him in command of the frigate and, in case the Germans came, sent him with a crew of twelve to French Polynesia.

"Ça suffit maintenant," the admiral with the great mustache said dryly into the brass tube, and swept displaced long tufts of hair over his balding head. He opened wide his tiny eyes, put his cap with the gold cording back on. *"Je m'excuse, Capitaine Pétard,"* he said, turning to the short, taut man beside him. "It is, after all, your ship."

Captain Pétard gave a tired smile. "But your fleet, Admiral." He leaned to the speaking tube and said to the engine room with a tone of familiarity, *"Merci, André. Laissez la reposer."*

The admiral combed his mustache with his fingers, buttoned his white *tunique,* and smiled with self-contentment.

"How long shall we stop, Admiral?" the captain asked, the tone of disgust barely disguised in his voice.

"How long does it take for them to see the smoke stop before they begin to worry? Begin to doubt their own eyes, their own minds? A few minutes? An hour?"

Captain Pétard pretended to busy himself with the charts, even though the course into the bay was without danger. The admiral felt his anger rise at being ignored, so he went on. "Let us wait until sunset. Then steam in slowly, just the black silhouette of the ship against the setting sun. Theater, Pétard. It's all theater. Wait for the darkness. The *indigènes* have a terror of the darkness. Let us feed that terror. It is the best way, don't you think?"

Of course I do, Pétard thought. Let us scare them all to death and have a jolly time. Or we could just pretend we're human, turn around and go home, and leave the poor bastards to themselves. Instead he quietly said, "We need to anchor before dark. It's hard to find good bottom in there even in daylight."

"Bien sûr," the admiral said dryly. *"Bien sûr."* Then he looked past Pétard at the cannon.

"This cannon the *indigènes* have," the admiral inquired, as if making small talk. "What kind of range would you say . . . ?"

"On target? I'd say maybe fifty yards. It's old. Bought from a Yankee whaler. Not much more than a harpoon gun."

"Good. Let's go in close, then, for a better show. Is there much roll in the bay?"

"There will be today," Pétard replied.

"Then they'll have even more trouble aiming."

With but little steam in her, the frigate sat and rolled in the beam seas.

Chapter 48

"It's all right," Joya said. "It's really all right."

Guillaume clutched her against his chest, mumbling, "Dear God. My God," and held her so tight she could barely breathe. He felt her blood pump against him from her chest. "I didn't know. How could I?" he pleaded. "We'll go . . ."

Joya pushed out a tired smile. "You're crushing me," she whispered.

Guillaume eased up slightly but placed his hand over the hole in her chest from where the blood was pumping.

"What a funny ending," Joya said.

"You'll be fine . . ." he sputtered. "The last person I expected in the world . . . Why didn't you say something?"

Joya touched his hand and clutched his finger. "If you had known it was me holding the gun . . ." she said. "I just wanted you not to shoot him. He has been good." She felt a hard deep pain; when it left, she went on. "He dreamt with my father of the day the French were gone . . ." She gasped for breath. "Something is crushing my chest," she said.

Guillaume tore off his shirt and folded it into a pad, then pressed it against the hole.

"I'm so tired," Joya said. "When the old priest died I had to be the chief. I couldn't be a girl anymore. It was hard being a girl. Now it's harder being a man."

"If only we could . . ."

"Run away . . ." She stopped when she saw the panic on Guillaume's face as he looked at her chest where the blood was already seeping through his shirt. "It's all right," she said, touching his grizzled face, "It's all right."

He looked into her weary eyes. The beauty of the woman of last night was gone. There was instead the spent face of a man. The flesh sagged, the eyelids slacked, the eyes took on a sadness overwhelmed by life.

She turned her head and looked out to sea. "My father said, look at the sea. It has been the same for so long. And it will be the same for so long again. In the end it doesn't matter. In the end . . . it's all right." She looked back at him and tears welled in her eyes, not for herself but at seeing Guillaume cry. "I'll never forget our nights," she said, her voice trembling. "Your tenderness. Such tenderness . . ."

The *demi*'s groan rose from the shack. It fell and there was silence and then it rose again. "The child soon," Joya said, and her eyes turned wistful. "How happy she must be."

They saw the old woman vanish into the hut and the groaning stopped, and then they heard a serene and lulling singing. "You must promise not to kill him," Joya blurted. "He's a father. The child."

"Shhh," Guillaume said. "Don't wear yourself out. Shhh."

"Promise?"

"I . . . promise."

She fell silent and her gaze grew distant. "You know, at first I hated being a girl. Then after a while I loved it. You know I loved it." She stopped and smiled and gave a tired laugh. "The only sadness I felt was that I could never have a child. Give birth to a bit of both of us."

He moved to gather her up. "I'll take you to the village."

"No," she protested. "Leave me here. No, don't leave me. Stay with me until . . ."

"But you'll—"

"I know. But I want to stay. A while."

"Just a while."

"Yes. Just a while."

They sat silently and he held her in his arms.

"Just a while," she repeated. "I'd like to stay to hear the baby cry."

They remained in silence until the shout came again, this time less shrill, more resigned, as if expecting to go on for some time.

"Do me something, Guillaume," Joya whispered. "Find me a fresh gardenia."

He lowered her with great gentleness to the ground. He walked a few steps into the jungle shade. When he came back she was smiling. "Put it in my hair," she said, and touched his hand. "Behind my ear. No, silly . . . my left ear. So when the stars look down, they will know I'm taken."

Chapter 49

The ship's bell struck four times. It was six o'clock. Dugger stood up with a sudden start on the foredeck and reached, without thinking, for something—anything—to do. He had readied the sails, set the sheets, fetched the halyards tight, and hove in the anchor chain until he felt the anchor flukes strain against the bottom. Then he waited. Every few minutes he looked up at the shore hoping to see Nello, but the shore was empty. Nothing moved and nothing changed, as if the world had resolved to remain unaltered until the end of time. When, at last, the sun fell and shadows deepened, the birds in the jungle grew incessant and loud, sounding their last trill and warble before the night.

He turned and glanced far out to sea, where the dark smoke now spread like a black fog on the water.

Kate stared at Testard's ankles. They were thin and white, even whiter than his cuffs, and so frail she couldn't imagine them holding him upright. She sat and rested her wounds and tried not to look at Dugger. I'm glad I'm not him, she thought. I'm glad I'm not the one who has to decide.

The Finn slept. He lay on deck near Testard's corpse, his face turned to the gunwale, and with the gentle pitch and rolling of the ketch he was lulled into a deep and distant dream. He was dreaming of a silent winter's night with a light snow falling, each flake aglow with moonlight, with wolves howling in the woods, and anxious cows stirring in the barn. His forehead started knocking lightly against the gunwale, and there was a thudding in his ears. He popped open his eyes, but the sound still stayed and his head kept knocking. "They're coming," he whispered. "Their propeller . . ." He fell silent when he saw Dugger.

The sun had just touched the curve of the horizon, and against its red orb there was a dark, deep scar. He saw it for an instant before being blinded by the sun, but every time he looked back, the dark scar seemed to grow. Above it, a gloomy mist spread across the sky, until little by little it darkened the last light.

"We should get the rifles from the fortress," the Finn said.

"Sure," Dugger said. "At least they'll pay for his burial."

"You keep a tight account, Captain."

"Oh, yes," Dugger mused. "I charge fourteen tons of gold per passage. But somehow I seem to never collect a dime."

They dug a grave for Testard in the sand at the base of the cliff, a few steps from the north wall of the fortress. The sand was easy digging, broken shells and pulverized lava, and they were already waist-deep in the hole when the frigate coasted into the bay, steered wide of the ketch and kept coming toward shore. The two of them dug while the priest washed the blood out of the flag, scrubbing the flag with sand in the sea, then he wrung it out. He told the Finn to hold one end, and they stretched the wrinkles from it. Then he draped it with ceremony, so the people on the frigate could see, over the corpse of Testard.

With much rattling of the chain, the frigate dropped anchor.

Its engine fell silent. The sun had set; lanterns were lit aboard. A squeeze-box began to play a wistful tune, then a ukulele joined in, and one by one the sailors started singing.

On the unlit bridge, the captain raised the binoculars to his eyes. At first he studied the ketch, and, seeing but a lone woman, turned his attention to the shore. The jungle and the bluff stood like a wall of darkness. He saw the two men chest-deep in a trench, and the priest near them kneeling piously, bent over a lump draped under the flag. With the priest praying, the diggers toiling and the candlenut flames sputtering, it seemed to him a proper burial.

"I don't see Testard," the captain said, and passed the binoculars to the admiral.

The admiral scanned the beach for a long time, stopping at the lump covered by the flag. "I think I do," he said.

The admiral ordered the lifeboats be launched and filled with food, rum, and anything else the natives might enjoy—kerosene lanterns, axes, matches, saws—and, as a final show of trust, an armful of new rifles.

With the lifeboats loaded, he ordered everyone to board them and to man the oars—the eight marines from the island and all the frigate's crew, the captain included. He ordered that torches be lit in the bows to give the floating procession a truly festive air, then he told the sailor to keep playing his squeeze-box and the others to sing, and be hearty about it.

"And you, sir?" the captain inquired.

"Oh, I'll stay here. Let the men make a merry feast of it. Wouldn't be much of a festive night with me hanging over them, would it? Give them extra rations, extra rum. And give poor Testard a proper Gaelic wake."

He climbed back onto the frigate's bridge and watched.

The sea flared purple-green just before the darkness, and the boats left folded wakes behind them as they went. Swirling purple eddies formed around the oars, as the men pulled in unison to the rhythm of their song.

In the lead boat, the captain sat in silence, watching the ketch with a longing for the time when ships had sails.

Lil'bit clambered down to the plateau of sacrifice, shouting about the smoke on the sea and the frigate coming, and where was Joya? Where was Ki'i? Where was anyone to lead?

Sleepy people came from the *meae,* some still numb from the night's *kava,* and listened without emotion, without a word of response. Finally her uncle Nataro said they should all go down to the village in the jungle, in case Joya or Ki'i returned. Go there before darkness came and the night filled with the spirits of the dead.

They gathered up their clothes and drums and went in a ragged line through the fading light.

On the silent plateau only an old woman remained, sitting beside the dead chief, who still lay where he died. She sat swaying, singing herself to sleep, so she wouldn't be awake when his ghost came in the night.

Holding Joya in his arms, Guillaume watched the shadows lengthen and a damp gloom descend from the mountains like a fog. The shouts from the shack below had become groans that diminished only with the dwindling light. On the far horizon a row of clouds marched on as if abandoning the world to the coming darkness.

There was a cry.

Joya had her gaze fixed far off on a shimmer on the sea. With her head on Guillaume's chest, she listened to his heart. At the cry she turned her head. It was a weak but willful cry, tiny but demanding, fresh, expectant, full of life. Hearing it, Joya smiled. Then she closed her eyes.

Chapter 50

The priest trod hard uphill, with the Zuo brothers behind him. The music of the sailors faded in the distance and they hurried through the canyon before they lost the light. All three were bearing gifts: one Zuo carried a small barrel of rum, the other a new fishing net, and the priest a wooden box packed with fragrant tea. Up ahead they could see the fires on the terraces of the village. They twisted up the narrow path when out of the gloom three figures—Nello, Darina and Lil'bit—stopped before them.

"Testard died," the priest gasped. "The frigate came . . . Finn told them a shark killed him . . . rescuing the lady of the ketch." He had to stop talking in order to catch his breath. "The crew . . . the captain . . . there's music and food and drink. A proper wake. They send gifts."

"And Dugger?" Nello asked.

"He's at the wake. The French sent these for the chief. There are a lot more gifts on the shore. All for the village: tools and rice, even guns for hunting. A show of goodwill. The admiral asks the village to come and share the wake. In friendship."

"Sounds like bullshit," Nello said.

"If you have no faith in God," the priest snapped, "you could at least trust your fellow man."

"I did, once," Nello said. "She pried the gold filling out of my tooth while I slept."

The priest ignored him. "Where's the chief?" he asked.

"The chief is dead," Lil'bit said.

"Oh, dear Lord!" the priest whispered. "Then where is Joya?"

"Joya is gone," Lil'bit said without emotion.

"Gone where?"

"No one knows."

"In heaven's name!" the priest exclaimed. "Who on earth is in charge?"

"No one," Lil'bit said.

The priest lowered the tea box to the ground and sat heavily on it, exhausted from the climb and from the madness of the world.

"How did he die?" he asked, and shook his head as if he didn't really want to hear.

"Joya's lover killed him."

"Who?"

"Her lover. The Frenchman."

"What Frenchman? There's no Frenchman on the island except Testard."

"There is now," Nello said.

"Lord help us," the priest said. "This is a slaughterhouse. Where is Ki'i?" he asked, his voice full of apprehension.

"We're trying to find him," Lil'bit said.

"I don't like this place," Lil'bit said, but kept leading them down the curving path to the lagoon. The path fell steep with switchbacks to the shore, where the shack on stilts threw a shadow over the water.

Darina followed her without a sound. She was walking, stumbling, no longer from strength or determination, but simply couldn't bring herself to stop.

She had over the years pictured, almost daily, the moment when she would again hold her brother in her arms: the tears, the sighs. And she saw a thousand times the fire in his eyes as they clutched each other, speaking with so much to say, about the long years they'd lived without each other—in body only, because in heart and mind . . . But now she couldn't think of anything at all; except the child. I'd like to see the child, she thought. The child with *his* blood . . . *my* blood in it. *Our* blood. The other woman was only . . . As for him, she thought. For him . . . A peal of laughter rent the air. It came on the sea breeze and echoed from the bluffs. She stopped and listened, but no laughter came again. She pushed Lil'bit aside and hurtled down the path, sliding on the blood-red soil, losing her footing, falling, and uttering a quick shriek not of pain but of surprise. Then she arrested her fall against a bush, pushed herself free, and went on down again.

Nello and Lil'bit stopped. "She doesn't need us," Lil'bit said.

"She doesn't need anyone," Nello said. Then he leaned on the rifle and said no more.

Lil'bit's shoulders dropped; her face was soft with calm. She smiled at Nello, looked down at his bandaged leg, his big hands resting, leaning on the rifle, then back up at his grizzled face, his tired, unguarded eyes. "I'm hungry," she said.

She stepped off the path into the tangled scrub, twisted two mangoes from their stems, and came back peeling the hard skin with her teeth, biting the fibrous mass so the juice ran down her hands and out between her fingers. She gave one to Nello. She was tearing her mango, the juice dripping from her chin, when from over the hill, as if disgorged from the sky, came a booming, hollow sound—the blast of a cannon.

She looked up at Nello, her eyes full of surprise. And he saw something else there, an unmistakable glare of bitter accusation.

She turned uphill and with forceful strides she climbed.

Nello drove the butt of the rifle hard into the ground and, pushing off with all his weight, hobbled up behind her.

Chapter 51

Darina stopped at the edge of the lagoon. The sun was setting directly behind the shack, smoldering through the thin cracks of its thin walls, making it seem to teeter on its stilts. And rising from the hidden sun, as if bursting from the shack, enormous shafts of sunlight shot between the clouds and fanned out across the sky.

She waded into the sea and pushed through its warmth. Someone in the shack began softly singing. The silky water around the shack reflected the oranges and yellows of the clouds on the horizon. The dazzling colors calmed her, and she hung her head and whispered, "Hail Mary, full of grace, the Lord is with thee." Then she forced herself to say, "Blessed art thou among women. And blessed the fruit of thy womb."

The sea oozed languidly as she pushed ahead. She was so near the shack that she could hear the singer taking short breaths as she sang. Pressing her forehead against the wall's bamboo slats, she looked in. Sunlight flooded the shack and bathed the naked woman, all alone, sitting on a mat leaning against the wall singing, slowly combing her hair.

Darina closed her eyes and let the sun blindness wear off. She moved around the shack to the front, to look through the door with the sun behind her. The *demi* sat with her hair golden in the light, and below her firm breasts there was her belly, flat except for a fold. Empty. There was no one else in the shack; no brother, and no child.

The *demi* looked up, squinted into the sun, and, not being able to see who it was, smiled a welcoming smile. Darina stared at a small bundle by the door—a bloody rag. She felt faint. She turned away and for support leaned against the door.

The *demi* stopped singing. Her hand with the comb stood still. With the sun now lighting Darina's face, she could see her pale forehead and great blue eyes. The *demi*'s smile went cold. *"Mon Dieu,"* she whispered. *"Mon cher Dieu."* She put the comb against her mouth as if to keep in the words that were trying to get out. *"Tu es lui,"* she said. *"Tu es lui."*

It took Darina a while to put the words in order, but then she understood. The *demi* had said, "You are him."

The *demi* regained her composure and, tapping the back of the comb against her lips, said, "You look like him before the tattoos." She let out a childish giggle. "If you get tattoos you'll look like him again."

"Where is he?" Darina asked weakly.

"How should I know?" the *demi* shrugged. "Killing the French."

"I meant your child."

"Oh," the *demi* said, as if it had already skipped her mind. "He took it."

"He took the baby?"

"Yes. He came, looked at it, then he took it."

"Took it where?" Darina asked, her hand tightening on the doorpost.

"Who knows?" Then she gave a hard laughter. "Maybe he

gave it to Lil'bit, for her sharks."

Darina pushed herself away. She felt unsteady standing in the sea. The sun had set; only a last sliver floated above the haze. She stared at the bloodstained cloth, crossed herself, and had started back toward the shore when she turned and called back, "The baby. Was it a boy?"

The *demi* snickered. "A boy? I would have kept a boy."

Darina ambled aimlessly up the bank, leaving deep footprints in the sand. Waves followed her, filled them, then washed them all away. She couldn't think of where to go, what to do. She stood dripping. If I could only sleep, she thought, forget everything and just sleep. She tried to console herself by conjuring up an image of her brother with the baby, holding it lovingly, tenderly in his arms, but the only vision she could muster—one that wouldn't go away—was of her brother near Connally's barn with blood-covered lambs dangling from his arms.

He was stomping in big boots across the rain-slicked glen, with the flock surging before him following a ram. The dog turned the flock across the ravine, leaving only the trampled grass and some straggling ewes behind. The ewes lingered to protect their newborn lambs. The lambs staggered and weaved. Her brother grabbed them, looking for sick ones, held them by their hind legs, and let them dangle headfirst, with their front hooves tap-tap-tapping on the ground. He put them down gently across the ravine. And there was only one tiny lamb left, with legs like twigs, just born, caked in blood and slime, bleating its tiny heart out, dragging its torn umbilical cord behind, and the mother running after it, her great milk-filled udders bouncing off her legs, and they too were stained with blood, and there was panic in her eyes as her lamb was lifted into the air. He swung it back and forth as if it were a rag, waving it at the ewes to turn them up the hill.

Darina had seen him swinging lambs before; on the cliff.

When they were sick beyond cure, or still weak and feeble a few days after birth, he would take them to the edge, where the wind howled with menace up the rocky face, and with a mighty swing launch them off the bluff over the sea, where anxious gulls and ravens waited far below.

The *demi*'s song floated in the cove. Darina didn't want to hear it anymore, so she pushed on into the jungle up the hill. She clambered shakily through the wet darkening air and didn't even notice when she ended up on all fours grabbing roots and the stems of ferns. Her knees were scraped and her fingers bled, but she pushed stubbornly on, slipping, and sliding when she ran into two legs.

The shoes looked familiar, but she didn't know from where. A hand reached down, holding flowers and a pistol. It pulled her up by the arm. "This way," a dry voice said. She recognized Guillaume.

His other hand was filled with fruit and he stood gray-faced, his eyes unfocused and solemn in the light. "This way," he repeated, his voice as brittle as straw.

She let him lead her, not caring where or why, and they traversed the hill into a clearing with a rock. She saw a figure lying on the rock, the head slightly tilted, staring out to sea. Both hands lay palms-up, unmoving, on the ground. There were flowers near the feet and a pile of breadfruit near the hands. Without a word, Guillaume knelt down and began to place the flowers and fruit he'd brought along the extended legs, then placed some around the head on the flat part of the rock. He worked slowly with much care, changing, arranging, as if he were laying a table for a feast. But he didn't let go of the gun.

"Food for her spirit," he mumbled. "If it goes hungry, it will be angry. Her ghost will come and haunt the place until the end of time."

Darina shuddered. "Do you really believe these tales?" she said.

He didn't reply until he had laid the last flower. "Do you believe yours?" he said.

"I believe in God's mercy."

"Then why don't you give her absolution?"

"I'm not a priest. I can't."

"She won't care."

"I don't have the power of God in me."

Guillaume uttered a laugh soft as a breath. "All these weeks at sea I wondered what was missing in you . . . So it's the power of God."

"I have to go," Darina said, and turned.

Guillaume grabbed her arm sand spun her around. "*I* have the power of God!" he growled. "Right here," and he held up the gun. "The true God. With the power of life and death. Now give her absolution or I swear you'll lie dead beside her."

Darina yanked her arm. "That would be a sacrilege. My soul would burn in hell."

"Damn your soul! And damn you!" And he pointed the gun at her.

"My absolution won't help her."

"Then say a prayer for her. Put in a good word with your God." When Darina didn't move, he clicked back the hammer. "I already shot her. Shooting you would mean nothing to me."

"*You* killed her?"

"I just shot her. Your brother killed her. Like he'll kill us all."

Darina stepped aside and knelt down near the flowers. "Our Father, who art in heaven, hallowed be thy name . . ." she went on, and after a while she could hear Guillaume murmur along with her, "and forgive us our trespasses as we forgive those . . ."

The darkness had fallen. Only the last light from the horizon reflected in Joya's eyes.

Darina rose and started across the slope toward the ketch.

"Not that way," Guillaume said. "He went up to the plateau."

As she came back past him, he held out the gun. "Take this," he said. "You might need two gods."

Chapter 52

A handful of sailors danced a lively jig, kicking up streams of sand into the flames. The others sang and swayed and took turns holding their tin cups under the spigot of a keg of rum that had been wedged smartly between two leaning palms. Dugger and the captain stood apart near the sea, drinking, talking about the ketch, her raked masts, her new-styled rigging, her sails, her hull, even the planks and the bronze fasteners that held them—all things concrete and blessedly inanimate. Then they fell silent and watched the sailors dance and the flames dance on the flag and on the steep walls of the grave. When the dance grew lewd, the captain looked out to sea.

"Is your wife all right?" the captain asked.

"She's better. The priest stitched her well."

The captain didn't turn back but kept staring at the ketch. "Is she alone?" he asked.

"Yes. Resting . . . Why?"

"Nothing," he said, and turned back toward the flames. "Just saw something move across your stern. A dolphin, I would say, looking for its dinner."

Dugger glared into the twilight, but there was only the dark ketch upon the purple sea.

"I should get back," Dugger said. "Thanks for the rum."

"Je vous en prie," the captain said. "Thanks for the company."

Dugger paddled the pirogue hard, pushed on by fear of something amiss aboard the ketch. Still blinded by the flames, he barely made out forms, the black mountains on his left, the ketch dark ahead, and the sky a deep purple all around it. The frigate lay with a single light no brighter than a candlenut flame shimmering in its bow, the cannon pointing rigidly at the shore.

He rested the paddle against the gunwales to steady his nerves and to catch his breath. The swells and the undertow turned the bow of the pirogue, and now he saw the shore, all dark except the candlenuts and the tall flames of the fire around which sailors leapt as if trying to stamp out the darkness at their feet.

Nearing the ketch, he used the paddle as a rudder, guiding the pirogue ghosting through the night. He drifted up alongside, and so as not to bump the hull in case Kate slept, he grabbed the rail of the ketch to keep the boats from banging. Hand over hand he moved the pirogue to the stern. He was at the last stanchion when he saw a quick movement on the sea. "Nello?" he called, but there was no reply.

He cleated the pirogue's painter and pulled himself aboard when something large and solid hit his head. Dazed, he fell. One leg went in the water and he dangled from the rail. He hung there, trying not to pass out. Big hands grabbed his arms and pulled him over the rail like a rag doll. He was lowered to the deck. He lay there facedown, trying to make sense out of the figures on the aft deck, while the smell of gunpowder swirled around his head. Only then did he make out the shape of a small cannon.

"Where is she?" Dugger said groggily.

"Shhh," a heavy voice replied.

"The woman. *Ma femme. Où est-elle?"*

"Elle dort," another voice said, the accent thick, not French.

Dugger started to push himself up, but the big hands pushed him down, and held the cool blade of a hatchet against his cheek. "What do you want?" he grunted.

"Some silence," a new voice said, thinner and with a lilt.

"You want silence, so you bring a cannon?"

No one answered. Along the stern rail three forms squatted as unmoving as statues, and a much slighter man was bent over the cannon. With a soft thud the breech of the cannon closed; then the slight man brought short blocks of wood and wedged them between the bed-logs of the cannon and the coamings. He tested the wedges holding the cannon by pulling the barrel sideways with all his might. The wedges held. The cannon stood immobile.

Seemingly satisfied, the slight man said something to the massive one kneeling, and the massive one quickly straddled Dugger's back, pulling Dugger's hands tight behind him.

"What the hell do you want with that peashooter?" Dugger snapped.

"If you talk, we will kill you," someone said.

"Not with that toy cannon you won't."

The slight man grabbed Dugger's hair, lifted his head from the deck. "Don't you care about anyone? Your friend ashore? The woman below?"

Then he let Dugger's head go and it banged on the deck. He tasted blood where he bit his tongue.

Three little girls burst from the canyon onto the beach into the firelight, the smallest one in the lead, the oldest one trailing, feigning disinterest. They had heard from the priest about the gifts that awaited: the food, paper and pencils, pots and pans, but all the little one wanted was a big floppy straw hat, and the big one a calico dress that tumbled to her ankles. When they saw the sailors dancing around the fire, they slowed, but edged toward the piles of sacks and boxes.

Older children followed, then some women arm in arm, others in groups, with the men trailing in fits and starts—all to gather up the alms without shame. They milled among the piles, lifting the lids of crates, untying sacks. Nataro headed for the rifles leaning against a lifeboat in the sand.

The captain approached, looked about for a leader in the crowd, but only Nataro seemed to command as he handled the rifles.

"Les cadeaux sont tous les votres," the captain called over the song and din, and spread his arms theatrically to include all piles spread along the sand. When they returned to their rummaging he said more quietly, directed at Nataro, "Testard is dead. Come and drink. To celebrate his life."

The sailors kept dancing, too drunk to really care.

The women untied the heavy sacks of rice. The smallest girl filled her arms with pomegranates, bit open the tough rusty rind of one, and grimaced when the acidic pulp reached her tongue, her lips, teeth, and the tip of her nose all red. The older girl, finding no calico dress, openly watched the awkward lurches of the sailors, the women passed around yams, and the men took cups of rum, then handled the new rifles, a kind they had not seen before. They were rifles with bolts instead of levers that you pumped, and they pulled and pushed the bolts and found the magazines empty. Nataro dug about for ammunition but there was only food, and bottles of rum.

THE FINN AND THE TALLER ZUO finished digging the grave, threw out their shovels, and the other Zuo reached down and helped them up. The captain handed them tin cups of rum, then he organized four sailors to lower in Testard. They spread the flag on the ground, and placed Testard, pale except for his blood-caked scars, atop it. Each sailor held a corner, and lifted him up and over the yawning grave.

"Saluer!" the captain ordered, and the music and dancing stopped. They all saluted where they stood as the flag with Testard in it was lowered out of sight. One young sailor saluted with his cup of rum.

Father Murphy edged his way slowly through the crowd, clasping the Bible. He paused near the cask of rum, murmured some words no one could understand then stepped to the grave-side.

The four sailors were on their knees, lowering in Testard.

The priest bent down, took a handful of sand, and, murmuring, "Ashes to ashes," sprinkled it into the hole. The captain stepped forward, said a few words about duty and service, then fell silent and there was only the murmur of the sea. He too picked up some sand and let it run through his fingers into the grave.

One by one the soldiers of the garrison did the same, then drifted back into the shadows. The others stood saluting. The sailor with the squeeze-box began a mournful Marseillaise. Someone sang. Others followed.

The blast of a cannon tore apart the night.

The sound of the cannon echoed around the bay. It had burst with a tongue of flame from the frigate and bounced up from the water, and then from the face of the dark mountain. The shell whistled overhead, a distant, silly sound, and slammed into the mountain somewhere high above. Some trees broke, some rocks fell, then the world returned to silence. The squeeze-box began to play. The villagers didn't move.

Then the cannon fired again.

This time, the shell whistled louder. More menacing. Lower. Closer. Then it hit. It slammed into the darkness just beyond the fire. By the light of the flames, they saw a shack rise off its pilings and explode into pieces. There was the violent sound of breaking, a woman screamed, and a stout man cried out, as the remnants of their house spread across the sky. Bits of poles, fronds, and mats fluttered to the ground. Some sailors stopped saluting. The captain turned away. The boy who saluted with his cup lowered his arm.

The man whose house it had been stood there as shards and shreds rained down over him.

The third shell came in quickly: the gunner had his range.

Chapter 53

When the fifth blast from the cannon came at the village, the boy who had saluted with his cup gave an anguished cry and flung the cup toward the shell whistling through the dark.

The shell hit Nataro's house, the largest of the huts. As it blew apart, a kerosene lamp burst and fiery pieces rained down, setting the nearby roofs ablaze. Nataro watched bits of his house smolder in the sky. He watched a corner post of ironwood tumble down, the one he had cut with his son on a three-day journey into the canyon of the ponds, the one they'd had a fine time searching for, cutting, and cleaning. They had brought the trunk of the ironwood out together, notched it and set it in place—the first post of the house—and Nataro's brother carved their figures into the pole, and so many times they had looked at it and remembered those days, that good time.

The post hit the ground. Around it fell planks every man in the village had helped hew, and the roof that for two weeks the village had braided—hard on the hands because it was *pandanus*, but worth the trouble because it lasted seven years instead of three, like palm fronds. Last to fall was the flaming mat Nataro's wife had woven with her sisters, singing all the while by the pond of the waterfall.

The village burned.

The admiral, his task eased by the blaze, shelled the village house by house like cleaning a cob of corn. Women shrieked and men waved empty rifles. The captain turned to them and apologized with all his heart, but there was chaos now and some children cried while others laughed, and the sailors backed away toward the lifeboats except for the boy who had thrown his cup. He now took a loaded rifle from the boat and aimed it at the frigate, but the captain gently pushed the rifle barrel down and said, "Forget it, son. It's not worth your life."

The captain ordered the sailors into the lifeboats, then he waded into the sea and pushed the first boat off into the dark. The second boat was overloaded and two sailors scrambled out to float it, then scrambled in again. Only the captain remained, thigh-deep in the sea. When the engineer put his hand out to help him aboard, he just stood there and watched the lifeboat drift away. The engineer called out, "Sir?"

And he still didn't move, didn't want to move, just wanted them all to go away, disappear, and never come to this beautiful place again. "It's your ship, sir," the engineer said quietly. The next shell hit, another house exploded. The captain gritted his teeth and waded deeper into the sea.

"UP SAILS," a big Kanaka barked, and Dugger stalled for time but hoisted the main. Two big Kanakas hauled in the anchor chain. The cries and shouts from shore and the cannon's roars drowned out its grinding.

Dugger hauled the halyard tight, sheeted it, and the ketch took off in the stiff breeze. He went to raise the jib. A Kanaka steered the ketch and the jib luffed hard and Dugger worked frantically, nearly blind with anger. When both the sails were set, he took the wheel and the ketch heeled hard to port with the cannon weighing it down, and headed at speed, straight toward the frigate.

The Kanakas gathered around the cannon. "You get one shot, you understand?" Dugger hissed. "Then I'm sailing out of here. They can't turn the ship without steam, and their boiler's out, but once they start it up again, we're all dead, so you get one shot and then we run."

"Me good shot," a young man said.

"Glad to hear it," Dugger said.

He steered the ketch over the rolling seas. Near the frigate, he fell off, aimed past its stern, and came about, finished resetting the sails, then sailed beam-on to the frigate less than thirty yards away. The young man was on his knees beside the cannon, sighting. He had the aft deck in his sights, then he sighted the main house, then the tilted stack, then the wheelhouse, then the kerosene barrels beside it, and now in his sight, he saw the base of the big cannon.

A swell jostled the ketch. He fired.

An enormous thunder shook the air. A column of fire from the frigate split the sky. Sooty flames roared on the frigate's deck as the burst kerosene drums caught fire and lit the remnants of the wheelhouse, now all blown to splinters, with only the wheel left standing in the open air. But the big cannon stood intact, with the admiral behind it, scorched, staring in astonishment at the wreckage at his feet.

"Dumb Kanaka bastards!" Dugger roared, and fiercely turned the wheel. He fell away from the frigate and let out sail, and had the ketch reaching, running out to sea. The Kanakas stood in stunned silence. Kate burst out of the hatch and blinked into the night.

"Brainless morons!" Dugger yelled, and slammed the sheets to the deck. "How could you miss from this close?" The ketch flew downwind, straight out of the bay. Then, with his jaw clenched, Dugger turned the wheel. He hauled the sheets ferociously and turned the ketch back, heading toward the frigate. He ordered the boy to the wheel, then ran to the foredeck, pushed the Kanaka away from the cannon, reset the wedges, braced the cannon tight, swearing all time, checked the sight, then threw open the breech to let fall the empty shell.

"Don't think I'm doing this for you!" he hissed. "That frigate is barely scratched and once they get up steam, they'll blow my ass to hell!" With a violent swing of his leg, he kicked the smoking shell into the sea.

They were coming up on the frigate as before. "Give me another shell!" he ordered. No one moved. "Come on, dammit, give me another shell!"

The boy stepped forward but stopped. "No more," he said.

Dugger stared. "No more what?" he said hoarsely. "No more *what?*"

"No more shell." the boy shrugged.

"No more shell?" Dugger repeated. "No more shell?" Then, for lack of anything else, he grabbed the boy by the neck. "No more fuckin' shell? You came to start a goddamn war with one goddamn shell! Is this a fuckin joke? Well, that's great! That's just jolly dandy! The war is started!" He pushed the boy violently away. "Now what? You gonna yell at them? Stick out your tongue? What?"

On the frigate, the admiral, his hair and eyebrows singed and uniform stained with soot, feverishly cranked the handle on the cannon's wheel, swinging the barrel around toward the ketch. The lifeboats came with chaotic churnings of their oars.

Without time to ease the sheets, Dugger rushed back to turn the wheel and the ketch fell away, but with the sheets still tight and the sails full, she heeled and buried the rail, plowing white foam furrows in the fire-colored sea. The admiral cranked the cannon to its farthest starboard range, flipped the lever, and fired. The shell flew and the sails shook, but it missed the mizzen. "You limp Frog!" Dugger grinned, his heart thumping in his throat.

The admiral stood helpless as the ketch sailed beyond the aim of the cannon and off into darkness.

The pirogue changed course to meet it in the pass.

The lifeboats reached the frigate and the sailors climbed aboard. As the admiral shouted orders to chase the ketch, some swung bits of canvas to suffocate the blaze. Others hoisted the anchor, still others the lifeboats, and the engineer headed below to fire up the boiler, but at the companionway the captain stopped him with his elbow. *"Doucement, Henri,"* the captain said. *"Doucement."* The engineer looked at his captain's tired eyes, then back to the shore, where the village was a row of leaping flames. He turned and went below and, without hurry, began looking for his shovel.

"Get off my boat," Dugger roared. "And take your goddam cannon!"

One by one, they slipped down into their pirogues and, with swishes of the paddles, vanished in the night. Dugger lifted the base of the cannon and rolled it overboard. He flashed a nervous smile toward Kate. "Alone at last," he said.

"And Nello?" Kate asked.

Dugger looked over his shoulder and said, "I don't know."

They sailed between the two dark points out of the bay. The swells grew long, and they sailed up moonlit slopes and down into dark valleys. The moon was clear and bright and on the sea was a dark pirogue heading for their bow.

Dugger tied off the wheel and went below for his pistol. When he came back the pirogue was so near he could make out two figures paddling with all their might. He untied the wheel and rested the pistol calmly on his arm. When they were just a boat-length off, he fired over their heads.

"Thank you, Cappy!" came a shout from the pirogue. "It's nice to be welcomed home."

Lil'bit held the gunwale of the ketch while Nello climbed aboard. When he turned, she was still there, saying nothing, standing in the dark. Nello leaned down and grabbed her wrist to pull her onto the ketch, but he felt her resist gently, clutching the ketch's rail.

"I wish I could stay," he said.

"Me too," she replied. Then she let go of the ketch. It sailed off, leaving her and the pirogue behind.

Behind them the frigate's smokestack belched its first dark plume.

They sailed with sails hauled tight but couldn't clear the point, so they tacked and beat across the wide mouth of the bay.

Sparks flew from the frigate's funnel. Halfway across the bay they tacked again. The bow was pointed barely past the point and Nello went to the high rail and stared ahead. The ketch strained, the blocks groaned, and the sea washed over the rail. Then he heard something slam hard into the hull. On the low side of the aft deck a figure clambered aboard.

Nello pulled out his knife and, leaping over the taut sheets, struggled aft. The figure, crouching, crawled toward the cockpit. Nello threw himself at it to push it over the side but held back in midflight.

"Madonna," he hissed in surprise. "You're coming?"

"A lil'bit," she said.

Chapter 54

With the wind whispering in the dark boughs above her, Darina climbed. She had left the village behind long ago, deserted, its fires down, with only a dog standing near a bucket looking down the path the villagers had descended. She climbed above the jungle into steeper open ground and could see up ahead the slope flatten to a saddle. The grip of Guillaume's pistol had grown familiar in her hand, its metal warm and sweaty, and she caught herself nervously fingering the trigger, not unlike what she had done so often at the Magdalenes' laundry, nervously fingering the beads of her rosary.

Throughout the climb, grisly thoughts of her brother and the child raced through her mind. To push them away, she rattled aloud the Apostles' Creed, skipped the Our Fathers because they reminded her of Joya's dead eyes, and raced into Hail Mary's with a feverish devotion, saying each word strong and clear to clutter up her mind. Breathless, sweating, but cold from fear, she reached the rim of the plateau. It stretched peacefully below her, aglow with tufts of mist in the gleaming moonlight. The point of land, like a silver spur, jutted out to sea, and the altar stones and platforms loomed, enormous and dark.

At the center of the plateau, something moved. A woman rose, straightened slowly with the caution of old age, and walked inland, leaving behind a corpse laid out in white, surrounded by mounds of fruit and flowers. She went to a creek where a nanny goat was feeding her wobbly-legged kid. Darina saw the old woman push the kid away and reach toward the nanny's sagging udder. Then, in the great stillness, she heard the sound of milk squirting into a tin cup. On the way back the woman drank from the cup, then she set it down beside a mound of flowers.

The plateau was still again. Nothing moved in the moonlight but the mist.

Darina sat under an overhanging rock, leaned against the still-warm stone, and waited. Her eyelids drooped. No matter how she tried, her eyes wouldn't stay open. She heard her own breath deepen, heard a purring snore. She dreamed long and unstoppably about Mr. Connally and her brother with the lambs. Her eyes opened only when she heard a baby cry.

She awoke with such a jolt she banged her head on the rock. Below her the plateau swam in hazy light. It was dawn. The old woman sat by the corpse with the wobbly kid now beside her. Darina's heart was still racing from the dream, and she reached for her rosary to calm herself but found only the gun. She clutched it under her breast, half to hide it, half to cling to it. Across the plateau, where the great stone platform rose and the banyan threw its capacious shadow, she saw movement. But when she looked, it stopped. Some terns dove and soared along the cliff's edge as if drawing pictures across the morning sky.

The movement came again. It was tiny at first, a small dark ball behind the platform in the shadow, but then it cleared the platform and stood clear against the sky, a dark, half-naked man, walking along the edge. She recognized the gait, the cautious way he held his head, and how he carried a small bundle in his arms.

Darina closed her eyes and hoped to God she was asleep. By the time she opened them again, he'd walked halfway to the spur. He was keeping to the edge of the cliff, heading toward that point of land that stuck so starkly out into the sea. "Michael," she whispered. "Michael."

She clasped her hands over the gun, laid them across her knees, and murmured, "Now and at the hour of our death. Amen."

She got up.

They had sailed west all night, running from the moonlight. At the first hint of dawn they had dropped all sails and packed them tight so they wouldn't reflect the sun when it rose. Dugger braced himself against the mizzen with the binoculars at his eyes, and looked in an arc straight aft of the ketch at the curve of the horizon. "Not a sign of them," he said, and, barely able to hide a grin, he handed the binoculars to Nello.

Lil'bit stood at the helm and watched the long swells pass under the ketch. During the night the wind had come up strong, with the swells growing higher every hour, and the ketch had run hard ahead of them and across them. Dugger managed now and then to catch a wave, and have the ketch raise her bow and surf on the hissing crest, feeling as if some giant had given her a violent shove. Lil'bit stood near him and, when she felt the ketch surge hard, made little sounds of joy. She let go of the rigging and bent her knees as if riding her board.

After a while Dugger pulled her into the cockpit. "Steer for those two stars," he said. "You surf better than me."

With sparkling eyes, she held the wheel. It took her a while to get the feel—she luffed the genny twice—but then she had the wind just right, and felt the press of each wave trough in her feet, through her thighs. She caught one and the ketch surfed well beyond her hull speed, and the rudder fluttered below when

Lil'bit finally lost the wave and the seas rushed by. All night she steered. And all night long she surfed. And each time she caught a wave she let out a squeal; like a child. Her arms tired by dawn and she asked Dugger to take over. She went and sat on the starboard rail, dangled her legs overboard, clutched the shrouds, and closed her eyes. She leaned against the shrouds and slept with a smile lingering on her face.

NELLO WORKED THE BINOCULARS a long time. He swept the dawn-lit north horizon from east to west in an ever-widening arc, back-tracking over the same piece of sea, then did it one more time.

On the cockpit seat beside him, Kate stirred. She had slept soundly all night and now rolled gently over and sat up. Her color had returned and she moved with aches but seemed fine. When she saw Nello looking incessantly aft, she turned questioningly to Dugger.

"We lost them." Dugger grinned.

Nello lowered the binoculars and handed them back without a word.

The horizon grew bright. The first arc of the sun burned a flat hole in the sky.

"What's eating you?" Dugger asked, looking up at Nello.

"Nothing. Just thinking."

"You're not thinking; you're worrying. Well, there's nothing to worry about. You saw for yourself; we lost them. Now we can go anywhere we like."

"I guess you're right."

"They saw us heading north. They must have thought Hawaii. So that's where they went."

"Except that frigate is twice as fast as us. We only had an hour's lead. After two hours they must have known they were wrong. They would have changed course. So they should be at least this side of the north horizon."

"But they're not."

"No. So where the hell are they?"

Lil'bit sat upright at the shrouds. She looked south, where on the bright sea lay a flat black cloud. "There," she said.

Darina felt the pistol tremble against her thigh. She pushed herself away from the rock and started down the path toward the plateau. "I believe in God, the Father Almighty," she whispered. "Maker of heaven and earth." She clasped her hands behind her back, over the gun, as if to hide it from the world. "Almighty and most merciful Father," she murmured, "we have offended thy holy laws. *I* offended thy holy laws. *He* was innocent. Let me atone for him. Do not let him commit the crime. My crime." She desperately missed the feel of her rosary. "Let the innocents be," she went on, running her fingers over the barrel of the gun. "I believe in the Holy Ghost, the communion of saints, the forgiveness of sins . . . and life everlasting. Amen. Take me," she whispered. "But save the child. And save what is left of his eternal soul."

She reached the plateau. The sun, an enormous disk of fire, rose behind her brother.

Her brother was walking slowly up ahead, but he must have seen her movement out of the corner of his eye. He stopped, craned his neck. Then, still looking back, he kept walking toward the edge. Darina stopped. So did her brother. Then, with that barely visible movement they had used to approach butterflies on a bush, she moved toward him. She neared and circled a few paces away, trying to get herself between him and the cliff's edge.

With the sun nearly behind him, his face was a blue halo, the glow of his tattoos. And the small white bundle lay motionless in his arms. She circled and he watched. When she was so close she could have touched him if she tried, she stopped. She blushed suddenly and with her free hand touched her hair. "You haven't seen it this short," she said. She bit into her lip and tried hard not to cry.

He was now exactly between her and the sun and he seemed to melt away in the circle of yellow fire. She looked down and stepped closer to the edge. The cliff lay at her feet and the wind whipped the sea mist past her, full of brine. The sunlight now lit half her brother's face. The tattoos hid his features, but the sunlight caught his eye. It was as dark and as blue as the sea below. She saw a tear swell, trip onto his cheek, and trickle down, confused, lost in the swirl of the tattoos, as if unable to find its way out of the maze.

His eyes narrowed and looked down at the gun. She tried to let it fall, but her fingers held on tight. Slowly she lifted her empty hand and touched his face. She heard him say as softly as the breeze, "If only you . . ."

Darina watched the tear meander down his cheek, through the tattooed spirals, across swirls and sharks' teeth, and then it dripped onto his chest over the drawing of a skiff, or maybe a curragh. Her eyes raced down his body, over pictures of tumbling bridges and cannons spewing fire, and stick figures lying dead, like cordwood. But among the images of destruction, wherever space allowed, were etched what looked like tiny birds and flowers. And on the left side of his chest, level with his heart, was etched in simple letters: *Darina.*

Her eyes welled up and the world shimmered into a blur. She felt her chest heave with uncontrollable sobs, and as tears poured down her face, all she could say was, "My dear."

She wiped her eyes with the gun in her hand. "Things never change, do they?" She smiled. "You shed one tear and I cry a waterfall." She kept her gaze down at his naked feet. They were the only part of him without tattoos. Burned by the sun, his toes were splayed out wide. She cringed at the distortion; the harshness of the change.

"Your toes," she whispered through a strange taste in her mouth, and kept staring at them with a mix of fear and hopelessness. Then she looked up suddenly into her brother's eyes. "The French sent a spy," she blurted. She looked for a reaction, but his eyes hadn't changed. "To kill you," and with a deft thrust of her arm she held out the gun. "Take this."

But instead of taking it, he pulled back in surprise. It was a short step backward, so his bare foot touched the edge and his body contorted as he teetered over the sea.

Startled by the lurch, the bundle stirred and out shot a tiny arm. It made a minute fist that rose toward the sky. A slight voice began a muffled, gasping cry. Darina froze. Some ancient instinct overwhelmed her mind. There was no thought. Only fear.

She lunged.

She reached for her brother with her arms extended, forgetting the cliff, the danger, her life; she saw only his frightened face and the tiny arm. She grabbed her brother's wrist and her fingers clutched the bundle. His tattooed fingers reached out and Darina fell against him. They hovered for a moment, contorted against the sky, then they fell toward the sun, the edge, and the far-below, heaving, crashing sea.

The old woman by the corpse gave a fearful cry.

Darina tried to stop her fall but found no solid ground. Crumbling rock and loose earth gave way under her feet. Blinded by the sun, she felt their arms entwine and smelled the acrid stench of the dying shark. With all her remaining strength, she tried to twist away, felt a tearing pain race along her spine, and her knees buckled. She twisted hard again, and with an ugly sound, like a pitcher cracking, her head hit a rock. She heard a gurgling cry, then saw the sun go dark, inward from the edges, until all that was left was a tiny ember at the unreachable bottom of an enormous darkness.

Chapter 55

The black smoke rose and grew dense on the horizon. Dugger sat down on the cabin. A crippling fatigue soaked him to the bone, a fatigue without redemption that only hopelessness can bring.

"I'm sorry," he said hoarsely to no one in particular. "Damn sorry."

"It's all right Cappy," Nello said beside him. "It can't be worse than being eaten by a flying shark."

They watched the smoke, but, even with binoculars, saw no sign of the frigate anywhere below it. Lil'bit leaned into the rigging and softly hummed.

"What now?" Dugger said, and exhaled in frustration. "What the hell do we do now?"

Nello went aft to the cockpit, confirmed their heading on the compass, and looked up to estimate the angle of the sun. He glanced over the side at the churning foam to verify their speed, unrolled the chart and studied it, then rolled it up again.

"Well?" Dugger queried.

"Well, what?"

"What do you think?"

"Think?" Nello said, as if it were the last thing on his mind. "Not a damned thing. Just keeping busy."

He came and sat beside Dugger, pulled out his marlinspike, and began to clean his nails. "I figure we have three choices," he said. "One: we show the French our stern, just sail the sticks right out of this poor ketch, and hope for the best. In that case they'll probably catch us in four hours and blow us all to hell. Two: we can head west right into that," and he nodded into the distance, where black squalls and great thunderheads darkened sea and sky. "We can go hide in the rain squalls. They should be so dense you can't even see the bow, and if we guess right and don't break anything, we might just lose them."

"And your *third* choice?" Dugger said.

"We drop the sails, have a nap, wait till they get here, invite them for tea, and tell them just what happened. How the Kanakas hijacked the ketch, tied us up, blew up their wheelhouse, then paddled to shore."

"And then?"

They glared at each other while the smoke spread across the sky.

"Haven't a clue what then."

"Or," Lil'bit interjected, "we can run for Rangiroa."

They turned toward her, but she just gazed through the rigging at the southern sky.

"What is Rangiroa?" Nello asked.

"The biggest atoll in the Tuamotus. It has one hundred *motus* around its lagoon. Big lagoon. Fifty miles across. A lagoon full of *motus*. With all those *motus*, no one will ever find you."

She looked at them out of the corner of her eye and a mischievous smile began blooming on her face. "Anyway, the French can't go in because they don't know the pass."

"What pass?" Nello said. "With one hundred *motus*, there must be a hundred passes."

"It's true," she said, and allowed the smile to spread. "But ninety-nine are so shallow you'd wreck even a canoe. Only one is deep. It is narrow and twisting and you can't see the bottom because the current runs too hard. But, if you know the way, you can get in without breaking up on the reef."

"Well, we don't know the way," Dugger snapped.

Lil'bit ignored him. "My uncle Nataro used to take the *Aranui* through it." When no one said a word, she added, "He used to take me with him."

Dugger and Nello looked at each other, their faces drawn with doubt.

Nello walked back to the cockpit and unrolled the chart. Over the myriad of islands was printed, *Dangerous Archipelago.* Unnamed atolls were scattered everywhere, rings of tiny islands enclosing lagoons, some oblong, some minuscule, some square, others round, and among them swirling arrows denoting giant eddies, and wavy lines denoting miles-wide currents, and everywhere the repeated phrase, *Unchartable water movement.*

He held the chart out to her. "Where is Rangiroa?"

Lil'bit didn't look at him or his chart. She stepped clear of the sails and, holding onto a shroud, studied the southwest sky. She looked at the low white clouds scattered all around, then she raised her arm and pointed at one, neither taller nor more billowing than the rest, and said in a hushed tone, "There."

They followed her hand in disbelief through the sky.

"Native humor," Dugger mumbled. Nello rolled up the chart.

"Should I make some breakfast?" Kate offered. No one replied.

Lil'bit's face flushed with a swift anger. "It's right there. Right there! Don't you see?" she insisted. And when none of their faces showed the slightest credence, she said firmly, "Look at the bottoms of the clouds. Dark. Like the color of the sea." When she looked around and saw they all agreed, she pointed adamantly.

"Now look at that one, with the three tall clouds beside it. Look at its bottom. Pale blue. That's the pale blue of Rangiroa's lagoon."

The more they looked, the paler blue the cloud seemed to become, until it glowed distinct from all the others, an unmistakable road sign in the sky.

"I've read about this," Dugger muttered.

Nello wanted to grab Lil'bit's head in both his hands and kiss her, but with the others around, he just said, "You're pretty damn smart."

She shrugged her shoulders with the innocence of a child. "I can see," she said.

Dugger looked at the cloud and then the smoke. "Can we get there before they do?"

Nello looked. "We can try."

Dugger ran aft to the wheel and swung the bow, while Nello and Lil'bit hauled halyards and tightened sheets. The ketch settled on a beam reach as steady as a plow, furrowing through the long and ever-rising swells.

"And the pass?" Dugger cried out. "Can you remember the pass?"

Lil'bit closed her eyes. In her mind's eye she could see herself in the long and curving pass, the bare spit of sand to starboard, a narrow palm-treed *motu* to port, and she could read the edge of the pass on either side of the eddies, as long as the sun was high, almost all the way into the lagoon. What she couldn't remember was how the pass looked from the sea. You had to count *motu*s from the first one you encountered coming from the east, eight or nine *motu*s. She couldn't remember which. Don't worry, her uncle used to say, just wait until you're there and then trust your eyes. They will find the way. She finished coiling the sheet, but instead of looking at Dugger, she looked timidly at Nello.

"Well?" Nello asked. "Can you remember?"

She took a deep breath. "I think so," she said.

Chapter 56

The darkness slowly cleared from Darina's eyes, as when daylight returns after an eclipse. Then sounds returned. She could hear the goat bray, and she could hear the wind scurry over the bluff, and from far away the rhythmic crashing of the waves and the faint grinding of stones as they rolled toward the sea. She lay crumpled facedown on the edge of the plateau, one leg tucked below her, the other over the cliff, and her arms clutching, protecting the tiny, squirming child below her breast.

The grass and the ground next to her face smelled like the bluffs of Inishturk. She smiled. She saw her brother's shadow there beside her; how comforting it was to have him standing there, how much more like his old self that shadow seemed to be than that tattooed face and body she'd seen in the sun. She saw the shadow lean down close to her, then she felt her leg being lifted gently onto the bluff. She pushed herself up and sat. The baby cooed. She began to turn to look at her brother, but the sun blinded her, so she turned away. She cradled the baby in her arms and rocked it gently; it curled up its toes, scrunched its face, and for a moment opened its eyes.

"My God, Michael," she said. "Did you see her eyes?" She felt a rush of warmth flow through her and she smiled. "She has your eyes." Then she said very softly, "Our eyes."

The shadow didn't reply.

The little goat came and with its pink nose gently nudged her breast. Darina pulled it close and held it against her side. The baby scowled. "And she has your scowl too," she said. "I bet you she'll be chortling before the day is done."

Terns and gulls shrieked below like some otherworldly choir.

She held the baby out and swung her gently, then sighed and pulled the baby to her breast.

"We'll be all right," she said. "We'll be perfectly all right. We'll give you lots of goat milk and papayas. And your daddy will catch lots of fish, he was always a good fisherman, and when you get some teeth we'll eat some roast goat and sweet potatoes. You'll love sweet potatoes. Of course you'll love potatoes, you have to, you're bleeding Irish." And she giggled and nuzzled the baby's belly.

"Then we can sail to a small island and build a little house in a beautiful lagoon—your daddy can cut the poles and I can weave the walls, and we can pile up palm fronds for the roof. Then dangle our feet in the water all day."

The baby kicked, then began to whimper. Darina whispered, "Shhh, my darling. Shhh."

She felt her brother lean down near her and the sea breeze brought the scent of coconut oil. Darina felt her breathing stop. She looked hard at the shadow for the first time—the shape of the head, the narrow shoulders—and a gnawing doubt ran like ice water down her back. The roar of the surf from below grew louder and she whispered almost without breath, "Michael?" When no response came, her voice trembled. "Michael. Are you there?"

A gust of wind flattened the grass. Then a very soft voice said something she couldn't understand. She twisted hard around. At the sudden movement the little goat took flight, crossing the plateau. Darina was on one knee now at the cliff's edge, the wind rattling the tatters of her shirt, and there before her, holding out the tin cup filled with milk, with eyes smiling in the creased and wrinkled face, was the old woman. Beyond her, the plateau was empty. Except for the white-robed corpse in its center with the small goat by its side.

Darina went pale and teetered on the edge. She had no fear of heights, but she didn't dare look down. She sat so she wouldn't fall. The baby cried. She buried it in her bosom and clutched it with all her might.

The wind fell. The air was still. Far below the terns shrieked, circling above something that had fallen and now rolled like a dead shark in the waves that climbed and slid back from the stony shore.

Chapter 57

Dugger wrestled the wheel to keep the ketch on course. The southeast swells loomed ever higher, and down in their troughs the wind eased and the sails flagged and the bow wandered and the ketch lost her way. Not until she climbed the next swell, ran its crest, and began sliding down its dark blue back did she regain her speed and good steerage. Then the next trough came.

He steered, shifting and jittery, through the surging and slowing. From atop the crests, he cast weary glances to port where the black smoke had changed course and neared. It was still distant, but each time the ketch slid into a trough, he convinced himself that the frigate had made miraculous speed and, when they climbed the crest, it would be right beside them.

Nello sat on the cabin top, binoculars in hand, forcing himself not to raise them to his eyes. He told himself the last look would be good enough for hours, little would change, but when he looked again he was sure the smoke was darker. He walked back to the wheel and handed the binoculars to Dugger.

"Let me steer awhile," he said.

Dugger went to the mainmast shrouds and started up the ratlines. Halfway to the spreaders, he wrapped an arm around the shrouds, and with the binoculars took a long look at the smoke with a small solid mass now visible below it. Then he looked west at the contorted black clouds and their rain squalls that grayed and blurred the sea. He came back and said quietly, so only Nello heard, "Ease her toward the squalls." When Nello gave him a weary look, he added, "In case we need to hide."

Ahead of the ketch, the cloud with the blue bottom seemed no nearer than when they began.

Lil'bit sat on her haunches on the foredeck, her gaze fixed on the blue-bottomed cloud until her eyes burned from the wind. Kate sat safely wedged in the companionway, leaning on the main hatch, her legs perched on the top rung of the ladder below. "These are the most beautiful clouds I've ever seen," she said.

Dugger leaned down and kissed her head but kept his eyes on the squalls. He had the unshakable sensation of the ketch standing still and the squalls standing still and the only thing moving in the world being the frigate—always nearing.

"How far are they, would you guess?" he asked Nello.

"Ten miles," Nello replied.

"And the squalls?"

"Maybe five."

"I make the lagoon ten. You?"

"Sure. Ten seems right."

"Then we might make it."

"We might."

Dugger handed him the binoculars. "What would you choose: the squalls or the lagoon?"

"Guacamole."

"What?"

"In that Mexican jail, they chopped up avocados and mixed it with onions and called it guacamole."

"Are you crazy?"

"No; hungry. They say a condemned man feels an insatiable hunger just before he dies."

"So which makes you less hungry, the squalls or the lagoon?"

Nello looked back and forth, calculating speed, time, distance, the direction of the wind, the change of course required in heading for the squalls and the loss of speed they'd suffer if they headed dead straight downwind. "If we keep going south they'll know we're trying for Rangiroa," he said. "But if we sail into the squalls, they might think we're headed for Tahiti."

"So better the squalls. Right?"

Nello stared at the dark clouds and thought of the cascades of rain that might blind them, flatten the sails, and choke off the wind. But the smoke was closing in. What he wouldn't give now for some guacamole. And a cold beer in his hand.

With her sails great swollen billows and her ropes and rigging strained, the ketch raced for an hour toward the wall of rain. The dark clouds sank, the blue sea dimmed, the horizon blurred, then vanished in the rain. Dugger tried to keep her surfing in the strong winds on the crest, but the ketch rolled, lost the wave, and slid back into the trough. They had turned fifty degrees northward; the gray smudge below the black smoke had changed course and followed.

They hurtled down a swell. The crest broke. The foam streamed by. The ketch staggered like a drunk and rushed down a wave threatening to bury her bow in the bottom of the trough, but Dugger turned her hard and she rolled and yawed and doggedly raised her head, and kept rolling rail to rail, shaking off the seas.

Kate ducked down. Swirling eddies swept by her on the decks. She turned her head and looked at Dugger in admiration. He tried smiling back. "It'll be cool under the rain," he said.

I wish Darina were here, Kate thought. It would be nice to have her murmur a Hail Mary.

The ketch sliced like a white knife across the dark blue sea. Nello went below. He loaded the pistols and rifles, wedged them tight into the bunks between the bedding and the hull, then, mumbling to himself, "What a waste of time," lashed a box of ammunition to the companionway ladder near Kate's feet. When he saw no one looking, he took a slug of rum.

Dugger steered. The frigate neared. He saw its shape; he could make out the cannon. Then the frigate vanished in a trough. Two miles, Dugger thought. No more than two miles.

The ketch climbed across the face of a heaving swell. It reached the crest and was broached by a blast of wind. Then he heard the boom of the cannon. Somewhere above, the shell whistled by. "Go below!" he yelled at Kate. "We have to tack. Hey, kid!"

He waved Lil'bit aft. She came with her hair tousled by the wind, her flat feet steady on the deck. The cannon roared again. A spout of water erupted a boat-length from the ketch. They staggered down a swell, the sails gushing water, and Lil'bit pushed her drenched hair from her eyes.

"Take the wheel," Dugger snapped. "Hold this course." When she did, he knelt down beside the compass and, looking through the misted air, took a last sight toward the blue-bottomed cloud of Rangiroa. "One-ninety," Dugger yelled. "Remember, one-ninety."

He felt cool air from the rain stroke his face, then bloated raindrops exploded on his skin. Through the sheets of rain, he saw the last flame from the cannon. A shell whistled loudly, closing in. The sea beside the ketch foamed white and opened wide. Then the world disappeared. The air turned to water and buried the decks and sails in an avalanche of rain.

A gust hit hard and the sails thundered tight. The sheets whipped loose, then sprung and rippled taut. They stood in the downpour, hanging on. "Go below!" he yelled at Lil'bit. "Take Kate . . . Tie her in a bunk . . . You too."

The ketch flew with wild abandon against walls of falling water. Dugger couldn't breathe. He steered with one hand and shrouded his nose and mouth with the other to keep out the spouts of slanting, pelting rain. He could see no bow, no mast, only the spokes of the wheel before him. A head burst out at him and he saw Nello's eyes, with his arm across his face like some coquettish woman trying to hide a smile. Nello stuck his head below and yelled into the gloom, "You two all right?"

"Never better!" Kate yelled.

Dugger wiped the compass with his hand and for a second saw the card, but it was swinging too wildly for him to be sure of their heading. "I'm going to head south," he yelled into Nello's ear. "Let the French go west."

Nello didn't answer; he went to winch in the sails. The main came in. The ketch turned. The headsail began to luff. Nello hauled it tight.

"We're headed dead for the atoll. Five miles, right? In a half hour we'll be on the reef."

Nello nodded in approval. He leaned across the bridge deck and stuck his head down the hatch. It was too dark to see the ship's clock on the bulkhead. "Could one of you ladies please tell me the time?"

Kate staggered forward in the heaving cabin. She grabbed the salon table, then the rail of the settee, and glanced at the ship's clock. "Twelve-eighteen," she shouted. Nello yelled it to Dugger.

Dugger clutched the wheel and steered with all his strength. All last night and all today, every flicker of his brain had gone into escaping from the frigate, running full speed ahead, but now he had to slow, to think of the unseen reef up ahead. He was tired.

Numb and tired. He turned his face up and let it be blasted by the rain.

"See that they're in the bunks with the leeboards fast," he shouted.

Nello went below to secure the women.

Six bells rang; the half hour had long passed. Dugger had to force himself not to turn the wheel and head back north to the safety of open sea. With every slat of the sails he tensed, listening through the downpour for the sound of a wave crashing on the reef, but he only heard the rain drumming on deck, hissing on the sea, gurgling out the scuppers, and pinging on the bell. He murmured a simple prayer, asking God to look after Kate, to bring her through this safely. And all the while he listened. He listened so hard he missed the muffled thunder of the wave upon the reef.

Kate lay wedged against the hull, with the mildewed canvas leeboard hooked to the underdeck holding her in. Inches from her ear the rain drummed on the deck, and the rush of the sea was right beside her head. All she wanted was to sleep, then wake up on dry land with no water in sight. She pressed her face against the hull. The wood felt solid, comforting. Then she heard something new; loud. With her ear against the hull, it was as loud as thunder.

"Dugger!" she shouted. "Dugger!"

Lil'bit sat in the bow, leaning against the cabin, her head down, as if asleep, in the rain. She only raised her head when a familiar smell had come, something that reminded her of home, her shack, her small closed lagoon. Fish, she thought. Dead fish.

Dugger saw her lift her arm and wave frantically to starboard. He looked over but all he saw was a hazy light breaking through the rain, and he thought she was just happy that the rain was easing, the squall ending, and they would soon be out of it, safe and free. He waved back.

She charged toward him, yelling, but water gushed over her lips and all he could make out was, "Fish."

Dugger stared in confusion.

"Turn!" Lil'bit pleaded. "I smell fish!"

Dugger, shocked, eased the pressure on the wheel and the bow swung and he had to fight to bring her back.

Lil'bit shivered. "I smell the reef!" she blurted. "You have to turn!"

The rain eased, the haze brightened, and dead ahead, a boat-length before the bow, rose a bright green swell. It curled and glowed translucent, its crest feathered by wind, then it toppled and erupted in a long string of white fountains, as it exploded into foam, crashing on the reef.

The next wave grabbed the ketch and hurled her ahead.

Chapter 58

Father Murphy sat barefoot by the sea in the drifting smoke of the smoldering bits of houses. The surf broke in long low curls along the shore, and people walked by in ragged clusters, carrying from the charred skeletons of their huts a dented pot, a length of singed rope, a shell, a half-carbonized pole, a handful of nails. Then they heaped them in small piles, each family its own heap, of the things they had once dreamed of and so proudly owned.

The children were gone. They had run off to the falls and now stood under the cascade, yelling, splashing, washing from their chests and faces tattoos they had painted with the soot.

Father Murphy looked out to sea and gripped the Bible lengthwise with both hands as if he meant to rip it right in half.

From the direction of the fort came the Finn with a burned ukulele in one hand and a tin cup full of rum in the other, and, without greeting, sat down by Father Murphy. He sipped. "Look at the bright side, Padre," he said. "The French are gone, your flock is back, and we're still alive to drink to our health." And, lacking another cup, he tapped his against the Bible. *"Prost,"* he said, and drank. Then he passed the cup to Father Murphy, wiped his mouth, and plucked at the remaining strings of the ukulele.

"Finn," Father Murphy began, as if dredging something with great effort from the depths. "Did you ever think of killing someone?"

"All the time," the Finn said. "I'm doing so right now. Why?"

"I've been thinking since last night, and I can't chase it from my mind, about that admiral, and the different ways I'd like to kill him. Not a very priest-like thing to do."

"Look, Padre. Some people need killing. That admiral, for sure. Even the Virgin Mary would vote a yes on that."

The children chanted something long in chorus.

"My job is to explain God's purpose to people. If I can't do that anymore . . .?"

The Finn emptied the mug, then at long last said, "I don't know. Maybe you should retire. Or maybe God should retire. *Or* you could both retire and leave the world to them." And he held his cup up toward the children. "And the Chinamen," he added. "Remember the Chinamen."

Where the stretch of curving sand touched the point, the Zuo brothers shuffled with woven bags in hand. They shoved their pirogue into the sea, and while the sun was still high and visibility in the depths still good, they paddled through the shoals to dive for black pearls.

The ketch reared. The bow rose on the last wave before the reef. With a violent swing of his arm, Dugger turned the wheel. The crest began to break and shatter on the coral as the headsail shed water and filled tight with wind. The ketch turned. As the wave broke, the lead keel slammed the coral with a bone-jarring thud as if they had fallen from the sky. Pots clanged and the ship's bell rang. Nello fell against a stanchion, Lil'bit flew across the bridge deck and lay crumpled at his feet, and Dugger was thrown with force against the wheel amid the muffled, endless grinding of the forefoot of the lead keel milling the coral reef.

A gust slammed the ketch and threw her on her side. The starboard deck was buried, the foot of the sails submerged. Nello dove into the water that churned where the deck had been and groped among the lines for the jib sheet. He found its cleat, tried pushing the loop off the horn, but the soaked line was too stiff, so he worked it with two hands, one hand pushing, the other clawing the loop. He was running out of air. As the rope softened, the loop opened wide. He left the line under the horn, eased it slowly out, and the ketch stood up and lifted him into air.

With the wind pushing the mainsail, the ketch twisted herself free and a spent wave pulled her from the reef and slid her seaward. The coral seethed under the portside rail, and to starboard yawned the blue depths of the sea.

When a boat-length from the reef, Dugger smiled with joy. Nello pulled Lil'bit to him and crushed her in his arms. Kate had unclipped the lee cloths and came up into the sun.

"We did it!" Dugger beamed. "We're here. Through the squall! This is Rangiroa. Right?"

Lil'bit glanced at the curved line of *motu*s, and the reef-bound shoals that stretched unbroken between them.

"Yes," she said. "Rangiroa."

"And the pass?"

She pulled out of Nello's arms. "Not far," she said, and made her way to the port shrouds and, with great apprehension, started counting *motu*s.

Dugger held Kate's hand as if a life's-worth of foreboding had fallen from his shoulders. He smiled. "We lost them in the squalls." Then he blew out a great sigh and let his shoulders slump. He was holding Kate close to him when he heard the whistle. "Never whistle on board," he growled.

"I didn't whistle," Kate said.

He looked over at Nello, but Nello shook his head. The shell whistled overhead and slammed into the reef, spewing a fountain of splintered coral high into the air. Out of the gray mist of the squall behind them burst the frigate. With its black smoke and long cannon, it came directly at them, then it dipped behind a swell and vanished as if sunk.

Nello grabbed for the sheet and trimmed the jib. Dugger kept the ketch running along the reef. "Where's the bloody pass?" he blurted.

Lil'bit stiffened at the harsh demand. "Soon," she said, staring straight ahead.

She scrambled up the ratlines for a better look. She counted the *motu*s she recognized, then stared helplessly when she came to one she didn't. She looked behind them and began counting again.

"Come on," Dugger pressed.

She shivered, finished counting, "Two more *motu*s," she said.

"You sure?"

She looked indignantly at him, then around at the huge swells, which, breaking on the reef, obliterated any coral heads she might have remembered. "Pretty sure," she said.

"That's great!" Dugger snapped.

"Come on, Cappy," Nello said, looking aft where, behind the swell, the frigate's bow now rose. Then he knelt down and cranked the winch, trimming the sail an inch.

With the sails full to bursting, the windward shrouds vibrating like violin strings, the ketch rode the waves along the foaming reef.

Lil'bit wrapped an arm around a shroud and the other across her chest to keep from shivering. Be calm, she told herself. Your uncle taught you to be calm. There is always something on a reef that will give the pass away. Just look. And if you're unsure, turn back to the safety of the open sea. There is no shame in turning back and trying it again. No shame, she thought, just the frigate with the cannon. Count, she told herself. Count well.

A school of silvery big-eye jacks darted past the ketch, disappearing in the glitter of the sea ahead. Two dolphins followed. Lil'bit smiled. There, you see? she chided herself. The big-eyes are running for the pass, knowing the dolphins don't like the lagoon. She recounted the *motu*s with greater confidence. "Two *motu*s!" she shouted.

Behind them the squall opened and a shaft of sunlight burned through the churning clouds, illuminating the cannon of the frigate. Lil'bit gazed at the small *motu* beside them with its wind-whipped palms and casuarinas on its shore. She waited until they passed, then she called out, "One *motu*."

One *motu*, she told herself. I'm sure it's one *motu*.

The squall cleared, but the wind stayed. Dugger glanced back and saw the men loading another shell.

"Can you see the pass yet?" he shouted.

"Yes," she replied.

The last *motu* was passing quickly by. It hugged the inside of the reef, with a white-sand beach that rose knee-high before the sand flattened among the palms. They all watched it so closely, no one saw the coral head awash before the bow. It jutted harshly seaward under a rising swell and only when it poked through the green did Lil'bit cry out, "Head out to sea!" and frantically wave her arm.

Dugger panicked. He spun the wheel and the ketch went too far; they jibed. The boom swung savagely to port and the sails whipped with it, slamming against Lil'bit, knocking her from the shrouds. She crawled to the ratlines and scrambled up again.

They were past the last *motu*.

She studied the reef beyond it, right below her now, for any curves or wear that waves pound out at the entrance of a pass, but the swells ran so high and the waves crossed the reef so white that it was hard to see with any certainty below the surface. She waved for Dugger to stand off seaward and he at once obeyed.

They sailed at speed along the reef. Dugger looked back. The frigate showed again, rolling and wallowing in the confused seas. It seemed in no hurry, staying a hundred yards behind. Why don't they fire? he thought. Why don't they just blow us to bits and get it over with? The ketch sank into a trough; the frigate vanished again. Because they're not stupid, that's why, he thought. They're saving their shells until there is less motion.

Lil'bit was staring directly down. She started to raise her arm but lowered it, then she slid down the ratlines and, with her head down, came aft.

"Well?" Dugger queried.

"That was it," she said, and pointed at their stern quarter.

Dugger spun. "That was what?"

"The pass."

Behind them the reef seethed white, but, just off the stern quarter, the water heaved unbroken right up to the bow, where the coral heads tore the seas apart again. The pass was no more than two boat-lengths wide.

"It's too late to turn now!" Dugger hissed.

Lil'bit looked sadly at him. "I know. I couldn't say to turn before," she said. "The trough was too deep; the pass was too shallow."

Dugger gripped the spokes and let his anger pass. "Now what?" he asked.

Lil'bit looked at Nello, then at the frigate still behind, and watched as a great swell loomed against the sky. Then, so softly Dugger barely heard, she said, "We can surf in."

Nello's face twitched. Dugger shut his eyes. She's a child, he told himself. Don't listen to a child. "If we turn around for another try, they'll blow us to rat shit," he said.

"Turn fast," Lil'bit said.

Nello jumped to the cleats. Dugger spun the wheel. The ketch did a violent jibe. A wave slammed them abeam and the ketch shuddered. The sails thundered and the masts bent, but Nello threw the sheet off starboard, then dove across the deck and hauled in on the port. "Get the staysail!" he roared, and Lil'bit clawed the staysail loose and fell to her knees beside him to haul the line. She turned to Dugger.

"You can surf in easy," she insisted, but her eyes were full of dread. "I'll tell you when to turn." She looked behind them and saw the next swell rise. "Start to turn slowly. Now," she said, hard and precise. Dugger turned the wheel and the bow slowly swung.

"Tighter!" Lil'bit cried.

Dugger made the correction and headed back along the reef, the bow of the ketch pointing at the frigate.

"Now!" Lil'bit ordered. "Turn hard now!"

Dugger saw a monstrous swell coming at them now; he turned and they hauled the sheets side by side. The ketch lurched. The wave curled. Dugger felt it propel them with great force at the reef. The wave has us, he thought. No; I have the wave. The ketch surfed, pitching and yawing, toward the pass.

"Stay in it! Stay in it!" Lil'bit commanded. And Dugger tried to play the helm but he felt no resistance. The crest of the wave neared too fast and he felt the ketch sink as the crest passed them by. He had lost the wave. Its bowsprit pointing skyward, the ketch slid stern-first down the back of the great swell, all the way down to the bottom of a trough. They could see nothing but the mountainous waves and sky.

"We missed it! Turn back!" Lil'bit shouted.

"Cappy, we'll break apart!" Nello cried. Over the side he could see the white-sand bottom of the pass. Dugger spun the wheel. The cable stopped it with a bang. The sea exploded on the reef around them. A shudder went through the ketch as the keel struck the outer coral, then she rose and turned free and sailed back into the deep.

The next swell came. The frigate sat atop it.

Lil'bit stood up. "Sorry," she said.

Dugger grabbed her arm and pulled her behind the wheel. "You surf," he said firmly, and put her hands on the spokes.

"But . . . "

"You surfed fine last night. You know the pass. You surf!"

"Cappy . . ." Nello protested.

"Our only bloody chance!" Dugger cried.

A flame burst from the cannon of the frigate. The shell shrieked, then the mizzen sail blew apart. It fluttered in shreds, like the tails of a hundred kites.

"It's all right," Dugger shouted. "We don't need it. Surf!" and he knelt down beside Nello to work the sheets.

Lil'bit, with her shoulders forward, began to turn the wheel.

She pointed the ketch directly at the frigate as if she meant to ram it. The frigate fired. The shell flew by so close, its airstream flattened the sails. Lil'bit didn't flinch. Her gaze was riveted on the swell that rose in a blue leap against the sky. She let it go by. The frigate was so close she could see sailors bucket water onto the cannon's breech.

The next swell came pure and blue. It glittered and curled, then its crest began to spume.

Lil'bit turned the wheel. The ketch swung.

As if some giant hand had grabbed it and hurled it forward, the ketch began to fly. Lil'bit bent her knees. She no longer watched the sea—she felt its movement in her legs—but watched the reef beyond the small *motu* ahead. She played the wheel, surfing the ketch at a savage speed across the wave. She could see the break in the reef and edged her way toward it.

She clutched the spokes, surfing wildly down, the pass gleaming shallow to port, so she cut back into the wave to gain some height, then cut back again, pointing at the pass. The mountain of water now inclined over her.

The curling wave hung like a blue vault over the ketch, and they sailed enclosed in its luminous blue glow, in a vast azure tunnel; a road to another world. Kate looked back. How beautiful, she thought. If this is death, I don't mind it a bit. And in all that roar and hissing she heard Lil'bit singing.

Then the wave collapsed and overwhelmed the ketch. Dugger held Kate as the sea tried to tear her from his arms; and the weight of the water pinned down Nello's chest, then the wave let him rise, only to slam him down again.

Lil'bit closed her eyes and surfed. Even with the sea upon her, she felt, through her legs, the shifting of the ketch. She nudged the wheel slightly to port as the sea around her exploded into fountains. The ketch wallowed, scraped bottom, shot forward again. A loose sheet hooked the reef, and the coral sliced it to shreds. The great wave pushed her on. Then the blue water drained away, sliding benignly from the cabin top and deck, then tumbling over the rail, back into the sea.

The ketch rose. Stood upright. The wave pushed her through foaming green-blue water, through the school of silver big-eyes, into the lagoon.

THE FRIGATE TURNED to line up the pass.

Chapter 59

The gunner plunged his singed hands into the bucket of water and cursed.

"S'il vous plaît," the admiral said, his voice as dry as chaff.

"My hands, sir," the gunner explained.

"It's all right, Blusson," the captain cut in quietly. "I will load."

"Hold your course," the admiral ordered.

"Holding course," the captain said.

They slid down the back of a wave and he waited for the next one to hurl them into the pass. Before them, the ketch wallowed, its sails slatting, its shredded mizzen tangling on the jackstays. The admiral factored in the range and rising swell, cranked the bronze handle to bring the cannon barrel down, then, out of breath but self-satisfied, he gave the order to load and hold.

The captain told the gunner to take the wheel while he loaded. The gunner steered and leaned close to him. "Shall we prepare the lifeboats, sir?"

A wry smile twisted the captain's lips. "It's too late for that, Blusson." He pushed in the shell and wet his hands before he cranked the hot breech shut. Then he took back the wheel. With a roar that drowned out the engine, a great wave broke and buried them in foam. A dim grayness blocked out the sun. The sea seethed over them. "Fire!" he heard coming through the din. He could barely make out the outline of the ketch. The frigate pitched. Then came up again. "Fire!"

God help us all, the gunner thought, as he pulled the lever down.

The ketch crabbed, rolling into the lagoon. Dugger was on his knees looking aft. Atop a towering swell he saw the frigate flounder, only its bow and cannon sticking out into the sun. It rode high on the wave as if, having taken flight, it wanted to dive onto the ketch from above. But the face of the wave it rode now grew sheer, kicking up the stern and pointing the bow down.

The frigate dove.

It dove in a deadfall, bow-down, onto the reef. As the wave around it shattered into foam, the sleek bow drove with violence into the coral. The cannon fired; the frigate blew to pieces.

The next wave rolled its shattered remnants on the reef.

Chapter 60

The old woman held the small goat under her arm while it lapped milk from the tin cup in her hand. Darina smelled the goat milk mingling with the smell of the sea. The old woman sat on her haunches beside her, talking softly, often holding her gaze, sometimes smiling as if she had just told herself a joke, at other times, frowning at the gravity of what she said.

Darina couldn't understand a word, but she sensed the meaning from the woman's gestures and her eyes, the tiny shrugs her shoulders made, and her rising and falling, ever-changing smile. Then the old woman fell silent and pushed the goat away. It bucked and leapt impatiently in the windblown waves of grass. She said a single word, then dipped two dark and wrinkled fingers into the cup, and crooked them as she pulled them out, to save the milk. She held them to the baby's mouth and let the milk trickle down her fingers. The baby closed her small lips over them, her chubby red cheeks hollowing as she sucked. The old woman now dipped her little finger and held it to the baby's trembling lips. The baby sucked and smiled.

After a while the old lady stopped and put the cup next to Darina. She said something short and firm. Then she pulled open a tear in Darina's shirt so her breast fell out into the sun, dipped her fingers in the milk, then raised them and let the milk run down Darina's breast, let it dribble to the tip. Then she guided the baby's head until the milky nipple touched the baby's mouth. The baby drank and, with her tiny hands, she poked Darina's breast.

A tear filled Darina's sun-reddened eyes. With great patience she dipped her fingers and dripped the milk. The baby fed.

The little goat came bounding back and poked its small head playfully at the baby's dangling legs. The baby gently kicked and the goat licked her leg, licked the rivulet of milk that ran down and trickled from her toes.

The wind blew without a sound over the plateau. Darina held the sleeping child softly to her breast. They stayed there for a long time, with the shadows of passing clouds washing over them.

Chapter 61

The ketch sailed all day across the calm lagoon, now and then passing a deserted *motu* with its ring of sand, a cluster of palms, and shoal seas all around it. The water around the ketch teamed with shifting colors as schools of zebra surgeonfish and lemon-peel angelfish, blue-green chromis and red-lipped parrotfish skittered quickly by.

They sailed under main alone, drifting, with Lil'bit sitting astride the bowsprit, directing them around coral heads that loomed just below the surface. By late afternoon the heads were hard to see. Ahead of the ketch the sun blazed on the water; behind her, the sea was filled with shifting shadows.

A crescent-shaped *motu* lay invitingly ahead, with flopping banana leaves yellowing the shore. Dugger eased the main; the sail fluttered, then hung still. Frigate birds came by, swooping, curious as the ketch drifted shoreward in water so clear and a sandy bottom so white that he could see every detail of her shadow. They dropped the anchor and watched it touch bottom, sending up a puff of sand. The chain fed out slowly through the rollers, then went taut. The ketch stopped. They dropped the main, crumpling, to the deck. Beyond the *motu*, the surf moaned on the reef.

LIL'BIT CAME BACK FROM A SWIM TO THE *MOTU*, pushing two coconuts ahead of her as she swam. The clouds blazed pink behind her in the west; in the east they towered red above the squalls, the colors of the sky rippling on the sea.

She crushed bits of coconut meat, mixed them with cut mangoes, and Dugger drowned the pulp in a deep pot of rum. They sat in the cockpit under a red-streaked sky.

They raised their tin cups and toasted to good health, then they toasted to the squall, then Kate lay in Dugger's arms and raised her cup "to the best surfer of them all." Lil'bit blushed visibly even in the twilight. The clanging of the tin cups sounded festive in the silence.

They drank.

Nello unrolled the chart, held it up to the fading light, and searched it for the crescent-shaped *motu* that lay before them. With the cup raised to her lips, Kate stopped. "What's that?" she said, pointing at a patch sewn with big stitches to its back.

At first Nello didn't seem to understand. He looked at the chart and saw only the normal lines, fathom marks and arrows indicating currents, until in the corner he saw stitches rise. Kate reached over and folded back the corner; a patch of paper had been sewn onto the back. On it was some writing and some faded curving lines, but she couldn't make things out precisely in the dusk. Dugger struck a match. Written were a few words, and below them, now faded but still possible to make out, a drawing of atolls and lagoons and, in the middle of one, an arrow pointing at the shape of a pear.

The match burned down and Dugger threw it in the sea.

"Guillaume's map," he said.

"And the writing?" Nello asked.

Dugger smiled and shook his head. *"Bonne chance* and *bon voyage."*

A sky full of stars danced on the lagoon. An albatross took flight from shore and headed west to try and find the sun.

Acknowledgments

This four-year voyage would not have been possible without major contributions from a vast array of people.

First were those who helped with historical and anthropological research: New York's Museum of Natural History, The Metropolitan Museum of Art, Tahiti's Musée de Tahiti et des Iles, and a team of New York-based researchers lead by Courtney Fitch and Heather Brown.

Invaluable assistance came from Sandy and the most gracious crew and owners of the passenger-freighter Aranui III, who were exceptional hosts and an endless source of stories and information. Huge thanks to Jonathan Reap at Tahiti Tourism who assembled dozens of jigsaw details into three months of unforgettable work.

A lifetime of thanks to my dear pal Starling Lawrence, W.W. Norton's scathing, gut-splittingly funny and—it kills me to say this—almost-always-right, Editor-in-Chief, for enduring another hand-to-hand, word-to-word battle, and clarifying, unraveling, and making intelligible such a complex narrative.

A huge thanks to Candace for her great sailing help in the Society Islands, her editorial travails and constant and encouraging companionship.

And much gratitude to my long-time cohort Céline Little who researched, plotted, dramatized, edited, criticized, and—thank God—patiently persevered.

The biggest debt I owe is to the wonderful people RW, CL and Lil'bit, for breathing life into this story.

Ferenc Máté
Tuscany, 2011

and ready living makes not good living.
The capital of -isms determines the form of your *frisson*:
Children, everyday is opposite day;
the opposite of knowing is play without play.
If you never think, you never have a thought;
cogito ergo sum ergo you *are* are not.
Words are yours, and there is a choice to be made:
Moderation enables Liberty, Freedom, and Will;
Rhyme, metre, and diction are the pure thrill
of fidelity to my lovely, lovely wife of thirteen years.
Miss, would you . . . yes, please, another beer."
Of course, nobody listened, his words lost
in the labyrinthine tropical foliage,
a solitary voice dying dying dying in the noise of Carthage.
And me, I tripped balls in the *ion* john
to move this picaresque tale along to its pen-
ultimate finale [DRAMATIC PAUSE]. Action:
I blew through the swinging doors chewing cheroot
between my teeth and looking mean;
from out of its zip, my unholstered schlong drawn
with the heroic elasticity of Plastic Man
(my homage to Montreal's Leonard Cohen)
shot across the room, pissing in shitee-soups,
one by one, when at last *oui-oui* my
ding-dong did settle in a seat at the table
of sad M. Hiver for a last nightcap.
Let Death's blow be executed with mannered
formality — even Michael Corleone
enjoyed the veal before whacking Captain McClusky.
My comic-western dick coiled around
Hiver's neck, choking out one last breath
as soft as a punning snowflake:
"Self-Pity is unbecoming of a poem, even more so of a Man

of water to the mystical washing away
of that Syrian General, Naaman, who,
swimming seven times in the river, cur
syphilitic soul; of the Roman harlot, Ch
clitoral tissue was restored
after a skinny-dip, as was her feeling fo
the feeling of *Love*'s deep-dick;
of 'Geffrey Chaucer,' who inked in the
that quill which scribbled his retractio
Heere taketh the makere of this book his
of Thomas Lodge, who, in the 'Preface'
to his *Prosopopeia* (1596), asked
to be 'cleansed, from the leprosy of my
lewd lines, in the Jordan of Grace';
of Dr. Donne who said young Jack was
who didn't know the first thing about Lo
'til he kissed the mouth of the Jordan;
of John Wilmot, libertine, esquire, his d
sembled powder-face, when splashed
with *nahr al-urdun*, collapsed into a rai
that floated downstream and with it
taking Rochester's memory of every ero
and a final image, or rather half-image
(a cold shadow forced the sun to shiver
before I could figure the total frequency
of the form) of he who I believed to be F
(Alessandro), the pornographic poet
('Why him?' I made out his pierced trag
and the tattoo of Kelly, Jill, on his neck)
sitting with his back to the bank; and if
he laughed or cried I could not tell the
by his convulsions. The meaning was lo
He sat, alone, waiting without hope, for m

ROLL CREDITS. I woke from my cell-
uloid slumber under the garden's dew-soaked statue of Dante
and *le cose belle che porta 'l ciel* —
a snail tickling my nose, I opened an eye
to both fear and admire the marvellous spiral.

Palindrome: After Dino Campana

Momentarily
The roses are deflowered
And the petals fallen
But roses I could not forget the roses
She was a rose I was a rose
We made roses
Our blood rose our tears rose
The dawn the sun rose
A brio of roses in the sun
In the thorny sun of the briar
Roses are deflowered
Petals fallen
We forget it all
Momentarily